ใจ

PASSIONATE PR
THE INHABITED

ใจ

"A gripping page-turner with a historical basis, an action tale with considerable depth that boldly dramatizes an inner struggle. Lavinia is the Everywoman of the 21st century."
—*Kirkus Reviews*

ใจ

"[This] is a passionate story of love, courage, solidarity, and death, where reality and legend blend harmoniously. The lives of the characters are intertwined with the destiny of the country and the struggle of a people for dignity. There is so much truth in this book that it is impossible for the reader to remain indifferent. This is a story that needed to be told and Belli does it with talent."
—Isabel Allende

ใจ

"Belli's poetic style intelligently and absorbingly links two seemingly different women, separated by centuries, demonstrating how, in the political and sexual arenas, the battle for freedom is never really won. Her message is to find the courage to fight anyway, since existence is hollow without it."
—*Los Angeles Reader*

ใจ

"A dynamic novel [that] revitalizes two literary genres—magic realism and social realism. This is Belli's triumph."
—*Hartford Courant*

ใจ

"Her writing moves events swiftly to an exciting climax."
—*Library Journal*

ใจ

"An inviting novel of love, politics, and history, steeped in magical realism, served in rich prose."
—*Booklist*

The Inhabited Woman

Gioconda Belli

TRANSLATED BY KATHLEEN MARCH

WARNER BOOKS

A Time Warner Company

La mujer habitada was first published in Spanish by Editorial Vanguardia, Managua, 1989.
First English language edition published in hardcover by Curbstone Press, 1994.

Warner Books Edition
Copyright © 1994 by Gioconda Belli
All rights reserved.

This Warner Books edition is published by arrangement with Curbstone Press, 321 Jackson Street, Willimantic, CT 06226.

Warner Books, Inc., 1271 Avenue of the Americas, New York, NY 10020

Ⓦ A Time Warner Company

Printed in the United States of America
First Trade Printing: October 1995
10 9 8 7 6 5 4 3

Library of Congress Cataloging-in-Publication Data

Belli, Gioconda
   [Mujer habitada, English]
   The inhabited woman / Gioconda Belli.
   p. cm
   ISBN 0-446-67206-8
  1. Title.
[PQ7519.2.B44M8513   1995
863—dc20

                        95-15221
                        CIP

Cover design by Rachel McClain
Cover illustration by Anthony Russo
Background art by Michelle DiCicco

The Inhabited
Woman

CHAPTER 1

✦ ✦ ✦

I emerged at dawn. What has happened since that day in the water when I last saw Yarince is all so strange. The elders announced in the ceremony that I would travel to Tlalocan, the balmy gardens to the East—verdant country, land of flowers caressed by gentle rains—but instead I found myself alone for centuries, enclosed by earth and roots, watching in astonishment while my body dissolved into humus and vegetation. I had been holding onto my memories so long: the sounds of maracas, the thundering of horses, rebellion, spears, the anguish of defeat, Yarince and the strong sinews of his back. But for days now I had been hearing the rain's tiny footsteps, the roaring of great subterranean currents drawing near my ancient dwelling, carving out tunnels, tugging at me through the porous dampness of the earth. I could see the world coming closer; I could see it in the changing colors of its layers.

I saw the roots. Their hands, outstretched, calling to me. The force of their beckoning attracted me irrevocably. I penetrated the tree, entered its circulatory system; I flowed through it like a long caress of sap and life, an opening of petals, a shuddering of leaves; I felt its coarse touch, the delicate architecture of its branches, and, joyfully, I unfolded into the hollows and passageways of my new skin, stretching out after so long, letting my hair tumble free, coming out to look at the blue sky with its white clouds, to listen to the birds singing as before.

I, too, sang with my new mouths (if only I could have danced), orange blossoms covered my trunk, and the scent of oranges was on all my branches.

I wonder if I have finally arrived in the tropical lands, the lands of plenty and peacefulness and the quiet, endless joy reserved for those who die under the auspices of Quiote-Tláloc, God of the Waters... Because it is not flowering time, it is time to bear fruit, yet this tree has taken on my seasons, my very life, the cycle of other twilights. It has been born again, inhabited by the blood of a woman.

There was no pain of childbirth, as there was when my head emerged from between my mother's legs. This time there was no uncertainty, no heartbreak mixed with the joy. The midwife did not bury my xicmetayotl, my umbilical cord, in the dark corner of the house. Nor did she take me in her arms to say: "You shall dwell within this house like the heart inside the body...you shall be the ashes that lie upon the fire in the hearth." No one cried when giving me my name, as my mother had, because ever since the fair-haired men, the men with hair on their faces, appeared in the distance, all the auguries had been sad and my parents were even afraid to call the soothsayer to give me a name, my tonalli. They were afraid to learn my destiny. My poor parents! The midwife washed me, purified me as she prayed to Chalchiuhtlicue, mother and sister to the gods, and in that same ceremony they named me Itzá, dewdrop. They gave me my adult name, not waiting for the time when I should have chosen it, for they feared the future.

Now, instead, everything seems quiet around me. There are newly-pruned bushes, flowers in huge pots, and a cool breeze that sways me, rocks me from side to side as if it were greeting me, welcoming me into the light after such a long period of darkness.

These are strange surroundings. Walls encircle me. Constructions with thick walls like the ones the Spaniards made us build.

I saw a woman. The one who tends the garden. She is young, tall, dark-haired, beautiful. Her features resemble those of the women who came with the invaders, but she walks like the women of my tribe, firmly, as we used to move and walk before the bad times. I wonder if she works for the Spaniards. I don't think she tills the land or knows how to spin. Her hands are slender, and her eyes large and bright. They shine with the wonderment of one who is still open to discovery...

Everything was silent after she left. I heard no sounds of a temple nor the movement of priests. The woman alone inhabits this dwelling and its garden. She has no family, nor master, yet she is not a goddess, for she is afraid. She closed and locked all the doors before leaving.

• • •

The day the orange tree bloomed, Lavinia rose early to go to work for the first time in her life.

Sleepily, she turned off the alarm clock. She hated its harsh lowing, like a ship's siren disturbing the morning's peace. She rubbed her eyes and stretched.

The scent wafted in from everywhere. The essence of orange blossoms pursued her relentlessly from the garden. Kneeling on the bed, she looked out of the window and noticed the orange tree was in bloom.

It was an old tree, growing right in front of the bedroom window. Her Aunt Inés' gardener had planted it a long time ago, swearing it would bear fruit year round because it was a graft produced by his skilled curandero's hands. A gardener wise in the ways of green, growing things. Her aunt had become attached to the tree, even though, while she was alive, it never showed any sign of trying to bloom.

It must be the late December rains, Lavinia thought. "Rains out of season, signs of miracles," her grandfather used to say.

Feeling lazy, she entered the bathroom. She turned on the radio as she went by, picking up the clothes she had carelessly dropped on the floor when she came home in the early hours of the morning and went to bed. She liked her room, decorated with baskets and brightly colored quilts.

With an architect's salary, she could improve on the folklorish decor, she thought, as she bathed, feeling enthusiastic at the prospect of her first day at work.

The scent of orange blossoms rained on her as it mingled with the water from the shower. It was a good sign that the tree had bloomed precisely that day, she said to herself, rubbing her long chestnut hair, then drawing the comb through it to straighten the tangles. She left the bathroom, drying herself with the huge beach towel, and, looking in the mirror, put on her makeup, making her eyes larger, enhancing the features of her attractive face. She would not have wanted to be like Sara, her best friend, who had features like a porcelain doll. Imperfection had its good points. Her face, which would have attracted little attention in another time, couldn't have been more in tune with the rock music, the hippie style, the miniskirts, the ongoing rebellion from the previous decade, the carefree modernity of the early seventies.

Yes, she said to herself, carefully choosing her clothes and shaking her head to coax her curls into place: the secret was in not combing her hair. She was typical of her generation. Over a month ago she had moved to Aunt Inés' house, leaving her parents' home. She was a woman alone, young, and independent.

Aunt Inés was the one who had raised her. She used to spend long periods of time in this house because her parents were preoccupied with their youth, social life and success. Only when they realized she had grown up, when they saw how she had bloomed, her breasts, her body hair, her curves, did they exercise their full parental rights and send her to Europe to study, as was the custom at that time among people of breeding.

Aunt Inés would have preferred not to see her go at all, but outranked by her brother's paternal rights, she had to be content with teaching her niece enough so she wouldn't let herself be talked into studying to be a bilingual secretary or an optometrist. Lavinia wanted to be an architect, and she had the right to be one, Inés told her. She had the right to build in real-life-size the houses she invented in the garden, the carefully constructed models made of matchsticks and old shoe boxes, the magical cities. She had the right to dream of being something, of being independent. And Aunt Inés paved the way for her before she died. She willed Lavinia the house with the orange tree and everything in it, "for when she wanted to be alone."

Lavinia finished dressing, taking a deep breath and inhaling the fragrant mid-January air, not noticing how nature's calendar had been altered, not suspecting the destiny that was marking her with its long, invisible finger.

She shut the bedroom door and went around the house checking bolts and latches. It was a very nice house, a smaller version of the enormous colonial mansions which face their inner patios.

When she arrived, it had been suffering from decrepitude and abandonment. The doors creaked, the roof leaked; it was ailing from the rheumatism caused by dampness and being closed up. She repaired it, using the money she made from selling the old furniture and her knowledge of architecture. She turned it into a jungle, filling it with plants, colored cushions and boxes, books, records. The orderly life style of pensioners who live alone was not for her. Today the untidiness was evident, after the weekend without Lucrecia, the maid, the only one who straightened things up, because Lavinia was used to the comfortable, easy life. It was only on the three days a week that Lucrecia came that the dust disappeared from the house and hot food was eaten. The rest of the time Lavinia was content to live on sandwiches, ham, cheese, salami, and peanuts because she didn't know how to cook.

The January wind scattered the oak's pink flowers along the gutters, tousling her hair when she went out and strolled along the wide sidewalks of her neighborhood. She hardly ever saw her neighbors. They were older people, her aunt's contemporaries, waiting silently for death, sheltering their memories behind their mansion walls, fading away in the shadows of their dwellings. It saddened her to see them sometimes in the afternoon, swaying alone in their rocking chairs behind the open doors of their old parlors. Old age seemed like a terrible and lonely state to her: she turned her head with a certain melancholy and looked back at her house, thinking about her Aunt Inés. Perhaps it had been better for her to have died before decrepitude set in, even though now she would have liked to see her aunt's elongated figure waving good-bye to her from the doorway as she left for school in the morning, all scrubbed and ironed. This time, she was sure, her aunt would have said good-bye woman to woman, living through her the dreams her time did not allow her to fulfill. A widow at an early age, she could never overcome the horror of loneliness. It was of little use to her to become the patron of poets and artists, a restless Maecenas, in an age of crinolines and modesty. The last image Lavinia had of her was their farewell in Fuimicino airport. They had spent two months vacationing together. Inés had confessed that she missed her niece so much she was dying of sadness. Lavinia didn't believe her and didn't suspect the deadly illness that was consuming her aunt because she wore a contradictory smile to hide it and insisted that the girl had to make the most of her time—one never knew what life would bring—and that she should stay a few months more to learn French. Inés was thin, and cried there in the airport. Both of them had cried as they embraced each other beneath the understanding gaze of Italians, sympathizers of expressiveness. Lavinia promised long letters. She'd be home soon, and they'd be together and happy. She never saw her again. When she died, she did not want to attend the terrible ceremonies of mourning. She would remember her Aunt Inés alive. She knew her aunt would have agreed with her.

The streets at that hour were empty. Lavinia hurried to get to the avenue, the boundary of her neighborhood of old people. At the corner she hailed a taxi. The shiny Mercedes Benz, all polished and repolished stopped beside her. She could never help feeling amazed at the paradox of Mercedes Benz taxis. In Faguas, the Great General gave his military officers licenses to import Mercedes Benz cars without paying duty. The military officers would sell the used Mercedes to the taxi cooperatives they belonged to, and then buy new models. Poor, dusty, hot Faguas had Mercedes Benz taxis.

As soon as she settled back in the fragrant leather seats, she became aware of the radio broadcast. The trial of the head of La Concordia Prison was on. The trial had been a common topic of conversation for the last few days, and she was tired of it. She didn't want to hear about all those atrocities any more, but she was captive in the taxi. The driver smoked and didn't miss a word as he stared at the traffic.

She concentrated on the window. From the heights, she could see the city, the distant silhouette of volcanoes grazing on the shores of the lake. The scenery was beautiful. So beautiful that it was unforgivable that the lake had been transformed into a sewer. She imagined what it would be like this morning if the city hadn't turned its back on the lake, if there were a boardwalk where lovers and nurses with blue baby carriages could stroll in the afternoon. But aesthetics had never mattered to the great generals. The city was a series of contrasts, with its walled mansions and wretched hovels.

She couldn't escape hearing the testimony of the military doctor, the forensic pathologist who was the key witness in the case. His steady voice was describing the scars of torture that had been found on the prisoner's corpse. He said that the dead man's brother—also accused of conspiracy—had been thrown into the Tago Volcano by the warden. It was an active volcano, with roaring lava in the crater. At dusk the rim appeared red. The Spanish conquistadors had thought it was molten gold. The man went on to describe the burns and lacerations of the brother, who had also been assassinated, as if he were an engineer explaining the effects of a seismic tremor. The account was full of technical terms.

She recalled how columns would break after the underground explosions in the documentaries the professor used to show them at the University of Bologna in Italy. But these were human beings, human structures being destroyed. "I should have stayed in Bologna," she thought, remembering her apartment next to the bell tower. That was her reaction every time she came into contact with the dark side of Faguas. But in Europe she would have had to be content with interiors, remodeling old buildings without changing the façades, the history of better times. In Faguas, challenges were different: it was a question of taming the volcanic, seismic, opulent nature, the lust of the trees piercing the asphalt.

Faguas stimulated her pores, her desire to live. Faguas was sensuality. A body open, ample, sinuous; wild breasts of women, made of earth, spread out across the landscape. Threatening. Beautiful.

She didn't want to keep hearing about death. She rested her head on the window, intensely observing the streets. What Faguas needed was life, she thought. That's why she dreamt of constructing buildings, leaving her mark, giving warmth and harmony to the concrete, replacing the stunted imitations of New York skyscrapers on Truman Avenue, where the taxi was slowly making its way through traffic, with designs that were in harmony with the landscape. Even though that was practically an impossible dream, she thought, as she looked at the sign on the recently inaugurated department store. From the street you could see the escalator, the only one in the country and a great novelty. The store had to post doormen by the entrance to keep out the ragged little newspaper vendors because in the first few days they had made the elegant ladies who were being electronically transported to buyers' heaven feel uncomfortable. The city was trying at all costs to become modern, using any outlandish method possible.

The dead were members of the clandestine National Liberation Movement. "They're the only people with courage in this country," Sara's husband Adrián had said. "How else could they get rid of the subversives?" the prosecutor was saying as the taxi pulled up. Lavinia looked at her watch. It was eight a.m. and she was on time. She paid the taxi driver, noticing how he was staring at her long legs. He smiled sarcastically while he wished her a good day after having forced her listen to that detailed description of local Golgothas.

She entered the lobby. The building was modern, a rectangular matchbox-style with gray walls and red trim. It had an elevator. A status symbol. Another artifice to convey modernity. There were only five or six elevators in all of Faguas. They were there to impress, sometimes in a building with only two floors, where only the top executives used them. At least here there were four floors. The elevator went to the elegant offices of doctors, engineers, lawyers, and architects.

The day she came for her job interview, Lavinia had stopped on every floor. They were all alike: huge wooden doors and signs with gold lettering.

She pushed the wooden doors of the firm called "Associated Architects, Inc." and found herself in the stark modern reception area facing the proper, green-eyed secretary who asked her to take a seat. Mr. Solera would see her in a moment.

Lavinia picked up a magazine and lit a cigarette. From somewhere inside the office, a radio was still broadcasting the trial. Fortunately she couldn't make out the words.

For the sake of professional appearances, she pretended to be engrossed in the magazine: houses it was nearly impossible to imagine human beings living in. They looked as if they were made for angels, heavenly dwellers far removed from such basic needs as resting their feet on the coffee table, smoking a cigarette, or eating peanuts.

In the interview, Julián Solera had spent a long time discussing the difficulties of being an architect in Faguas. It wasn't like Europe, he told her. Ladies came in with their clippings and ordered designs from *House and Garden* and *House Beautiful*. They would fall in love with a mountain hideaway in the Alps and decide to apply the design to a summer home on the beach. One had to convince them that they were in a different country and had to think about the heat, the building materials. But Lavinia was a woman, he said, and would be better at explaining those things. Women understood each other. She smiled as she recalled that, thinking how she'd cheerfully persuaded him that he was right. At first he had looked at her, not totally convinced. When she had come into the office the week before, he'd looked her over from head to toe, sizing up her obvious "pedigree," the length of her miniskirt, her tousled curly, hair. He was a man in his forties, with alert eyes and a pragmatic attitude, but he had the need-to-seduce characteristic of Latin men his age. Soon after their first greeting, when she took out her portfolio and showed off her exquisite academic preparation, her elegant university projects, her criteria for what Faguas needed, defending her love of architecture with a vehemence befitting her twenty-three years, Julián succumbed. Like a boy doing tricks on a bicycle, he explained the local complications of the profession and it wasn't long before he was convinced that she would be a good addition to the office. She felt no remorse about using the age-old weapons of femininity. Taking advantage of the impression polished surfaces made on men wasn't her responsibility, it was her heritage.

She had to wait for a long time. A tall man of medium build and gray eyes crossed the room and entered Solera's office. The green-eyed secretary told Lavinia she could go in. The office was modern. Leather chairs. On the walls abstract drawings framed in aluminum. A floor-to-ceiling window overlooking the lake. Volcanoes grazing. Enormous mammals. Mr. Solera came over to greet her. She liked his old-fashioned courtly air, although his formal behavior made her uncomfortable.

"This is Felipe Iturbe," said Solera. The man was standing in the middle of the room like a well-constructed building. He shook her hand firmly, and Lavinia noticed his muscular forearm, his sinews, the way they were covered with what almost looked like black pubic hair. He was younger than Solera and looked at her teasingly while Julián talked about her academic qualifications, the advantages of having a woman in the group, and explained to her Felipe's role as coordinator, in charge of assigning and supervising all the work. Architect Iturbe, Solera said, would be responsible for familiarizing her with the norms and procedures of the office.

The two men seemed to enjoy their role as fatherly employers. Lavinia felt she was at a disadvantage. She made a mental bow to masculine complicity and hoped that the introductions were over. She didn't enjoy feeling as if she were on display. She remembered her return from Europe, when her parents took her all dressed up to parties and let her loose so the little animals in suits and ties could sniff at her. Little domestic animals searching for someone to give them strong, healthy children, cook for them, and keep their homes tidy. Under crystal chandeliers and extravagant lights they put her on display like Limoges or Sèvres china in that Persian marriage market that made her feel like she was being auctioned off. And she had hated it. She didn't want any more of it. She was here to escape it. She shifted uncomfortably. Finally Mr. Solera finished the introduction, and she followed Felipe out.

They walked through the hall toward the bright drafting room. A large window extended from one end of the room to the other, filling it with natural light. It had a modern decor, with burlap-covered dividers that separated the areas into cubicles for the architects. "Because she was a woman," Felipe said, she would have the privilege of having an office next to the window. He opened the door to show it to her and then led her to the one that was his. It was slightly larger. On one of the walls was a simple poster of pastel colors from a graphic arts exhibit.

There was a fairly old black radio on the cabinet behind the desk. Lavinia wondered if he had been the one listening to the trial, but she didn't say anything.

She sat down in the chrome chair with sand-colored fabric in front of the desk, while he leaned on the high bench of the drafting table over to the side.

"You have an odd name," he said, in a casual manner.

"My mother was fond of Italian names," she replied, making fun of her mother's whims.

"Do you have brothers or sisters with names like that too? Romulus, Remus...?"

"No, I don't have any brothers or sisters. I was an only child."

"Ah!" he exclaimed, insinuating the usual things: only child, well-off, spoiled...

She wasn't intimidated, and even joked about it herself: What could you do? Birth was fortuitous. She wanted to ask him if he would have made fun of her if she had been a man and had a name like Appolonius or Achilles, which in fact was common in Faguas, but she preferred not to confront him, at least not today. There would be time for that, she told herself. She directed the conversation toward professional topics. Felipe knew his job. He told her he had studied for several years in Germany. Besides working during the day, he had taught night classes at the university. As they talked, they found they shared similar ideas about the harmony of concrete, trees and volcanoes, the integral nature of landscapes, the humanism of construction. She thought they would get along professionally. An hour later, she felt he was looking at her differently. He seemed to have forgotten her miniskirt. The telephone interrupted them. Felipe picked up the receiver and had a monosyllabic conversation, one of those that people generally have when they don't want to talk in the presence of another person.

Lavinia tried to seem preoccupied by looking around until he hung up and said he had to go out, leaving her with a set of blueprints by the door of his office.

Alone in her cubicle, she sat down at the drafting table. She spun around several times in the swivel chair, enjoying the feeling of being an "architect" for the first time. It was hot outside. Haze vibrating above the asphalt. The haze would climb to the heavens to form immense towering clouds at dusk. Magenta and orange cumulonimbi that would travel across the sky before the light disappeared, erasing her first day at work.

She spread out the blueprints, trying to examine the similarity of the nomenclatures. This was the "practice." In "practice," the theoretical terms were transformed. Little by little she began to visualize the shopping center, the tiny houses in rows for the new development. The design was the usual boring one. It would make no difference if it were in any American suburb or in Faguas. The topography looked promising. The unimaginative angular lines were such a pity. She began to draw circles, allowing her impulses to guide her.

"I would like your opinion," Felipe had said.

She wanted a cup of coffee. She got up and left her cubicle. The secretary, Mercedes, a young woman, dark haired and opulent, was solicitous. "I'll get it for you," she said. And she walked away swaying her hips under the watchful eyes of the draftsmen. Lavinia stood in the door a moment, smiling at the ones whose eyes met hers when they looked up from their blueprints. Mercedes returned with a steaming cup.

"Here you are, Miss Alarcón," she said.

"Call me Lavinia," she replied. "'Miss Alarcón' is too formal. Do you know if Felipe will be back soon?" she asked.

Mercedes flashed a playful smile.

"We never know when he'll return when he leaves like that in the middle of the day," she said.

He came back in the early afternoon, and Lavinia hurled her ideas at him. "You should go see the place," Felipe said.

CHAPTER 2

She returned at sundown. She opened all the doors and windows. She seemed happy. As happy as I am, after spending the day getting to know the world again, breathing in and out through all the leaves of this new body. Who would have thought this would happen! When the elders spoke of the tropical paradises that awaited those who died in the water, under the sign of Quiote-Tláloc, I imagined transparent regions created from the substance of dreams. Reality is often more fantastic than the imagination. I don't wander through gardens. I am a part of this garden. And this tree is alive with my life. It was all battered, but I have sent sap into all its branches and when the right time comes, it will bear fruit, and then the cycle will begin anew.

I wonder how much the world has changed. Probably it has changed a great deal. This woman is alone. She lives alone. She has no family, no master. She behaves like a high dignitary who is only accountable to himself. She came and threw herself into the hammock, near my branches. She stretches her body and thinks. She has time to think. Time to be there like that, not doing anything, just thinking.

I am surrounded by high walls, and I hear strange noises. There is the clanging of carts, as if there were a road nearby.

This loud peace seems strange. I wonder what happened to my people.

Where is Yarince? Has he taken shelter in another tree, or is he wandering the sky like a star, or has he become a hummingbird? I still seem to hear his cry, his long, desperate cry, piercing the air like a poisoned arrow.

I wonder what is left of us, I wonder about my mother, whom I never saw again after I left with Yarince. She never understood why I could not simply stay at home. She never forgave Citlalcoatl for teaching me how to use the bow and arrow.

• • •

When Lavinia opened the door to the house, she noticed the fragrance, the smell of orange blossoms, and the smell of cleanliness. The house shone. Lucrecia had been there. She found the note scrawled by the maid, telling her that she'd be there early on Wednesday to see her before she left for work and to make her breakfast. She smiled, thinking how Lucrecia spoiled her, how her presence, three times a week, kept her life in order. She went into the kitchen and poured herself a rum and coke. She went out to the hammock in the patio. She sank into the soft manila that took the shape of her body. The patio was fading into the gentle shadows of dusk. Darkness slid silently over the still objects. The white blossoms on the orange tree were phosphorescent in the twilight. She rocked herself gently with her foot. It felt good to be there, at peace. All by herself. Although now she would have liked to talk over the day with her Aunt Inés, she thought. She would have liked to see the enthusiasm in her luminous and caring eyes. See the love so visible in her expression when as a little girl she told her about her childhood adventures. Or maybe she should have visited Sara. But Sara would not understand her happiness. She did not understand the pleasure of being oneself, of making decisions, of having one's life under control. Sara had gone from the father-father to the husband-father. Adrián bragged in front of her how he wore the pants in the family. And Sara listened to him with a smile. For her that, too, was "natural." The parties where the young women were exhibited were "natural," necessary for mating, just like the courting dances in the animal kingdom. Sara had gotten married with elegant wedding invitations. Lettering and phrasing recommended by Emily Post. Lavinia remembered how Sara had left the church in a vaporous cloud of tulle, with a bouquet of white orchids in her hand, long gloves. She would reproduce, century after century, in her noisy, fat grandchildren. That would be her life, her ultimate goal. That was what Lavinia's parents had wanted for her as well. But the club parties bored her. She preferred other types of entertainment.

Perhaps some day she would like to get married, but not now. Getting married meant limiting yourself, giving in. A very special man would have to appear along the way. Maybe not even then. They could live together. They wouldn't need "papers" to legalize their love.

The air was getting cooler. The moon displayed her yellowish light. The sound of silence seemed almost threatening. Maybe she should have gone to see Sara after all, she thought, listening to the silence that hid among the branches of the orange tree. Sara loved her and she loved Sara. They had been friends, best friends, since they were little girls. They accepted each other in spite of their differences. For a moment she was sorry she had chosen to be alone, but she had decided to learn to be by herself. It was her way of paying homage to her Aunt Inés. "You have to learn to be good company for yourself," Inés used to say to her.

She got up and turned on the television. On the tiny black and white screen they were reporting the trial. The warden had been found guilty. The soldiers looked at the doctor who so undauntedly implicated him. It was a Pyrrhic victory for justice. A few months later, the warden would be out of prison for good behavior and would kill the doctor on a deserted road.

There was a time when Lavinia thought things could be different. A time of effervescence when she was eighteen and was spending her vacation with her parents. She found the streets plastered with the posters of the opposition party. People sang the Green candidate's song with genuine enthusiasm. There was the illusion that the electoral campaign could result in a victory for the opposition. All those dreams were dispersed on the last Sunday of the contest. An enormous demonstration wound through the streets demanding the resignation of the ruling family, the withdrawal of the candidacy of the dictator's son. The leaders of the opposition spoke enthusiastically to that sea of people. No one was to leave. No one was to go home. Peaceful resistance in the face of tyranny. Until the soldiers with their riot helmets began to descend down the avenue in the direction of the multi-colored group agitated by the speeches. Afterward no one could remember when the shooting began, nor how the hundreds of shoes appeared, the shoes Lavinia saw strewn about the ground as she ran amid what seemed a stampede of runaway horses toward where her Aunt Inés stood waving her hands and calling to her.

That night families waited anxiously, listening to the shots of snipers ringing out in the dark. Dawn arrived amid heavy silence. The radio stations announced that the Green candidate and his collaborators had taken refuge in a hotel and had requested the protection of the United States ambassador. There was talk of three hundred, six hundred, countless dead. They would never know exactly how many people died that day, taking with them to their graves the last hope many had of getting rid of the dictatorship.

The repression increased.

Since then, the little flyers had begun: "Our only alternative is armed struggle." Flyers would appear furtively underneath doors. Groups would take over barracks far from the cities in the northern towns; there were ardent speeches in the universities; power became more and more concentrated, and the deaths of "subversives" were the order of the day.

"This is madness," commented her father. "The only thing we can do is resign ourselves," while her mother nodded assent.

Even her Aunt Inés had become discouraged. It gave Lavinia chills when she remembered how close she had come to a useless death.

The news concluded with a commercial for nylon stockings. "Provocative freedom for just nine pesos," the announcer offered. Lavinia smiled, thinking how in Faguas modernity had now reached women's legs, offering panty hose at "popular" prices, freedom through stockings. She turned off the television and got in bed with a book until sleep overcame her, and once more her grandfather appeared, inviting her to try on wings.

✦ ✦ ✦

It is night. The dampness of the earth penetrates me through these long veins of wood. I am awake. Will I never sleep again, never surrender myself to dreams, never again know the deciphered auguries of slumber? There must be many things I shall never feel again. As I watched the woman there in the garden, looking so thoughtful, I wished I could have known what she was meditating about, and there were moments when I felt her nearness, as if her thoughts had mingled with the rustling of the wind.

Ah! But I was soon distracted by the moon coming up in the distance. It looked large and yellow, a ripe fruit rising into the firmament, becoming brighter, shining white as it traveled toward the highest point in the sky. And once more the stars with their mystery. The night was always a magic time for me. To see it again after so many katunes (how many, I wonder) was enough to rid me of the sadness I was beginning to feel because of all those "nevermores" that await me. I should thank the gods for my having emerged again, breathing in so many branches in this ample green dress they gave me for my return.

I began to sway in the air, swinging and feeling weightless. More than once I had thought that trees looked so erect and graceful in spite of their great trunks, as if the trunks didn't weigh them down. Roots give you a feeling that is quite different than that of feet, they are diminutive legs that extend into the earth: a part of my body has sunk into the earth and gives me a strong sense of equilibrium that I never had when I walked upon its surface, when I only had feet. It is night, then, and the fireflies hover about the sleeping birds. Life bubbles within me as if I were pregnant, a cloak of butterflies or the slow gestation of fruit in the corollas of my blossoms. Funny to think I shall be the mother of oranges. I, who had to deny myself children.

• • •

The next day, Lavinia left earlier and went to the construction site indicated on the blueprints for the shopping center. It was a warm day. The January wind was blowing, stirring up the dust. The taxi went down avenues toward the lake. As she came nearer to the site, Lavinia looked out the window to see the part of the project already in progress. She saw the foundations of countless houses all made according to a single model. She got out of the taxi and began to walk through the recently laid-out streets, brushing off the lime which, mixed with dust, whitened her pants. Here and there she found groups of workers busy setting blocks to mark the foundations where the walls would go up. They looked at her as she passed, forgetting the cement to whistle or let fly a "hi, babe" at her. It ought to be illegal, Lavinia thought, the harassment women encounter in the streets. The best thing was to take no notice, although at some point she planned to stop and ask them how the work was going. She paused to look at the blueprints. She couldn't find the site where the shopping complex was to go up. Only when she went over them again did she realize that the sketch pointed clearly to the other side of the street. She looked up and saw again the row of cardboard and wood slab dwellings. Barrios like that occupied the periphery of the city and occasionally they were able to infiltrate the more central areas.

At least five thousand people must live there, she said to herself. The neighborhood looked peaceful. It was the peacefulness of poverty. There were naked children, children in short pants filling buckets of water from a common faucet, and barefoot women hanging clothes made of thin, worn cloth along wires. Over there a woman was grinding corn. On the corner, a fat man tended a vulcanizing workshop.

According to the blueprints, the corner of the shopping center would hypothetically crush the vulcanizing shop. An ice cream parlor would replace it. The walls of the new construction would cut through the small gardens of banana and almond bushes.

And the people? What would happen to the people? she wondered. More than once she had read in the newspaper about people being evicted from their homes. She never thought that she would have to be a party to it.

She looked around her. The January wind rustled the weeds growing in the half-finished sidewalks. Several workers were pouring cement into the foundation of one of the new houses. She went up to them.

"Do you know a shopping center is going to be built across the street?" she asked.

The workers looked her over from head to foot. One of them dried his sweaty face with a dirty blue kerchief he wore tied around his neck. He nodded.

"But what about those people?" Lavinia asked.

The group was expressionless. Well-dressed young white woman asking questions. The men were strong. Well-built workers. Sweat glistened on their dark, naked chests. They were barefoot. Their feet were white with lime, like their hands.

The one who had pointed before had a sneer on his face. He shrugged his shoulders in an eloquent expression of "who knows?" and "who cares?" Breaking the silence, a worker with a red kerchief tied about his forehead said, "They're going to move them somewhere else. They're going to get them out of there because they're squatters."

"And how long have they been living there?" she asked.

"Whew..." exclaimed the one with the red kerchief, "for years! Since the lake flooded."

"And what do they say?"

That indifferent reaction again. Now it was from the whole group; a simultaneous reaction, in unison.

"Ask *them*," said the one with the red kerchief. "We don't know a thing."

"Thank you," she replied, walking away, knowing they weren't going to tell her anything more. As she crossed the street, she felt the eyes of the man with the red kerchief on her back.

She was sweating. The sweat ran down her legs, making her pants stick to her skin. Her red T-shirt clung to her back. Her makeup smudged the kleenex she used to dry her face. Lavinia went over to the wooden hut that served as a vulcanizing shop. The fat man was putting a tire in a barrel of water. He was watching the water and waiting for the bubbles that would indicate where the hole was. Poor and primitive but accurate methods of diagnosis. She said hello. Farther inside, a thin man was pounding an inner tube out of the tire's rubber covering. He looked at her.

"You know they're planning to build a shopping center on this land?" Lavinia asked the fat man.

"Yes," he replied, stopping. The tire gave off bubbles on all sides. He was on his guard.

"Are you in favor of it?"

Once more the same reaction as the workers. Lavinia asked herself why she was asking questions: what was it that she wanted to know?

"They say they're going to move us somewhere else, they're going to give us land. I've been here five years. That's my home over there." He pointed toward the dirt streets of the neighborhood. "We argued with the land developer, but they say the land doesn't belong to us. As if we didn't know we don't own anything! We came here when the lake water forced us out from over there," he said, pointing to an indefinite spot in the direction of the lake. "For five years no one bothered us. We invested here. We even got together and put up a school. But they don't care! Nobody pays any attention to us. If we don't leave, they'll send the army after us. That's what they told us! And who are you?" inquired the man, suddenly looking at her with distrust, as if he were sorry he had talked so much. "Are you a reporter?"

"No, no," clarified Lavinia, feeling uncomfortable. "I'm an architect. They asked me to check the blueprints. I didn't know about this situation."

"In this country no one knows what they don't want to know," the fat man said, as he noticed the blueprints under her arm, and turned back to the tire in the water.

Lavinia walked away. She walked a little while on the path beside the settlement, seeing the dirt streets disappear into it, flanked by houses of wooden slabs, newspaper-lined folding screens, roofs of palm, tile, zinc, wood. Variations of degrees of poverty. Pot-bellied kids, dirty and naked, stood in the doorways next to scrawny dogs. There were banana plants growing here and there and chickens strutting about. In the distance was the shack that served as the school. Children sat on the ground. The teacher, who wore a threadbare dress and plastic sandals, stood in front of the blackboard. Lavinia felt pity and discomfort. It wasn't the most pleasant way to get to know "the practice," she thought, sensing she was part of the destructive apparatus that would force these eternal gypsies to migrate once again. Why hadn't Felipe warned her? she wondered, heading for the avenue in the middle of the suffocating heat and the wind that sent dust scurrying.

She returned to the office in a Mercedes Benz taxi.

When Lavinia went through the big wooden doors, she was hit by the gust of air conditioning. Silvia, the receptionist, noticed she was sweating. She told Lavinia such an extreme change of temperature was dangerous and she could catch a cold.

Lavinia went into the bathroom and dried her skin with a towel. The dust on her arms turned to mud as it came in contact with the water. She looked pale in the mirror. She took out her blush to redo her make-up before speaking with Felipe.

She knocked on his door. "Come in," said Felipe's voice. Lavinia entered. She was aware that her T-shirt was still damp. It was sticking to her skin and her nipples were erect in the cold air-conditioned room.

"Did they throw a bucket of water on you?" he asked jokingly, grinning from ear to ear with his wide mouth and slightly uneven teeth.

"A bucket of cold water. Right. Why didn't you tell me about the site for the shopping center?"

"I thought girls like you didn't care about things like that," responded Felipe, again with his teasing expression.

"Well, now you know you were wrong. You really hold my birth against me. Of course I care about those poor people. I don't like the idea of starting my "practice" by designing buildings that are going to force almost five thousand souls, as the priests say, out of their homes..." She shook her T-shirt, blowing inside it, trying to cool off her breasts. She was very hot.

She felt her cheeks blush and her skin redden because of the contrast between the temperature of her body and the artificially cold environment. She sat back in the chair. She didn't like Felipe's attitude.

"I think it's good for you to get rid of some of your romantic ideas about architecture," he said.

"You could have given me more time..."

"Maybe. I think it's harder later on. The blow is harder then... Let me get you some coffee. You're all sweaty and the cold might be bad for you."

Lavinia looked at him. His expression had become slightly softer. He went out of the office and came back with a steaming cup of coffee, which tasted good. She thanked him, contemplating the mixture of ferocity and gentleness Felipe displayed, abruptly changing from one to the other.

"What struck me most was the way the people are so resigned," Lavinia said, remembering the expressions of impotence while she slowly sipped her coffee.

"They have no alternative," Felipe said. "Either they leave, or they are thrown out with the help of the army."

"That's what one of them told me."

They continued talking until lunch. Felipe invited her to have lunch in a nearby cafeteria.

"Let's go some other day," she said. Now she needed to change. She didn't want to catch a cold with her damp shirt and the wintry chill in the office.

Felipe was strange, she thought, as she headed home. He had given her a long talk about the "realities of the job." According to him, he had tried to persuade the land developers to change the site for the shopping center, but to no avail. The lots, which had been bought from the mayor for a bargain price, were "state" land. The mayor made a profit from the transaction. Besides, the blueprints were finished. "I only wanted your opinion," he told her. She wouldn't have to design the walls that would flatten the fat man and his vulcanizing shop. He only wanted to "bring her down to earth." It was better to walk with one's feet on the ground, he told her.

CHAPTER 3

✤ ✤ ✤

I am slowly beginning to understand these times. I'm getting ready. I have observed the woman. Women don't seem to be subordinate any more but are important people. They even have their own servants. And they work outside the home. She, for example, leaves for work every morning.

I don't know how advantageous this is. At least our mothers' sole responsibility was caring for their homes, and that was enough. I would say that maybe it was better then because they had children to prolong their heritage and a husband who made them forget the narrowness of the world, embracing them at night. But she has none of these joys.

There no longer appears to be any cult to the gods. She never lights ocote branches, nor bows in ceremonies. She never seems to doubt whether Tonatiú will light her mornings. We were always afraid that the sun could set forever because what guarantees do we have that it will shine tomorrow? Perhaps the Spaniards found a way to be sure. They said they came from lands where the sun never set. But none of that was really true, and their strange and thick tongues told lies. It did not take us long to discover their odd obsessions. They were capable of killing for gems and gold from our altars and our clothing. Yet they thought we were impious because we sacrificed warriors to the gods.

How we learned to hate that language that robbed us of everything and kept on destroying everything we had always been!

And now these people have a language similar to the ones who came before, only theirs is sweeter, with some intonations like ours. I dare not think about winners or losers.

My sap continues its frenzied task of transforming the orange blossoms into fruit. I already feel the embryos being covered with the yellow flesh of oranges. I know I must hurry. She and I will meet each other soon. The time of bearing fruit, of ripening, will come. I wonder if I shall feel pain when she cuts them.

• • •

Lavinia spent the entire first month getting used to her job while Felipe, with his ubiquitous presence, took on with gusto the mission of "getting her feet firmly planted."

She had gotten used to the daily routine of going to work, getting up early, even if every morning she was hard to abandon the cool, comforting sheets. She could never understand why schedules weren't modified to honor the morning, the cosiest time for sleeping. For her, they also had the lure of transgression. Sleeping while the city was waking. Sleeping while delivery trucks, buses, and taxis greeted the dawn from the streets as they transported their cargoes of people and milk and bread and butter. Sleeping despite the fact that the sun was pouring mercilessly into the room through the chinks in the doors.

But her drowsiness did not last long. Now that she was part of the hubbub punctuated by the staccato pulse of office typewriters, she understood why people got great satisfaction from their problems, the tight deadlines for signing contracts and completing projects.

It was a way of feeling important, she thought, an excuse for leaving the domestic world and entering the world of balance sheets, where there was risk, a chance of gain and loss. That way life became an interesting business, a constant gamble, and you could pretend that time wasn't slipping through your fingers, that something was being accomplished during those extended hours, those days that were implacably repeated, one after the other.

She got out of bed and once again performed her rituals: she put on the water for coffee, she looked out the window to check on the rebirth of the tree, now occupied with transforming flowers to fruit—the future oranges already looking like tiny green spheres among the branches—she went to the bathroom and looked at herself in the mirror. She thought of her morning face, so strangely distant and ugly. She knew that thankfully it would soon return to normal. She turned on the shower, feeling the water wash away her sleepiness, announcing that the day had begun. She enjoyed scrubbing the soap along her skin until foam embroidery clung to her naked body. She liked to see her pubic hair turn white, liked to inspect the body that had mysteriously been assigned to her for an entire lifetime—her antenna to the universe.

"You have to love it," Jerome would say while making love to her among the gnarled olive trees beside the sea, during those jaunts away from dorms for students of French. Taking a shower reminded her of Jerome and how she had discovered the texture of green fruit in his masculine body, his strong muscular body rubbing against the softness of her thighs. That was how she had realized that her skin was ready for caresses, that it could make sounds which linked her to cats, panthers, and jaguars from her tropical forests.

She closed her eyes beneath the shower. In her mind she clearly envisioned Felipe's image superimposed upon her occasional love-affairs. They were attracted to each other by something more than architecture. They played cat and mouse, stalking one another, then pretending to flee, creating imaginary antagonisms that were a pretext for long consultations in each other's offices. Since the day he had sent her, unwarned, to see the eviction that would result from the construction of the Shopping Center, there had been constant arguments. Although she understood the limits of her romanticism as the weeks went by, she did not stop insisting that, despite the fact that those who had money weren't exactly humanists, they, as architects, had control over the ultimate form and design. It was difficult to resign herself to accepting the clients' requests, some of which were boring, some flamboyant, others in bad taste. Felipe helped her reach compromises, showing enormous patience for their long discussions. Only once in a while did he criticize her "spoiled girl's" attitudes, practically shouting as he told her again that they were paying her to please clients, not to argue with them, especially if it became obvious that arguing was useless.

She was certain that Felipe enjoyed the arguments, even if he pretended to be exasperated when he saw her appear at his office door with a belligerent expression.

During meetings, their eyes would meet and turn away. Still, they both tried to put on a show of professional coolness, barricading themselves behind buildings, houses, roofing and siding material, talking on the periphery of things, avoiding the personal.

More than once she was tempted to invite him home, but she hadn't even been able to get him to repeat the lunch invitation of her first days there. She felt trapped in a contest between magnets and iron filings.

Felipe seemed to be one of those men who flirt with attraction, shying away from the possibility of plunging into the vertigo of abandon. Although it was hard to imagine that nothing would happen. One day the game would have to be defined. Both their gazes revealed the naked night when they would cast off their moorings and be shipwrecked together. But, perhaps, Lavinia thought, he was more traditional, he enjoyed the postponement, the give and take, throwing bread crumbs at each other like pigeons in a plaza, only to flutter their wings and break the spell at five o'clock, the time they parted.

Or perhaps she was a victim of romantic speculation, she told herself, as she slipped her stockings over her legs, and the truth was that Felipe was having an illicit love affair with a woman whom she imagined waiting anxiously for the husband to leave so she could make those mysterious telephone calls that sent Felipe catapulting out of the office at mid-morning or mid-afternoon. Or maybe he was a Don Juan in disguise, with several women responsible for the "study sessions" at night, the students who "needed" him, because no normal person had so many things to do, nobody seemed to have so many busy hours outside the office as he did.

The telephone rang, putting an end to such disquieting speculations. It was Antonio, inviting her to go out dancing that night. She accepted without hesitation. She needed some distraction.

When she rushed into the building, she found Felipe waiting for the elevator. They entered side by side, standing silently among men and women with preoccupied faces. Lavinia thought about the curious phenomenon of elevators. Their tense accumulated silence. In an elevator, people resembled silent fish, afraid of closeness. Fleeting swimmers heading toward open doors. Different destinations. Floors. When they left the confined space, they breathed, filling their lungs, like someone surfacing for a deep gulp of air after being under water. Elevators. Fishbowls. Objects of the same family.

When they got off on the fourth floor, she mentioned it to Felipe. He laughed at her idea.

Silvia was already behind her desk, saying good-morning to the late arrivals.

Lavinia joked about the insidious way the bed had refused to let her go that morning. She felt completely integrated into the jovial, creative ambiance of the office. The first day's formality seemed so distant to her. Mr. Solera was now Julián. Her male colleagues respected her—she was the only woman with a substantive job; all the rest were secretaries, aides, cleaning staff. It hadn't been easy, she thought, as she left Felipe in the hallway and went into her cozy office, now decorated with plants and posters. At first they had listened distrustfully to her opinions. When it was her turn to present projects or designs, she was subject to an intense barrage of questions and objections. She didn't let them intimidate her. She recognized the advantage of her birth: she owed something to having been born into a social strata that believed it owned the world.

Julián's attitude toward her helped soften the others' efforts to impose their masculine supremacy. He frequently referred to her creativity and professional ability; he used her as an example of the concern one should have for achieving higher levels of quality, even when that meant making meetings with clients longer.

She left her purse on her desk and opened the curtains of her picture window, picking up the pencils to sharpen them in the electric sharpener. Mercedes came in to bring her coffee and place the daily papers on her desk.

Lavinia enjoyed few things as much as she did that first hour in the office, "psychologically" preparing herself for the bustle of the day.

She opened the papers and scanned the daily news, sipping her coffee. Soon Felipe came in to review the week's work. It was Friday, and they would get together with Julián that afternoon, as they usually did, to evaluate and plan the work for the coming week.

At one point in the conversation, she mentioned her plans for the evening.

"Don't you like to dance?" she asked Felipe.

"Of course," he said. "When I was a boy I used to win the school contests," and he looked at her with a wide smile. Lavinia thought that she hadn't seen him in such good humor for days.

That night while she was dancing with Antonio on the dance floor of the "Pink Elephant," she saw Felipe at the bar, having a drink and watching her. For a moment she lost her concentration, surprised to see him there surrounded by the smoke and strident music, a Cheshire cat appearing and disappearing between the couples crammed on the tiny dance floor.

Lavinia kept on dancing, letting the bongo drums and the percussion guide her. Seeing Felipe, as he watched her from afar, energized her movements. She let herself be seduced by the feeling that she was being watched. She could see Felipe through the lights and smoke; his gray eyes penetrating her, tickling her. She danced for him, pretending she didn't see him, aware that she did it to provoke him while she enjoyed the exhibitionism, the sensuality of the dance, the euphoria of thinking that they would finally meet outside the office. She was wearing one of her shortest miniskirts, high heels, a shirt that fell from one shoulder—the perfect image of sin, she had thought to herself before going out—and she'd smoked a little grass. Now and then she liked to do that. Although in Italy she'd already embraced and discarded the ephemeral high of escapism, here in Faguas her friends were just discovering it, and she went along with the trend.

When the music changed, she had already decided to take the initiative; she wasn't going to risk having Felipe just stay by the bar watching her from a distance, entrenched, as usual. Antonio wasn't surprised when she told him she was going to say hello to her "boss." He went back to join the gang at the table while Lavinia went over to the bar.

"Well, well," Lavinia said teasingly to Felipe as she sat on the empty bar stool beside him. "I thought you were too 'nice' to hang around these dens of iniquity."

"I couldn't resist the temptation of seeing how you do in this environment," Felipe said. "I see you fit in very well. You dance very nicely."

"I probably don't dance as well as you," she answered, teasingly. "I never won a contest."

"Because girls like you don't participate in those things," he said, slipping from the stool to the floor and holding out his hand. "Let's dance."

The rhythm of the music had changed. The D.J. was playing a slow bossa nova. Most of the couples had left the dance floor. Only a few remained, embracing. She accepted, amused. She talked without stopping, hating herself for feeling so nervous. Felipe held her close to his broad chest, holding her tight. She could feel his thick black chest hairs through his shirt. They began to sway. Their skin touching. Lavinia's legs brushed by Felipe's trousers.

"Is that your boyfriend?" he asked, referring to Antonio, when they passed near the table.

"No," Lavinia said, "boyfriends are out of style."

"Your lover, then," he said, holding her more tightly against him.

"He's my friend," Lavinia said, "and once in a while he takes care of me..."

She felt a vibration in Felipe's body, responding to her attempt to shock him. He was holding her so closely it almost hurt. Lavinia wondered what had happened to the married woman, the night classes at the university. She had trouble breathing. She could touch the buttons on his shirt in the middle of his chest with her mouth. This dance is getting serious, she thought. Barriers were crumbling. Brakes were being released. Their hearts were accelerating. Panting. Felipe's warm breath on her neck. The music moving them in the dark. The sphere covered with tiny mirrors in the sweep of the spotlight lit up the surroundings, the smoke, the sweetish smell of clandestine grass smokers coming out of the bathrooms.

"You like to smoke grass, don't you?" Felipe asked in a whisper from above, without letting go of her.

"Once in a while," she agreed, from below, "but I'm over that stage now."

Felipe held her tighter. She didn't understand the abrupt change. He suddenly seemed to have dropped any pretense of indifference and thrown himself openly into an almost animal seduction. She was disconcerted. Felipe emanated primitive vibrations. It was something that came from deep within him. Different than the others. Her friends. There was an intensity filling his whole body; it was in his gray eyes as he looked at her, holding her now ever so slightly apart from him.

"You shouldn't go around smoking grass," he told her. "You don't need stimulants. There's life inside you. There's no need to go around borrowing it."

Lavinia didn't know what to say. She felt dizzy and was moving without taking her eyes from his. Suspended in that smoky gray gaze. She said something about sensations. Grass heightened your sensations.

"I don't think you need anyone to heighten anything for you," he said.

The soft music ended. It changed again to heavy rock. Felipe didn't let go of her. He kept dancing to a music of his own, following the rhythm his body demanded, oblivious to the noise. It seemed to Lavinia that he was even oblivious to her. He held her tightly against him again with the force of a shipwrecked man clinging to a board in the middle of the ocean. He made her nervous. She saw Antonio gesturing to her in the distance, but she closed her eyes. She liked Felipe. She wanted this to happen. Time and again she had repeated to herself that this was going to happen some day. They were not going to spend their whole lives glancing at each other in the office. They had that something that animals have when they sniff each other, the emanations of instinct, the magnetic attraction, unmistakable. She didn't think any more. She couldn't. She was engulfed by the waves of his skin washing over her. She saw herself set in the middle of the music, saw Antonio's leaping and contortions, Florencia, the rest of the dancers, and the two of them there moving to their own rhythm. In a fascinating bubble far from everything. Like a balloon or a space ship disappearing into the ether. Lavinia smelled, touched, perceived only the absolute of Felipe's body, swaying her from side to side.

Antonio thought he should rescue her and came over to try to break the spell. He was jealous. Felipe looked at him. Lavinia thought Antonio looked so fragile, so volatile beside Felipe.

She, amused, excited, compliant, female, on the edge of the dance floor, heard Felipe tell Antonio that they were going to leave, they had an appointment, and Antonio needn't worry about her.

Afterward he told her to get her purse and she obeyed, incapable of resisting the fascination of that air of authority, leaving Antonio's astonished stare in her wake. They entered the house in the dark. Everything happened so quickly. Felipe's hands rose and fell along her back, slipping toward all the borders of her body, hands that multiplied and were alive, exploring her, making their way through the obstacles of clothing. She felt herself respond in the penumbra, still aware that a part of her brain was trying to assimilate what was happening without managing to do so, blinded by a touch that created high tides of trembling in her skin.

In the silvery moonlight they found their way to the bedroom, while he completely opened her blouse and the zipper of her miniskirt, until they reached the territory of the mattress, the bed beneath the window, the barriers to nakedness. Once more Lavinia stopped thinking. She sank against Felipe's chest, letting herself slip into the wave of warmth that emanated from her womb, drowning in the waves that crashed one upon another, oysters, mollusks, cuttlefish, palm trees, the subterranean passageways giving way, the movement of Felipe's body, her own body, arching, tensing, and the sounds, jaguars, reaching the tip of the wave, the bow letting arrows fly, flowers opening and closing. They barely spoke between one onslaught and the next. Lavinia tried to smoke a cigarette, to speak amid Felipe's kisses, but he wouldn't let her. Again, she felt as if she weren't there. She spoke to him.

"Look at me," she said. "Do you see me?"

"Of course I see you," Felipe said. "Finally I am seeing you. I think I would have gone crazy if this hadn't happened tonight. I was already thinking I would have to prescribe cold showers for myself in order to stand the office."

And he rose to Lavinia's laughter when she finally decided to just enjoy it, to put aside her amazement at the strength of the passion, freed with such determination in a single exhausting night during which she lost track of everything else and feared Lucrecia would find them at dawn, both dead of a heart attack.

✦ ✦ ✦

Today a man came. He came in with the woman. They seemed to be under the spell of love potions. They made love madly, as if they had been holding themselves back for a long time. It was like reliving it all. Living again Yarince's bonfire piercing the memories, the branches, the leaves, the soft flesh of my oranges. They sized each other up like warriors before a combat. Afterward the only barrier between them was their skin. Her skin grew hands to embrace the body of the man lying on top of her; her womb strained forward, as if trying to bring him home to nest, bring him inside her, make him swim within her in order to give birth to him once more. They made love the way Yarince and I used to when he returned from long explorations that lasted many moons. Over and over again until they lay exhausted, stretched out, quiet on the soft mattress. He gives off strong vibrations. He is surrounded by an aura of hidden things. He is tall and white, like the Spaniards. Now I know, however, that neither he nor she is a Spaniard. I wonder what race this is, this mixture of invaders and Nahuas. Could they be the children of the women in our tribes, dragged into promiscuity and slavery? Could they be the children of the terror caused by rape, the insatiable lust of the conquistadors? To whom do their hearts, to whom does the breath in their bodies belong?

I know only that they make love to each other like healthy animals, without garments or inhibitions. That is how our people loved before the strange god of the Spaniards forbade them the pleasures of loving.

• • •

Lavinia awoke at eight that morning. She opened her eyes and sensed Felipe's body there, entwined with hers in the rumpled bed. She didn't move, fearing she would wake him. It took her a moment to notice the time, to realize no one would come, and they didn't have to go to work because it was Saturday. The night before she had completely lost track of time.

Calm now, she smiled as she looked at Felipe's peaceful slumber. It was fun to watch people sleeping, she thought. He looked like a child. She imagined him as a little boy playing with a top, and without moving, she fell asleep again until Felipe woke her.

"It's really late!" he exclaimed. "I have to run."

"But we don't have to go to work today," she said. "We can have breakfast together."

"I can't," he said, as he went into the bathroom. "I've got a meeting with my students. I promised to help them for an exam."

He came out and dressed quickly.

"You're always busy..."

"No, not always," he said, winking at her.

She said good-bye to him in the doorway. She watched him leave, walking quickly, growing smaller in the distance. She went back to the bedroom. Alone now, she looked at herself in the mirror. She had the face of a woman who was well loved. She smelled of him. If it were up to her she wouldn't bathe, she'd have kept his scent all day. She liked the smell of semen, of sex. But she got under the shower to get rid of her languor, her desire to go back to bed. Sara was expecting her for breakfast.

CHAPTER 4

+ + +

She awoke singing. She is singing while she bathes. I am glad that she is happy. I am, too. I am bearing fruit. The oranges are still tiny and green. In just a few days they will be round and yellow. I am glad I found this tree. It was one of the few good things the Spaniards brought. Yarince and I used to steal oranges when we went by their plantations. Not everyone liked them, but we would devour them because their juice is cool and refreshing. It is not like the mango, which leaves you thirstier. Though I wouldn't have minded coming out in a mango tree. But I had good aim. I do not know what I would have done if I had emerged in the cactus right nearby. I do not like cactus. They only remind me of legs being scratched.

The pulp of the orange is fleshy and carefully structured. It has thousands of tiny containers, soft skins to wrap the flesh in, another skin to separate the sections, then the rind and many seeds: the possibility of tiny trees left to the whims of nature.

I hope my seeds find good soil.

I can see the inside of the fruit so close. I can be in it, in its flattened ends, its roundness. "The earth is round and flat like an orange." That was the great discovery of the Spaniards. That makes me laugh. The earth is like me.

• • •

When Lavinia arrived, Sara was doing her gardening rounds. She and Adrián had been married now for six months, and Sara played the role of housewife perfectly.

They lived in a colonial house with four corridors and large bedrooms with ogive windows. In the inner garden was a malinche tree taller than the roof that provided cool shade for the house. Around the tree, which bloomed fiery red just once a year, Sara had hung ferns and planted all kinds of begonias, jalacates, and roses.

The garden showed its gratitude for this care by producing beautiful flowers.

The two friends were in the habit of having breakfast together on Saturdays. The table was set: hot coffee, toast, marmalade shining in its glass container, butter in its silver tray, new china, a new table cloth.

The air of wedding gifts still lingered in the house.

"Madam," Lavinia said in a joking tone as she came over to the table. "I see you have everything ready for our breakfast."

"I didn't make pancakes this time," Sara said. "And because you're punctual, you never ruin my efforts. The coffee doesn't get cold on me, and the toast doesn't get hard the way it does with Adrián, who right at dinner time decides he can't leave his book or is in the bathroom endlessly 'washing his hands'."

They laughed as they sat down at the table and Sara served the steaming coffee in white porcelain cups.

Lavinia looked at her eighteenth century lady's face, with its fine, delicate features, her "porcelain skin," as Sara jokingly called it. Her blond hair was pulled back in a bun. Everything about her was soft and delicate.

"How's your work going?" Sara asked.

"Fine," Lavinia answered. "I'm still getting used to the idea that dreams are only dreams. I think Felipe was right about that trick he played on me with the Shopping Center. The business world is rough. Nothing could help the poor squatters. The developers weren't about to give up the land they'd just bought. They are hardly philanthropists."

"That's life," Sara said. "Don't worry about it. Anyway, those people are used to it. What are you designing now?"

"A house," Lavinia replied, sipping her coffee, thinking how everything was so "natural" for Sara. "You know Felipe? Well, it happened," she added, unable to keep her secret any longer.

Sara's face lit up. Ever since she had heard her talk about Felipe and found out he was a bachelor, she had begun to act as matchmaker, something Lavinia didn't want her to do, telling her to stop trying to marry her off, like her parents. But Sara didn't stop trying. She always asked about Felipe.

"And how was it?" she asked, trying to hide her curiosity so as not to put her friend on guard.

"Wonderful. But I don't want to get too enthusiastic. It all happened so fast. I'm afraid to fall in love before I have a sense of the whole picture."

"You really complicate things," Sara said. "Love is the most natural thing in the world. I don't see why you should be afraid..."

"Well, it's just that there is something peculiar about Felipe. He often gets strange telephone calls. He leaves in a rush. He's always 'busy.' To me it sounds like there's a married woman... I don't know. Maybe it's just my imagination."

"You always did have a fertile imagination."

"Could be," Lavinia said thoughtfully, angry at herself and feeling just like one of those jealous wives, thinking about Felipe and his Saturday morning "classes." "And how are you doing with Adrián?"

With a demure expression, Sara drew an imprecise picture of her relationship with Adrián, the oral portrait of a perfect marriage. They still had problems in their intimate moments, Sara confessed. Adrián was a little "rough." He didn't understand how important tenderness was.

Lavinia had always had trouble imagining Sara making love. She was so ethereal, almost mystical. She'd even spoken at one time of entering the convent and devoting herself to "loving God."

"I don't know if it's because I'm too romantic. Or if I've seen too many love scenes in the movies," Sara said as she shifted her position in the chair, leaning forward to butter her bread.

Lavinia smiled.

"The love you see in the movies is just an illusion," she told her friend. "Actually, it must be awful. Imagine: under those lights, those cameras, and with the possibility they'll say Cut! at any moment! The constant threat of *coitus interruptus* if the director doesn't think you're doing it right..."

They both laughed. Tenderness in men was generally repressed, Lavinia said. One had to teach them. She thought Sara should teach Adrián, but preferred not to mention it to her. Beginnings were always difficult, Lavinia said. Crude imitations of what was to come once the skins deciphered each other. That is what had happened to her, at least with Jerome. Although Sara and Adrián had been together for six months now, she thought. She told Sara how it was important to get over one's shyness. She had to teach Adrián about the hidden maps, give him the compass.

They talked until noon. Adrián would be home soon, and Sara said she had to take a shower. She didn't want her husband to find her just the same as when he left.

Lavinia took advantage of the chance to leave in spite of the invitation to stay for lunch. She wasn't in the mood for Adrián's sarcasm and lectures. That afternoon she wanted to make up for not having slept, she wanted to read and think.

The week went by with the amazing speed time usually has when it is crowded with events.

Since the beginning of her relationship with Felipe, the days at the office had become a blur. It was hard for her to concentrate on her work because he invaded it with comments and gestures that wouldn't let her forget their recent intimacy. Even though since then they had only seen each other once to go to the movies and then for a few beers, both that time and their single night of unbridled love were foremost in her mind, along with the daily caresses they furtively exchanged during work hours.

Felipe liked to talk about his past, but he seemed to avoid giving any details about his present.

Lavinia had been able to catch an imaginary glimpse of him in the distance, on the long voyage across the Atlantic, on his trip to Germany, picturing him dressed like the sailors in old photographs. Or strolling along the streets of Hamburg, the famous port where "women of ill repute" stood naked in the windows along the *Reperbahn* and were sold to the highest bidder. Her imagination had stopped in particular at Ute—the woman who, in words whose meaning she didn't completely understand, taught Felipe, among other things, that he should "return" to Faguas. She imagined a tall valkyrie with long blond hair, experienced in life and the art of making love. She could almost visualize the red-brick house, the chimney, and Ute teaching Felipe how to make love. At seventeen, Felipe had signed on a ship in Puerto Alto, where his father worked in the shipyard. The adventure turned into a nightmare. Determined not to return at the mercy of the slave-driving captain, he stayed in Germany and nearly died of cold and starvation. Ute saved him. "Mother and lover in one woman," he had called her. She took him in, deciphered the language for him, taught him "the importance of lighted streets for women who were alone," the study of architecture and the body. What Lavinia could not understand was Felipe's grateful tone when he told how she had explained to him the need to "return." She felt as if she were listening to Ulysses talk of his return to Ithaca. She couldn't understand how Ute, who was no Penelope, seemed to have been so set on his returning to his country. Why did she convince him to return if she loved him so much?

It was just another one of his mysteries, Lavinia thought, placing books in a bookcase she had recently bought, just like the phone calls and the evening duties which he insisted were university "responsibilities."

That weekend Lavinia didn't go to have breakfast with Sara. She had gotten paid the day before and spent Saturday morning buying furniture and other things for her house. That night she was going out with the "gang" and the next day Felipe had promised to come over for coffee in the afternoon.

She looked out the window at the garden. She saw the early spring of the orange tree. The shiny leaves gleamed in the sun. The oranges were nearly ripe. Every day they looked larger and yellower. She empathized with the tree and felt its rapid growth along with her own. It was a happy tree, fiercely embracing life, proud of the force of its flowering. For this she had given up Bologna, the bell tower, and the archways. Ever since she was a girl she had loved the greenness, the rebellious tropical vegetation, the stubborn plants that resisted scorching summers and hot suns that baked the earth. Snow was something else: it was white, cold, and inhospitable, she thought as she turned back to the bookcase. She had never gotten used to European winters. As soon as spring began, she felt her own personality returning. In winter she would retreat into her own body and grow silent. Her thoughtful, nostalgic side appeared. In contrast, in Faguas no snow would afflict her bones. The warmth invited her to come out of herself, to find happiness in the landscapes she held within her eyes as if inside a fine porcelain jar. That was why the tropics, this country, these trees, were hers. They belonged to her as much as she belonged to them.

"Saturdays are slow," she thought, feeling alone.

+ + +

I'm striving. I am at work in this laboratory of sap and verdure. I must hurry. An occult wisdom nourishes my purpose. It says that she and I are about to meet.

This morning the hummingbirds and other birds came. They frolicked among my branches, tickling me, chattering amid the fullness of my growth. They make love. Theirs is the love of growing things. Perhaps the spirit of Yarince lives in the quickest one of all, the one that flies in search of pollen with its little beak held high. Everyone knows warriors return in the form of hummingbirds to fly in the balmy air.

Ah, Yarince! How I remember your strong, tanned body after the hunt when you used to return, a splendid tired puma looking for the shelter of my lap. We would sit beside the fire in silence, watching the flames cluster and fade away, their blue centers, their red tongues biting the smoke and filling the air with hot crackling. Those silent nights were so long when we crouched in the wild innermost heart of the mountain, hiding in ambush. The Spaniards did not dare follow us. They feared our trees and animals. They knew nothing of the venom of the serpents, and they were not familiar with the jaguar nor the tapir or even with the flight of the nocturnal pocoyas, which scared them because to their ears they were like "suffering souls." And still they sent the thunder flashing from their sticks, frightening the parrots, scattering the flocks of birds, making the monkeys screech as they passed above our heads in droves. The mothers carrying their young that since then have had a scared expression on their faces.

But you embraced me while we were surrounded by those thundering volleys. You put your hands over my ears, held me close in the thickets, managed to ease my fear with the weight of your body, making me forget the nearness of death by holding me close to the palpitation of life; your body taking shelter in mine until the beating of our hearts was the loudest sound in the hills.

Ah, Yarince! Perhaps it was all in vain. Perhaps not even the memory of our battles remains!

• • •

The next day Lavinia struggled between waking and sleeping from early morning. The habit of getting up early had been implanted like an invisible clock in her chest, but the idea of Sunday begged for pillows and the right to drowsiness. It was nearly eleven when her hunger won out over her laziness and the bed. She got up, barefoot, wearing her aquamarine silk kimono. On Sundays she felt she was one too many in the world. It was an uncomfortable day for single people. Sundays, she thought, were meant for family outings in the car, the kids and the dog, looking out through the back window, or for getting up late: the father in his striped pajamas sitting at the table, reading the newspaper and the kids waiting for the scrumptious breakfast. She remembered the full refrigerator in her parents' house and felt nostalgia.

Since that day at lunch when she had announced that she was going to live "her life," and move to her aunt's house, she hadn't seen them. She still remembered the cataclysm amid chicken breasts in white sauce, water goblets, the spotless tablecloth. Her father's and mother's faces predicting dishonor, gossip, shame. Horrors of the world that awaited her outside the four walls of her home (in spite of her years alone in Europe). The peril of strangers. Men who would try to rape her, take advantage of her. Society's disapproval of women who lived alone. From magicians' hats they had pulled out all the sacrifices they had made so that she would have a good education, so she could be happy, like any other self-respecting, decent girl. During dessert they tried with a conciliatory tone to persuade her not to move out. It was time for them to get to know one another and learn to love each other.

Too late for Lavinia. Aunt Inés and her grandfather had been her mother and father. For her real parents she had only the affection that comes from biological ties. The distance between them surfaced when they became convinced that they could not dissuade her. Instead of persuasion they tried threats and in the end forced her to pack up all her things "so she could leave immediately if her mind was so made up." While her father, trying to avoid conflict, withdrew to his room, her mother stood by the door, and, like an exterminating angel brandishing a sword of fire, expelled her from paradise.

That was how the full refrigerators and bountiful Sunday breakfasts had disappeared from her life. That was how she had lost the last privileges of an only daughter. And also the possibility of primal love. She felt an orphan's nostalgia. It always happened on Sunday.

To forget about them, Lavinia decided to give herself a treat. Prepare a Sunday family breakfast just for herself.

The kitchen smelled empty. She was sorry there had been no one to initiate her in the culinary arts. Neither her mother nor her Aunt Inés, each for different reasons, had been devotees of the kitchen. She was following in their footsteps. But a woman didn't lose anything by knowing how to cook, she thought. She personally admired those who could. To her they were like magical alchemists, who were capable of turning a red, almost repulsive piece of raw meat into an appetizing dish that not only tasted good but looked wonderful as well, its golden color in perfect harmony with the green parsley and the red tomato.

The cabinet shelves were tidy, and various cans dozed along them with the inertia of inanimate objects. There was the unopened box of "Aunt Jemima." She took milk, eggs, and butter out of the refrigerator, mixed the ingredients together and began to beat the slowly thickening white batter in a bowl.

She set the coffee on the burner, put bread in the toaster, and spread an Italian cutwork tablecloth over the rustic wooden table in the kitchen: it had white and red checks. She put on some music, getting caught up in the rhythm of her own activity.

Only the orange juice was missing. That was too bad. Why not make some even if the oranges are still a little green? she said to herself. Bitter juice wouldn't taste so bad. The yellow color in the glass would make up for it, at least from an aesthetic point of view. Besides, that way the menu would be complete: a family Sunday breakfast, just for her.

She got the keys to the gate, unlocked it, and went out to the patio. The orange tree was glowing. The eleven o'clock sun, nearly overhead, gleamed upon the intensely green, shiny leaves. She looked at the tree and patted its trunk. Lately she had begun to talk to it as if it were a cat or dog. They said it was good to talk to plants. She looked up at the leafy crown and saw some oranges beginning to ripen, with yellow stripes along the curved green surface.

With the help of a stick she knocked down one, two, three, four oranges.

They fell with a dry thud on the grass.

She went into the house and returned to the kitchen.

She took out the sharp, polished knife from the cupboard where the utensils were kept.

She put one of the oranges on the cutting board and looked at it, putting it into the right position so she could slice it in the middle. As she sank the knife into its flesh, the yellow interior of the orange unfolded before her. Yellow faces, one after another, looking up at her.

They looked juicy. She cut all four, licking her lips in anticipation, inhaling the scent of golden pancakes mingling with the aroma of coffee and toast.

She squeezed the oranges until only the empty rinds remained. Their juice flowed yellow into the clear glass.

✛ ✛ ✛

And it happened. I felt they were pinching me. Four definite, round pinches. Like the feeling on the tip of my fingers when I felt the sharp edge of the arrows. Nothing more. No blood, no sap. I was afraid when I saw her come out to the patio with the obvious intention in her eyes and in her movements. My leaves quivered. Slightly. But she did not notice. In her linear time, events are linked by logic. She does not know that my leaves trembled before she shook them with the long wooden stick. I thought everything would be over when the oranges fell to the grass. But no. I found myself watching myself from two dimensions. Feeling that I was both on the ground and in the tree. Until her hands touched me, and then I understood that, without leaving the tree, I was in the oranges, too.

O the gift of ubiquity! Just like the gods. I couldn't contain myself, I was so amazed (I couldn't contain myself I was so multiplied). There was no "me." All of that was me. Endless prolongations of my being. A lake. A stone. Endless concentric circles, forming and dissolving. The paths of life seemed strange to me.

She split us open with a single slice. A dry, almost painless scratch. Then her fingers were grasping the rind and my juice was flowing. Pleasurable. Like breaking the delicate inner tension. Similar to crying. My sections opening. My soft peels freeing the gentle tears they held within their round worlds. And then she was setting us on the table. From within the transparent vase, I watch her. I wait for her to hold me to her lips. I wait for the consummation of the rites, the joining of the circles.

Outside the sun shines upon my leaves. It travels into the afternoon.

• • •

The warmth of the food was comforting: the fluffy pancakes, the coffee, the toast. The music and the glass of orange juice on the table were comforting. Contrary to custom, she preferred to drink her juice at the end, finishing with the taste of oranges in her mouth. She usually ate very quickly. But Sunday, she thought, had to be in tune with the day's cadence, *allegro ma non troppo*.

Would she see Felipe today? He was supposed to come at five that afternoon. If he couldn't, he'd phone her. The night before, Antonio had asked her about him. She had forbidden him to fall in love, but it was inevitable. He was jealous. He had been her most constant companion. Lavinia didn't disclose anything more than what was essential, but several times during the loud party at Florence's house she lost touch with the smoke and rock music. Antonio couldn't persuade her to stay. She wouldn't have liked Antonio after Felipe. She didn't want to feel the difference. To superimpose a minor cadence.

That Sunday afternoon, she thought if only she had a car, she would have liked to take Felipe to "her" lookout. Go up the road to the sierra. Walk on the shady path beside the coffee groves. See the landscape from that place of hers near the top. They would feed the clouds from the palms of their hands and watch flocks of parakeets paint splashes of green across the blue. They would remember childhood. That place always reminded her of the beautiful engraving from one of her favorite children's books: the girl in the straw hat and gauzy flowered dress, her elbows resting on the ground, looking toward the infinite horizon, the plain with winding paths and wheat fields. And the caption beneath the picture: "The world was mine and everything in it belonged to me."

She used to climb up to the lookout when they spent vacations on her grandfather's farm. The association of the landscape with the engraving was immediate. Since then, the phrase had stuck in her mind.

It was around that time that she started to look for a world that would be more propitious for her dreams. "Las Brumas" was a large house with thick adobe walls, enormous rooms and tubs in the bathrooms, with a garden full of milflores and a fountain in the middle. They drank chocolate to warm themselves from the late afternoon chill. Sara and her cousins devised competitions, where they would race their bicycles down the steep hill that led to the house.

It was then that her grandfather showed up with the Jules Verne books.

She was entranced by those pages with the text set in two columns, and they became a thousand times more fascinating than bicycles, the dress-up games, or the battles between cowboys and Indians.

In the introductions to the books it said that Jules Verne had never left France, and yet he had still managed to reach the moon with his imagination and predict many of humanity's deeds and discoveries. That was what she wanted: to be able to travel as far as her imagination would allow her. To do that, she often preferred to be alone when she was a little girl.

She liked to go down along the abrupt slope behind the hacienda to look at the smoking volcano in the distance, go to the lookout or walk alone toward the dam and the waterhole. There she would linger, looking at the circle from which the waters flowed unceasingly. She wondered about the source of the water that flowed from the hole, the crystalline water that welled up in circles like breathing or the tide. She imagined a subterranean sea, the one in the center of the earth, with its immense waves and that indiscreet hole revealing its existence.

She felt nostalgic again. Daydreaming, she sipped the orange juice and savored its bittersweet taste, similar to that of her memories; she thought of her grandfather. Plunging her eyes into her memory, she saw that tall, thin man with the long nose and the small, clear, piercing eyes; she saw, through the translucence of his skin, the fine red veins like small deltas of great interior rivers.

Her grandfather used to wear wide khaki pants and a long-sleeved white shirt. He wore hanging from a watch chain a prodigious pocket knife, which he used in order to make slingshots out of wood, toys the kids used for hunting birds or playing war.

She preferred him when he was resting, when he would sit still in a rocking chair and talk to her. His knowledge was broad and ranging: he knew about the constellations, the planets and the stars. "There's Mars," he'd say, or the Seven Goats, the constellation of Orion, the Centaur, the Scales, the Southern Cross... He knew about the phases of the moon, the equinoxes and the tides; he knew ancient legends of Indian chieftains and princesses. He was a lover of books. His photographic memory allowed him to quote entire passages by heart.

A widower since he was thirty-five, he lived alone, but his love affairs were famous. Although Lavinia's mother was his only "legal" daughter, Lavinia would never forget the countless aunts and uncles who appeared the day of her grandfather's funeral. The sisters and brothers who didn't know each other got together on that occasion for the first and only time. She still didn't know exactly how many there were.

Shortly before he died, grandfather made a will for his few belongings. He left Lavinia a brief note that he recited from memory on his last birthday: "The Greeks called the beginning and the end the Alpha and the Omega. Now that I am nearing Omega, I leave you this legacy: nothing that is done in the name of universal culture is ever a waste. This is why you must venerate books, sanctuaries of the word; the word which is the highest expression of *homo sapiens*."

He died on a New Year's Eve, as firecrackers, rockets, and parties were bidding him farewell along with the old year. He died from a rare diaphragm ailment that made him sneeze to death.

His funeral was practically a political rally. Lavinia recalled the hot afternoon, the flowers in the cemetery, and the number of workers who stayed until he disappeared beneath the tombstone because her grandfather, holder of liberal socialist ideas, rabid opponent of the dynastic regime of the great generals, had established the eight hour work day, social security, and job safety before the existence of a labor code. And he had also discovered the ancient ruins of Tenoztla.

For her, grandfather was her childhood and the awakening of fantasy. She still met him in a recurrent dream: they were both on a lofty mountain, very high, with snow on the summit and spring on the slopes. Her grandfather would fit enormous wings of white feathers on her back—like the ones she wore as a girl when they dressed her up as an angel in a Holy Week procession—and he would blow a strong wind, encouraging her to fly. She flew in those dreams. She felt happy, like a bird, and safe, because her grandfather was waiting for her on top of the mountain, where he enjoyed watching her fly.

It was only lately that she had begun to have nightmares in which the wings turned into aluminum, and she crashed to the ground.

The minutes passed. The music stopped. Lavinia went back to the empty plates and the empty glass of orange juice. She got up to clear off the table. She would take a shower and wash the nostalgia away.

✝ ✝ ✝

I traversed rosy membranes and entered Lavinia's body like an amber cascade. I saw the uvula go by before I descended a dark, narrow tunnel leading to the forge of her stomach.

Now I swim in her blood, traverse the wide expanse of her body. Her heartbeat is like an echo in an underground cave. Here everything moves rhythmically: exhalation and inhalation. When she inhales, the walls distend. I can see the delicate veins that look like the outlines of a handful of long arrows launched into the air. When she exhales, the walls close in and grow dark. Her body is young and healthy. Her heart beats evenly, without resting. I saw her powerful interior. I felt the force propelling me through her inner caverns from one small space to another. This is how the hearts of our warriors beat when the priest wrenched them from their breasts. They beat furiously, expiring. I felt pity when I saw them being torn from their dwellings. I thought the gods ought to appreciate this gift of life. What more could we give them than the center of our universe, our best, our most valiant hearts?

And still...one could say we were defenseless in the face of the beasts and firesticks the Spaniards had brought. Perhaps the gods would have preferred our gold, too. Our wailings did not seem to move them. They left us to face the fury of the heartless monsters. So many red hearts for nothing. They seemed to surrender to the god of the newcomers, the one they said entered the spirit through water.

Yarince had himself baptized to test the word of the Spaniards. Also so he could see what skills he could learn from their god that would be useful to our people. But the god of the Spaniards did not touch his spirit. We realized that their god cared nothing for us, either. Maybe he asked the Spaniards for "Indian" sacrifices.

Lavinia contains great spaces of silence. Her mind has wide regions which are dormant. I submerged myself in her present and could feel visions from her past. Coffee bushes, smoking volcanoes, gushing springs, wrapped in the thick fog of nostalgia. She is trying to understand herself. This fountain of echoes and visions is complex. I cannot find any order in the succession of images that emanate from these soft white surfaces. They disconcert and overwhelm me. I must rest. My spirit is uneasy.

• • •

The distant cathedral clock struck five. Lavinia looked out the window, waiting for Felipe, and saw the old pensioners sitting beside the doors of their houses, enjoying the cool air in their usual immobility.

The house looked clean and inviting. Not for nothing had she spent the weekend working, arranging the new furniture, dusting, watering the plants, organizing old papers. She wondered if love generated domesticity, but felt satisfied with her effort. She put on jeans, a comfortable blouse, and sandals. She smiled, thinking that she must look like a young homebody girl with a pony tail.

Felipe didn't come, and by six her impatience was devouring her. The telephone didn't ring. A bad mood threatened to overtake her. But she tried not to be impatient, thinking about how he might have run into traffic problems, possible hold-ups. Though he should at least have called her, she thought, let her know he'd be late. It wasn't such a great effort to pick up the phone and call, especially for someone like him who was so addicted to phone calls. She grabbed a book and threw herself into the hammock. Reading would help her pass the time. But she couldn't concentrate, and at seven o'clock she got up from the hammock in a terrible mood. She went about the house, pacing like a caged animal, not knowing what to do. Maybe she should go out, she said to herself. Not wait any more. She dialed Antonio's number and no one answered. He must not have gotten back from the outing to which he had invited her. Sara and Adrián weren't home either. The day's solitude loomed darkly in the silence. She put on some music. Even though last week she had resolved not to speculate about Felipe's "occupations," she couldn't help it now. She wondered if she hadn't been the victim of a common Don Juan or at least of someone with a difficult relationship for which she'd been chosen as a "substitute" or savior. It happened in real life, so it wouldn't be that unusual. And yet Felipe's feelings toward her seemed sincere. She made a rum and coke. She wouldn't be upset any more, she told herself, wouldn't wait for him any longer. Tomorrow she would try to straighten everything out once and for all. She was not going to keep on pretending his mysterious doings didn't matter. She'd ask him directly. Though in truth they didn't have any understanding, nothing that gave her the right to pry. But thinking like that was a trap, she said to herself. The trap women afraid of the terrible accusation of "domineering" or "possessive" always fell into. She couldn't help looking toward the window. Her ears were alert for approaching footsteps.

The clock struck nine. It was clear Felipe wasn't coming, she told herself one more time. Aunt Inés used to say men were capricious and impenetrable, like deep, dark, starry nights. The stars were the cracks through which women looked into their hearts. Men were the cave, the fire among the mastodons, the security of broad chests and big hands that supported their women during love-making. They were beings with the advantage of having neither fixed horizons nor the limits of confined spaces. The forever privileged. In spite of the fact that they all came from a woman's womb and depended on her in order to grow and breathe, for nourishment, their first contacts with the world, learning to recognize words; later they seemed to rebel with strange fierceness against this dependency, subjugating the feminine, dominating it, and denying power to those who had given them life and the universe through the pain of open legs.

She turned on the television. There was a bad movie on. On the other channel, a nondescript soap opera. In Faguas there were only two TV channels. She turned it off, as well as the lights around the house. She closed the garden gate, undressed, and got into bed to read. The clock struck eleven. Her head ached, and she felt terribly sad, betrayed, angry at herself, at her ability to build castles in the sand, her romanticism. Finally the peaceful solitude lulled her to sleep. Enormous white clouds with faces of chubby, playful children. Her tall, tall grandfather put the huge white feather wings on her. The flight over immense flowers, heliotropes, gladioli, gigantic ferns. Dewdrops. Magnificent, huge drops of dew where the sun was shattered, opening marvelous kaleidoscopes. Her grandfather's beard and gray hair covered with dew. The thick wings spraying water as they flapped in the wind. She was getting wet. The dew was drenching her. The wet wings were heavy. The effort greater and greater. Holding herself afloat over the precipice of immense flowers, she tried again and again to return to her grandfather, beating her wings desperately until the effort woke her and everything was dark. Only the orange tree's shadow stood out in the glow of the moonlight against the window.

+ + +

Night swaddles my branches, and crickets chirp their monotonous song amid the entourage of fireflies. I barely managed to reach her in her dreams and mark my name, Itzá, dewdrop, upon her visions of flowers and flights. I, too, once dreamed of flying, when I saw the birds rise in flocks at the sight of the beasts and bands of smelly, hairy men. How tiny the birds were and how great an advantage they had over us.

I am confused by all these events. Being in her blood was like being inside myself. My body must have been like that. I miss having veins, entrails, lungs. But her thoughts were a family of parrots flying in circles, making lots of noise, piling one on top of another boisterously. Still, for her there was order, I am certain. One image reflected another and then another, like a mirror that reflects to infinity. I remembered being fascinated by mirrors. The Spaniards managed to trap our attention with them. At first we thought that image was a joke when it imitated all our movements. Until we realized we were seeing ourselves for the first time. Clearly, so clearly, not like the fleeting ripples of the river waters. And we were intrigued. What can be more fascinating than to see yourself for the first time? To see who you are? Yarince was furious when he caught me looking at myself in the little mirror. But until then I had not known I was beautiful. And I liked to look at myself.

• • •

CHAPTER 5

Lavinia was beginning to fall asleep again when she suddenly heard the noise. She froze in the darkness. Outside the wind blew wildly, whipping the tree branches about. At first she thought the blustering wind was rattling the door. But the pounding was rhythmic, strong, urgent. Frightened and suddenly wide awake, she quickly put on her aquamarine kimono and went out to the living room. She was turning on the lights when she heard Felipe's voice. It sounded hoarse, like the voice of someone trying not to shout.

"Open up, quick, open up!" he said.

Lavinia slid the bolts, thinking: Felipe here, at this time of night, so upset, his voice muffled like that...what could it mean? She had to move away because the door, unlocked now, opened with a heave from outside by the weight of a body. A man came in, bent over and leaning on Felipe's arm.

She had no time to wonder what was going on and had barely made out Felipe's worried expression when he went by her, leading the stranger toward the bedroom without a moment's hesitation, without looking behind him.

"Close it tightly. Lock everything and turn out the lights," he told her.

She closed it. Dazed, she turned off the lights. What was going on? she wondered. What did that sudden interruption in the middle of the night mean? The two men smelled strange, of danger, of desperation.

She went toward the bedroom, the adrenaline humming in her ears.

As she followed them in the dark, she noticed the spots on the floor, barely illuminated by the light coming from the bedroom. The spots were wet, large, red.

She went into the bedroom. She felt weak; her legs were like water. Felipe was circling around the man.

"Do you have any sheets, something we can use for bandages, something for a tourniquet?" Felipe asked, holding a towel that was turning red where it covered the wounded man's side.

Without a word she went into the bathroom. There she kept disinfectants, cotton, simple first aid items. Her hands were shaking. She came out with the sheets, more towels, scissors, and laid them on the bed.

The man made a strange sound when he breathed. He held the towel over his arm, pushing it tight against his waist. Lavinia saw the trickles of blood running down his pants. She felt as if her eyes were growing rounder in their sockets.

"He's badly hurt. Did he have an accident? We should take him to the hospital, or call a doctor," she said, stumbling over her words.

"That's impossible," answered Felipe, dryly. "Maybe tomorrow. Help me. We have to stop the hemorrhaging."

She came over. The man was removing the towel so Felipe could apply the tourniquet. A little above the elbow she saw the skin on the arm, the round hole, the raw flesh, the heavy flow of red that would not stop. Scattered images came to mind: war movies, bullet wounds. The dark side of Faguas invading her very home, unexpectedly, like a sudden storm. How else was she to understand that they hadn't taken the wounded man to the hospital? She finally understood Felipe's mysterious phone calls, his sudden departures. It couldn't be anything but that, she thought, feeling the terror grow within her, trying to calm herself, and thinking she shouldn't jump to conclusions so quickly. But why, then, would Felipe have had to bring that man to her house? Reproaches, fear, washed over her as she looked numbly at the wound and the blood, trying hard to control her dizziness, her desire to vomit.

Felipe wrapped the piece of sheet around the arm and began to tighten it hard.

Lavinia tried not to look at the wet spots staining the white sheet red; she concentrated on the man's face, his strong features, his olive complexion, his pallor, his clenched lips.

Who could he be? she thought. How could they have wounded him? She would rather not think about it. She felt trapped, couldn't do anything except watch them, help them. There was no way out. Her head throbbed like a big pounding heart.

"He's been shot," she affirmed, without looking at Felipe. She said it out of the need to say it, to get it out. Felipe was working with the tourniquet, grasping it tightly. The white cloth was turning red, a frightful, bright red.

The man was panting slightly. His head was turned, expressionless, toward Felipe's hand. He watched the operation as if it weren't his arm. He was young, of average height, with slightly slanted eyes and thick lips, his hair was brown, and there was a lock falling over his forehead. He looked strong. The outline of his muscles and his big, strong veins was readily visible. When he heard her speak, he turned toward her.

"Don't worry, compañera," he said, speaking for the first time, looking at her. "I'm not going to die on you in your house," and he smiled almost sadly.

Felipe was sweating profusely, tightening and loosening the tourniquet.

At last he tore off another piece of sheet and tied it tightly on the arm.

He wiped the blood off with a towel, which he then used to dry the sweat from his brow.

"Well," he said to the man, "I think you'll survive this one. How do you feel?"

"Like they just shot me," answered the other with a smiling yet calm expression, and he added: "I'm fine, don't worry, take care of the compañera. She looks really frightened."

"I'll tend to her now," Felipe said, "but I don't think you should move from this place for the time being. The compañera is 'clean.' It's better if you stay here. It's safer. Now you should have something to drink and get some sleep. You lost a lot of blood."

"Well, we'll see. We don't even know what she's going to say," and he looked at her.

Only the wounded man seemed to notice her presence. Felipe was finishing cleaning up the bed. There was no doubt about it, Lavinia thought, after hearing Felipe's concerns about the unknown man's safety. He could have kept her out of things, in the dark, she thought. Not force her to face such a situation so suddenly, without warning.

"Do you have anything we can give him?" Felipe asked, turning to her. His face looked hard and expressionless, dominated by a single, fixed idea.

"I can make him some orange juice. There's milk, too," she replied, pressured by Felipe's air of authority. She felt clumsy, numb.

"Milk would be better," the wounded man said. "Oranges give me heartburn."

Felipe caught up to her in the kitchen.

"I think it would be better to warm it up a little," he said.

"I don't think so," Lavinia said. "I've read that heat isn't good for hemorrhages. We'd better give it to him cold. Tell me what happened, who is he?"

"His name is Sebastián," Felipe answered. "Let's get him the milk and then I'll explain." He left her and went over by the window. The wind was still blowing. There were stray dogs barking. An occasional car went by. She saw him check the locks, and the door chain.

Sebastián drank the milk. He handed the glass to Lavinia and lay back in the bed, closing his eyes.

"Thank you," he said, "thanks, compañera."

Something about his serenity reminded her of fallen trees.

She left the bedroom with Felipe. The living room was in shadow. The lights on the patio threw off a faint white glow. The shadow of the orange tree moved over the bricks. Felipe collapsed on the sofa and laid his head back, closing his eyes. He put his hands over his face in a gesture of exhaustion, like a person trying to get his strength back for the next episode.

"Lavinia," Felipe opened his eyes and indicated he wanted her to sit down next to him. His expression had sweetened slightly, in spite of his wrinkled brow and authoritarian glance.

She sat down beside him and was silent. She didn't want to ask. She was afraid. She thought it would be better not to know anything. In Faguas it was better not to know anything; but Felipe was talking.

"Sebastián was detected by the army. They riddled the house he was in with bullets. He managed to get out by jumping over back fences and walls. Three other compañeros died..."

Silence. What could she say? Lavinia thought. Felipe had a wary expression on his face. She couldn't react. She felt like running. The idea of the army chasing them terrified her. The methods they used were well known: torture, the volcano... And she was a woman. She imagined herself being raped in the dungeons of the Great General. The sounds of the night seemed ominous and foreboding to her. The wind...

Felipe shouldn't have done this, she thought, breaking in like this without notice, into her house. Maybe he had no choice, she told herself, but he had no right to plunge her into danger, in the shadow of the three "dead compañeros"...and the wounded man was sleeping in her bed...

What could she do? she thought desperately.

"Now you know why I couldn't come, what my occupations and the phone calls are," Felipe said, looking at her gently, putting his hand on hers. "I'm sorry you have to find out like this. I would never have come here if it hadn't been an emergency. I couldn't leave Sebastián in my house because there are other people there. They would have realized what had happened, and if somebody denounced him, it would be fatal...I'm sorry," he repeated. "I couldn't think of anything better than to bring him here. He's safe here."

In the dark she saw how pale Felipe was, the sweat gleaming on his face. It was hot.

"And what are we going to do?" Lavinia asked, speaking in a whisper, too, as he had done.

"I don't know. I still don't know," mused Felipe, smoothing his hair with his hands.

Lavinia felt his confusion in his heavy breathing, his body sprawled over the cushions, his long legs stretched out on the floor as if they were dead weight. Suddenly Felipe straightened up and began mechanically cleaning his glasses, speaking without seeing her, talking to himself:

"You never get used to death," he said. "You never get used to it."

He knew the three dead compañeros, he said; one of them, Fermín, had even gone to high school with him.

He had been called to a meeting in the afternoon. That was why he had missed his date with her, he added, as if it still mattered. The meeting lasted until nine that night. Fermín had been joking about how peaceful the neighborhood was. They felt safe there, in the little house recently rented with the few funds the Organization had (and he spoke of "the Organization" as if she knew what that meant). It was a poor, marginal neighborhood with houses made of wooden slats and latrines in the patios. The people who lived there were peasants who had emigrated to the city in search of a better life. "Who could have denounced them?" Felipe asked, looking at her without seeing her. At nine o'clock he'd left to go home.

"I didn't notice anything, not a thing," Felipe repeated, as if blaming himself for something very serious. He tried hard to reconstruct the details of the street's normal appearance:

men and women sitting by the doors of their houses, stray dogs, buses going by, their old chassis rattling. "I didn't notice a thing," he said over and over, while he told her what Sebastián had told him, how suddenly the soldiers had appeared: "They heard the screech of the jeeps' brakes and the 'You're surrounded, surrender' almost simultaneously," he said. And they didn't have much ammunition: just two submachine guns. While they hurried to take their positions to shoot, loading their pistols, they decided that Sebastián should try to get out and escape, he had to survive in order to carry on.

And they shouted "we're coming" to give him time. It was the last thing Sebastián heard as he was jumping over their garden wall.

"At nine tonight they were alive," Felipe said, taking off his glasses and pressing his thumbs against his eyes.

"And now nothing can be done for them," he added. "Nobody could bring them back. Their dreams will continue living, but they are gone."

Felipe was silent. He put his arm out to embrace her, as if he had been drained and needed the nearness of another human being so as not to slip into the deep, dark hole of despair.

Touched, unable to speak, she cuddled against Felipe's chest, touching and hugging him, not knowing how to console him.

She would have liked to shelter him, give him the protection of her woman's body. She rested her head on Felipe's chest. She felt his rhythmic breathing, the soft niche of his being, the solid, muscular flesh that was, however, still easily penetrable: a piece of lead launched at a certain speed and Felipe would break. This skin she was touching, everything his skin held inside, would jump its course, the dam would burst in a thousand pieces, the waters would flow. The murmuring would cease, along with the waterfall that sweetly raised and lowered the level of his underground currents. She felt a chill when she thought how nearby death had been circling. Felipe had only left the house at nine. What if he had stayed? She pressed closer against him, thought about his friends, the ones she now would never meet.

She felt like crying because of what she imagined he was feeling, the numbing pain of death, impotence.

And they could all die, she thought. She herself could die. Fear gripped her, overcoming sadness. And Felipe had told his friend they would stay here. They wouldn't leave until the next day. She shut her eyes tight. She wished it were already the following day. Then she could watch them leave her house. Be alone, at ease, again. Forget what had happened. But she was ashamed to have Felipe see she wanted him to leave with his wounded friend. She didn't look at him. She was still nestled against his chest, while he entangled his hands in her long hair, and she could feel the tension in his arms, his hardened muscles.

Will they come after them? wondered Lavinia. What'll I do if they come looking for them...?

The glow of dawn began to slip through the door to the garden. Felipe got up and went to stand beside the window. Outside roosters were crowing in the distance.

"We're members of the National Liberation Movement," he said, confirming Lavinia's suspicions. "You know what that is, don't you?" he asked.

"Yes," Lavinia said, "yes," she repeated, "armed struggle."

"Yes." Felipe said, "That's right. Armed struggle. We couldn't continue to work only in the mountains. We're growing and now we're beginning to operate in the cities. They won't be able to stop us. Resignation is not the solution, Lavinia. We can't keep allowing the army to control the people with force. Do you remember the squatters? We can't keep letting that happen. The only response to violence is violence."

As he stood, leaning against the edge of the garden door, he spoke without seeing her. Lavinia studied his profile,

Felipe's eyes looking with determination toward a point in space. "It's the only way, the only way," he repeated, pacing back and forth, opening and clenching his fists.

He was recovering his strength. The process was almost visible; it was like watching a sick person rise out of bed, determined to live, after the terrible news. She should have suspected it, she thought. Although, looking back on Felipe's attitudes, she couldn't say his ties were obvious. The truth was, she wouldn't have guessed, in spite of his many "duties." She would have kept suspecting illicit love affairs or would have attributed his absences to the traditional male fear of "commitment." It was a pity, she told herself, to see him surrounded by such danger. She looked at his face, the face of an intellectual, his thin-framed glasses, his big gray eyes... It was crazy for him to take chances like this; he could have a bright future; he had worked so hard to earn his degree in architecture...

It was crazy, she thought, that they'd convinced him the only solution was armed struggle.

"But they have no future, Felipe," she said. "They'll kill them all. It's unrealistic. And you're a rational person... I never imagined you would believe in those things..."

He turned toward her, about to say something. She would never forget that look of raging Zeus about to hurl his thunderbolt. He must have seen the fear in her eyes because he stopped.

"Let's make some coffee," he said.

While they were sitting on the rough kitchen benches, smelling the sweetish aroma of freshly-made coffee that wafted up from their cups, he came over to her and took her hand.

"Lavinia," he said, looking at her intently, "I don't want to get you involved in this. I don't want to ruin your peace of mind. In fact, I like it. I like this pleasant house, this peacefulness. Selfishly, I like them," he said, as if talking to himself. "I don't ask you to understand, nor agree with this. You might think it crazy, but for us it's the only way. I'm just asking you to let Sebastián stay here until we can move him. Your house is safe. No one will look for him here. Sebastián is very important to the Movement. I swear we'll never ask you to do anything else."

"And you, what are you going to do?" Lavinia said.

"I'll stay here with him tomorrow to see how he's doing. Afterward I'll take him with me. I'm not the problem. I'm fairly clean. The problem is that we don't have great resources: houses, cars, that sort of thing. We have to think carefully about where to take him."

"Then the Movement isn't very big?" Lavinia asked.

"It's growing," answered Felipe, with another flashing glance. "What do you say, will you do it?"

It was hard for him to say it, she thought as she looked at him, to have to ask, almost beg her. His eyes shone. He had let go of her hand and was waiting anxiously for her to say something.

I'm trapped, she thought, I can't say no. But she couldn't be romantic now, she told herself, her relationship with Felipe didn't mean she had to get involved. It was no game. It was real blood and death.

She had never imagined anything like this could happen to her, especially to her. Not in her wildest dreams or worst nightmares. The "guerrilla fighters" were something distant for her, like beings from another planet. In Italy, like everyone else, she had admired Che Guevara. She remembered her grandfather's fascination with Fidel Castro and the "revolution." But she came from different stock. She was certain of that. It was one thing not to agree with the dynasty and another to fight with weapons against an army trained to kill without mercy, in cold blood. It took another type of personality, other mettle. Her own personal rebellion against the status quo, her demand for independence, to leave her home and hold a professional job, was one thing, but it was quite something else to get involved with this mad adventure, this collective suicide, this extreme idealism. She had to admit they were brave, sort of tropical Quixotes, but they weren't rational, they would keep on killing them, and she didn't want to die. But she couldn't turn her back on Felipe either, she thought, nor his friend. She couldn't make them leave her house. Even though she felt the urge to flee, for everything to be over, to erase this night from her mind.

"You haven't said anything," Felipe was saying. "You haven't answered me." His voice had recovered the tone of authority of the previous night.

"I know I can't say no to you," Lavinia said finally, "though I'd like to. I know you all have reasons for doing what you do. I just want to make it very clear that I don't agree with them. I'm not cut out for these things. Sebastián can stay, but I have to ask you to move him somewhere else as soon as possible. I know this must sound terrible to you, but I don't feel I can do anything else. I have to be honest with you."

"I understand," Felipe said. "That's all we want you to do, for the time being."

"No, please," Lavinia said. "None of that 'for the time being.' For me it's one thing to respect your bravery, like a lot of people do, but that doesn't mean I agree with it. I think you're mistaken. It's heroic suicide. Please, I beg you not to get me into any of this."

"All right, all right," Felipe said, cleaning his glasses again.

Lavinia leaned over the table, put her head on her arms and closed her eyes. She felt tired, exhausted, and a sense of shame welled from deep within her. Strange images of burning villages, dark men fighting off wild dogs—ghosts of daytime nightmares—clamored in her mind.

"We should get some rest," she told Felipe, lifting her head. "I think I'm starting to hear voices."

✛ ✛ ✛

CHAPTER 6

Oh how I would have liked to shake her to make her understand! She was like so many others. So many others that I knew. Afraid. They thought to stay alive that way. So many became mournful skeletons of women or scullery maids or were beheaded when they exhausted themselves during forced marches, or ended up on one of those ships that set sail to build distant cities, carrying off our men and taking our women to satisfy the lusts of the sailors.

"Fear is a bad advisor," Yarince used to say when people objected to his bold strategies. Felipe emanates the strength of courage; she swims in a sea of confusion. Her images were lukewarm, her blood dissolved inside her as when one cuts oneself in the water. She clings to her world as if the past did not exist and the future were but a brightly-colored tapestry. It's like those who were baptized, thinking the water would cleanse their hearts; that there was nothing they could do against the horses, the firesticks, the hard, glistening swords; that there was nothing left to do but surrender or wait because their gods seemed more powerful than our own.

It seems as if I can still hear their moans after the battle five days' journey from Maribios... We had received news of the expedition led by the Spanish captains. They wanted to conquer the villages around the place where they were building their houses and temples. They were erecting a city so they could settle in our territory. It was a desperate moment. In those days we attacked them constantly, by night and by day, with surprise assaults, taking advantage of our knowledge of the terrain and its hiding places. But we were losing many warriors. After their initial surprise, they brought out their animals and shot fire from their sticks. They hurled themselves upon us and forced us to disperse.

Then a strategy occurred to Tacoteyde, the ancient priest, that would surely make the Spaniards retreat.

For two days and nights we discussed it around our campfires, hidden deep in the forest hills. I did not agree. It seemed like a useless sacrifice to me, although I could not stop thinking about the effect it would have on the Spaniards. But our elders deserved a better fate. Yarince, Quiavit, and Astochimal argued fiercely. Some were in favor, others against.

Finally Coyovet arrived. He was the elder we all respected, the white-haired one, and he made us decide by contest.

I can still see the tight circle of warriors in the night around the three leaders. Ocote tree torches had been set in the angles of the trees. Coyovet and Tacoteyde were sitting on the ground smoking their tobacco.

The warriors shot their arrows. The air vibrated in the bows. Those of Yarince and Quiavit landed far off. Astochimal lost. He lowered his head and moaned deeply.

That night the warriors selected forty elders, men and women, from the communities. They led them to our camp, their faces still heavy with sleep, wrapped in their blankets. They began to chew tobacco seated in a circle. Tacoteyde spoke to them and told them that the Lord of the Coast, Xipe Totec, had spoken to him in a dream, telling him that in order to get rid of the invaders from the sea, it was necessary to sacrifice wise men and women. Afterward the warriors were to don the skins of the sacrificed, placing themselves in the front line of battle; in this way the Spaniards would be frightened and flee. They would give up the idea of building their cities in Maribios. He told them that they had been chosen for the sacrifice. They were to be offered up to the gods at dawn.

I watched from my hiding place in the bushes because women were not allowed to be present at the services of the priests. I should have stayed in the tent, but I had already challenged what women were supposed to do anyway, going to fight in battle with Yarince. I was considered to be a texoxe, a witch who had cast a spell over Yarince with the scent of my sex.

That is what I saw in the mist of dawn. The elders wrapped in their blankets, side by side, their faces furrowed with wrinkles, listening to Tacoteyde. They were silent. Then one by one they prostrated themselves on the ground, lamenting loudly. "Let it be done, let it be done," they said. "Let it be done, let it be done," until their voices resembled a chant.

I felt as if a vase had been broken in my heart. I saw the figures of our elders who were to die the next day. With them the history of our people would die, and our wisdom—so much of our past. Many were the parents or relatives of our warriors who watched it all with faces of obsidian.

Those sacrifices made us suffer so much! When at dawn the next day Tacoteyde wrenched their hearts out one by one on a quickly raised altar to Xipe Totec, we all felt a weight upon our shoulders, and the hate for the Spaniards was like fire in our blood.

Tacoteyde removed their skins. One by one, forty of our warriors donned those terrible cloaks, some finally giving off deep moans. When they were all dressed that way, it was a vision that made even us shudder.

Our pain lessened when we imagined the Spaniards looking at what we saw. Surely they would not be able to stand it. Certainly their beasts would be afraid. We were going to win. The sacrifice of our elders and relatives would not be in vain.

We had not calculated the hardness of their guts. They must have been frightened. We saw them back away and, as they did so, many fell, pierced by poison arrows. But afterward they seemed to swell with fury. They attacked us, shouting that we were "heretics," "infidels." They made the terrible din of death with their horses and harsh tongues, their firesticks.

Later, hidden again in the mountains, we didn't even want to look into each other's faces. That was the night that many said their teote gods were more powerful than ours.

Yarince threw himself face down on the ground. He covered his face with mud and would not let even me get near him. He was a wounded animal, like Felipe thinking about his dead friends. But he too arose from his crumpled body.

I recognize my blood, the blood of the warriors, in Felipe, in the man who lies in Lavinia's room, clothed in serenity, with the air of a chieftain. Only she flickers like a wick in oil and is unable to sustain me within her blood. I had to call her, hide within the labyrinths of her ear, and whisper to her. Now she feels guilty.

• • •

A little before seven in the morning, Lavinia awoke with a start at the sudden notion of Monday. Work, the normal routine of the week, would continue, indifferent to the arrested time within her house. Lucrecia soon would be there. She would have to stop her, invent an excuse to keep her away. She sat up on the mattress that smelled like old rags. Felipe had sent her to rest in the room that some day she planned to make into a study but which was still nothing but a storage place for extraneous objects. She had barely managed to doze for a while. Through the half-open door, she observed him pacing about the house at dawn, keeping watch over the street and the wounded man.

She heard the murmur of his voice coming from the other room. He was talking with Sebastián. She sat up straight, then bent her knees and rested her head on the angle formed by her legs, squeezing them against her chest. Reality was worse by day, she thought. Now nothing was the same. Her life, so peaceful until yesterday, would never be the same again. She would have liked to stay in the fetal position, look for a refuge where she could feel safe, far from the danger of those voices crawling toward her through the walls, the cracks in the doors. But she got up quickly, dressed, and went to stand beside the window. It was seven o'clock. There was a dewy dampness covering the lawn. Outside everything looked peaceful.

Lucrecia was arriving. She had come early to prepare her breakfast. Lavinia opened the door, pretending to look at the garden. She thought up excuses and pretexts, then discarded them. Finally, she acted as if she had just noticed Lucrecia's presence when she came nearer. She greeted her and, trying to be assertive, explained to her that people from the office were coming to her house to work on a special project. She didn't need to clean, she said, they would have to put papers on the floor and would make a mess. It would be better if she returned on Wednesday. Lucrecia insisted, saying that meanwhile she could make coffee, straighten up. It wasn't worth it, Lavinia repeated. They would be there in half an hour. "I'll see you Wednesday," she smiled, "I have to take a quick shower." Looking as if she didn't understand what was happening, Lucrecia accepted it and left.

Lavinia went back to the house. She had not been at all convincing, she thought; but Lucrecia would not be too surprised. She would think it was some peculiar demand of her job. She caught a glimpse of Felipe, who was hidden, as he peeked out the window. He must have been startled when he heard the door open. When she came in, he wasn't in the living room anymore. And now, what do I have to do now? Go to work? She would have to consult with them. She went into the bathroom to wash, splashing water on her face over and over.

Should she go to work? she wondered once more, feeling afraid again. It was difficult to think that everything would be the same outside. Nothing would have changed: the buses, the taxis, the people in the elevator, in the office. She, on the other hand, felt naked, fragile, afraid of their glances, afraid that they would see in her face the night before, the secret, the blood.

She'd rather stay home, she said to herself. The problem with Lucrecia was resolved, but someone else could knock on the door. What would happen if Felipe opened it...with Sebastián, the wounded man, there in her bed?

In the mirror she saw the dark circles under her eyes. Her face, the same face as always, only just a bit tired, like after a night out partying. Looking at it, you could not tell what a mess she was mixed up in, she thought.

She went out and decided to knock on her bedroom door.

She heard Felipe's voice saying, "Come in," and as soon as she entered he asked her who she'd been talking to. Lavinia explained.

The wounded man was sitting on the bed. He had a clean bandage on his arm. The hemorrhaging had stopped. His face was still pale.

"Good morning, compañera!" he said. (He insisted on calling her "compañera.")

"Good morning," she replied. "How do you feel?"

"Better, better. Thanks."

"I wanted to ask you both if you think I should go to work or stay home."

The men exchanged questioning glances.

"It would be better if she stayed, don't you think?" Felipe said to Sebastián.

"No," Sebastián said. "I think it's better if she goes. It's not a good idea for both of you to be absent from the office."

"But if you need something," Lavinia said, "if anything happened..."

"Are you expecting anyone else today?" Sebastián asked.

"No, no one else."

"Then don't worry. We're pretty safe here. It's better if you go to the office... If they come looking for you, if they suspect something, Lavinia can fill us in," he said, turning to Felipe. "She can bring the newspapers and find out what people are saying. If the house is locked, it'll look like there's no one here. It's better if she goes," and turning to look at Lavinia, he added. "It's not good for them to associate your absence with Felipe's."

Sebastián's tone was calm, serene. He talked as if he were referring to everyday events, like going to the beach on Sunday and not what he had said: bring the newspapers (the photographs of the dead compañeros, Lavinia thought); find out if they had been looking for Felipe (and if they had, what would she do?); listen for rumors, comments.

Lavinia would rather have stayed. She didn't feel capable of "investigating" those things. Her face would give her away—it was an open book. It was easy to read her because she got nervous easily. But she didn't say anything; Sebastián's expression, his calmness, made her feel ashamed.

"You can also go to a drugstore and buy antibiotics, any strong antibiotic. The wound could get infected," Felipe said.

"So you're not going to get a doctor today, either?" Lavinia asked.

She didn't understand them, she said, a bullet wound in the arm could be disabling. They could pretend it was an accident.

They calmed her down. They'd get a doctor, but it couldn't be just any doctor. They'd talk about that when she returned.

Sebastián asked her for the radio to listen to the news.

Lavinia got her clothes and left the room.

It was hot in the street. The warm, damp breath of the earth, mixed with wind and dust, enveloped her. Each year the summer was worse; each year more deforestation. The oak tree looked ashen. Lavinia quickened her pace, looking at nearby houses as she walked. In the distance, a gardener lopped at the grass with his large machete. Everything remained the same, she thought. Only she felt strange in the quiet atmosphere of that weekday. She walking to the office. Walking quickly, feeling her legs move as if they belonged to someone else.

Fear opened eyes all over her body. As if it were a nightmare, she remembered the phrase Felipe had repeated so many times the night before while he told her the circumstances of Sebastián's flight: "I didn't notice anything, I didn't notice anything." And what if they were there? What if the security agents were near the house, waiting for the right moment to surround it?

She reached the elevator and went up alone. At that hour the building lobby was empty. She saw her reflection in the metallic walls. "Nobody will notice," she reassured herself. "I'm the same. The same as every day." But she wasn't really convinced; inside, her blood circulated rapidly in a torment of adrenaline.

She said good morning to Silvia and headed toward her cubicle, greeting the draftsmen as she passed. Everything as usual. "Act natural," Felipe had said. He'd hugged her before she left. He told her again that he was sorry he had gotten her involved. And yet, she thought, they kept involving her, asking her to find out the rumors, the terrible possibility that the security forces would come looking for Felipe (it was very remote chance, Sebastián assured her), asking her to bring them the newspapers and buy medicine.

She would have preferred not go back home. To stay with Sara or Antonio till the others had left. To stop being responsible, "humanitarian," not to feel compelled to do as they asked, or heed that inner voice that told her "Don't be a coward, you can't leave them all alone, you can't run the risk of their being killed." To not feel the strength of her love for Felipe...even though this was something more, she thought, something more than her love for Felipe. After all, she wasn't even sure that love existed, if you could talk of love in a relationship so recently begun, and that, after what had happened, maybe it would be better not to continue.

She called Mercedes and asked for the newspapers. She was surprised to find herself lying to her:

"Felipe isn't coming in to work. He called to ask me to tell you he's having stomach problems."

Mercedes looked at her with a knowing smile. She went to get the cup of coffee and the newspapers, moving flirtatiously as usual, swaying on her high heels. Lavinia imagined her walking through the draftsmen's room, smiling as she went by, aware that they were looking at her. Was she in on the secret? Lavinia thought. Who else was in on it? Which of those people, acting so normal every day, also led a double life?

The young woman came back with the coffee and papers and put them on the table.

"Did you hear what happened?" she asked.

"No," Lavinia said without looking at her, afraid of giving herself away (the question made her heart skip a beat), beginning to leaf through the newspapers.

"Well, you live pretty far from there," Mercedes said, "but from my house you could hear the shots. You should have seen it: airplanes, tanks... It was like war. The army was going crazy! And there were only three kids! Imagine! Three kids..." And she turned to leave, closing the door behind her.

Lavinia sat back in the chair. Closed her eyes. The lack of sleep made her feel as if she were under water. She swallowed the coffee in big gulps, thankful for the shelter and privacy of her little office, putting off reading the newspaper.

What would she do there all day? she wondered. Pretend she was working? This was not for her, she said to herself again, she couldn't stand the tension, her stomach all knotted up; it was as if she had a fist clenched in the middle of her chest, and she felt unable to breathe.

Finally she bent over and looked at the photographs of the soldiers posted in front of the house and the headline: "Terrorist Hideout Discovered. Army Makes Successful Sweep" and farther down, the photo of the three dead guerrillas. Which one was Fermín? she thought, looking at the corpses: two men and a woman, young, shot to pieces, with blood and gaping bullet wounds everywhere, and the photograph of the house full of huge holes.

Felipe's friends, she thought. And Sebastián had been with them, and now he was in her house. One of them. In her house. She read avidly to see what was said about him. Nothing. There was nothing. And yet he had leaped over the walls of the neighboring houses, through the patios. But no one had denounced him.

The distances were becoming smaller. She no longer felt the vague sadness that these photos of young people riddled by bullets had always given her; these were dead people who were close to her, dangerously close. Their unknown faces, now disfigured and strange, had entered her life.

Their phantoms were real to her. The night before, hugging Felipe, she had suffered these deaths; if it were not for the fear, she certainly would have even cried over them. Like other times, she felt like reproaching the dead for letting themselves get killed, for dying, for believing they could stand up to the Great General's army with those childlike faces. The rickety weapons lying beside the cadavers formed a contrast with the helmets, radios, machine-guns, planes, and tanks of the army.

And now they had her involved in their suicidal bravery.

Doña Nico, the woman in charge of refreshments and cleaning, came in to bring her the carrot and orange juice that Lavinia usually had at mid-morning. When she put the glass on the table, she glanced sideways at the newspapers.

"Poor kids," she said, in an nearly inaudible whisper. "It was in my neighborhood," she added, as if justifying her comment.

"And what happened?" Lavinia asked, without knowing very well how to approach her, how to go about that "finding out what people were saying..."

"I don't know," said the woman, nervously wiping her hands along her apron. "I don't know what happened. I was minding my own business in my house, washing clothes, when I heard the shots. It was a terrible shoot-out. It lasted almost until midnight.

"We thought there were a lot of people in the house, but it was just those three. That's all I know."

"And did you know them?" Lavinia asked.

"No. I'd never seen them."

"And how could the army have known they were there?"

"I don't know. I haven't the slightest idea," said the woman, backing towards the door and hurrying out.

That was the dictatorship, Lavinia thought. It bred fear: like the woman saying she didn't know a thing and she saying she didn't want to get involved. It was better not to know anything. That was the safest thing: to ignore the dark side of Faguas. Leave as Doña Nico had, clearly showing she didn't want to talk about it. The need for survival was stronger than the heaviness in her voice as she said, "poor kids." How could you blame her when she had four children and was raising them alone?

But Sebastián had escaped and no one had said a thing.

After reading the newspapers, Lavinia tried to work, to concentrate on the plan for the elegant house she was designing with tiled baths and interior gardens. She couldn't take her mind off the photo of the dead. They became confused with the lines of the blueprint; they appeared in the big bedrooms, among the exposed beams of the ceiling, the façade. She imagined Felipe's and Sebastián's reaction when they saw them, when they opened the newspaper and found the photos of their dead friends.

In spite of everything, she felt calmer. The quiet, uneventful surroundings of the office slowly returned her to a feeling of normality. Nobody came to look for Felipe. Everything's fine, she told herself, nothing has changed. But the hands of the clock advanced through the hours. It would soon be five o'clock. She would have to leave, walk to the pharmacy, buy the antibiotics, return home, return home with the newspapers.

One of the architects stuck his head in the door, asking if she knew when Felipe was coming.

"What's the problem?" she asked, tense, trying to conceal her jumpiness.

"Nothing special. Just wanted to ask him something."

"He called to say his stomach was bothering him," Lavinia said, recovering her aplomb... "Guess he ate something that disagreed with him," she added with a smile.

She had lied on the spot, almost without thinking.

+ + +

I can't help feeling tenderness about her fear, now that I can distinguish the past and the present in the white dunes of her brain. At first it was difficult to tell them apart. An event, to be assimilated by her, must make its way through past references. These constant comparisons confused me until I noticed the color. When she experiences an immediate sensation, the color is bright and shiny. It does not matter if it is dark or light. The blackness of the present is the wing of a crow in the moonlight; red is blood or the sun at sunset. On the other hand, the past appears opaque: black like volcanic rocks, red like our sacred paintings. In the past, objects and persons emanate a dull, round echo that contains superimposed nostalgias and hollow smells. In the present, the images and sounds are smooth, flat, with the rotund odor of spear tips before combat. This is how I have learned to read the signs and guide myself through her labyrinth of sounds and images.

Many events are incomprehensible to me because of the time that the world has traveled through. But there are a great number of immutable relationships; the primary ones are still essentially similar. I am confident that I understand peace and restlessness; love and uneasiness; longing and uncertainty, vitality and sorrow; faith and mistrust; passion and instinct. I understand heat and cold, humidity and roughness, superficiality and profundity, sleep and insomnia, hunger and satiety, comfort and abandonment.

It is the untouchable landscape. Man with his deeds can change features, appearances: he can sow or cut down trees, change the course of rivers, make those huge dark roads that trace snaking paths along the earth. But he cannot move volcanoes, lift up the canyons, interfere in the dome of the heavens, prevent the formation of the clouds, change the position of the sun or the moon. The same untouchable landscape is the inner substance of Lavinia. That is why I can understand her fear and imbue it with strength.

• • •

The corner pharmacy gave off an odor of old jars, the sweetish aroma of vitamins, flasks of alcohol and peroxide. The wooden shelves contained exhibits of small boxes labeled with strange names. The glass jars with shiny brass covers paraded their full bellies of cookies, sweets, and Alka-Seltzer. The pharmacist with his waxed mustache, a Mexican charro in a white coat, was reading the newspaper as he rocked lethargically in a wicker chair in the late afternoon shadows.

Lavinia asked the druggist for a "strong" antibiotic, making up a story about a neighbor woman who had cut herself with pruning shears.

"And is she vaccinated against tetanus?" asked the druggist, preening his mustache.

Lavinia said she was. She just had to be careful about the possibility of an infection. Since the wound was deep, they thought she needed a strong antibiotic.

In Faguas the druggists often acted as doctors. The people preferred them because they didn't charge for their consultations, only the medicines.

She saw him walk toward the drawers on the back wall and fill a paper cone with a large number of black and yellow capsules, moving with the circumspection appropriate to his profession.

He gave them to her, explaining that her friend should take one every six hours for no fewer than five days. He had prepared the complete dosage.

She left with the medicine in her bag. The afternoon was slowly turning to evening. Tropical twilights were always a spectacle, with reddish clouds, strange slashes across the sky, an orange glow.

She got out of the taxi on the avenue. As her steps took her closer to her home, her body tensed, her muscles stiffened; her heartbeat became alert, nervous. If she could be sure this was all nearly over, she thought, that she would arrive with the medicine and find Sebastián and Felipe ready to leave, to tell her good-bye at the door and return her to her usual nighttime tranquillity. But it wasn't going to be like that. She calculated that there would be at least two more days of this, and she would have to go around with that double personality for two, maybe three more days.

And yet, she said to herself, she had crossed still another border. Aunt Inés used to say that in life growing was a question of going beyond your personal limits and trying out abilities you never knew you had. She'd never have imagined she could survive a day like this, lying without guilt, bare-facedly, without calculating, as if the words were stored away for that purpose, ready for her to put them to use. At the office, in the drugstore, nobody would have ever known.

She always felt bad about lying. As a girl, when she went to confession, she always accused herself of lying. It had been a great effort to stop doing it because she enjoyed lying. And that's how it was: a quick impulse. She didn't even know how she made up the lies. They came out of her mouth like goldfish that lived independently inside her. They were insignificant little lies, told for the sheer pleasure of feeling that she could play with the adults' world, alter it slightly. Only afterward, when the lie was living outside her and was going around in her mother's or her nursemaid's mouth, did she feel bad. "Lying is a sin," the nuns at school said. "Thou shalt not bear false witness, thou shalt not lie," said one of the commandments. She stopped lying out of fear, fear of the torments of hell that Sister Theresa described with an abundance of macabre detail. She made them light a match and quickly stick their finger in the flame. That was hell but over the whole body, that fire over the whole body, burning without killing for all eternity. Later on, the lie lost its meaning of sin and became a negative value for her; honesty was something adults had to strive for. That's why she had felt guilt whenever she lied while living with her parents after returning from Europe. She was uncomfortable when she had to deceive them, to pretend she led a more conventional life.

But this was different, she thought, as she inserted the key in the lock and entered the dark interior of the house.

The darkness smelled of heavy silence. It was an expectant silence. Tigers crouched. In the patio walk under the orange tree, she saw Felipe standing with his hand on his hip, alerted by the sound of the door as it opened. A pale moon projected the tree's shadow over the flagstones.

She turned on the lights. Felipe came over to meet her.

"How did it go?" he asked in a soft voice.

"Fine, I think," she replied, holding out her arm with the newspapers, looking at him, thinking about those faces, the friends that now he would never see again.

Felipe took the newspapers with an abrupt gesture, and right there, next to her, read the headlines, the news on the front page, looking at the photos without saying a word.

She was silent, not knowing what to do, whether to stay there beside him or leave discreetly, as friends do at funerals when the moment of looking through the tiny window of the coffin for the last time arrives.

"Murderers! Bastards!" Felipe finally said, in a silent cry that echoed inside him. Lavinia imagined the shout projected inside his lungs, dispersing throughout his chest, his arms, his legs.

She embraced him from behind without saying a thing, thinking about how useless words were in the face of death. Sebastián appeared in the doorway to her room. This time he didn't greet her. He looked as if he had recovered. He had a clean bandage and was dressed in one of the men's shirts that she wore. He walked to where Felipe was and stood beside him, looking at the pages of the outspread newspaper.

"They don't mention that someone escaped," Felipe said, as he passed him the paper, offering him the pages with the photos of the dead compañeros. Silently he went to the kitchen and returned with a glass of water and drank it in big gulps, while Sebastián continued to read in silence.

Lavinia moved aside respectfully, feeling that she was in the way. She slipped toward the garden gate without saying a word, looking out to see the night, the patio, the serene, calm air around the plants, the orange tree exhaling its citrus smell. "Fortunate is the tree that hardly feels at all," she remembered. She would have liked to be a plant at that moment.

She heard Felipe coming over to her.

"Nothing odd happened at the office, no one came to ask about me, you didn't hear anything strange?" He spoke in a low voice, so as not to perturb Sebastián.

"No. Nothing unusual occurred. They all knew about what had happened, but they didn't talk much. They commented on the display of force used by the army against just three kids. Doña Nico told me it had been in her neighborhood, but she wouldn't say anything else. She only said "poor kids" when she saw the photos, but she seemed afraid to speak. I told Mercedes your stomach was bothering you," Lavinia said in a whisper.

He didn't reply. He left her and went back to Sebastián.

They talked for a bit. Sebastián said, "Excuse us, compañera," and they both went into the bedroom, closing the door.

Of course men didn't cry, Lavinia thought leaning on the door-frame, staring fixedly at the trunk of the orange tree. Tears were burning in her eyes. And she hadn't even known the dead! After all, she was a woman! she told herself ironically. The two men could look at the newspaper with dry, steady eyes, reading it carefully in spite of the photographs.

Felipe seemed to have recovered from his pain of the night before. "You never get used to death," he had said in the vulnerability of weariness. Now she saw them accept death without drama, without losing their composure, yet with anger. Evidently, for them, what mattered was how they should proceed, now that they knew no one had mentioned "the other one," the one who had jumped over garden walls, wounded, fleeing.

It gave her a chill to see them armored with that strength, armored, as if death or sadness bounced off their skin, unable to penetrate them. She remembered a conversation with Natalia, a Spanish friend, about the justice of the Basques' actions against Francoism: both factions killed in cold blood. What was the difference between them? In war, how did men differ? What basic difference was there between two men who each had a gun, ready to shoot to defend the position that both considered just?

Natalia had been furious at her "philosophical and metaphysical" questions. But she couldn't stop asking them even when she was aware of the differences between aggressors and victims; between the French "maquis" and the Nazis, for example. In society, as on an individual level, there existed a collective "self-defense" as a justification for violence; there were different human qualities, people who killed to kill and people who killed for life, to defend and preserve what was human in the face of bestiality and brute force. But it was still terrible to have to resort to bullets and weapons, one group against another. All those centuries had not managed to change the brutal way human beings battled each other.

In Faguas it was easy to justify the guerrillas; injustice was too blatant; it was easy to tell the difference between what one group and another defended; easy to see the lack of alternatives against the Great General. Just seeing today's newspaper, for example, one had to take a stand between brute force and idealism. One had to choose the cause of those who had been killed, even if only on an abstract level.

But she couldn't get rid of her doubts. Seeing Sebastián and Felipe made her think about the dangers of becoming hardened to death.

Although if they had started to cry, perhaps she would have thought they were weak. But no, she said, why? She always thought it was terrible and absurd to consider it a weakness for men to cry. But in reality she had never seen any of them cry. Maybe she wouldn't be able to stand it in this case. It would increase her sense of defenselessness. Maybe they did not need to cry, they only had to do something. Something to avoid the hardness. That hardness that made her apprehensive, as if there were a delicate equilibrium which, if it ever were destroyed, would return the world to the wild beasts.

It was then that she heard that horrible sound she would always remember coming from the partly-opened window of her room: Sebastián's hoarse voice, breaking off, breaking into thick, dry, sobs, producing the sound of a pain she had never known.

✛ ✛ ✛

I see her looking at me. I feel her thinking. There she is in the middle of the night like a lost firefly, floating among us yet unable to reach the place where she belongs. Inside the house, the men are talking. I hear the low murmur of their voices, like the many times I listened from the darkness to the councils between Yarince and his warriors. Those councils where I was not allowed to participate even though they took me into battle.

After the battle at Maribios—the battle of the Flayed Ones, as the invaders called it—there were moments when I felt my sex was a curse. They spent days discussing how to proceed, while I, charged with hunting and cooking their meals, hovered on the fringe.

When I went down to the gently flowing river to get them water, I waited there with my legs open for the surface to become smooth and motionless so I could look at my sex. The cleft between my legs seemed mysterious to me, like a fruit with fleshy lips and in its center, a delicate rosy seed. That was where Yarince entered me, and when he was inside, we formed a single image, a single body: together we were complete.

I was strong and more than once my intuition saved us from ambush. I was caring, and often the warriors came to me to talk about their feelings. I had a body capable of bearing life in nine moons and withstanding the pain of birth. I could fight, was as skilled as any with my bow and arrow, and also I could cook and dance for them in the placid nights. But they did not seem to appreciate these things. They left me out when they had to think about the future or make life-and-death decisions. And all because of the cleft, the palpitating flower the color of medlar fruit which I had between my legs.

● ● ●

Lavinia stood a while longer watching the shadows in the garden sway in the wind. The sobbing had tapered off into the murmur of a conversation under water; the sound of the men talking was like a conversation between two fish, scarcely louder than the sound of bubbles.

The wracking sobs weighed heavily on her heart. She was sorry she had doubted the feelings of those two strange people, invaders of the peace of her home, those undaunted dreamers, "the brave ones," as Adrián had called them.

Their pain so nearby made her want to protect them. What could she do for them? she thought. Practically nothing. Then she remembered they hadn't eaten. She could make them something, even though she wasn't hungry. Eating hadn't crossed her mind until that moment. She went to the kitchen, thinking about what to make for the three of them. In spite of the pain, Sebastián and Felipe had to eat, to live, to nourish themselves.

She found an empty sardine can in the sink. Poor things! she thought, feeling ashamed of her empty cupboards.

She prepared the only thing she knew how to make decently: spaghetti with sauce.

She was setting the plates on the table when Felipe appeared in the kitchen doorway.

"How's Sebastián's arm?" Lavinia asked, pretending she hadn't heard a thing, just as she was pouring the last of the water from the spaghetti into the sink and putting butter on it.

"It's inflamed," Felipe said.

"He should see a doctor," Lavinia said, pouring the sauce.

"That's what we wanted to ask you," Sebastián said, appearing behind Felipe to watch her serve the plates. He was composed now; only his nose was a little reddish.

"We wanted you to go get a compañera who is a nurse. We'll also arrange my moving tomorrow with her."

"Why don't you tell me about it while we eat something?" Lavinia said. "You two have to eat."

She was pleased to see Sebastián smiling a little as they sat down to the table.

Flor—that was the compañera's name—had a car. Lavinia would only have to take a taxi and return with her to the house. Just that. Afterward she would be free of them.

"At least of me," Sebastián said, flashing his teasing smile again.

They ate in silence. Sebastián and Felipe didn't appear to have much appetite. Lavinia looked out of the corner of her eye at Sebastián. Without letting her refuse, with his soft, firm voice, his tree-like appearance, he had gotten her to do things she never thought she would. He acted with a sort of deep conviction that she would agree, wouldn't refuse him. His confidence in her was more imperative than an outright command.

Tomorrow her life would return to the safety of the ordinary, she thought. She could forget about the fear, the suspense, those confusing feelings.

The idea of crossing the city in a taxi, at night, didn't appeal to her, but she was willing to do it; she'd do anything to get her life back to normal.

"Have you gotten over being afraid?" asked Sebastián.

"More or less," she replied.

"It's normal," he said. "We all get afraid. What matters is not that you feel the fear but that you overcome it. And you've gotten over it very well; you've been brave."

"I had no choice," Lavinia said, a slight smile hovering on her lips.

"That's how it is with us," Sebastián said with a sad expression. "We have no choice."

"It's not the same," she said, slightly uncomfortable at the comparison. "You know why you're doing it. That's something different. I'm sorry about your friends."

"They died like heroes," Sebastián said, looking at her with an expression that was serious as well as kind, "but they were people like you and me."

"I think Lavinia should go get Flor," Felipe interrupted. "It's getting late."

• • •

CHAPTER 7

It was nine o'clock. The clear March sky boasted a yellow moon. The taxi sped along, weaving in and out of the light traffic. The streets, emptier than usual at that hour, were the only visible sign of the effect of the recent events. Leaning to one side against the door of the vehicle, Lavinia glanced backward, as Sebastián had indicated, to ascertain that no suspicious car was following them. The taxi headed toward the eastside neighborhoods. The poorly-lit area flashed by the window in a series of pink, green, and yellow dwellings: simple houses, all alike, decorated only by the loud colors of their walls and an occasional garden.

Inside the vehicle the driver was smoking and listening attentively to a sports program.

Lavinia, alert, didn't recognize herself in this guise of a vigilant woman. If all went well, the nightmare would be over tomorrow. She nibbled at her nails. Traveling in a taxi at night always made her uneasy, gave her the feeling that she was taking a risk. Except this time she wasn't afraid of the taxi driver, she was afraid of the darkness surrounding them in the badly-lit streets, the possibility she'd be followed... Silently she prayed that nothing would happen to her, that she'd find the woman named "Flor" and return to her house safe and sound.

Crossing a bridge and turning left, they entered an unpaved street. On both sides there were houses made of roughly-cut boards. Jumbled together precariously, separating here and there to form doors and windows, they lined the street. At the end she saw some houses made of concrete. One of the last was where Flor lived. From the taxi she saw the tile roof, the small hacienda-like structure of the building, and the rough wall that Felipe had described to her.

When the taxi entered the street, she looked around carefully. Sebastián and Felipe had warned her about supposedly innocent passersby, drunks sleeping on the sidewalks, parked vehicles occupied by necking couples: any of those signs could mean danger, might mean that security agents were watching. She didn't see a thing. (Felipe hadn't seen anything either, she thought, praying that nothing out of the ordinary would happen.)

"This is it," she said to the taxi driver.

She paid and got out of the taxi.

The bell made a shrill screech. A moment later she heard footsteps and the sound of slippers shuffling toward the door.

The woman on the other side of the iron gate looked at her. Lavinia saw her eyes follow the taxi as it drove off, stirring up dust as it headed toward the paved avenue.

"Yes? Who are you looking for?" asked the woman, coming up to her.

"For Flor," Lavinia said.

"I'm Flor," said the woman. "What can I do for you?"

Lavinia held out the paper Felipe had written at her dining room table and then folded in an odd way.

He had said that just by seeing the way it was folded, Flor would understand. Nevertheless, the woman opened it and read it before opening the door to let her in. The weak light from the bulb on the eave allowed Lavinia to observe her. She had dark, wavy, shoulder-length hair; her features were dark and fine; she was around thirty; her face was that of a stern nurse.

She still wore her white uniform. She had only removed her stockings and shoes and was wearing plastic slippers.

"Come in," she said, giving Lavinia a slight smile that softened her features almost like magic.

The gate opened with a rusty creak, the hinges crying out for oil.

"Sorry for making you wait," Flor said. "Nowadays we have to be more cautious than ever."

They went down a corridor with many urns. Plants with huge leaves: ferns, violets, and begonias brightened and warmed the old, rundown house. Flor led her into a pleasant, cozy living room which made Lavinia think she might have been mistaken about her first impression of her as a stern person. There were records, books, rocking chairs, more plants, paintings and a poster of Bob Dylan on the wall. A huelenoche vine hung above the hallway window.

Only a few fat medicine books on one of the shelves and the anatomical model of a woman indicated what the profession of the house's owner was.

"Wait just a moment," Flor said. "I just have to put my shoes on, grab my things, and we'll leave."

She gestured to Lavinia to sit down and disappeared behind a flowered curtain. Rocking and drumming her fingers on the arm of the chair, Lavinia waited. Her head ached.

Flor came out soon, dressed in a simple, comfortable outfit of light blue and carrying a medical bag in her hand. She was obviously worried.

She turned off the lights and closed the windows. Lavinia followed her to the small garage where an old Volkswagen was parked.

"Did you countercheck everything coming here?" Flor said, opening the car door.

"What?" Lavinia asked, not understanding.

"Did you check to see that no one was following you?" explained Flor.

"Yes, yes. I didn't see anyone."

Overwhelmed by the accumulation of sensations in the last few hours, she reacted slowly, a novice to that strange, dangerous world. She didn't resemble them at all, they seemed such expert conspirators, she thought. She watched Flor take the vehicle out, then close the garage doors. Just like Sebastián, she too had the air of a serene tree.

It seemed unreal to her to suddenly be in contact with these beings. She had always imagined them with sharp faces, their eyes illuminated by chimerical visions, fanatics, samurai of a sort. Ridiculous clichés from the movies, she reproached herself, feeling shame. She never suspected they would be normal people, everyday people. Felipe, no less, had turned out to be one of them. Maybe it was only her romanticism that attributed an air of peace, firmness and balance to Sebastián and Flor. It was probably her imagination that endowed them with penetrating expressions, although she couldn't deny the chameleon-like appearance of Flor who, as she got into the vehicle and started the engine, now looked nothing like the nurse at the door.

They left the dark streets of the east side and entered the avenue that led to Lavinia's neighborhood.

"It's lucky Sebastián is all right," Flor said. "I was very worried. We had no news of him."

"Have you known him for a long time?" Lavinia asked.

"More or less," Flor said, evasively. "And you're Felipe's friend, right?"

"Yes. We work together."

"But you didn't know anything about this..."

"No."

"You must have been frightened..."

"I never imagined..."

"That's how it is," Flor said. "When we least expect it..."

Yes, Lavinia thought, when one least expects it, one walks through the mirror into another dimension, into a world that exists hidden away from everyday life. Suddenly you find yourself, riding in a car talking with a unknown woman who has crossed rebellion's firing line. For Flor, Lavinia's protests, her rebellion against being married off, against parents, social conventions, were just chapters out of children's fairy tales. Flor wrote history with a capital "H"—while her history, on the other hand, was no more than that of a young rebel without a cause. She looked at

Flor as she drove. Flor was talking. She commented on the traffic, the lights, trivial things. She didn't look at all nervous. Lavinia felt a tinge of admiration for her. How did she feel? she thought. What was it like to live the 'heroic' side of life? She recalled her old admiration for the feats of heroes, born from the Jules Verne books. It was but an adolescent admiration. In today's real world it wasn't easy to find people you could admire. That's why it was easy to turn them into mythical beings, as Adrián did when he admired them for their bravery. She should be careful, she thought. Especially being so close to Felipe. She shouldn't even toy with the idea of being one of them. She had nothing in common with "the brave ones," who like Flor could calmly drive a car at night in the middle of a city with dark streets where the FLAT (the jeeps belonging to the Forces for the Struggle Against Terrorism) drove around, in order to go treat a wounded guerrilla with a complete stranger who had handed her a folded piece of paper.

Flor was asking her questions. Lavinia gave in to the temptation to talk about herself, talk with someone who listened so intently, a woman, someone subject like her to an ancestral fate, and who, however, lived on such an unusual plane of reality, involved in conspiracy as if it were a natural habitat, apart from the preconceived notions of femininity. She thought about asking her what that sort of life was like, but the trip wasn't long enough.

"That's the house," she said, pointing it out.

Flor went by the house without stopping and parked several blocks away, explaining to Lavinia that it was better not to park at your destination in order to avoid being detected.

They started walking, Their steps echoed along the empty sidewalks. The noble ghosts hid in the silent houses. A few dogs scavenged among the garbage cans.

Lavinia looked at the silent, thoughtful woman walking beside her carrying a black medical bag. She didn't know a thing about Flor. She had skillfully managed to avoid talking about herself. That was certainly how they functioned, Lavinia thought. When they entered the living room where the men were waiting, she wondered if Flor had known the other three who were dead, the ones who floated in the atmosphere of the house. The newspaper was carefully folded on the dining room table. They embraced: first Sebastián and then Felipe embraced her. An embrace of shipwreck survivors, and Flor with her eyes closed.

Then the three of them broke the tenuous circle of affection and silence, talking about Sebastián's arm. Flor said his hand looked slightly swollen. They went into the bedroom with her nurse's bag. Lavinia went in with them, not wanting to stay outside, apart, alone.

She created the excuse for herself that maybe they would need her for the cotton or peroxide. They didn't seem to avoid her presence.

She stood there while Sebastián, sitting on the bed, let Flor remove the improvised bandage.

"It's quite inflamed," she said. "Did you give him an antibiotic?" she asked, turning to Felipe.

"Yes," he said, "ampicillin," and he explained the dosage.

With professional precision, Flor opened the black bag and took out cotton and bandages. Lavinia couldn't help feeling her blood run cold when, amid ampules, syringes and flasks, she saw two black pistols on the white bottom of the bag. And she had crossed the whole city with that woman in the car, she thought, with those pistols covered only by gauze and bandages...!

"Ah, good! You brought them," Sebastián said, without changing his expression. He had seen them too.

The questions, the reproaches assaulted Lavinia again. She felt like scolding them for having involved her in all this. She thought about Flor's innocent, serene air when they were in the car; when she asked her about Italy, the remnants of fascism, the concerns of the students. Unaware of what was in the bag, she had had it at her feet the whole time and had even offered to carry it for Flor while they were walking to the house.

The pistol's black outline made her afraid again, but her fear dissolved in the curiosity she felt, watching them.

✛ ✛ ✛

It is hard to keep her fear anchored, to prevent it from spreading freely through her blood. Fear is both dark and shiny. It envelops her thoughts like a net that clutches, immobilizing her, like the bite of the yellow snakes in our jungle. I was afraid many times. I remember the first vision of the beasts the Spaniards rode when they arrived. At first we thought they formed a single body. We thought they were gods from the underworld. But they died. Their beasts died, and they did too. We were all mortals. When we finally discovered that, it was too late. Fear had played tricks on us.

• • •

Flor finished cleaning the wound. The bullet had entered through the back of the arm, where the hole was smaller, coming out a little above the elbow in a jagged opening. The entire area around it, including the hand, had darkened.

She asked Sebastián to do a series of movement with his arm—which he did without hiding the pain it caused him. Convinced the bullet had not affected his movements seriously, Flor said she had to suture the wound to make sure it would heal and thus avoid the danger of serious infection.

"Lavinia, could you please boil some water?" she asked.

They sterilized the curved needles for suturing in the boiling water.

Flor removed them carefully.

"Could you help me?" she said to Lavinia. "I do these things better with women. Men get nervous."

Lavinia nodded. When she was deciding on a profession, medicine had been another possibility. As a teenager she had devoured novels about doctors and hospitals. But her father was totally opposed. Too many years of study, he argued. She'd end up an old maid, he said, or at best her husband would leave her if she had to go out to attend to emergencies in the middle of the night.

She helped Flor set out what she would need on the bed, spreading out a white towel. The nurse's fine, clean hands worked efficiently, passing the black thread from one side of the wound to the other and joining the skin together. It must hurt, Lavinia thought, but Sebastián barely grimaced. Only his neck showed his tension; the fine sets of veins stood out like slender wires on his neck.

Felipe watched the operation in silence. Once in a while he'd crack a joke to distract Sebastián.

Holding the towel with the instruments, Lavinia had the feeling she was living someone else's life. This is not real, she told herself. She couldn't believe that she was in her own bedroom (the records, the mattress on the floor, the colored blankets rolled up in the corner) watching Flor's hands going across Sebastián's skin over and over with the suturing thread.

Except for Felipe, these people were totally unfamiliar to her. They could have passed her in the street, and she would not have noticed them. Perhaps she would only have shared the brief, ephemeral moment, when your eyes meet another's in the crowd, and glances cross like distant ships in the fog, and faces disappear without a trace, lost forever when they reach the corner and your eyes are distracted by the bright colors of the tray resting on the legs of the woman selling sweets. She never would have imagined this night with them, she thought, with the thick March heat, the silence of camaraderie and concern for Sebastián's arm, for the pain he was suffering. Something bound them together now: intimacy, as if she'd known them for a long time. The fabric of danger, death crouching low, stalking outside in the still, dark streets, made them a family, a group of people who needed each other in order to survive. They were like the people in the caves, sensing each other's presence in the dark, listening to the breathing of bison outside. She lifted her head, alert to the sound coming from the street. It was just a car. The four of them looked at one another and then continued watching Flor in silence. They didn't need to know much about each other, Lavinia thought. Their common concern did away with convention; their eyes were tuned to the same frequency; vulnerability and strength lived side by side, alternating in rising and ebbing movements, a sea-tide in which they all swam together, shipwrecked in this moment, this bubble.

Flor finished. Sebastián looked at his arm, with the black criss-cross design of the stitches. Felipe softly grasped Lavinia by the shoulders and steered her out of the bedroom.

"You should sleep in the other room," Felipe said, when they were outside. "Don't worry anymore. We have to talk about moving him tomorrow. It'll be late when we finish. You ought to sleep a bit."

"Felipe," Lavinia said, "if it's necessary, Sebastián can stay. I wouldn't want anything to happen to him because he was taken out of here."

"Thanks," Felipe smiled, "but I don't think it's a good idea. Keeping on the move is important in situations like this. We don't really know if anybody gave him away. We don't know if they're looking for him. Maybe they didn't say anything so we'd let our guard down and give ourselves away... Don't worry."

He gave her a fatherly kiss on the forehead and disappeared behind the bedroom door.

She lay down on the mattress with the odor of old dreams in the other bedroom.

She stretched out face-up, fully dressed, with the light off. The shadows of things she stored in the room surrounded her like silent icons. The underwater voices from the other room glided indistinctly in through the crack of light under the bathroom door.

She knew she should go to sleep, and not think about them any more, not think about the possibility that Sebastián would accept the offer to stay. She didn't know why she had offered, how the words had come out of her mouth; maybe because it saddened her to see them leave, see them abandon this island, the island where they had been together as if they had known each other for a long time. That's why she said it, she thought, even if it didn't make sense, even if she would undoubtedly regret it tomorrow and would be afraid again. But she told herself she wouldn't think about anything, that she was going to sleep. She had hardly slept at all.

She felt alone. Felipe was with them, he belonged to them; the three of them belonged to one another. Only she was alone in the empty room, immersed in a dense mist of images and thoughts that would not let her slide into sleep. She tried to erase them by thinking about the sea. When she couldn't sleep, she usually thought about the sea.

She was walking along the beach, listening to the sea gulls, the waves flinging their curly white locks about. She was walking on the deserted beach in a light gauze tunic. And there was the beating of wings, flight. She was flying again. Her grandfather waved to her while the immense sea grew tiny in the wide open space.

When she opened her eyes the next day, light was streaming in through the high window. Beside her, fully dressed, Felipe was smoking a cigarette.

"They left," he said.

Lavinia sat up on the mattress. She rubbed her eyes. They're gone, she thought. I don't have to be afraid any more; and she felt like crying.

"Now we ought to take a shower and go to work," Felipe continued. "They asked me to thank you. They told me you were very brave."

She didn't say anything. She got up and took the sheets off the bed, folding them carefully without knowing why. They would return to work. Sebastián and Flor had left. Normality would return. Nothing had happened. Everybody

safe and sound. She breathed deeply to control her desire to
cry.

Felipe looked at her, expectantly. Maybe he thinks that
everything will end between us now, she thought, going by
herself into the bathroom. She closed her eyes under the
shower, letting the water fall in a heavy stream on her
head. She felt as if she were convalescing from a long illness.

When she came out, Felipe had nearly finished
straightening the bedroom. The bloody sheets were carefully
piled on the bed.

"It'd be better to throw them away," suggested Lavinia, as
she dressed. Felipe was smoking another cigarette, standing
beside the window.

"That's dangerous," Felipe said. "They might find them
and use them as a clue. It's better to leave them hidden
somewhere and wash them when you're alone. I'll help you."

They hid them in the top of the closet behind the old
suitcases.

Before she left, Lavinia went through the house closing
doors and windows.

"I hope Sebastián doesn't have any more problems," she
told Felipe before leaving, her conscience suddenly bothering
her for the vehemence with which she had wished he would
leave so she could recover the peacefulness of her home, the
untranscendental days, her blessed routine.

"Let's hope not. Thank you," he said, hugging her.

Lavinia hugged him tightly. It made her feel bad to see
him so worried, watching her, afraid she'd tell him she
never wanted to see him again.

"I love you," she whispered. And she thought how, in
spite of everything, she couldn't leave him.

Lavinia spent the day absorbed in a strange, calm
happiness. The routine of blueprints, draftsmen bent over
their tables, Mercedes swaying around the office, the
steaming coffee on her desk, seemed like special events to
her. She had the feeling of having returned after a long
journey. During the day she thought several times about Flor

and Sebastián. They seemed so distant that the memory had already turned to nostalgia. She thought about the fox's speech in *The Little Prince*, the part about the ties of affection. In such a short time she had come to care for them. She didn't want anything to happen to them. If anything happened to them she would feel a profound sorrow, she told herself. Not the sorrow you feel for two slight acquaintances, because something chemical had happened between them, a certain complicity in their glances, that sense of being close to one another. It was the solidarity of danger.

But now that time had turned the corner, it was better to be able to remember the moment, knowing it was part of the past. She didn't think she could go through another experience like that.

When Lavinia got home, she found the house clean. It was Wednesday. Lucrecia had come. She turned on the patio lights, looked at the orange tree laden with fruit, poured herself a drink and lay in the hammock.

She was there for a long while listening to music, feeling the cool night air, treasuring the calm. Only when she got up to call Sara and Antonio did she feel uneasy for a moment. This was her beloved state of normality, and yet she felt as if her house and her life had been suddenly drained of their contents. With the receiver in her hand, slowly smoking a cigarette, she imagined the mundane conversation that was about to take place and wondered what she really loved about this "tranquillity." Did she really love it or was the notion of independence, of the woman who lives alone and has her own job, a room of her own, an incomplete option, a half-hearted rebellion, form without content?

Now nothing would happen, she thought; she could predict how her days would be, one after another.

This space was an island, a cave, the benevolent imprisonment of a blind statue in a Roman garden: conquering solitude was her most outstanding achievement. She could stay in here while the world unleashed the rain, and Sebastián, Flor, and Felipe and who knows how many others,

were there outside battling windmills, with their air of
serene trees.

+ + +

She is standing before the threshold of questions. She
cannot respond. Only I, here, hidden as I am, can dream, can
glimpse conjunctions, the forks in the roads. Only I feel the
imperatives of her legacy, while she only intuitively senses
changes in her heart which she cannot name.

The Spaniards said they had discovered a new world. But
our world was not new to us. Many generations had flourished
in these lands since our ancestors, worshipers of Tamagastad
and Cippatoval, settled here. We were Nahuatls, but we
also spoke Chorotega and the Niquirana language. We could
measure the movement of the stars and write on strips of
deerskin. We cultivated the land, we lived in great
settlements beside the lakes, we hunted and spun, we had
schools and sacred festivals.

Who knows what all this territory would be like now if
the Chorotegas, Caribs, Dirians, and Niquiranos had not
been killed...?

The Spaniards said they had to make us "civilized,"
make us give up our "barbarianism." Yet they defeated us,
they decimated us barbarously.

In just a few years they made more human sacrifices than
we had ever made in all the history of our festivals.

This country was the most populated. And yet in the
twenty five years I lived, it lost so many men. They sent them
in great ships to build a distant city they called Lima. They
killed them: their dogs tore them to pieces, they hung them
from trees, cut off their heads, shot them, baptized them;
they prostituted our women.

They brought us a strange god who did not know our
history or our origins and wanted us to worship him in a way
we did not know.

And what good remains of all this? I wonder.

Men are still running. There are bloodthirsty governors. Flesh is still being torn, they are still fighting.

Our legacy of beating drums is still pulsing in the blood of these generations.

It's the only thing left of us, Yarince: resistance.

CHAPTER 8

● ● ●

Lavinia raised her eyes from the blueprint and saw the landscape at dusk, reddened by the April burn-offs.

She had cramps and felt tired. Menstruation made her feel like that: sensitive and languid. She would rather have been somewhere else, in some other time, she thought, be a lady from the eighteenth century, a friend or lover of one of the romantic poets, prone to fainting, weak, sitting beside the hearth during a wintry April. But nothing romantic had happened to her lately.

She was in a bad mood. A little while ago, Felipe had come in to explain why it had been impossible for him to come to her house yesterday: an emergency meeting, he couldn't let her know, there was no telephone there.

She had waited for him all night—at first, dressed, her makeup on, her hair carefully brushed, impatiently reading any old book; afterward, in bed, awake through dawn, fearful of falling asleep and not hearing the knocks on her door, until sleep finally overcame her.

Since the incident with Sebastián, Felipe had been avoiding talking with her about the Movement. It had become tabu between them. He responded to Lavinia's questions, her desire to understand, her half-hearted attempts to get closer, with evasive answers and a paternal air. At first she preferred that. She didn't know what would have happened if Felipe had tried to involve her in the Movement immediately after the incident. It took her weeks to recover from the impact, to get over her uncertainty as to whether or not to continue her relationship with him, to feel that the space in her house was whole again and her solitude was productive, to feel that her usual friendships were satisfactory, to take up her relationship with Felipe again in spite of...

Deep down, however, she wasn't able to understand his attitude; it disappointed her. Felipe had been too accepting of her fears and her arguments that it was better to keep everything as it was, not to contaminate the relationship with discussions or actions that were a matter of individual choices... He had been receptive to the many reasons she wielded, when, fearing that he would catch on to her doubts, she sat him down the nights following Sebatián's departure, in the patio next to the orange tree, hurling argument after argument to convince him not to insist on something that he, in fact, seemed to have no intention of insisting upon.

She recalled how Felipe had listened in silence, nodding, agreeing with her.

"I know we can't swim together," he had said at last. "You are the shore of my river. If you swam with me, where would the shore be?"

He admitted—to Lavinia's dismay—that he needed the oasis of her house, of her smile, the quiet certainty of her days.

"That thing with Sebastián was an emergency. I didn't do it to get you involved. Believe me," he told her.

Convincing him to desist, Lavinia thought, had been excessively easy. It was obvious that Felipe didn't want to see her involved at all, and she had, unsuspectingly, paved the way for him.

It wasn't logical, Lavinia thought. The logical thing would have been for him to try to share with her what gave purpose and meaning to his life. To try, even if she resisted.

Deep down, she blamed Felipe for her own fear, for not helping her struggle against the sharp terror that the possibility of getting involved caused her (although Sebastián had said she was brave, and she would have liked to believe that). In fact he made it worse with terrible stories of tortures and persecution. Or it could be her contradictory spirit, she thought, because she also wasn't sure whether an attempt by Felipe to recruit her would not have separated them, put her on her guard, made her flee, not only from the Movement but from him as well.

Lately Lavinia couldn't figure herself out. She couldn't understand why it angered her that Felipe would not speak to her about the Movement. She didn't want to belong to the Movement, she told herself over and over. And yet, talking, asking about it, had become an irrational attraction for her, a constant temptation, an inexplicable incitement. And she had never imagined Felipe holding her back, stopping her, denying her the knowledge.

The only true thing was that she felt confused. She felt alone even when he was with her, alone in a sort of existential solitude, like a vacuum chamber. She was with a man whose goals were nothing at all like hers, a man who obviously considered her just a "pleasant refuge" in his life. A man who could disappear any day, swallowed up in the conspiracy. She should leave him, she thought. But she couldn't. If she had been attracted to him before, that attraction had now been doubled. The halo of mystery and danger appealed to her in spite of herself. She didn't want to remain on the periphery, but she did not want to take the deadly leap, either. Maybe if he insisted, she would consider it. Sometimes she wished he would. She asked herself if life demanded more of her than just her personal independence and a room of her own. But Felipe avoided the subject, and lately she hardly saw him.

The city was alive with protests. The Great General had ordered an increase in the prices of public transportation and milk. The people, goaded by groups of students and workers, were holding demonstrations and night rallies in all the barrios. Besides protesting against the new prices, the people demanded the release of a professor who was accused of collaborating with the Movement and who had begun a hunger strike in the prison.

At the university, buses were burned, bonfires were lit at night. The Great General had imposed censorship on the press. The climate in the streets was belligerent and fiery.

She was sure Felipe was participating in the revolts, while during those days there was nothing for her to do but wait for him, struggling inside herself, trying not to feel that love was turning into anguish and oppression.

She did not want to make Felipe the center of her life, to become a Penelope weaving the strands of night. But even so, in spite of herself, she saw how she was trapped in the age-old tradition: the woman in the cave waiting for her man during the hunt and the battle, fearful of the storm raging around her, imagining him trapped by gigantic beasts, wounded by lightning or arrow; the woman without repose, leaping alertly as she hears the grunt calling to her in the darkness, grunting in response, her heart joyful as she watches him return safely, happy to know that at last she would eat and be warm until the next day, until the man left again to hunt, until the next terror, the fear, the picture in the newspaper, the breathing of the wild beasts.

Penelope never had her sympathy. Perhaps because all women, sometime in their lives, could be compared to her. In Lavinia's case, it wasn't a matter of being afraid that Ulysses wouldn't cover his ears to escape the sirens' song, as with most of the modern Ulysses. Felipe's problem wasn't the sirens; it was the Cyclops. Felipe was Ulysses battling the Cyclops, the Cyclops of the dictatorship.

And her problem, as a modern Penelope in spite of herself, was to feel herself locked in the narrow pigeonhole of the lover, with no other right to knowledge about life beyond that of her own body; the abundant sensuality they shared, the private petals that Felipe plucked each time he entered deeper and deeper in her most intimate self, kneeling to open her legs and gaze at her moist sex, drink from it like a cup of pollen, like a bee poised over the corolla of a flower, inhaling the salty perfume until she opened the gate for him, surrendered the subterranean passageways, the castle moats surrounding the tiny tower of pleasure that his mouth laid siege to with an army of spears, conquering her entire flesh, entering her womb until the final wave tossed them panting, exhausted, upon the moan of surrender.

But she could not penetrate him. She could not even reproach him—his desire to confine her, to keep her to himself in order to create the illusion of an oasis with its palm trees. She couldn't blame him for using her to satisfy the logical need of a man to have a normal space in his life: a woman who would wait for him. To do so would have meant making a decision which she was neither ready for nor sure about, or else leaving him once and for all. She couldn't choose between the alternatives, and her inability to make a decision forced her to wait.

In vain, Lavinia thought, the centuries had ended the terrors of the caves: Penelopes were condemned to live eternally trapped in silent nets, victims of their own shortcomings, reduced, like her, to their own private Ithacas.

She was angry at herself. Lately that was her predominant feeling. She wasn't even in the mood to see Antonio, Florence, or the others, who had tired of calling her. Their world had shrunk, overshadowed by the conflicts she dared not resolve.

Night had descended about her. The office had become silent and dark. The sound of silence interrupted her daydreaming. She was startled to find herself there alone so late.

She left quickly, grabbing her purse, rushing fearfully through the halls to the elevator and into the street where she finally shook off the strange sensation of being trapped, locked in.

"It's nearly seven," she thought, looking at her watch while she walked to the parking lot and the car she had recently bought. She didn't feel like going home, but she didn't feel like visiting Sara or her group of friends either. The impossibility of sharing her uncertainties with them made her feeling of loneliness greater. She recalled how badly she'd felt the previous Sunday during their outing at the hacienda that belonged to Florence's father. She had somehow felt uncomfortable with the peasants who observed the group of rich young people from the city. She couldn't get the images of Sebastián and Flor out of her thoughts. She couldn't help wondering what they would think if they saw her on these spoiled kids' outings.

And it happened to her often. She would see Sebastián and Flor as in a movie. It was as if the invasion of that episode into her life had fractured the order of an apparently unalterable world. Why did it haunt her so? she wondered. It had even invaded her sleep, for at times she dreamed of wars and dark men and women. It was becoming an obsession, a vertigo whose attraction she resisted.

✛ ✛ ✛

She is wrestling with her contradictions. Day after day I have felt her waver without managing to escape, unable to flee, like someone looking out over a cliff. I don't know if I should insist. I don't know if I can. The relationship is not clear to me yet. I know that certain images from my past have entered her dreams, that I can frighten away her fear by setting my own resistance against it. I know that I inhabit her blood like that of a tree, but I feel it has not been granted to me to change her substance, nor take over her life. She must live her own life; I am only the echo of a blood that also belongs to her.

• • •

The worst part was not being able to talk to anybody about all that, not being able to talk about her feelings, her uncertainties. The conversations with Sara had taken on the ethereal quality of half-truths. Lavinia could not even mention her dissatisfaction with her relationship with Felipe without explaining the reasons. On the other hand, she couldn't answer Sara's questions about the plans and dreams that are normal for couples, even when this aspect was easier to justify according to "modern" criteria. Lavinia thought how paradoxical it was now for her to want traditional things like security and stability in a relationship that allowed no more future than an instant. Felipe had warned her it was possible he would have to "go into hiding" at any time. She replied by quoting a love sonnet by Vinicios de Morais, the Brazilian poet-musician: "let it not be immortal since it is a flame, but let it be eternal as long as it lasts," defending the beauty of the moment, of living the present. But she had to admit how difficult it was to live with the future engulfed in uncertainty, without being part of the goal, without being able to share her insecurities with anyone.

She had no choice but to keep her doubts to herself, she thought, as she got into her car, noticing that it still smelled new.

She started the engine without knowing which direction to take and considered going for a drive along the highway to get rid of the sensation of the abyss, loneliness, of being helplessly stranded in no-man's-land.

She drove along streets and avenues, missing her Aunt Inés, wishing for a person who could understand her, someone she could talk with.

The image of Flor, her wavy hair, her dark features, the woman-to-woman empathy Lavinia had felt the only night they were together, came to mind with the flash of a distant beacon.

But...should she go? she thought. The night Flor had been in her house, they didn't even say good-bye. Flor wasn't just anybody, someone one knew and could visit anytime, without even having to call first. She belonged to another world. But, why not? she said to herself, if she doesn't want me to visit her, she'll certainly tell me.

Decisive, Lavinia turned the steering wheel to the right, away from the street she had been about to take, concentrating her attention on remembering the way to Flor's house.

She took the route to the eastside barrios. The rickety old buses were picking people up at the stops, men and women whose faces melted into the night, huddled together wearily under the brightly-colored shelters advertising soap, coffee, rum, and toothpaste.

"I could have been any one of them," she thought, riding in her soft car seat. "If I had been born somewhere else, had different parents, I could be there, waiting in line for the bus tonight." Being born was such a chance occurrence. People talked about the fear of death. Nobody thought about the fear of life. The innocent embryo takes shape in the mother's womb, without knowing what awaits it at the end of the tunnel. Life is created, and just like that, you're born. "It's lucky we aren't aware of anything then," she thought. Because you could be born into love or rejection, into want or abundance, although life itself was certainly not to blame. The vital principle did its job when it united egg and sperm; it was people who created the conditions in which life followed its course. And human beings seemed marked by destiny to trample one another, to make life difficult for one another, to kill one another.

"Why must we be like that?" she thought, when she reached the corner near the bridge, where a commercial establishment was located, a sort of big store that had a sign saying: "Divine Providence Shop." How could she not remember it? she smiled.

She turned left and found the bridge that marked the entrance to Flor's street.

Again the doubts assailed her, doubts as to the kind of welcome Flor would give her. But she was so close now, she told herself. She couldn't let her doubts take over, immobilize her. She couldn't let herself lose the confidence she had been so proud of since she had been a teenager.

The wheels of her car entered the unpaved street. She recognized the wooden dwellings. Some of their doors were open now. Looking through them you could see the whole house: the single room, the stove at the back, the family sitting outside on wooden chairs, enjoying the cool evening air, and barefoot children playing.

She parked her car beside the rustic wall of Flor's house. She saw her car was in the garage, and there was a light on in the house. The doorbell made a shrill sound and again Lavinia heard the slippers coming. Mentally she prayed Flor would let her in. Flor came to the door and her face showed pleasant surprise when she saw Lavinia.

"Hi," she said, opening the lock on the gate, "what a surprise!"

"Hi," Lavinia said. "Before I come in, I wanted to ask if it's all right for me to visit you... I didn't know if I should or not..."

"Now that you're here," Flor said, "don't be so formal; come on in."

And she smiled warmly.

They went into the living room; there was the Bob Dylan poster on the wall.

"Want some coffee?" asked Flor. "It's already made."

"Yes, thanks," Lavinia said.

Flor went behind the flowered curtain. Lavinia sat in the rocking chair, rocking and lighting a cigarette to kill time until Flor returned with the coffee. She looked at the shelves of books: *Madame Bovary, The Wretched of the Earth, Hopscotch, Nausea, Woman and Sexual Life*...familiar and unfamiliar titles... Quite unusual reading for a nurse. Who was this woman? she wondered.

She was the one returning with two enameled cups which she set on the table.

"So how is it that you came to visit me?" asked Flor, stirring the sugar in the coffee, looking at her with her gaze of a tree.

"Well, I don't know how it occurred to me," replied Lavinia, slightly intimidated. "I needed to talk with someone... I thought it might not be the best idea, coming here without warning, but I also thought you'd tell me if..."

"Well, usually it's better for you not to come like this, without warning," Flor said. "But you didn't have any way of letting me know, either, did you? So let's not worry about that right now. You're here, and I'm really glad to see you."

And what was she to say now? Lavinia thought. How should she start talking, what was it she needed to talk about?

"How's Sebastián?" she asked, for something to say.

Flor said he was all right. He had recovered better than she had expected. He could move his arm well. It hadn't gotten infected.

"The truth is," Lavinia said, "I don't know why I came. I felt lonely and thought of you, thought you would understand."

Flor looked at her with a kind expression, encouraging her with her glance to continue, but not helping her much with the conversation.

"I feel like I'm in no-man's-land," Lavinia said, "I'm confused."

"Don't you talk about it with Felipe?"

"Lately I haven't seen much of him. At night I don't do anything but wait for him, in case he comes. I feel like Penelope."

Flor laughed.

"He must be busy, right?" she said.

"You mean," Lavinia said, "that whether the man you're with is a guerrilla fighter or a refrigerator salesman, a woman's place is to wait for him?"

"Not necessarily," Flor said, smiling again. "It depends on what you as a woman want to do with your life."

"And how did you come to be what you are?" Lavinia asked.

Between sips of coffee, expressive gestures, and nostalgic silences, Flor told Lavinia her story. She, too, had a relative who had been important in her life, but not in a positive sense of Lavinia's Aunt Inés. Her uncle had taken her from her mother's shack up in the mountains to give her a "city education." He was a man who had made his fortune during the coffee boom, a bachelor and a degenerate. He took her along on his trips abroad to see museums and fast-living, outlandish people. "He more or less adopted me," Flor said, "but not with good intentions." She had already noticed how he looked at her when she entered her teens, and how he watched her bathing in the river. "He waited for me to grow up to make me his lover. As I stand before you I swear I left my virginity in San Francisco," Flor said, smoking and sipping coffee with a firm expression on her face.

She hated him. And to oppose his lasciviousness, she entered the university, flirting a lot, going to bed with anyone who was willing ("There was never a lack of them," she added, looking at Lavinia almost defiantly.) The only one who hadn't been willing was Sebastián. Flor recalled how he had confronted her, how he had shaken her to make her see the self-destructive process she had gotten into, confusing her deep-seated anger against her uncle with anger directed against herself.

"I resisted," she said, "but then I began to think and to cry." And between the arguing and crying with Sebastián, Flor went on, it just so happened that one day the army attacked the university. "Here, hide this pistol in your purse," she remembered Sebastián had told her in the horrible moment when they heard the sirens drawing up to where they were holding the rally, and just as the arguments broke into a fist fight between one student group and another. "Get out of here fast. Go home and wait for me to come tonight," he told her. She left in a daze, explained Flor, amazed that he would trust her, that he wasn't afraid she would give him away if they caught her with the pistol in her purse. "He trusted me and made me go through one of the worst moments of my life," she added. Hours later, Sebastián had shown up at her house as if nothing had happened, claiming the pistol she had hidden in her underwear drawer.

Without much preamble, he convinced her to leave her uncle's house, use the money she had saved to buy the house where she lived now, and collaborate fully with the Movement.

"His confidence in me was what did it," Flor said. "Either I accepted it, or I continued being the ridiculous thing that I was, just to get revenge on my uncle."

Afterward she had had to go through countless trials by fire to convince herself that the Movement wasn't—and this was what Sebastián told her constantly—a "therapy group," that it shouldn't just be a mechanism to give her "something to live for." She finally managed to not only make peace with herself but also assume a collective responsibility. "If only so that no peasant mother has to "give her children away" to rich relatives, thinking that it's the only way to help them "become something," she said.

Flor leaned her head back against the chair. Lavinia, very moved, had listened to her story in silence, astonished that Flor had confided in her.

"It wasn't easy," Flor added. "These decisions are never easy. It's just that sometimes things happen, and they find you at the right moment...but nobody makes the decision for you. Your problem is not Felipe."

"I know," Lavinia said defensively, "but it seems to me that he has some responsibility, since he's the person closest to me."

"Obviously what he wants is 'the warrior's repose,'" smiled Flor, "the woman who waits at home for him and warms his bed, happy that her man is fighting for a just cause, providing silent support for him. Why even Che Guevara said at first that women were marvelous cooks and couriers for the guerrillas—that was their role... This is a long struggle."

"But I don't want to be just the shore to his river," Lavinia said.

"Well, if you want, I can give you some pamphlets so you can familiarize yourself with the Movement and what it is trying to do," Flor said. "That way you won't have to go to him, if that's what makes you uncomfortable. That way you can make your own decisions, and you can wait for him 'on the bank of his river' with a bow and arrow."

Lavinia began laughing. The laughter brought tears to her eyes. Even she did not know why it suddenly burst from her chest. She couldn't hold the laughter back. She had visions of a woman tensing her bow, delighted, playful, waiting for the man's head to emerge from the water.

She gradually calmed down.

She didn't know if she would find the answers in the pamphlets, Lavinia said, but that was all right, she'd read them. Felipe deserved to have an arrow shot at him.

"Be careful," Flor said. "This is your business, not Felipe's."

Lavinia left Flor's house with the papers in her purse.

Was that what she had come to find? she wondered. She had been about to tell Flor no, not to give them to her. It wasn't for her, she couldn't, she was afraid. But she couldn't refuse; she had already gone too far. Without knowing why, she had been toying with the idea, chasing it the way a cat chases its tail. After all, she needed to make up her own mind at least, find out if her uneasiness was legitimate or just her way of disguising her sense of disappointment that Felipe hadn't included her in what she felt was something so fundamental in his life.

She had to take good care of the papers. If they caught her with them she could go to jail, Flor had said, giving her several mimeographed pamphlets. They told the history of the Movement, its program and statutes, their security measures (it wasn't a bad idea for her to know them, Flor said, especially because of her recent experience with Sebastián). After reading them, Lavinia was to return them to her.

She held her purse tightly as she got in the car, putting it close beside her on top of the emergency brake. Flor waved good-bye from the doorway. Lavinia thought about the trees again; at the end Flor's voice even rustled a bit when she advised her about the pamphlets, as if someone had been walking on leaves.

Lavinia started the car and headed out toward the avenue. She was crossing the night in the direction of her house when she saw the police car on the corner. Her heart leapt and her blood began to flow quickly, making her feel warm all over. She grasped the steering wheel tightly, reduced her speed, and prayed to all the saints not to let them stop her. "What have I done?" she thought, flushed. And what if the police saw the papers in her purse while they asked for her license? And what if they noticed how nervous she was?

She went by the police, slowly, without looking at them. They didn't stop her. She kept going. She could barely control the shaking in her legs, her desire to cry.

"This is not a toy," she thought as she touched the bag of papers over and over, while she made sure nothing irreversible had happened. "I'm not carrying a doll," she said to herself, continuing the childish regression caused by fear, slowly calming herself with various thoughts.

She remembered the dolls she used to take out of the closet her Aunt Inés had carefully arranged, the ones she secretly carried to the cabinet where the sewing machine was kept, her favorite hiding place, where she could check them out and find their hearts. "She's a destructive child," her mother would say because Lavinia bathed them until the paint washed off and they only had faded mouths or one blue eye and one brown one; she would comb them until their hair fell out, and she looked them over from head to foot trying to find a human feature, something that would give meaning to the cooing she made to them, to the caresses of a girl who had to play by herself, an only daughter, trying to find someone her age for company.

She remembered her disillusion when in doll after doll, her eyes encountered hollow chests, when she understood that she was wasting her fondling and caresses and lullabies, when she understood that not one of the dolls had a heart.

What would her mother say if she saw her? Lavinia thought, nervously accelerating at the green light, anxious to get home, feeling the whole city knew she was crossing it with a load of clandestine literature.

When she arrived, she found Felipe asleep in front of the television set. She hadn't expected to see him. Recently she had given him a copy of her house key so she could avoid uselessly waiting up at night, afraid of not hearing his knock at the door. But it was the first time he had used it. She moved cautiously so as not to awaken him and went into the bedroom thinking of a good place to hide the papers.

She looked around her and her eyes rested on the dusty old doll on the top shelf of the closet. Associating it with her recent thoughts, she took it down, took off its head, put the papers in the hollow chest and put the head back on again. "Now it'll have a heart," she thought. She went back to the living room where the white light coming from the television glowed intensely. The actors continued their performance, oblivious to the sleeping viewer.

She looked at Felipe. He resembled a fallen, defenseless statue. She liked to watch him as he slept. Sleep was an odd state, she thought to herself, like going off the air: a "little death." According to oriental beliefs, while a person is sleeping, the spirit separates from the body and makes astral voyages to other planes of existence. Where was Felipe right now? she wondered. She leaned back against the cushions, amusing herself by watching him. The midnight news report was on television: the Great General was inaugurating a so-called agrarian reform program for the peasants. He spoke of "revolution" in the countryside. He tried to wring the meaning out of the word, appropriate it for himself, decontaminate it. He was a repulsive man, of average height, big-bellied, white, with black hair and an artificial smile, carefully polished teeth, carefully-groomed hands. He carried himself like a person of power, of benevolent superficiality, surrounded by his entourage of ministers smiling their servile smiles.

Nothing was said about the neighborhood rallies, the buses burned in the streets...

Lavinia thought about the papers inside the doll. She looked at Felipe.

She decided she wouldn't tell him anything. She would keep him outside the sphere of her decisions. She'd condemn him—as he did her—to the margins of the page, keep him absent from one of the centers of her life, keep him in innocent ignorance as men did with women. Because although it was true that had it not been for him, if Felipe hadn't brought Sebastián to her house, she wouldn't even have had the doubts she had now; it was also obvious that for Felipe what had happened had been nothing more than a chance event, a subtle alteration in her daily routine that ought not to be of consequence in their relationship. Most likely without intending to, he had led her to the threshold of that other reality, then tried to lead her away from it. "Felipe is not your problem," Flor had said. And precisely for that reason she had to make her own decisions, she told herself, not tell him anything about her involvement...

What am I thinking of? she suddenly wondered, frightened at herself. What involvement? She was just trying to keep better informed, she told herself, unable to fully believe it.

Felipe was still sleeping. Absorbed in her thoughts, Lavinia looked toward the orange tree swaying in the wind. The night followed its course. From the doll's heart the papers made their presence felt, floating in the quiet air of the house.

✛ ✛ ✛

She looked at me. In her eyes I felt the force of a battle raging in her lungs and entrails. The wind sways me from side to side. Soon it will rain. The earth has begun to give off the remembrance of the scent of rain; it beckons to Quiote-Tláloc, in whom the rain resides.

I think now that perhaps my remote ancestors who fled Ticomega and Maguatega and populated this land, also remained in the earth, in its fruits and vegetation during my lifetime. Perhaps it was one of them who inhabited my blood with echoes; perhaps one of them found life within me, made me leave my home, led me to the hills to join the combat beside Yarince.

Life has ways of renewing itself.

CHAPTER 9

• • •

The next day Lavinia awoke with the Saturday heat. It would rain soon, she thought, longing for the coolness of the rainy season, the gentle mornings and the snuggly cloudy days. Felipe was gone. She found a note on the night stand that said: "Didn't want to wake you. Got some work to take care of. I'll try to get back this afternoon. Love, Felipe." She vaguely remembered having led him to bed. He only woke up to take off his shoes. He had slept beside her as if they were a bored married couple.

She stretched, rubbing her legs in the last coolness of the sheets. Her eyes rested on the doll up in the closet: round blue eyes, turned-up nose, dark curls. Sole dignified survivor of the infantile exercise of her motherly love. Its glass eyes reflected the window where the orange tree held out its branches. Leaning to one side, she looked indecently limp.

She should read the pamphlets, Lavinia thought. This morning there would be no breakfast with Sara—she would stay home and read.

She called her friend to tell her she had urgent work to do. She lied again with aplomb. Sara understood, sparing her further excuses.

In her pajamas, with a glass of orange juice, coffee and a piece of bread, Lavinia settled herself on the bed, took the doll's head off, and removed the papers.

The clock said two fifteen in the afternoon when she turned the last page. Spread out all over the bed like black and white insects were the clandestine pamphlets that had been mimeographed, with rough stencil drawings.

She closed her eyes and rested her head against the wall.

Is it permissible to dream like that? she asked. To recreate the world? To make it from nothing? Worse, she thought, worse than nothing, to make it from the landfill where garbage is tossed, the sad, empty field that accommodates refuse and scrap metal. Was it permissible, rational, that there should exist people in the world who could invent it anew with so much determination, describing sadness in small paragraphs, delineating hope point by point, like in the program of the Movement, where they spoke with such conviction of all the unobtainable things that had to be achieved: literacy, free health-care for everyone, housing, agrarian reform (real, not like the television program with the Great General), women's emancipation (And Felipe? she thought, and the men like him, revolutionaries but male chauvinists too?), the end of corruption, end of the dictatorship...the end of everything, just as when the lights come on and the bad movie is over. That was what they wanted: to turn on the lights. They said just that: "the end of darkness, emergence from the long night of the dictatorship." Turn on the lights and not only that, but the rivers of milk and honey—she liked the Biblical language—the utopia of a better world, Don Quixote riding again with his long lance held high. The rules for the new Quixotes, the statutes, the countless tasks, the few rights...the statutes for a new, generous, fraternal, critical, responsible man, a defender of love, capable of identifying with those who suffered. Modern Christs, Lavinia thought, willing to be crucified for spreading the good news, but not willing to fail each other. There were sanctions and punishments for traitors, even the firing squad was being considered (would they really do that? she wondered, sitting on her bed, looking at but not seeing the head of the doll beside her with its round blue eyes open beneath their pitch-black lashes).

But, she thought, one could forget the anguish and hope of the majority. Here in her house, with the cushions, plants and music, or in the discotheque with her friends, in bed with Felipe, at the office in the morning with the air conditioning. So many people did forget. All her friends did. Widespread poverty did not dull the shine of the crystal chandeliers at the club or in the discos, or even Sara's life of sweetness and light, or the assiduous, busy social calendar of her parents.

She could choose to live in the world parallel to the one in which she had been born. Not see the other world except from the car as she passed, turning her eyes away from the slums with their board and dirt floors to look at the beautiful clouds on the horizon or the fringe of volcanoes beside the lake.

So many people managed to ignore poverty, accepting inequalities as a fact of life.

And that was how things had always been. Who would dare dream of changing all that? Why think that these dreams written down with such effort (the mimeograph was run in the middle of the night and there was always the danger of being arrested) could change the state of things? The "natural" state of affairs, as Sara would say.

And how long would she wrestle with herself? Lavinia wondered. It would be better to accept once and for all that she could not allow herself to be enveloped in this romanticism. It's true she also liked to dream. She had done that since she was a child, since Jules Verne. Who didn't? Who didn't dream of a better world? It was logical for her to be attracted by the idea of imagining she was a "compañera," being involved in conspiracies like the heroine of some romantic novel, surrounded by those people whose expressions were deep and transparent, their serenity like that of a tree. But that had nothing to do with reality—her reality as a rich girl, a high-class architect with pretensions of independence, and a Virginia Woolf room of her own. She should stop this constant interrogation, she said to herself, this coming and going between her rational self and her other self, with her ardent desires for justice that were flavored by a childhood that had been too full of heroic stories, impossible dreams, and grandfathers who invited her to fly.

✛ ✛ ✛

Ah! How she doubts! Her position allows her to do that. She thinks too much. There are thick bandages over her eyes. In our time, when the war came, there were too many women who had to awaken and realize the disadvantage of having spent so much time cultivating idleness and docility.

I was fortunate. Although my mother would get furious, I was always attracted to the games the boys played, their bows and arrows.

She could not understand how women could go to war along with their men.

That afternoon when Yarince arrived in Taguzgalpa with his men, the day our eyes met and were forever bound together, she knew it. She knew that at dawn I would leave with him to fight against the invaders.

She was waiting for me beside the fire. And as I drew near, she looked at me with the mournful expression her face had acquired since the battles with the Spaniards had ceased being news from afar.

Her strong hands were busy kneading the corn dough, pushing it into rounded shapes. "You have been with the warriors," she said to me.

And her voice was saying: "What you did is wrong; it is not a woman's place; they have intoxicated your blood."

"They come from afar," I said. "They are Caribs. They say we should rise up, fight. If we don't, everything is finished. The Spaniards will kill us for our lands, our lakes, our gold. They will destroy our past, our gods. Many men will go with them tomorrow to join the fight. We must put an end to our old enmities. We must unite against the light-haired men. I want to go, too."

"I've told you the battlefield is no place for women. This is the wisdom of the world. Your umbilical cord is buried beneath the ashes of this hearth. This is your place. This is where your power lies."

"Yarince is their leader. He said he would take me."

"Yes," said my mother, "I saw how he looked at you in the square. I saw you looking at him as well."

I lowered my eyes. Nothing could be hidden from my mother's heart.

"It's the destiny of woman to follow the man," she said. "It's not a curse. If he loves you, he has to arrange a ceremony with your father, he has to make the offerings. Obtain the blessing of the tribe."

"We're at war. That's not possible now. We have to leave tomorrow at dawn. Mother, don't curse me. Give me your blessing," I said, kneeling upon the ground.

"You're being guided by your instinct," she said to me. "Itzá, are you going to give me still more reasons to curse the Spaniards?"

"We only have two roads, mother," I said, standing up again. "Either we curse them or we fight them. I must go. It is not only because of Yarince. I know how to use a bow and arrow. I cannot endure the stillness of the long days, waiting for what I know is to come. Deep inside I feel that it is my destiny to go."

I remember her extending her hands, her palms were white from pounding the corn, shaping the tortillas. She raised them and lowered them again. She bowed her head, deciding not to speak any more. Telling me to kneel down, she invoked our creators, Tamagastad and Cipaltomal, Quiote-Tláloc, god of rain, to whom I had been dedicated.

Strong as a volcano by the light of early dawn, her soft silhouette etched against the light that entered through the doorway, I still seem to see her that last morning when I left, waving good-bye to me with her outstretched hand, a hand like a dry, desperate branch.

She was my only doubt, she who taught me how to love.

• • •

The telephone rang.

"Hello. Yes? Who's calling?" Lavinia said.

"Lavinia?"

"Yes, it's me," she said. She didn't recognize the voice on the other end, although it sounded strangely familiar.

"Lavinia, it's me, Sebastián."

The name suddenly brought back the disorder in her bed. What did Sebastián want? What was going on?

"Isn't Felipe with you?"

Her heart began to pound. No, Felipe wasn't with her. He had gone to work and left a note.

"To work? On Saturday? But I was supposed to meet him for a beer over an hour ago!" replied Sebastián, speaking matter-of-factly.

Felipe stand Sebastián up? Lavinia thought, feeling confused as fear slowly welled up within her.

"He told me he was going to work," she insisted, not noticing the efforts of the other to camouflage the conversation. Her brain began to manufacture terrible speculations.

She couldn't understand why Sebastián was laughing on the other end of the phone, why he made that comment about 'that Felipe' who would never learn—who would ever think of going to work today? They worked enough during the week.

Lavinia began to understand that she should pretend it was a normal conversation, but she couldn't manage it. The words would not flow.

Finally, Sebastián seemed to notice.

"Don't be like that," he told her. "Let's do this. I'm in the phone booth near the Central Hospital. Come pick me up and we'll talk. I'll be waiting for you in ten minutes. Just remember, I can't be out in the sun for long," he added ironically.

When she hung up the receiver, Lavinia felt her legs shaking. Jumbled images were wrestling inside her, and she was seeing things through a foggy haze.

"I mustn't think," she told herself, unable to avoid the vision of the newspapers and the photographs of bullet-riddled corpses. She jumped up and threw on her rumpled clothes from the day before. "I have to get hold of myself," she said, while she ran a brush through her hair, grabbed her purse and keys, and went out to get into the car.

She was starting the car when, in an effort to calm down, she exhausted the reasons for possible delays and transportation difficulties that her mind produced in an effort to relieve herself of her anguish. She remembered the paragraph about punctuality being the inviolable rule for clandestine contacts. She had just read it in the security measures: the margin for waiting could not be more than fifteen minutes. And Sebastián had waited for an hour.

She accelerated on the lightly traveled Saturday streets. The rhythmic sound of her heart beating was the only thing that interrupted the silence of fear.

She caught a glimpse of Sebastián standing on the corner with a newspaper under his arm and wearing a truck driver's cap. He was talking nonchalantly with a fat fruit vendor in a white apron. The sidewalk was full of passersby carrying bundles and packages on their way to visit the sick.

She eased the car over to the curb and called to him: "Sebastián!" she shouted, since she couldn't honk the horn in the hospital's quiet zone.

He lifted his head, said good-bye to the woman and got in the car with a serious, upset expression on his face.

"Don't ever do that again," he said, settling into the seat.

"Do what?" Lavinia asked, momentarily forgetting her concern for Felipe.

"Call me by that name in the street, in public like that. You don't know if that's really my name."

She remembered the pamphlets, the pseudonyms. Then Sebastián's real name wasn't Sebastián; it was a pseudonym. Maybe Flor wasn't really named Flor, and Felipe wasn't Felipe... Maybe tomorrow in the newspaper she would see a photograph and find out that Felipe's real name was Ernesto or José. How alien everything seemed to her! She was no good at this, she thought, her depression mounting.

"I'm sorry," she said in a repentant tone. "So Felipe's name isn't Felipe, either?"

"Felipe's real name is Felipe," Sebastián said. "His name is 'legal.'"

Because there were "legals" and "clandestines," as Lavinia had recently learned.

She asked Sebastián if she should take him to her house. He nodded and looked worried.

"But what do you think could have happened?" Lavinia asked.

"I don't know, I don't know," Sebastián replied. "It's strange. Felipe is always very punctual. Well, punctuality is one of our rules. And that's why I don't know what could have happened to him. Let's go to your house and wait another hour. If he doesn't show up by then, I'll tell you what we're going to do. Try to calm down," he said, touching her arm.

While Lavinia concentrated on driving carefully ('We have to make sure the police don't stop us for a traffic violation,' Sebastián had said) and was trying not to notice how worried he was because it sent chills through her, Sebastián began to speak in a calm voice.

You have to control your fear, he said, not let it get the best of you. That was how he had managed to survive years of clandestine activity in the Movement. One had to be optimistic. Have faith, he said, not lose hope. That was what kept them going, he added. He understood that she should be upset. He knew the anguish of waiting, he knew it in the worst way, while he was in hiding, without being able to move freely, having to go from place to place dressed as a hippie or medical salesman. "You should see how good I look in some of those get-ups," he said, to make her laugh. And he wouldn't tell her not to be upset, he added, just to stay calm. Nobody could avoid those sorts of feelings, just as they couldn't avoid other kinds. What's more, it was important, especially for them, not to allow their defense mechanisms to make them insensitive, turn them into cold mechanical people, harden them. Danger, death could not turn them into invulnerable beings. Though there was a high price to pay for keeping one's sensitivity. But it was necessary not to lose touch with everyday feelings: that would be like losing touch with the people, he said.

Lavinia listened silently. Sebastián seemed willing to speak to her as if she were already a "compañera." She wasn't a "compañera," though. She didn't want to suffer. She didn't want them to kill Felipe. If anything happened to Felipe, she would hate them, she thought. Him, Flor, the whole Movement, hate them for going around throwing away their lives, disposing of them as if they meant nothing.

They were getting near her house. Sebastián told her to drive around several times before parking in the garage. They had to make certain nobody was following them.

She followed the instructions, alternating between furious rebellion against sacrifice and the feeling of closeness. It was a closeness like the one she had wanted to feel, like the time Sebastián had come to her house badly wounded. A sense of belonging.

All during the drive, possessed by conflicting waves of hope and fear, Lavinia had prayed to Aunt Inés' saints that she would find Felipe when they opened the door. Now, as she inserted the key in the lock, she closed her eyes, thinking that when she opened them she would see him sitting in the garden in the soft shade of the orange tree. But the door to the garden was still locked and the house was silent. It was just as she left it. Nothing moved. Nobody was waiting in the shadows.

They went in, and she told Sebastián to sit down while she went to the bathroom. She didn't want him to see how her eyes were moist with disappointment. She wanted to calm the tears weighing on her heart. She felt frantic and had a desperate desire to scour the streets looking for Felipe. If it hadn't been for Sebastián, she thought, she would have gone up and down the avenues, she would have gone everywhere looking for Felipe.

She left the bathroom after splashing water on her face, refusing to let herself cry. She thought if she started to cry, she would never be able to stop; she would cry forever. And she was ashamed to do that in spite of what Sebastián had said in the car.

She was afraid she would add insults to her tears. Afraid she would condemn them for their suicidal vocation. She went to the kitchen, explaining that she was thirsty and needed a glass of water.

"Would you bring me some water, too, please?" she heard Sebastián's voice from the living room.

Lavinia came back with the glasses and set them on the table.

"Sit down," he told her. "You have to try to calm down. Felipe may have run into some problem. This delay doesn't necessarily mean that he's dead or that he's been captured."

She nodded and sat down. She wondered whether there wasn't something they could do, someone they could call, someone with "connections" who could inquire concerning Felipe's whereabouts.

"You should get the radio," Sebastián said, "to see if there's any news."

He's nervous too, Lavinia thought.

They put the radio on the table in the middle of the room. 'Radio Nacional'—the official station, the one that gave the communiqués regarding subversive actions—had a jazz program on. Duke Ellington was skillfully blowing his trumpet.

Outside, cars drove by from time to time, interrupting the silence kept by the two people leaning against the cushions that served as a sofa.

Friends with connections, Lavinia thought. She remembered one person in particular, a friend of her parents. Every Christmas he would send them expensive, extravagant gifts: miniature radios, fountain pens with built-in watches.

That man could certainly do something, she thought. He had dealings with the government. He was a friend of the

Great General. But how could she do it? she wondered. It would mean calling her parents and explaining to them. She rejected the idea. She couldn't explain anything to them. "I'm not going to have anything to do with those people," her mother would say.

And Julián? Lavinia thought, not giving up. Maybe Julián knew someone. Felipe and Julián loved each other. She even suspected that Julián was in on the secret. When Felipe left the office too often, Julián called his attention to it in a friendly way.

"Sometimes he exasperates me," Felipe would tell her, referring to Julián, whom he had known since they were teenagers when he used to go to the city to visit relatives. They had shared their first experience with a woman. First one, then the other, had gone into the poorly-lit room of the Moulin Rouge," a red light district whorehouse with mysterious high walls that Lavinia remembered having stared at with curiosity from the street. Felipe had depicted it vividly for her, describing its musty smell and the woman still buttoning up her dress when he went in after Julián.

Felipe had said she was a young, attractive woman. She seemed to enjoy watching him unzip his pants nervously, as if she felt she possessed some ancient power. She observed him with the expression of someone who watches a child make his first scrawls in a dog-eared notebook.

He had always imagined the women in whorehouses as being sad and withered, but Terencia had a beautiful smile and said that in her job a person had to have a sense of humor.

Felipe had recalled that it was only when he was on top of her, almost immediately overflowing at the mere thought of being between a woman's legs, feeling the warm, moist tunnel enclosing his sex like a cobweb, a mysterious hand arising out of Terencia's womb, that she got tense and aggressive, growling with a muffled rage she had kept concealed. He told Lavinia that Terencia had pushed him off her, saying "Now you know what it's like, now you can feel like a man." And Felipe admitted that even though it had been a sad way to feel like men, Julián and he had left the whorehouse feeling prouder, bigger.

Julián could do something, Lavinia thought.

"Felipe has a friend, our boss at the office, Julián. Maybe he can find out something," she said, leaning toward Sebastián, busy trying to locate the daily news on the radio.

"It's not a good idea to arouse suspicion, stir up a hornet's nest before we have to," Sebastián said. "You can't be impulsive in matters like this. It's dangerous... There's nothing on the news," he said, adjusting the dial again to Duke Ellington and the *Radio Nacional*. "That black fellow plays well. He's good on the trumpet. Do you like music?" he asked, turning to Lavinia.

He's trying to distract me, Lavinia thought, as she told him yes, she liked music.

Didn't you see that film, *Woodstock*, at the movies?" asked Sebastián.

"Yes," she said, "I saw it with Felipe."

"Ah, then it was you... Felipe told me he saw it with a woman he liked. That was about two months ago, right? I should have guessed it was you. How long have you been seeing each other?"

"Since a little before you were shot," Lavinia said.

"So my bullet wound is a kind of reference date for you two?" smiled Sebastián, touching his arm, already healed. (He wore a long-sleeved shirt to hide the scar.)

"Yes," Lavinia said, "that's true. What's more, I could say my life is divided into before and after your getting shot."

"That's an honor," Sebastián said, "but I was just a passing scare."

"No," Lavinia replied, "it wasn't just that. Since then, I've been troubled about life, doubting..."

"Doubting what?" asked Sebastián.

"I don't know... I'm confused. Sometimes I hate you all for being so brave. Sometimes I want to be like you. What I used to think was rebellion seems weak in comparison now. You all seem to have so much determination and seem to be so sure of who you are, where you're going... But I'm afraid to get involved. I'm not like that."

"A person *isn't* one way or another. You make yourself. I think you are very involved," Sebastián said, with a smile that seemed slightly ironic to her. "It doesn't matter if at you rebelled in your own way first. For many people that's the first step. In Faguas, you can't keep your eyes closed, even if you want to. As much as you may not want to avoid seeing the violence, violence searches you out. Here we all have a dose of it guaranteed to us as a national right. Either they do something to you or you do something yourself. Or, in any case, if they don't do anything to you, they do it to someone else...and that's where political awareness comes in, because if you let them do it to others, you become an accomplice, intentionally or not."

Duke Ellington was finishing a solo. The long note spread through the living room. He was right, Lavinia thought. She was having doubts about what was already an accomplished fact. The reality was that she had lived the anxiety of participation, even if she believed she was still weighing whether to become involved or not. Violence had touched her own home. Home delivery, courtesy of the Great General and Felipe.

+ + +

In times of war nobody lives in remote regions. The invaders might still take some time to arrive, but they will arrive. That was what Yarince said. That was what we used to say in the places we passed through. We told those who thought their world would never be touched. Ah, but so many did not listen to us! Sebastián speaks wisely. His words penetrate the resistance that she has set up, the walls she has erected and which are beginning to weaken.

• • •

"I went to Flor's yesterday," Lavinia said. "She gave me some pamphlets about the Movement so I could read them. I read them today."

There was a look of surprise on Sebastián's face. She wondered if she could be causing problems for Flor.

"And is this the first time you've read literature about the Movement?" inquired Sebastián.

"Yes," Lavinia replied.

The conversation inevitably led to Felipe, the circle closing around Felipe. Sebastián didn't understand why he hadn't at least put her in contact with the Movement's literature. The return to the riverbank was inevitable.

"Right now it wouldn't matter to me," Lavinia thought, if I always had to be the shore to his river." She was willing to be the shore to his river for centuries on end, just as long as Felipe showed up again. She even justified his behavior.

"I understand his need to have a space in which to lead a normal life," she said, glancing at her watch.

Forty-five minutes had passed. It was getting harder and harder for her to concentrate on anything except the implacable hands of her watch.

Sebastián began to say something about the "problems the compañeros had," but suddenly stopped. He lifted his head like an animal perking up its ears. Lavinia also heard the steps coming close: the steps she knew so well from having waited for them in the night. The heels clacked heavily on the pavement. They didn't move until the key entered the lock, and Felipe appeared in the room intact, safe and sound, blinking, unaccustomed to the light.

He looked at Sebastián and Lavinia, unable to figure it out.

"What are you doing here?" he asked Sebastián.

He looked blankly at Lavinia. She didn't make a sound, unable to recover from his sudden presence.

"You ask what I'm doing here?" Sebastián said, obviously bothered by Felipe's tone, "when you don't show up like we'd planned. I wait for you an hour, I call you thinking you're with Lavinia and there's no sign of you anywhere... We thought something had happened to you..."

"But I went to the meeting point," Felipe said, "at the agreed time." I waited for you, too. I was worried, too. I made a number of detours before coming back here because I thought something might have happened to you..."

The two men argued with each other, each one speaking of the confusion about the point where they were supposed to have met. Felipe insisted that it was the corner by the park; Sebastián, the entry to the hospital. Forgotten by the two men, she, invisible, disappeared, felt as if she were melting, not knowing whether to laugh or cry.

One mix-up and the world could change entirely. That was how life was when you lived on the brink. Someone gets confused, makes a mistake, arrives later than the designated time, and the scent of death begins to filter into every breath. But Felipe was alive. There would be no photograph in the newspaper. It had been a simple error.

They went on talking, referring to the note Sebastián had sent with the "courier."

"I'm positive you wrote 'on the corner by the park.' Too bad I burned the paper," Felipe said.

Little by little, the two men began to calm down until at last they laughed and embraced, saying what a good thing everything was all right, they'd had quite a scare, and just look at Lavinia, poor thing, what a state she's in: give her a hug.

Hours later, in the shelter of Felipe's arms—he was sleeping placidly—Lavinia could not sleep.

After the wait, after clearing up some of the confusion (because they hadn't definitely figured out which one had made the mistake, altering the equilibrium of the world), Felipe still had to go out to take Sebastián somewhere. She remained in the house by herself. And when she'd found herself alone, she thought she had imagined Felipe's return. Panic seized her again until Felipe returned.

They made love softly and tenderly, and she finally let herself cry over the possibility of his death—that tangible creature lying in wait as they kissed, touched. She cried for herself, for the image of the carefree young girl she had been until a few months ago, now dissolving, leaving her disconcerted, possessed by a woman who had not yet found identity, purpose, security. She cried, feeling helpless before love, cried at the dilemma of violence, at the evidence she could no longer avoid that she was just another citizen. And, without warning, at the deepest moment of their coming together, when their sweaty bodies were hurling themselves into the trembling space just before the finale, for the first time in her life, her womb grew in the desire to have a child. She felt a desperate desire to keep Felipe inside her germinating, multiplying himself in her blood.

Calm at last, unable to sleep, she evoked the animal sensation, the instinct that had taken hold of her, over-powering reason, constructing the image of the child—she saw it so clearly—appearing suddenly in her imagination. What had made her think of it? she wondered. For her, motherhood had been an notion she'd put off for some distant future. Given the course her life was taking now, that future seemed more imprecise. Day by day her life seemed increasingly entangled in unpredictable events. Day and night were unknown territories—disappearance, death, a daily possibility. Under these conditions there was no choice but to give up the idea of prolonging herself in another. There was no room for a child in the midst of such uncertainty. It was foolish. As long as she loved Felipe, it was impossible. She shouldn't even think about it. She'd have to renounce the idea. Renounce it as so many others had before and would after her, renounce it as long as Felipe was the figure that appeared, disappeared, that blinking light.

Her womb ached. The pain turned slowly to rage. A nameless rage springing from the image of a child who would never be.

How many children would be up there floating in the ether, denied life because of situations like this? How many in Latin America? How many in the world? She looked around, trying to recover her sense of reality. Felipe slept heavily. In the dark bedroom, shadows were sketched in the moonlight, that filtered through the window. Outside the bent branches of the orange tree swayed in the wind. Somewhere she had read that the desire to give birth was the strongest in times of natural catastrophes when death was grinning.

That was what probably was happening to her, she thought. It wasn't rational that such an idea had occurred to her in these circumstances, and yet she'd seen the image of the smiling child; deep inside she felt the anger and instinct unleashed in the night calm.

Sebastián was right, she said to herself. She was already involved. Why fool herself with long personal battles about whether she should or shouldn't talk with Flor, or whether she should simply return the pamphlets to her like someone returning a book they've read to its owner? Her uncertainty made her unable to resist the desire to deceive herself; her anxiety arose from a vain hope that she was still able to choose. The truth was that the sound of death was already riding her nights, the violence of great generals had invaded her world like a giant evil shadow. She could no longer avoid it: she already had the quota of violence that was hers by "national right," as Sebastián had said.

She would begin the journey, she told herself. The shoreline faded away in the mist of her dreams. At peace, she fell asleep beside Felipe.

✦ ✦ ✦

We refused to give birth.

After months of heavy combat, the warriors were dying one after another. We saw our villages being razed, our lands being given to new owners, our people forced to work like slaves for the encomenderos. We saw the adolescents ripped away from their mothers, sent into forced labor or to the ships that never returned. The warriors they captured were subjected to the cruelest tortures: they were torn to pieces by the dogs or drawn and quartered by horses.

Men deserted our encampments. Stealthily they would disappear into the darkness, finally resigned to the slave's fate.

The Spaniards burned our temples; they built gigantic bonfires where they burned the sacred codices of our history; our legacy was a net full of holes.

We had to retreat to the farthest inland regions, the high forests of the north, to the caves on the edges of the volcanoes. It was there that we went around looking for men who wanted to fight, there we prepared spears, made bows and arrows, recovered our strength so we could hurl ourselves into combat again.

One day I received news from the women of Taguzgalpa. They had decided not to sleep with their men any more. They did not want to give birth to slaves for the Spaniards.

That night there was a full moon, a night for conceiving. I felt it in the warmth of my womb, in the softness of my skin, in my deep desire for Yarince.

He returned from hunting with a large iguana the color of dry leaves. The fire was burning, and the cave glowed with reddish brilliance. He drew near me after we had eaten and caressed my hips. I saw his burning eyes reflecting the flames of the fire.

I took his hand from my waist and slipped away toward the back of the cave. Yarince came up to me, thinking it was a game to excite his desire. He kissed me, knowing that his kisses were like juicy pulque upon my lips; they inebriated me.

I kissed him. Images surfaced in me: water from the ponds, tender scenes, dreams that had been with me many a night: a warrior child, rebellious, indomitable, who would prolong us, who would look like us, who would be a graft of us, bearing our kindest expressions.

I pulled away before his lips defeated me.

I said, no, Yarince, no. And then I said no again and told him about the women of Taguzgalpa, my tribe. We did not want to bear children for the encomiendas, children for the constructions, for their ships; children to be torn to pieces by the dogs if they were brave warriors.

He looked at me with crazed eyes, He backed away. He looked at me as he left the cave, staring at me as if he had seen a terrible apparition. Then he ran outside, and there was silence. I could only hear the crackling of the branches in the fire, burning and dying.

Later I heard my man howling like a wolf.

And later still he returned, scratched by thorns.

That night, embraced, we cried, containing the desire in our bodies, enveloped in a heavy cloak of sadness.

We denied ourselves life, prolongation, the propagation of our seed.

How I hurt to my very roots simply remembering it.

I don't know if it's raining or if it's me crying.

CHAPTER 10

● ● ●

It was raining in Faguas. The rainy season, winter in the tropics, was beginning. The week was drawing to a close. Since Sunday Lavinia had been putting off her decision, putting off going to see Flor.

Sitting at her desk, she looked at the rain-bathed window. The drops slid down forming rivulets, pushing one another downward, creating cascades over the glass. During the rainy season the afternoon sky was covered with storm clouds, and floods of wet fury broke loose. The earth surrendered to the pleasure of the tempests. A sharp scent arose from the soil, announcing future births. The land turned intense shades of green. The trees shook their thick tops, their wet manes of hair. It was the time for orgies of birds, the time for swift-moving streams, when the city lost its usual appearance and coexisted with mud, winged ants, leaks. The old folks complained about their rheumatism and damp bones, and in the morning the beds were cool, the sheets were cool against warm bodies.

"You would think we've returned to the beginning of the world, and soon the dinosaurs will appear," Lavinia thought, contemplating the flowering greenery of the landscape.

The beginning of the world. Dinosaurs. The world was spinning. Orbits and ages followed one after another. And men and women weaving stories.

She couldn't put the matter off any longer, she thought. It was agonizing and affected her work, decreased her ability to concentrate. Nothing was worse than indecision. It was Thursday. Flor had given her her phone number at the hospital. Lavinia called, and they agreed to meet after work.

In the afternoon, when the distant cathedral clock struck five, she grabbed her purse and left to carry out the final ritual.

Standing on the misty look-out of her childhood, now shrouded with the fog and drizzle of winter's dampness, Lavinia looked at the city's vague, whitish outline, at its lakes, its volcanoes. Standing there alone she discarded all possibility of turning back, deeply inhaling the cold, damp air of the mountain and the peacefulness of the landscape where everything had sprung up green. She watched the decline of that imperceptible Thursday and finally pacified by the misty taste, the womb's taste of the world, she crossed the bridge that brought her to the rocking chair where she was now swaying, listening to the wet leaves rustling in Flor's voice.

Flor spoke softly. She looked tired, her eyes were ringed with dark circles. The hospital work was exhausting, she said. There were many people needing attention and too few to take care of them.

Flor inspired respect. Felipe thought she was "hard." He said that Sebastián talked of his experience with her, comparing it to that of a fisherman sinking his knife into an oyster to extract the pearl it held in its center. Looking at her, Lavinia imagined, looking at her, the interior of an abalone shell. It must not have been easy for her, she thought, that uncle loving her with the kind of passion Lewis Carroll felt for Alice. It had scarred her, made her suspicious. She didn't think that Flor was "hard," even though she had the air of a fortress about her, typical of those who have suffered and know themselves to be vulnerable. But Lavinia could feel Flor's tenderness in the way she spoke, trying not to frighten her, telling her they would do things little by little. First, Lavinia had to read more. Her convictions could neither be weak nor blind, she told her. She wanted her to understand, to be aware of the possibilities—the ones Lavinia called the program's "dreams." She had to be able to use the tools better, Flor said, in order to understand the world differently, to decode the certainties that had always surrounded her, to see the deception of certain universal "truths," be able to understand the negative and positive aspects of reality and how they could be switched around to suit different interests.

After that they went on to practical details. Flor said she should keep the pamphlet on security measures.

"Now you must learn them by heart," she added, "like a school lesson. At first they will sound exaggerated to you, they'll seem like strange, extreme precautions. But they are essential not only for your own security, but for everyone's. Today you begin to substitute "I" for "we." You must be concerned above all with the security of your clandestine compañeros, like Sebastián, for example. And don't talk with anyone about your activities, absolutely no one who isn't linked to you through work in the Organization.

"And can I talk with Felipe?" Lavinia asked.

"Not with Felipe, either," Flor said.

"It's better that way. I wouldn't want him to find out about my decision."

"Whether or not you tell him about your joining is up to you," Flor said, "but that's all he should know. If you want, you can tell him about it."

"I don't want to," Lavinia said.

Flor smiled.

"And now we have to give you a pseudonym. What would you like to be called?"

"Inés," Lavinia said without thinking twice.

"Sometimes for specific jobs we give ourselves other pseudonyms," Flor said. "And you know it is only to be used among ourselves, or for whatever you're told to do. Never mention this name in public."

Lavinia told Flor the story about calling to Sebastián in the street.

"I felt so stupid," she said.

"You'll get used to it," Flor said. "It's a learning process. As time goes on, your senses get keener. Adrenaline works better for us than many hormones. And you see, in spite of everything, sometimes we make mistakes like the one on Saturday between Sebastián and Felipe. And they have a lot of experience."

Flor went on talking. Explaining. The wind rippled through the huelenoche vine that could be seen from the living room. Bob Dylan watched pensively. A rain-laden breeze was blowing. The sky lit up with distant flashes of lightning. Lavinia realized that Flor was tired when she fell silent.

"You're tired," Lavinia said.

"Yes," Flor said, pushing her hair away from the sides of her face.

Before saying good-bye to her at the door, Flor turned and gave her a hug.

"Welcome to the club, 'Inés,'" she said, smiling, as a bright flash of distant lightning lit up her face.

+ + +

I feel Lavinia's blood, and I am invaded by the fullness of the winter sap, of recent rain. In a strange way, she is my creation. She is not me. She is not me come to life again. I have not taken possession of her like the spirits that frightened my ancestors. No. But we have lived together in one blood; and the language of my history, which is hers, too, has begun to sing in her veins.

She is still afraid. I still hear at night the vivid colors of her fear. Images of death haunt her, but now she too belongs, she is getting a foothold on solid ground, she is growing her own roots: now she no longer wavers like a wick in oil.

It is difficult to transcend the ashes of the hearth, the hands that tend the fire, the grinding of corn, the mat of the warrior.

At first Yarince wanted me to stay in the camp waiting for them. I managed to avoid it by using my own weakness as a strategy. And if the Spaniards came? I asked. What would be my fate? How many things could happen to me while I was alone, waiting?

I preferred to die in battle rather than be raped by the men of steel or die chewed to pieces by jaguars.

I convinced them. I got them to assign me a place in their formation, a protected position from where I shot poisoned arrows.

I had good aim, so they finally gave me a place in battle, even though afterward I had to cook and tend to the wounded. Then, when we retreated to the caves of the North to recover our strength and continue the combat—several chiefs had already joined the invaders, having been bent like reeds in the river current—Yarince sent me to the outlying areas to enter the homes and speak with the men, urging them to join our struggle. "Do not bring women," he told me. He demanded that of me, even though I got furious. He said it was harder for men to fight if they were thinking about the women being exposed to the firesticks. I had not thought about that. He never told me he was afraid for me in battle. I was touched by his concern and did not insist any more.

But it was a mistake to send me. The men did not trust me. The only thing I managed to get was corn so we could have tortillas once in a while.

The women would gather around me and listen to my stories. They wanted to know about the war with the Spaniards. Yet none of them asked if she could join us. I don't think they thought it was possible. To them I was a texoxe, a witch.

I told them about the decision of the women of many tribes not to bear children so as not to give the Spaniards slaves. They lowered their eyes. The youngest ones laughed, thinking I was going mad.

Those were difficult times. I would return sadly to the caves. I even began to think I was made of an odd substance, that I was not made of corn. Or maybe, I said to myself, my mother had a spell cast on her when she was carrying me inside her. Maybe I was a man with the body of a woman. Maybe I was half man, half woman.

Yarince laughed as he listened to me. He would caress my breasts, smell my sex and say, "You are a woman, a woman, a brave woman."

• • •

The storm broke while Lavinia was driving back home. An electric storm with white slashes and the sound of the sky cracking, expanding, the wind shaking the trees, and dust thickening the night. She saw some people running in search of shelter from the imminent rain. In contrast, she, in whom there should have been a storm unleashed after making her decision, after talking with Flor, drove unusually calmly, indifferent to the lightning bolts. The rain began to fall on the windshield of her car: scattered drops, large at first, timid in the first few moments, and suddenly pelting with incredible force, sounding like stones on the thin, metal roof.

Sheltered inside the vehicle, she thought about her sense of peace, the calm after the storm, the way her uncertainty had ended, how she had accepted her own decision, the result of having finally transcended the weeks of indecision. Later on, if she didn't feel she could do it, she would have to recognize that she had made a mistake and own up to it. Everyone had the right to make mistakes.

How would her life change now, she wondered. What would happen? It was so hard to imagine. She couldn't share her speculations over what would happen with the people she knew. She was alone. She couldn't overwhelm Flor with her questions. She couldn't do it to Sebastián, either. She couldn't take advantage of them, nor give the impression she was naive and ambivalent. It was the type of ignorance that she had to traverse without company. Would she be able to resist the temptation to tell Felipe? she wondered. She would like him to know, like to make him feel bad for not having been the one to bring her into the Organization, for not having thought she was capable. "Don't go turning it into a sort of revenge," Flor had said, and she had denied that was her reason for not saying anything to Felipe. But there was something of that in it; she couldn't deceive herself. In fact, deep down she hoped Flor or Sebastián would tell him and make him feel ashamed.

In her opinion, men involved with the business of being revolutionaries shouldn't act that way. Would Che Guevara have acted that way? Flor said that Che had written that women were ideal for being cooks and couriers for the guerrilla forces, although later, when he was in Bolivia, he was with a guerrilla named Tania. He changed, Flor said. Who had Tania been? Had Che loved her? she wondered, while she turned the corner in the rain, driving through streets that were suddenly full of muddy torrents. She had to take the corners slowly in order not to make waves and risk flooding the engine and having the car stall.

Who cared about Che's love life? History paid no attention to those details. It wasn't interested in the private lives of heroes. It was "feminine" to always wonder about love. Why was it so hard for men to recognize the need for, the historical importance of, love? she thought, as she saw two dilapidated taxis stalled in the middle of the street. The drivers were trying to push them out of the mud. Water ran crazily everywhere in the city.

In time, Felipe would recognize that he had been wrong about her, that he had acted selfishly. She admired his intelligence and honesty. She couldn't deny the fact that he struggled to overcome the male resistance to giving love its rightful place, even though he might be boxed in by tradition. He had his aspect of a playful, happy elf, his lovable, understanding side, which she adored. It was sad to see him imprisoned in dissonant patterns and behavior that contradicted the development achieved in other areas of his life. It wouldn't hurt him to learn a lesson. She enjoyed knowing that now she had a secret, something he could not penetrate unless she allowed him to.

But she did not want to think about him anymore. She hadn't done it because of Felipe, she told herself again, watching the oak trees in her neighborhood bend beneath the rain. No, she hadn't done it because of Felipe. This was her country, too. She, too, dreamed it could be different. She loved its greenness, its round white clouds, its soft rain. Faguas deserved a better fate.

No, it wasn't just because of Felipe, she repeated to herself as she arrived, parked the car in the garage and ran with her purple umbrella through the rain to the porch.

"Why are you so quiet?" Felipe asked in the patio. He had arrived a few minutes after her, and had discovered her lying silent and thoughtful in the hammock. Now he was sitting in the white wicker chair, facing her, watching her, playing absentmindedly with the nearby leaves of the orange tree that held out its green and silver foliage, laden with rain.

"I don't know. I guess I'm tired," she replied. She was exhausted, still tense. She saw Felipe through a crystal dome, as if he were far away.

"For some time now I've noticed you have been very distracted," he said. "It seems as if you're not here, your mind is far away. At least you could tell me what's going on. Maybe I can help."

"I don't think it's a question of *helping*," she said, feeling she would rather be alone so she could get used to the idea of having the name 'Inés' and think about whether she had made the right decision.

"When a person is going through a crisis, it's always good to share it with someone else," he said.

"And why do you think I'm going through a crisis?" she asked defensively, leaning back in the hammock. Felipe's self-sufficient, paternalistic attitude annoyed her.

"Don't jump on me like a tiger," he told her. "I'm not accusing you of anything. We all have crises."

"It's hard for me to believe you've had any. It seems as if you knew everything from the moment you were born," she said, picking a leaf from the orange tree and biting it until she tasted its bitter citrus flavor and smelled the aroma oozing from its veins.

"Don't be unfair. You've been with me in several crises...the one with Sebastián, when they killed our compañeros..."

"That's exactly what I mean," she said. "You go through crises when things happen outside you, but as far as your feelings are concerned, you seem to have everything under control."

"It's just that I'm good at hiding it," he said, staring at her. "But I can assure you I have my inner battles. And often I wish I could be more communicative, could share them, but I've been trained to survive the floods by myself, to control my weaknesses."

"The bad thing about that training is that what comes to the surface is an air of self-sufficiency that separates us," Lavinia said. "It's very hard to be with perfect people...or ones who act like they're perfect."

Felipe came close, bending over her. Smiling, he caressed her hand.

"But you know I'm not perfect, don't you?"

"Nobody is. That's exactly why it bothers me. That façade of yours, of always being so sure of everything, bothers me. It's as though you never have any second thoughts. You're always giving me advice, but you never ask for any," she said sullenly. She needed to scold him, aggravate him. Somehow the resentment had to manifest itself, her anger at not being able to share the dangerous journey.

"Maybe. Maybe it's because I've had to survive on my own. Maybe it's also because I've had to get used to keeping so many things secret," Felipe said.

"You never survive 'on your own' in life, Felipe. You should know that better than I do. Other people play an important role, they have an influence on you. We imitate models."

"Well, it's true one has references. After all, as you pointed out so well, we are social beings. I was referring to the fact that the crises in my life have been ones of action rather than reflection. I haven't had much of an opportunity to meditate on 'existence.' I've had to solve the problems that have come up in my own way...and most of the time, they are practical problems."

"But haven't you ever wondered or been worried about yourself, about what you want, who you are, what you're doing in the world?"

Felipe was silent. Lavinia saw him try to remember, try to find the questions in his memory.

"The truth is I haven't," he said at last. "Reality has always been imposing its answers on me without my having had to interrogate it. I knew who I was, knew I wanted to study, and then, with Ute's influence, I realized I should return and fight to improve the situation in my country...and that's what I try to do in the world. It has never been very complicated for me."

Maybe it only happens to me, Lavinia thought, because I have options, I can choose.

"But you could have stayed in Germany," she said to him. "Didn't you wonder if it was worth it to return, if it was feasible to 'struggle to improve your country's situation'? Didn't it seem like a romantic or utopian idea?" she asked, teasing him.

"Life in Germany was horrendous for me. Even though I had my architect's degree, I had to work as a gardener. Over there, competition for jobs is hard. The only thing that could have made me stay was my relationship with Ute, but she was convinced it was more important for me to return to my country and 'do something.' She knew compañeros from the Movement there, passers-through who traveled to seek support, money, political contacts to get the word out about the struggle. She shared their point of view. It wasn't hard for her to persuade me. I knew from my own experience how bad things were here. I don't know if it will seem romantic to you, but one of the most overpowering motives is a sort of faith that sends its roots into you. You read the history of the struggle in Faguas, and you feel the energy that has been gathering, its capacity for resistance. You become convinced that it exists, that it's nothing more than a matter of awakening it and guiding it correctly..."

"Don't you think it's practically impossible?"

"No. I see it as difficult, but I don't see it as impossible. I'm absolutely convinced that what we're doing is right and that there's no other way..."

"But I don't think human nature is so generous. How can you give yourself so completely to the struggle? Don't you ever think about yourself?"

"No, because there's something else to keep in mind: one isn't only motivated by knowing that the cause is just; one gets personal satisfaction from it. For example, what you said about what a person does in the world... You know you're not devoting all your energy just so one day you can sit in your own home, with a car, a good job and a pretty wife and think, 'Now what?' I believe the mere fact that we exist implies a certain responsibility to the future, to what comes after us. If we can build airplanes, submarines, and space satellites, then we should be able to transform the world around us so we can at least live decently. It's almost inconceivable that in this age of technology there are people starving to death, who've never seen a doctor..."

"But you like the idea of leading a normal life, don't you? Didn't you tell me the other day that you envied ordinary people who haven't a worry in life except coming home and sitting down to watch TV?" Lavinia said, incisively.

"Yes. Sometimes I feel this way of living's unnatural—flirting with death, conspiring. And it is, in fact. It shouldn't be this way. We shouldn't have to die or risk dying because we want to put an end to misery and dictators. What's unnatural is that these things exist, but since they exist, there's nothing else to do but fight against them. You have to go against your own nature, resort to violence because life is constantly subjected to violence, not because you like the idea of suffering or dying before your time."

"So you mean to tell me that the idea of a 'normal life' doesn't appeal to you?"

"I'm not saying that. Sometimes, contrary to what I said before, I'd like to think I have nothing to worry about, that I'm a normal man with a steady job and average life, that I'll reach old age surrounded by grandchildren... But then I go out in the street, look around me, and realize that would only be possible if I had no feelings. I don't think anybody who has the least bit of humanity could enjoy a banquet with hundreds of starving children begging beside them. The people who do it have convinced themselves they can't do anything about it, and they think it's natural for there to be kids starving. They accept this type of violence and can't understand that we feel the need to take up arms, that we can't accept it, that we don't consider it natural."

"But, coming back to that thing about 'normal' life," Lavinia said, "don't you think it's wrong for you to have managed to enjoy both worlds? With me you have a 'normal' life and with your compañeros you can feel the satisfaction of doing something 'special'..."

"I don't see what's wrong with that," Felipe said, genuinely surprised at her question. "If I've been fortunate enough to find you and have a relationship with you, I don't see why I should deny myself. It's not a masochistic calling, either. We're all normal human beings who love life, we have a right to love and be loved... Anyway, I don't quite understand what you're getting at..."

"Maybe I should reformulate the question," Lavinia said, "and ask you instead if it doesn't bother you that I, the person who shares your life, am one of those 'normal' persons who go to banquets alongside starving children...?"

"But I don't think you are that type of person," he said, his expression showing the confusion of wanting to understand, unsuccessfully, the direction of Lavinia's words.

"I think you, as my companion, share my feelings... We've talked about it many times since we met..."

"Maybe I do share them in some way," she said. "But it's a completely passive sharing. Doesn't that bother you?"

"If I remember correctly, since that time that I brought Sebastián here when he was wounded, you said you understood us but didn't want to get involved, you didn't feel you could, you were afraid. You didn't agree with our 'heroic suicide.' That was what you said, if I remember correctly."

"And if you want so much to transform the world, don't you think you should try to transform me? Instead you've decided to agree with me, including reinforcing my fears when you've heard me express my opinion, my uneasiness about my own ideas, my passivity... Don't you think that unconsciously that might have something to do with your desire to keep a part of your life 'normal'?"

"I think, Lavinia," he said teasingly, "as Juárez said, that 'peace is the respect for the rights of the other person.' You're an intelligent person, and you have the right to think the way you do. I can't force you to join the Movement. It wouldn't be right on my part. I can't tell you not to be afraid because what we do is dangerous and certainly does make one afraid. I can't deceive you so you'll join us, inviting you as if it were a party. The Movement is not a plaything... I don't think the fact that I have respected your way of thinking has anything to do with that so-called 'desire for a normal life' that you seem to see in me."

"But would you or wouldn't you like me to join the Movement?"

"What a question!"

"You forget you've told me I'm the shore of your river, that if both of us were to swim in it, there would be no shore to welcome you home?"

"But I only told you that so you wouldn't feel bad about your own indecision...so you'd feel that in some way, by loving me, you could do something useful..."

"No, Felipe, don't tell me that. You know that's not how it is. Every time I've mentioned the remote possibility—and it's true I've done it with lots of uncertainty—of joining, you get all cuddly and tell me that thing about the shore of your river..."

"But that's a joke, woman, so you won't feel bad, because I know how difficult the idea of joining is for you."

"You're right. It is difficult," she said, assuming a thoughtful, silent pose, waiting for Felipe to try to convince her to join the Movement so she could tell him about her recent decision. If he had ever thought about doing it, this was the moment. She had served it to him on a silver platter, on purpose. She wouldn't tell him about it until he overcame his resistance to suggesting it to her.

But Felipe didn't say anything, He came close and hugged her, stroking her hair. Then he said it was late, and it was time for 'normal' couples to make love. That was what he said.

Lavinia said nothing about her disappointment. Lately she had observed the contrast between his beautiful discourse and his refusal to invite her to share 'the transformation of the world.' She wasn't going to use these stratagems any more, she thought, feeling worn out, falling asleep after telling Felipe no, no, she was tired.

She would reveal her secret to him at the right moment, she told herself. It would be a pleasure to see the surprise on his know-it-all face.

In her dreams, Lavinia soared far from Felipe.

✛ ✛ ✛

Silently, life weaves its fabric. I hear the rustle of thread shaping pattern of strange colors; events are drawing nearer, which I can only intuit.

• • •

CHAPTER 11

Monday. Lavinia was designing a luxury bedroom. Her work had taken on touches of routine. Seated at the drafting bench, placidly sketching rooms, thinking up colors and textures, it seemed unreal to her that she was part of the underground, part of the secret life of a city with a false bottom, inhabited by people who could only be seen by the eyes of a few.

The contrasts, the feeling of unreality, sometimes overwhelmed her.

She had spent the weekend with old friends. On Saturday she had had breakfast with Sara, and in the evening she had gone to a party with Antonio and the gang. At one point she felt herself split, felt herself disembodied, out of place. She left the group, pretending she had to go to the bathroom, wanting to go home. In the bathroom, she washed her hands over and over, studying the white tiles with intricate ochre drawings, the geraniums in pots beside the sunken bath, the mirrors on the walls. As she listened to the strident music outside, she thought how this world floated above the real one, but she also wondered which was more real. Whether or not it was her, shut up alone in the bathroom, who was drifting off in a balloon, without direction, on the lookout for monsters and ferocious, wild animals.

"Since you've been hanging out with that Felipe, you're different," Florencia had said.

She wondered if she weren't turning into another person, if she weren't slowly ceasing to be what she had been. The days of carefree living seemed so distant now. Obviously she was changing. The problem was she didn't know which direction the changes were taking. For now, she had to get used to being three persons. One for her friends and her job, another for the

Movement, a third for Felipe. At times she was afraid of not
knowing which of these persons she really was.

At least in the office she continued to reap professional
kudos. Her work routine was frequently altered by the
appearance of the "wives," whom Julián had assigned her to
convince not to import garish fabrics and carpets from Miami
or insist on "Swiss chalets" for a tropical climate.

These women caused a lot of work and headaches for
Lavinia, but she couldn't deny that their extravagant tastes
amused her, giving her unlimited material for gags and jokes,
pathetic portraits of the incongruities of the times.

And that day in May two of those women came to the
office to alter Lavinia's routine forever.

Mercedes announced their arrival. She opened the door,
stood in front of Lavinia's desk with a humorless expression,
and said:

"The boss wants you. I should warn you he's with two
'mummies.'"

And she left without another word.

It was no exaggeration. They were two truly dry women
with rouged cheeks, their faces theatrical with thick makeup. Bracelets jingled on their thin arms, giving the
impression that it was an effort to gesture, to lift their arms
weighed down with so much gold. One talked nonstop while
the other nodded her head.

When Lavinia entered, they looked at her with the
expression of indifference certain women assume when facing
specimens of the same gender whom they consider
subordinate. They must think I'm the secretary, Lavinia said
to herself. For this type of woman, secretaries are the
enemies, the ones who steal their husbands.

"Hello," she said to them.

They returned her greeting.

Turning to the visitors, Julián introduced her.

"Lavinia is one of our best architects," he said.

When they heard her name and qualifications, their expressions changed completely. They softened into broad smiles.

"Allow me to introduce Mrs. Vela and her sister, Miss Montes," added Julián.

She shook their hands with the usual "very nice to meet you." They had slender, lifeless hands which they extended with affectation. All their bracelets couldn't hide their lack of social grace.

The surname Vela sounded familiar to Lavinia, but she couldn't quite place it.

To give her a quick orientation, Julián turned to her, explaining that the Vela family wanted to build on a site that they had recently acquired, situated on one of the hills bordering the southern part of the city.

"The terrain is quite irregular," he said, spreading out the plan. "Nevertheless, it has very attractive possibilities."

"It has a wonderful view," Mrs. Vela said. "I can't imagine how a house can be built there, but my husband says it's possible. I wish he could have come, but he's very busy these days, so he asked me to get some ideas about what kind of house could be built there." The woman sighed with resignation.

"She should be pleased that her husband allows her such freedom, right?" smiled Miss Montes, looking at Julián and Lavinia, trying to cover over what she must consider a subtle complaint on the part of her sister.

Amused, Lavinia watched them. Mrs. Vela was younger than her sister, who had the air of a flirtatious spinster, one of those who always have an opinion and are always meddling. She probably took care of the children, too.

"How many people will live in the house?" Lavinia asked.

"My husband and myself, our two children and my sister...and the servants, of course. But we want a big house, with plenty of room."

"General Vela likes a social life," said the made-up Miss Montes.

General Vela! Lavinia said to herself. That's why the name had seemed familiar! He was none other than the recently promoted Army Chief of Staff! The newspaper had emphasized his unconditional loyalty to the Grand General. Before he was promoted, General Vela had been the chief of police—the incentive the Grand General offered his loyal followers before elevating them to a higher military rank, so that they could accumulate great sums of money while in charge of license plates, fines, and driving permits.

And now she'd have to design his house! she thought. Now, of all times!

"We've decided we'll need to have several drawing rooms, dining rooms, and extra bedrooms," Mrs. Vela was saying. "We also want a swimming pool for the children, a play area... Plus, my husband would like a place to shoot pool..."

Lavinia kept asking questions, observing them now with another sort of curiosity. The sisters interrupted each other, rattling off the list of features and rooms the house should have. They weren't long in opening their purses and taking out clippings from magazines, mentioning their desire to have "imported" materials, since Faguas couldn't supply the styles that would satisfy their requirements. Lavinia leaned over the table to look at the sisters' clippings. At least it was Raquel Welch's summer home and not Ursula Andress's Alpine cottage.

The actress was posing on impeccably white furniture in a room with a round bed and a tiger-stripe bedspread.

Mrs. Vela mentioned her "dream" of having a bath with an oval tub and Jacuzzi. Miss Montes explained the passion the Velas' teenage son had for airplanes, birds, and everything that could fly. "General Vela wants to give some direction to the boy's dreams. Instill in him a pilot's vocation," she said.

"My husband is worried about the boy's being such a daydreamer. We think his room could be decorated with warplane motifs," Mrs. Vela said.

Then they mentioned fountains in the garden, walls with "weeping" rocks, mirrored walls in the bathrooms...

Lavinia and Julián looked at each other from time to time, pretending to follow the sisters' flood of ideas attentively.

They knew it would be expensive, clarified Mrs. Vela, but money was no object. The "General" had worked very hard all his life. He deserved it. Besides, the house was something his children would inherit.

Finally Julián—ever courteous and smiling—scheduled them for the next week to present an initial sketch and continue the conversation.

The women marched off to the tune of their jangling bracelets.

Lavinia collapsed on Julián's office couch. The women's harangue, their nouveau riche self-assurance, had left her dazed. Before she wouldn't have felt any conflicts but simple professional ones. Now that she had joined the Movement, she wondered if this weren't the moment to carry out her first display of recently acquired political awareness.

"General Vela, no less," Julián said, closing the door.

"Incredible!" Lavinia said.

"They don't know what to do with their money," Julián said.

"And are we going to work for them?" Lavinia said, testing him. "Are we going to accept their corrupt money?"

"Don't be a romantic," Julián replied, as he rolled up the plan. "Most of the money we get is ill-gotten. The only difference with this money is that it's more obvious. Besides, it seems the Great General has decided to make his faithful followers richer in order to ensure they'll be satisfied and defend him. I imagine that's how he plans to deal more effectively with the discontent and rebelliousness of the people. After this job, there'll probably be others."

"So you're willing to make a profit on them?" Lavinia asked, still not able to decide what position to take.

"Don't try to play the moralist with me now." Julián said. "If they want to spend their money, let's help them. After all, it's better if we earn it. We're more honest. In this case I won't even ask you to convince them to avoid extravagance and bad taste. Don't even worry about it."

"That's not what bothers me," Lavinia said, sitting up straight. "It's just that I don't know if I feel like helping them think about ways to spend their money."

"The money will be spent anyway. If we don't spend it, there'll be others who will. We aren't going to keep it from being spent. Besides, principles don't enter into business."

"I don't like the idea. Wouldn't you consider assigning the job to another architect?" Lavinia asked, getting up to leave and thinking how her principles were starting to take hold.

"No, Lavinia," Julián said, looking at her seriously. "I couldn't assign it to anyone else. There's no one better than you for this job. If we let ourselves be ruled by principles, we might as well stay home."

"Haven't you considered they might not like it if I'm in charge?" Lavinia said, turning to a more persuasive tactic. "They must know from my last name that my family is from the opposition party..."

"On the contrary," Julián said. "They'll be thrilled. Those people are impressed by aristocratic names. They don't care if they're rivals or not. Their dream is to be like you. The truth is—and don't take it wrong—for them the only serious opposition are the guerrillas..."

Julián opened a folder on his desk and began to look over the papers, as a sign that the conversation had ended. Lavinia picked up her notebook and started to leave.

She had her hand on the doorknob when Julián lifted his head.

"I will supervise this job personally. You and I will work together. Felipe already has too many projects going."

Julián knew about Felipe, she thought. He didn't want to force him to work with General Vela. He must know he'd refuse to get involved in this one. Once she was in her cubicle, Lavinia picked up the phone and dialed Felipe's extension. She didn't want to risk having Julián see her entering his office and thinking she was indiscreet.

"Felipe?"

"Yes."

"It's Lavinia."

"I recognize your voice," he answered in a curt, preoccupied tone.

"I've just met with General Vela's wife. They're asking us to design their house. Julián wants me to do it."

Silence.

"Felipe, I don't think I should do it."

Silence.

"I think," said the voice on the other end, "that you should do it. Yes, definitely!" he added more emphatically.

"But..."

"Why don't we talk about this later? I'm busy now," he said.

Lavinia hung up and contemplated the distant landscape. It would feel good to go into Julián's office and tell him she wasn't willing to design the house. She imagined the reaction of the other architects and the draftsmen, the buzz as the news spread through the office. The young people who secretly criticized the government without daring to confront its corruption or insane demands would realize that the road to rebellion was open. She was sure Felipe would understand when she explained it to him later. And she had no doubt that Sebastián would support her. Pleased with herself, she got up, sat on the stool by the drafting table, and continued her work, humming softly.

"But why are you so sure I should accept?" Lavinia asked Felipe. "I'm almost certain Sebastián would agree with me."

"Don't be naïve," Felipe replied. "Your 'rebellion' would be squelched immediately. They'd simply give the design to someone else, or fire you. It's odd that Julián has even assigned it to you. He knows about us..."

"I don't understand..." Lavinia said, looking at him.

Felipe had arrived when she was already in bed. He took off his clothes and got between the sheets, saying he was sorry for being late. He asked her to tell him everything about the job for Mrs. Vela and her sister. She told him. She explained her plan to protest, to refuse to do the job. He insisted on the importance of her accepting.

"Don't you realize he's the Army Chief of Staff?" he repeated.

"Of course I do," Lavinia said. "That's precisely it."

"Don't you realize you could have access to a great deal of information about his habits and routines, his family? Don't you realize you would be designing his house, his bedroom, his bathroom...?" Felipe exclaimed, finally exasperated.

Lavinia was silent. She began to understand.

Her mind flashed on a series of images: terrorist attacks, Aldo Moro, men dead in bedrooms. She felt ill.

"Are you going to kill him?" she asked, unable to express it any other way.

"That's not it," Felipe said. "But it's extremely important to have information on these people, to win their trust, don't you see?"

She did see. But it was a confused picture, blotched by spine-chilling images. She thought about the spinster, the conciliatory sister.

She imagined the bomb blowing the woman to pieces.

"I see," Lavinia said. "I see it's information that can be useful for doing away with them."

"Lavinia, we don't see this as a matter of killing people. If we did, we would already have taken care of the Great General. What we want are changes greater than a mere change of persons."

"But then what use would all this information be?"

"One of the golden rules of war is knowing the enemy, how he lives, how he thinks. What is done with the information is no concern of yours. What you would have to do is get it, earn the family's trust, be able to enter the house...get documents."

"But that would be dangerous," she said, feeling him out.

"It could be," he said. "That's true. But it's important. We'd protect you."

"I'd have to join the Movement," Lavinia said, looking him straight in the eye.

"Or get all the information to me," Felipe said.

"It would be about the same."

"Not necessarily," he said. "You wouldn't have any more responsibility than passing the information to me."

"And if I were to tell you I already joined the Movement?"

"I wouldn't believe you."

"Well, I'm sorry to inform you that I did."

Lavinia waited for Felipe's reaction. She saw him looking at her, incredulous. They sized each other up in silence. She didn't look away.

"It hurts me that you kept it from me," Felipe said finally.

"I was going to tell you sometime. I wasn't sure when."

"But when was it, when did you decide, how?" Felipe was asking.

Lavinia gave him a brief run-down of her meditations, her conversations with Sebastián and Flor.

"And why didn't you tell me anything?" Felipe demanded.

"I tried to," Lavinia said, "but you didn't help any. I had the feeling you didn't want me to participate, that you were always going to say I wasn't ready."

"That's true," he said, visibly shaken. He still thought she wasn't mature enough to join officially, he said; she had too many doubts, she didn't really know what she wanted.

Lavinia admitted her doubts, but were only those who had no doubts allowed to participate in the Movement? she asked. It was only Felipe who seemed to think so. His attitude contrasted with that of Sebastián and Flor.

"Because I know you better than anyone else!" Felipe said, raising his voice. "You're going to tell me that you don't think we're suicidal, that a minute ago you weren't horrified at the idea of passing information about the General because it could put his life in danger, as if his life was more important than those of many of our compañeros? As if they cared about our lives?"

"That's what makes us different from them, isn't it?" Lavinia said. "For us, lives aren't disposable."

"Of course," Felipe said, put on the spot. "But it's not a matter of protecting people like Vela, either."

"I don't think you understand my misgivings," Lavinia said, staying calm, her voice soft. "And you don't understand me, either. You would never think I'm ready for the Movement. It's not convenient for you. You want to keep your niche of 'normality,' the shore to your river, century after century, your little woman collaborating under your guidance without growing or becoming someone on her own. Fortunately, Sebastián and Flor don't think like you."

Lavinia was losing control as she spoke. The cracks were widening, revealing her pent-up resentment: the nights lying awake waiting for him, his superior, paternalistic attitude.

"I don't give a shit what they think!" he said, furious. "They can think what they like. They don't live with you. They don't have to put up with your little rich girl's antics! That's what you are: a little rich girl who thinks she can do anything. You don't even see your own limitations."

"Nobody asked me where I wanted to be born!" Lavinia said, in a rage. "I'm not to blame, you hear me?"

"You want the whole neighborhood to hear us?"

"You're the one who started shouting."

She had sat up on the edge of the bed. Naked, her legs spread over the sheets, she fell silent, looking at her feet.

Whenever she didn't know what to do, she stared at her feet; it was like observing herself from a distance, seeing a strange, distant part of herself, her long toes tapering gradually to her tiny little toe. They resembled her mother's feet...what fault was it of hers that she had a mother like that, with those aristocratic feet...even her little rich girl's antics...? I don't have a little rich girl's antics, she said to herself. The only thing she couldn't stand was going by bus or taxi. She liked having her own car. But who didn't like that?

Besides that, she couldn't think of any other "antics." She barely ate, nor did she care about eating anything in particular... And she didn't like the parties at the club.

She wiggled her feet, stretching her toes. The tense silence was spreading between the two of them like something physical, crouching tigers, naked upon the sheets, waiting to see whose claws took the next swipe at the other. She didn't want to look up, didn't want to see him, she wasn't going to say any more, she'd wait...

"Have you lost your tongue?" Felipe said, in a softer voice.

She kept looking thoughtfully at her toes.

"And who brought you into the Movement, Sebastián?"

"Flor," she said, without looking up.

"Of course," he said. "I should have figured," he added.

Some of the paint on her nails was a bit worn; she ought to remove it.

The thick silence set in again. Outside, the wind was beginning to blow hard, moving the branches of the orange tree whose shadow ran along the window, sprinkling dark designs across the wall.

She lifted her head ever so slightly, just a bit above her big toe. Felipe was stretched out on the bed, his arms under his head, looking intensely at the ceiling.

How long would they stay like that? Lavinia wondered. How long would it take Felipe to acknowledge that he'd made a mistake? She wasn't going to do a thing, she thought. She didn't have to be the one to start up the conversation again.

She wouldn't talk to him. He would have to be the one to speak.

"So it's already done," he said, as if talking to himself.

"Yes," she said. "I'm not going to back out when I've only just started. Especially now."

"I guess you're right," he said. "It shouldn't bother me, quite the contrary, but I can't help it."

He leaned on his side on the bed and looked at her. He held out his hand and timidly touched hers.

"You should be happy," she said. "Don't you think it's strange that it's got you so worked up?"

"That's what I was thinking about," he said. "What bothers me is not that you've decided to join, but that you've done it without saying anything to me."

"But I already told you..."

"Yes, yes," he interrupted, "maybe you're right. Maybe I didn't want to get you involved, maybe I let myself become too protective because I didn't want you exposed to danger... But not the thing you keep mentioning, my hankering to lead a normal life..."

She looked at him without saying a word.

"All right," he said. "You win. I'll try to get used to it and help you."

"So I'm a spoiled little rich girl?" she said provocatively.

"You sure are," he said, barely lifting his head, his body sideways over hers. He was looking playfully into her eyes.

They grew calmer. They caressed each other. The tension didn't vanish completely, but it was camouflaged by kisses and timid I love yous.

Felipe nibbled her shoulder. Lavinia thought how Felipe, with bites and kisses and his hand between her legs, always got his way, how he could suddenly change, say he'd "help" her and how she preferred to believe him, preferred to give in, to accept the reconciliation, the path of moans and erect nipples, wings buzzing in her ears.

They agreed she should talk to Flor and Sebastián. She would design General Vela's house, if Sebastián agreed.

• • •

CHAPTER 12

On Wednesday, Sebastián and Flor not only agreed, they advised her to give the project her undivided attention, work her way into the milieu as completely as possible, and report everything she observed and noticed about the Vela family.

"Everything," they said. No detail should seem unimportant.

They thought like Felipe. Their arguments finally convinced her.

She didn't dare continue brandishing her reservations.

What's more, they insisted that she had to keep up a social life, her friendships, the club circles, and attend the next ball. She shouldn't isolate herself, they said. It was absolutely necessary for her to be seen. When General Vela inquired about her, he should have no doubt that she was an active socialite, accustomed to the company that was hers by birthright.

What a paradox, Lavinia thought after the meeting, that her "work" in the Movement, which she thought would change her existence, would be to play the role of herself.

When she got home, she realized the house had not been cleaned. It was stuffy and messy. Lucrecia hadn't come to work. The morning coffee cups were still on the table and the bed was unmade.

It had rained in through the half-open windows. Tiny particles of water glistened on the floor when she turned on the lights in the room. The orange tree swayed from side to side, scratching at the windows.

"Hi," Lavinia said. "Now you've really gotten soaked!"

Speaking to the tree had become a habit. Seeing how green it was, and how laden with oranges, she was convinced that people who claimed it was good to talk to plants were not mistaken. This tree, anyway, seemed to appreciate her greetings.

She took off her shoes and put on her slippers. She gathered up the empty cups and the glass of water beside the bed and began to wash the dishes in the kitchen.

What would happen with the Vela family? she wondered, as she scrubbed and slid the sponge in and around the glasses and cups. And what could be wrong with Lucrecia, who was always so reliable? Was she sick?

She worked until the house looked tidy. She was in no mood for disorder. I hope Lucrecia won't fail to come tomorrow, she thought. She must have had some problem.

Lucrecia didn't come the next day. Nor the next.

"You ought to go find out what's wrong," Felipe said at the office in the morning.

"I already thought about that," Lavinia said. "I'll go look for her after work."

In her purse she had the piece of paper where Lucrecia had jotted down her address. It was hard to make out the crude, primitive scrawl (Lucretia had only been able to attend two years of elementary school), but Lavinia managed to figure out the name of the neighborhood and the street. She thought that would be enough. The neighbors would know her.

As she drove down the main highway near the area, she saw in the distance the poor neighborhood with its bumpy streets, the board houses, the remote outline of the church framed by the setting sun.

She turned off the main road onto the unpaved one. The street lights ended where the houses began. The only illumination for the alley-like paths came from the open doors of the poor crowded dwellings. Almond trees and banana shrubs dotted the patios.

She arrived at the small square in front of the church, the only cement building in the area, and entered the back streets. The children stared at her as she drove by. The car bounced along the bumpy surface; pigs and chickens crossed the muddy path. Through the doorways she could see the tiny, unhealthy interiors of the one-room dwellings. Families of as many as six or seven lived crammed into tiny spaces. Fathers often raped adolescent daughters when they were drunk.

How do they manage to live like this? she thought uncomfortably, feeling guilty.

One had to go only a few kilometers outside the area of tree-lined streets and comfortable, well-lit residential neighborhoods to enter this sad and miserable rural world. She imagined Lucrecia walking through the dirt streets in the early morning hours to catch a bus at the main road, rickety, packed buses; jostling, pickpockets. She thought once more of the injustices of birth. Death was much more democratic. Death evened everything out; whether buried in a crypt or in dirt, everyone's body decomposed the same way. But what was democracy good for then?

Lavinia stopped in front of a group of young people who were talking on the corner. She asked for the street where Lucrecia lived. They knew which one it was. She had to go a little bit farther, they told her; Lucrecia's house was the one next to the store, farther back.

Daylight was fading. A barefoot woman with olive skin was struggling up the steep street, pushing a cart full of firewood, with several children sitting on top.

She passed her in the car. The children looked at her surprised. At this time of day, few cars must go through here, Lavinia thought to herself.

She reached Lucrecia's house. From a distance, she saw the woman with the cart watch her as she got out of the car. She felt bad, out of place, in her linen pants suit and high-heeled shoes. She knocked on the door.

A girl of about twelve opened it a crack.

"Does Lucrecia Flores live here?" Lavinia asked.

"Yes," said the little girl, hiding behind the door, looking inside the house as if seeking protection. "Yes, she lives here. She's my aunt."

"And is she in?" Lavinia asked.

"Aunt, there's someone looking for you," shouted the girl as she turned toward the interior of the dwelling.

The door opened a little more. Lavinia could see the roof that had no ceiling, with the electric wires strung across the zinc and a single light bulb swinging from the beam where it had been tied. There were mattresses hanging folded over a joist. They would take them down when it was time to go to bed. There was a rickety old chair in the corner.

"Who's looking for me?" said Lucrecia's voice.

"It's me, Lucrecia. Lavinia," she said from the doorway.

"Let her in, let her in," came the voice from inside.

Obediently, the girl stepped out of the way. Lavinia entered the tiny room that seemed to serve both as living room and bedroom. From one side of the room, behind a wooden partition and a dirty, frayed curtain, she heard Lucrecia telling her to come in. The place smelled of dirty rags and confinement.

Lavinia pushed the curtain aside and found Lucrecia lying on a canvas cot, her head covered with a towel that gave off a strong camphor odor.

"Oh, Miss Lavinia," said the woman. "I feel so bad you've come to get me. I couldn't come because I've been so sick. You should see the fever I've had!"

Lavinia came over to her and saw her red eyes. Lucrecia looked pale and her lips had a strange bluish tint.

"But what's wrong with you, Lucrecia?" she asked. "You don't look well at all. Has a doctor seen you yet?"

Lucrecia covered her face with her hands and began to cry.

"No," she said between sobs, "nobody's been here. I don't want anybody to examine me. Rosa, get her a chair, go on now," she said to the girl while she continued to cry.

Lavinia sat down in the chair beside Lucrecia, the same chair she'd seen when she came in, the only one she could see in the whole house.

"But why don't you want anyone to examine you?" she said, while Lucrecia sobbed. "Come now, stop crying. When did this start?"

The woman, young but aged by poverty, covered herself with the sheets while she ordered the girl to go look for her mother.

"Lucrecia," insisted Lavinia, "tell me what's wrong with you so I can take you to a doctor. Don't cry any more. The doctor can cure you. We can go now, if you like..."

"Oh, Miss Lavinia! You're so kind!" Lucrecia said, "but I don't want anybody to examine me!"

"She doesn't want anyone to examine her, and those fevers are going to kill her," said a voice from behind Lavinia.

She turned around and saw a fat woman, an apron tied about her waist, beside the curtain. It was Lucrecia's sister, the girl's mother.

"Tell her. Tell her once and for all," the woman continued. "You can't go on like this, just crying in bed and burning with fever until you die. If you don't tell her, I will."

Lucrecia's crying intensified.

"I told her not to do it," said her sister, "but nothing would convince her."

Finally Lucrecia, intermittently breaking into tears, told Lavinia the story of the abortion. She didn't want to have the baby, she said. The man had told her she could not count on him, and she couldn't consider quitting work. She wouldn't have anybody to take care of the child. Besides, she wanted to study. She couldn't raise a child. She didn't want to have a child only to leave it alone, badly cared for, ill-fed. She'd thought about it carefully. It hadn't been easy to decide. But finally a friend of hers had recommended a nurse who didn't charge much, and she did it. The problem was that the hemorrhage wouldn't stop. Now she smelled bad all over, like something rotten, she said, and she had this fever... It was God's punishment, Lucrecia said. Now she was going to die. She didn't want anybody to examine her. If a doctor saw her, he'd ask her who had done the abortion, and the woman had warned her not to tell. The doctors knew it was illegal. They'd know. She could even get arrested if she went to a hospital, she said.

Lavinia tried not to be overwhelmed by the image of the women with their drawn faces, Lucrecia huddled under the sheets, the ignorance, the fear, the tiny room without ventilation, the smell of camphor, the girl sticking her frightened face around the edge of the curtain.

"Go on out and play, Rosa, I told you to go play," her mother said, losing her patience and pushing the girl, raising her hand as if she were going to strike her, so that the girl ran out.

She had to figure out what could be done, Lavinia told herself. She had to overcome the queasy sensation in her stomach, the desire to cry with Lucrecia, who finally fell silent, sobbing quietly.

"I have a friend who's a nurse," Lavinia said. "I'm going to go get her."

She'd bring Flor, she thought. At least Flor could tell her what to do.

She got up, managing not to let the smell of camphor, the fever, the pain, the infuriating injustice of poverty get the best of her.

"Thank you, Miss Lavinia," Lucrecia said, starting to cry again.

When she went out into the dark street, Lavinia took a deep gulp of air. Night was settling over the wooden walls of the neighboring houses. Washed clean by the rain, the sky was full of stars. There was no light to compete with their splendor. Lucrecia's sister, standing stiffly in the doorway, straightened her hair with her hands.

"I'll be right back," she told the woman. "I'll be right back." And she got into her new-smelling car.

On the road, Lavinia had to stop because the tears in her eyes formed iridescent halos around the headlights of the vehicles coming from the other direction.

Two hours later, Flor disappeared with Lucrecia behind the door of the emergency room. Through the glass Lavinia saw them go inside and then lost sight of them. She walked toward the waiting room, wearily dragging her feet.

The roof was high and the neon lights that were set over the ceiling—most of the bulbs were burned out—barely illuminated the area. She collapsed onto one of the wooden benches. If it hadn't been for the smell of medicine and anguish, the typical hospital smell, the waiting room would have resembled the worship area of a Protestant church. Rows of simple wooden benches occupied the center and sides of the room. Women with dirty, sick children, others who were alone, a few men, all were waiting in silence. Lavinia rested her arm on the corner of the bench and rubbed her eyes. Her head ached. Her neck was stiff.

Fortunately, Flor had taken control of the situation with her usual serenity. She had friends at the hospital, doctors used to situations like Lucrecia's. "There are thousands of cases like hers," Flor had said.

She kept her eyes closed for a good while, hoping to doze a little to shorten the wait. But sleep didn't come. She opened her eyes and looked around the room. She noticed the other people in the room were watching her. They turned away as soon as she looked up, but their eyes had been on her, observing her, as if they were all in a theater, and the spotlight was fixed on her.

She felt ill at ease. To keep herself occupied, she stared at the floor. She scanned the row of feet facing her. Dirt had accumulated beneath the benches. The feet of an older woman shifted. They were thick and heavy. Varicose veins could be seen rising from the top of the coarse, black leather. The front of the shoe had been cut out so its inadequate size wouldn't cramp the toes of its new owner. The toes, with broken, purplish nails, were grotesque. Lavinia looked at the next pair. A much younger woman. Thirty, perhaps. Sandals that had once been white. Brown feet. Rough. The nails had old, flaking polish, almost violet. The veins protruded. Farther down were the worn soles of a man's shoes. Short socks. The elastic sagging. A rip near the top. Hypnotized, she studied the row of sad feet. Lifted her eyes. They were looking at her. She looked down again. Her own feet came into focus. Her feet—refined, white, peeking out from her heeled sandals, the soft brown sandals, Italian leather, the red toenails. Her feet were pretty. Aristocratic. She closed her eyes again.

She had pledged she would fight for the owners of those rough feet, she thought. Join them. Be one of them. Feel the injustices committed against them in her own flesh. These were the "people" the Movement's program referred to. And yet here, being with them in the dark, dingy emergency room of the hospital, an abyss separated them. The image of their feet couldn't be more eloquent. And their distrustful glances. They'd never accept her, Lavinia thought. How could they ever accept her, believe she could identify with them, not distrust her delicate skin, her shiny hair, her manicured hands, her red toenails?

Flor put an end to her meditations when she appeared with the doctor. A middle-aged man, robust, with a good-natured face. Lucrecia was all right, they told her. They'd had to give her blood and do a D & C. It was lucky they'd brought her to the hospital today. One more day and nothing would have saved her.

She went into the gynecology section with Flor. The "J" ward was long and narrow, with rows of bed on both sides. Somber women's faces followed her as she walked through the aisle toward the bed where Lucrecia was sleeping. They took stock of her clothes, her purse, they looked her over from head to toe. She tiptoed, wishing the earth would swallow her up, feeling awkward, offensive, guilty, an intruder in other people's suffering.

Only Flor smiled as she encouraged her to go over, bend over Lucrecia and place her hand on her brow. She said Lavinia should remember the number of her bed in order to tell her sister. She'd be much better tomorrow, Flor said. They could visit her from three to five in the afternoon.

Days later, at the office, Lavinia struggled against depression and weariness while she was sketching possible options for the Vela house.

She felt that her life was becoming uncontrollably tangled. Her two parallel existences crashed into each other, shaking her, threatening to erase every vestige of her identity.

That night in the emergency room would not vanish from her memory and continuously haunted her. It grew sharper with afternoon visits to the hospital during the next three days, as she sat next to Lucrecia, her sister, and her niece under the high windows of the gynecology ward. She couldn't forget the women's faces framed with white sheets, staring at her in a quizzical way, looking uneasy when they saw her appear among them.

In that arbitrarily divided world it was terrible to find oneself armed solely with good intentions. To bear privileges in the face of so much injustice, to feel branded by wealth as if with a hot iron, setting her apart from the owners of the rough hands and feet, from those women lying in bed, their insides torn apart by botched abortions, or cradling children who, like her, hadn't chosen where they were to be born and who, because of the randomness of birth and the social inequalities, would grow up in dark rooms with the stench of dirty clothes, stacked up in wretched dwellings with brothers and sisters, aunts and uncles, fathers and mothers.

Lavinia's pencil stopped drawing arches and doors and slipped into sketching hands and feet. She lifted her head and heard the buzz of the drafting lamps, the conversation of the apprentices, the clatter of coffee cups, the purr of the air conditioning. By now Lucrecia would be back in her house, happy to have survived. She was probably having a cup of liver broth, washing the camphor from the sheets, waiting for her sister to return from her stand in the market so she could knead the tortillas that Rosa, the girl, would go out to sell around the neighborhood in the afternoon, her tiny voice hawking:

"Tortillas, get your torr-tiii-llas."

All her life Lavinia could remember flashes of this other reality, insinuating itself shamefully, surreptitiously—motionless portraits from which pain stares out at you. Faded, yellowed moments packed away in silence until now, when they were beginning to float in her conscience like bottles cast into the sea. Messages tossed up on the beaches of her mind, shaking her.

If I were one of them, she told herself, I wouldn't trust someone like me, someone who looked like me. Nothing good could come of it.

• • •

CHAPTER 13

Looking at her garden of ferns and jalacates, Sara talked non-stop about the time she spent buying vegetables, decorating rooms, upholstering furniture... "I'm a good wife," she said. "And I like being one. It's as great a pleasure as any other, cleaning the house, welcoming my husband home." What was curious, she said, was to feel oneself enclosed in a kind of indolence, in a continuum of time belonging to her alone, in which Adrián barely had a place. When he came home at night, with his news about work and world events, it was hard for her to change roles, to have an "interesting" conversation. It was even harder, she went on, to go to bed and play the seducing games he liked, to break through the chrysalis, the quiet refuge of her domestic duties, and soar like a butterfly every night, to be a sensual woman.

"I almost feel as if I should pretend. I have to force myself to break out of my indolence, accelerate the rhythm, listen to what he says with an interested expression." It was easier, she said, when he left, and she stayed behind in the protection of her quiet world, in the garden, with her domestic chores.

Sometimes she thought "her world" allowed her to find peace and meaning in the daily tasks, so apparently irrelevant and simple; or perhaps it was because she really liked the exquisite slow-motion life of her kingdom, the realm of domesticity.

What struck her most, she added, was that the sensation seemed to be common to women in her situation: they spent the day apparently devoted to their husbands' happiness, but these men who appeared at night and left in the morning weren't really part of their lives.

"Hadn't housewives for centuries found their own personal universe, where they presented themselves for the nighttime intruders and then went about their own business by day?" Sara asked, looking at Lavinia

"I don't know if you understand me," Sara said. "For people like you, home life is a desert. That's the way men see it, too. The fact is one invents one's own oasis. You enjoy what you do. I like to talk with the butcher; it amuses me to haggle over prices in the market, work in the garden, watch the begonias grow. I enjoy the daily routine. What begins to feel strange to me is sharing my bed, my bathroom, the shower, with someone who comes at night and leaves in the morning, who leads such a different life..."

"Well," Lavinia said, "that's exactly what it's all about. Women are given the routine of daily life, while men reserve the arena of great events for themselves."

"What I'm trying to tell you, Lavinia, is that even though it may not seem like it, in their own way wives banish their husbands, too. Husbands become intruders in the domestic world..."

"Don't kid yourself, Sara," Lavinia said. "If husbands didn't exist, housewives wouldn't either, and that world you talk about would be different..."

"I'm not saying there shouldn't be any husbands. Don't get me wrong. The fact is they exist. What I'm saying is that, just as a man has a satisfying life at work, we 'housewives' have our own rewards, too."

"I don't doubt it," Lavinia said, "but still, a job with no salary, no social recognition..."

"Everyone in my neighborhood likes me," Sara said. "They know me and respect me. All my friends acknowledge my place in society..."

"The way they respect any housewife," Lavinia said.

"That doesn't bother me," Sara said. "Being a housewife is respectable enough. I'm not trying to tell you I don't enjoy it, it's just this thing of discovering that..."

"The only thing you've discovered is the division of labor," interrupted Lavinia, in exasperation.

"No, Lavinia. You'd be surprised to hear how 'housewives' talk among themselves about their husbands. We tend to them as if they were strangers. They have nothing to do with us, with the discussions about the spots on the tablecloths, how long it takes to cook the meat, tending gardens... The strange thing is that men think the world exists for their benefit, and I honestly don't think there's any place where they are less important, even though everything seems to hinge upon them. The housewives' space is one which, contrary to what everyone thinks, only returns to normal when the men leave for work in the morning. They are the interruptions."

"And the reason for that space existing," Lavinia said. "Any feminist who heard you would be furious..."

"Don't you see it as a way women have of establishing a territory of their own?"

"No," Lavinia said, categorically. "It seems to me the 'indolence' you're talking about and your seeing men as 'intruders' are nothing but examples of unconscious rebellion."

"But don't you think we women control a more important territory, with an incredible, real power...what's been called 'the power behind the throne'?"

"That's something men invented."

"What happens is we've never exercised that power as power, only as submission. Beneath its appearance of being controlled by men, the domestic empire has solid structures. And men, you see, are just inevitable reference points."

"Could be," Lavinia said. "What I think is you're coming into contact with the female reality of 'housewives', with their defense mechanisms. That's the way it has always been. And the truth is we haven't changed anything in the world to our benefit..."

"You have your ideas, I have mine," Sara said.

Lavinia decided not to argue with her anymore. Her mind was preoccupied with other concerns. She'd talk with her about it some other time. Maybe Sara was beginning to feel unhappy with Adrián and was afraid to admit it.

It was nearly dusk. The shadowy light bathed the garden and the low branches of the malinche tree in the middle of the patio. The two friends fell silent, each one submerged in her own reflections, sipping the iced tea in tall crystal glasses.

"And how's your social life?" Lavinia asked at last.

"A lot of bridal showers," Sara said. "It seems as if all our friends are going to get married soon...and in two weeks there's the annual Country Club Ball. Did you finally decide to go, or are you still determined not to frequent such places, to 'retire from the madding crowd'?"

"I'll probably go," Lavinia replied. "Lately I've been feeling lonely. I don't think it would be bad to have a little social life again."

"Of course, it would be good for you," Sara said. "And this year they say the club's going to go all out; more than twenty debutantes are going to participate. You'll have a good time. It's different than the discotheques, but it's fun too..."

"It's such a spectacle," Lavinia said. "That's what I never liked. The feeling of being on display, offered to the highest bidder."

"I never felt that," Sara said. "It's the normal, natural way for young people to get to know each other and find a mate. But probably you're not going to feel like that this time. You'll enjoy yourself more. People are wondering where you've been."

If they only knew, Lavinia thought, they'd die.

After her experience with Lucrecia, the shack, the feet in the hospital, it would be hard to enjoy the ball. But it wasn't worth telling Sara. It wasn't even a good idea, for the image Sebastián had insisted she should present. He stressed how important it was for her to frequent the fancy club circles, not only for a "cover" as an impeccable "socialite," but because she could get important information from those circles for the

Movement. "We're interested in knowing what those people think and what plans they have," he'd said.

"Maybe I'll feel better now," Lavinia said, trying to sound convincing. "Now that I can sit on the sidelines and not feel that I'm the 'offer' of the year."

"We can go together if you like," Sara said. "I'm sure Adrián would be glad to take us both...and Felipe, he won't get mad, will he? I don't think he can come with us..."

No, of course not, Lavinia thought. Felipe wouldn't be allowed in. To be admitted into the club was a long procedure. Not only did you have to have the money to pay the high membership fee, you also had to pass the scrutiny of the club's board of directors. They met and discussed the "pedigrees" of the applicants at length. They voted with black and white balls. Not even the upper echelons of the Great General were admitted. The majority of the aristocrats were "Green." The "Blue" party, which was the Great General's, and its members, were considered "low class," "uneducated policemen," "nouveau riche." At least on the social level, the "Greens" were still in control. It seemed to satisfy them. Smiling as she remembered the absurd selection criteria, Lavinia said:

"Don't even worry about that. Felipe would only get black-balled if he tried to be admitted. But of course, it wouldn't even occur to him. I don't think he'd be interested at all," and she smiled, imagining Felipe's comments.

"You never know," Sara said. "When they become professionals, people with humble origins like Felipe would usually give anything to be members. Of course, he wouldn't admit it, knowing that he doesn't have the slightest chance, anyway. It'd be different if you two got married..."

"You think that the whole country would like to join the Country club, don't you, Sara?" Lavinia said, unable to hide the disgust she felt at her friend's words.

"I don't see why they wouldn't," Sara said, "but in Felipe's case, since he's a young professional, it'd be a great advantage for his career. Nobody can ignore the fact that everybody who is anybody in this country goes to the club."

"Maybe," Lavinia said, "if I can make him see that by marrying me he can be admitted to the club, he'll propose."

"You have to admit it would be to his advantage." Sara said. "More than to yours."

Sara was impossible, Lavinia thought, and she didn't want to go on listening to her; she didn't want to watch her friend growing smaller and smaller.

"I ought to be going now," she said, standing up. "It's almost six, and I still have to go to the grocery store. I don't have anything to eat in the house."

"Then it's decided? You'll go to the ball with us?" asked Sara.

"I don't know if I have a dress that's right," Lavinia said sarcastically. "Everyone's already acquainted with everything I have."

Sara accompanied her to the door. She shouldn't worry about the dress, she told her, not noticing Lavinia's sarcasm. That was the least of her worries. She could get away with it because they'd all be so glad to see her they wouldn't notice.

Yes, Lavinia thought, entering the supermarket, she could get away with it: Sara and Flor. One kind of life and another.

She looked at the sterile, brightly-lit interior of the supermarket. Its recent opening had been a real social event. "The biggest selection in the city." "Even supermarkets from the United States can't beat it," the newspapers said. She took the shiny new cart and pushed it through the aisles, sensing the wave of temptation from the products, the cans with labels in French and English, the different colored jellies in delicate crystal jars, smoked oysters, squid in their ink, red and black caviar.

She bought bread, ham, and cheese. There were few people there at that time. A few women were discussing baby food in the children's aisle.

Women like Sara, she thought, remembering her friend's theories.

The cashier quickly rang up her items, smiling and commenting on how little she had bought. She didn't say anything. Could she have said, Lavinia asked herself, that she was tired, depressed at how she was quickly drifting away from Sara, from what she used to consider 'normal,' without knowing where she was heading, and feeling that the people for whom she now wanted to fight wouldn't accept her either. Of course not, she told herself. The woman would only stare at her uncomfortably without knowing what to say; she would consider her confidences out of place, weird.

She went out. A barefoot boy with patched pants came running to her car. "I watched your car for you," he said, holding out his hand. Lavinia took out a few coins and gave them to him. The boy had snapping black eyes. "Maybe he'll have a chance to be a doctor or a lawyer," Lavinia thought, fitting this image among the others. She didn't understand clearly what was happening to her. The whole street was shouting at her, the landscape was being transformed. It had all been here since she was a little girl, she thought: this state of things. She had always seen it. She even remembered her Aunt Inés, pointing out the contrasts to her, based on her Christian sense of charity. And she'd walked along these streets, indifferent, in the hubbub of her friends, going to and from parties and picnics. If she had looked down on the clubs and fancy salons, it had been because her attitude was one of "To hell with them all." But now her feelings were different, they were sharp and penetrating. It was as if in the theater of life she had changed her comfortable spectator's seat for the actors' stage, the heat of the lights, the responsibility of knowing that the play should end successfully, with the public's applause.

Darkness descended upon the oak trees along the street. She entered the penumbra of her house, thinking about the new sensations she'd experienced on becoming part of the invisible underground fabric of faceless men and women, people crouched and waiting. She thought how different it would be to go to the ball now, how paradoxical it was that they had told her to go, to infiltrate her own people.

She put the bag from the supermarket on the kitchen table. Before putting what she'd bought away in the refrigerator, she took out a bag of bread, ham, and cheese, and made herself a sandwich. She went out onto the patio corridor to eat and read the newspaper.

Felipe wouldn't come today. She felt it in the leaves, in the air. She trusted her intuition, her ability to read what might be in the weight of the atmosphere, the way the flowers moved and the direction of the wind.

Felipe wouldn't come today, and it was better that way, she thought. She was tired.

The stars twinkled in the distance like roguish eyes opening and closing the holes in the universe. "I'm alone," she thought, looking at the immense abyss of darkness. "I'm alone and nobody can tell me for certain if what I am doing is right or wrong." This was the amazing thing about running one's own life, she thought: that chiaroscuro substance shifting in time whose individual duration was a chance like everything else.

÷ ÷ ÷

Now she will not leave the earth like flowers that perish without a trace. Omens are hidden in the night, and she moves among them, at last unsheathing her obsidian, her oak. Little remains now of that dormant woman whom the scent of my blossoms wakened from the heavy sleep of indolence. Slowly Lavinia has touched her depths, reaching the place where lie the noble sentiments the gods give to humans before sending them to live on earth and sow corn. My presence has been a knife to carve away indifference. But hidden within her were the sensations which now flourish and that some day will intone chants that will never die.

• • •

CHAPTER 14

The Vela sisters arrived at the office the next day.

Lavinia was blowing her nose. During the rainy season she often sneezed.

"Do you have a cold?" asked the unmarried sister.

"It's an allergy," she replied, putting the notebook on the desk.

"My husband is allergic, too," Mrs. Vela said. "People prone to allergies have to be careful this time of year. There's a lot of pollen in the air."

General Vela was allergic to pollen.

"And how are those ideas coming?" asked the unmarried sister, whose name was Azucena.

Lavinia took out the initial sketches.

"I've been working a little based on our conversation from the other day. These are some designs for the main areas. Just some ideas to get started." To reduce the amount of bulldozing needed and to make best use of the declivity of the terrain, the house would have three levels. The top level for the entertaining area, then the bedroom area, and then the service area.

She pointed to the main entrance in the blueprint, the stairway system from one level to the other. Every level would have a good view of the landscape, including the one with the service area.

Mrs. Vela had put on a pair of glasses with a thick frame set with tiny sparkling stones. She frowned, running her index finger over the lines in the drawing as if she imagined herself wandering through the house.

Miss Azucena looked intermittently at the plan and at her sister. From time to time she raised her head and smiled. She was one of those people who made an effort to be friendly to everyone. She didn't seem to have any interests of her own; she lived to oil the lives of others to avert friction and squeaking.

Lavinia felt a mixture of sympathy and compassion for her.

"I see you put my husband's study next to the living room," Mrs. Vela said.

"Yes, so he has a good view," replied Lavinia.

"But it seems to me it would be better to put the music room there. My husband doesn't read very much. He prefers to listen to music. If he's going to read a book, he reads it in bed or in the living room..."

"He's not a great reader..." added Miss Azucena.

"And couldn't the billiard room have a view also?" asked Mrs. Vela.

"Well, it's just that there's practically no more room where the view is," replied Lavinia.

"But look at all the service area," Mrs. Vela said. "It's a waste. What do the servants need a view for?"

"If we put the servants' quarters inside, we'll have ventilation problems," explained Lavinia. "During the rainy season the clothes won't dry," she added, so as not to sound too worried about the maids.

"I don't think so. There are windows on both sides," Mrs. Vela said.

"But the air wouldn't circulate enough," insisted Lavinia.

"Well, it would be a bit warm. That's not a big problem... The clothing can be dried outside on the line, and they can bring it in when it starts to rain."

"And if we move the service area to the back of the second level?" asked Azucena.

"We can try," Lavinia agreed. "As I said, this is only a first draft."

"Let's try," Mrs. Vela said.

The bedroom area was only sketched in, Lavinia explained, because she needed to know a little more about the family's habits.

At that moment Julián walked in.

The two women settled in their seats, smiling demurely. Mrs. Vela's bracelets jangled as she straightened a lock of hair.

They liked Lavinia, but Julián was a man.

"How are you doing?" he asked condescendingly.

"We're just beginning," said Azucena, "but it seems that everything is going to go very well. Miss Alarcón has some interesting ideas."

"Very interesting," Mrs. Vela said.

"I don't doubt it," smiled Julián, coming over to look at the blueprint.

"I was explaining about the different levels," Lavinia said. "They wanted to find a way to situate the billiard room so it would have a view. The problem is the ventilation for the service area..."

Julián looked closely at the sketch while Lavinia indicated the possibilities for the location of the laundry room, the ironing room and the maids' room. She noticed the women were watching Julián's expression, as if he were a god about to pass judgment.

She recalled her conversation with Sara. How could she have thought men were not important to housewives?

"General Vela has had a passion for playing pool since he was a boy," Azucena was saying.

"It's his way of relaxing," added Mrs. Vela. "As soon as he gets home he plays a game of pool."

Lavinia imagined him in his T-shirt, the fat man aiming at the multicolored balls, forgetting the "business" of the day: the raids, the firing squads pursuing guerrillas in the mountains, the villages burned by napalm. What did he think about while he played pool?

"I can well understand it would be a good idea to have a picture window with a view of the landscape," Julián said. "I don't think it'll be too difficult. The service area can be put on the first or second level, or we could study other alternatives to distribute the space. As I'm certain Lavinia explained to you, this is only a preliminary sketch. What we're most interested in at this stage is knowing what you think about the style of the design, the solution of building on several levels."

"I think it's fine," Mrs. Vela said. "I'm sure my husband will like it."

"Would you like some coffee?" Lavinia asked, going toward the door.

"No, no thank you," Azucena said. "We only drink coffee in the morning. We go to bed early. If we have coffee now, we won't sleep. Thank you very much anyway."

"I would, please," Julián said.

Lavinia came back after asking Silvia to bring the coffee. She had prepared a minutely detailed list of questions about the family in order to determine the placement and size of the rooms.

"You told me your oldest child is thirteen, didn't you? And that the girl is nine?" she asked.

"Yes, that's right," Mrs. Vela said. "Remember what I told you about the boy's room? About the decoration with aviation motifs? It's important."

"Yes," Miss Azucena said. "He's a very ethereal boy. His love of birds exasperates my brother-in-law. He says if he's interested in flying things, he ought to think about airplanes."

"He *does* like planes," Mrs. Vela said, looking at her sister with a censuring eye. "It's helicopters he's afraid of."

"Yes, yes. That's right," corrected Miss Azucena. "He'd like the room to be decorated with airplane motifs."

"We don't want the girl and the boy to be too close," Mrs. Vela said, putting an end to the strange discussion of birds and planes. "Because of the age difference, they fight a lot. Besides, it's not convenient for the future, when she becomes a woman."

"Besides, they should each have their own bathrooms put in," Miss Montes said.

"And for your daughter's room, do you have any special idea?" Lavinia asked.

"I think it should be a little bigger. You know, we women need more space," Mrs. Vela smiled with feminine complicity. "Something with a coquettish design would be all right."

"And won't your husband want to see the designs?" Lavinia asked, smiling in agreement.

Julián looked at her out of the corner of his eye without saying a word.

"Not the sketches," Mrs. Vela said. "He wants to see the finished preliminary design."

"He wants us to take care of the details. He's a very busy man. He travels a lot, all over the country," added Azucena. "We'd rather save him the trouble."

Lavinia was still smiling imperceptibly as she went back to her office after saying good-bye to the Vela sisters. It was really incredible all that you could find out about people when you designed a house for them.

She was supposed to pick up Sebastián on the corner near a neighborhood cinema.

"At exactly six," Flor had said, "not a minute before or after six." The car radio was tuned to "Radio Minuto." Minute by minute, the radio gave the time they used as the Movement's "official" time. In the background, while the music played, you could hear the persistent tick tock. Every minute the announcer interrupted to give the time in a mechanical voice that resembled a telephone recording.

Following instructions, she drove aimlessly for a while until she was certain nobody was following her. It was hard to get used to constantly checking the rear-view mirror. She didn't feel it was really necessary.

Who would suspect her? But Flor insisted on the need to follow the "security measures" to the letter. She was never to take anything for granted. And she didn't want to make a mistake. She tried not to miss anything, making sure the red car turned at the corner and didn't keep following her.

She miscalculated the time. She reached the meeting place five minutes ahead of the appointed time. She didn't see Sebastián. There were only a few people at a street vendor's stand.

On the radio, with the tick tock in the background, Janis Joplin was singing "Me and Bobby McGee." The tick tock added an urgent note to the music. She drove on past several corners and streets. Darkness was beginning to settle over the city. Women were sitting in rocking chairs at the edge of the street enjoying the cool air. Life, with its dogs and cats, its children playing hopscotch on the sidewalks, continued on its course of days and nights, and those five minutes seemed endless.

Finally the announcer's voice said: "It is exactly six p.m." She turned the corner and entered the street where the cinema was. There, wearing a truck driver's cap, was Sebastián, at the designated place.

She drove towards him until she stopped at his side. She stuck her head out the window, pretending to recognize a friend and greet him. Sebastián came up also pretending it was a casual encounter.

"Where're you heading?" she asked.

He mentioned some place.

"If you want, I can give you a lift."

Sebastián got into the car, and they pulled away from the curb.

"Did you check everything well?" he asked Lavinia.

"Too well. I've been driving around for almost fifteen minutes. I got here too early."

"That's better than getting here late," he said. "You'll get better at calculating the time more accurately. It's not a good idea to arrive too early, nor too late. It can look suspicious if you drive around too much. If you arrive too early, the best thing is to take a long swing outside the contact area and return two or three minutes before the designated time. You have to understand the real meaning of kilometers per hour and know the city well, so you can figure out your travel time. But you'll learn all that little by little. Miscalculating is normal at first. Now take the south highway and don't forget to keep checking the rear view mirror. How's Vela's house going?"

"We turned in the first sketches. I proposed to go and explain them to the general, but his wife suggested that we wait until we have the complete preliminary sketches. Apparently Vela's on a trip in the countryside."

"He's in charge of the counterinsurgency campaign," Sebastián said. "How long does it take to build a house?"

"That depends," replied Lavinia. "From the time the blueprints are approved, it can take six or eight months. It depends on how efficient the contractor is..."

"So if the blueprints are approved next month, the house could be finished in December?"

"Yes."

Sebastián was silent.

"General Vela is allergic to pollen," Lavinia said, proudly offering her information. "He plays pool after work; he doesn't like to read, he'd rather listen to music. It seems his teenage son likes birds and that exasperates his father. He wants to turn the boy's interest to airplanes. But the boy's afraid of helicopters... The family goes to bed early."

"Very good...very good," Sebastián said, smiling. "Don't get too close to the car ahead of us. We always have to keep a good margin to maneuver in case of an emergency, especially if there's a clandestine person in the car."

Lavinia obeyed. She felt the wave of fear, her adrenaline rising and falling. It was so easy to forget that Sebastián was a "clandestine." Easy to think she was riding with a person like herself, practically without a care in the world. She looked in the rear view mirror, recovering her sense of caution, amazed to think she was the one transporting a "clandestine" in her car.

"From now on," Sebastián said, picking up the thread of the conversation again, "you will write a report on each one of your meetings with the women. Try to do it as soon as possible after every meeting. There are important details you can forget if you let too much time go by. Make just one original, with no copy, without mentioning any names, and give it to me every week. As Flor said, every detail is important. When the project is further along, insist on the meeting with Vela, in his house. You can also try to get in good with his sister-in-law, the old maid, try to get to know her better...make her trust you.... By the way, are you ready for the ball yet?"

"Yes, but I don't really know what I'm supposed to do there."

"Be nice."

"Hey, Sebastián, don't joke around..."

"I'm not joking. I mean it. You should give the impression you're happy to be at the ball, happy to return to those circles. It's important for the people who know you to think your rebel-without-a-cause stage is over. That's the most important thing. As for the rest, you should be alert and listen to people's comments, anything that seems useful. Once you're there you'll get a feeling for what's important; you'll develop your conspiratorial skills, you'll get information."

The climate changed as they went up the mountain road. A cold wind filtered through the windows and made the trees sway and lean out over the dark highway.

"And how do you feel?" he asked her, changing his tone, taking off the truck driver's cap.

Sebastián never ceased to amaze her. He displayed a constant mixture of toughness and tenderness although perhaps it wasn't exactly toughness. It was more like an executive's tone, precise and exact when he dealt with matters related to the Movement, then noticeably softening when the conversation turned to personal things.

"I'm fine," she replied.

"I know you're fine," he said, "I can see that. But how do you feel? How are your confusions coming?"

"So-so," she said, thinking about Sara, the ball, the remarks of her friends, the feet in the hospital, Lucrecia. Things that would seem like unimportant details to him; they'd bore him.

"And how did Felipe react when he found out you were involved?"

"Badly at first. He said I wasn't mature enough; I should go on collaborating through him, but he finally had to accept it."

"It'd be nice if someone invented a 'maturity meter.' Maybe they'd throw all of us out of the Movement..."

They laughed.

"Now you shouldn't give into the temptation of consulting him about your tasks. It's good that he's informed in general about the Vela house business, but you should keep each other compartmentalized. That's how he'll come to respect you and come to see whether you're mature enough or not. Usually we men have difficulty accepting the idea that we should share certain things with women. It affects our competitive spirit. There's a degree of satisfaction in feeling important in front of the women you love. That's machismo, you know."

"You don't seem like a male chauvinist," Lavinia said, smiling as she looked at him.

"Of course I'm a male chauvinist. It's just that I hide it better than Felipe. I'd like to have my little woman waiting for me too..." he said in a slightly teasing tone.

Lavinia wondered if he had a girlfriend. She knew nothing about him, nor would she know anything about him, she thought. She could surmise that he was from a poor background because of some small things about his behavior: a certain dragging of his s's that rural people had, things he said. Sebastián avoided answering personal questions.

"You don't give me that impression. Flor told me how you got her to join..."

"We're all chauvinists, Lavinia. Even you women. It's a matter of realizing we shouldn't be. But it's easier said than done. I try..."

"I don't agree that we women are chauvinists," Lavinia interrupted. "The thing is we've been forced to get used to a certain type of behavior...you men..."

"It's the eternal question of the chicken and the egg. Which came first, the chicken or the egg? What's certain is that women teach their sons to be chauvinists. I say that out of my own experience."

"I'm not denying that, but it's not that we women are chauvinists, it's that that's how men arranged the world...and then they want to blame us... Could you close your window a bit? I'm cold."

"I don't know, I don't know." He closed the window. "If I'd been a woman, I think I'd have tried to inculcate a different kind of behavior in my children even if in just in my own self-interest."

"I think you'd have done just like your mother."

"Perhaps. These are matters for endless discussion. The only thing that's clear is that we have to try and change the situation. The Movement's program talks about women's liberation. For the moment, I try to avoid discriminating against my compañeros who are women. But it's hard. As soon as you put men and women together in a safe house, the women take on the household chores without being asked, as if it were the natural thing to do. They go around asking their compañeros for their dirty clothes..."

"You have to take that road over there to the right," he added.

They drove along a narrow, unpaved road that curved through coffee groves and hemp brake. The car windows became tinged with the mist. Where could we be heading? Lavinia thought, recognizing they were in the vicinity of the coffee haciendas near her grandfather's.

"Let me off here."

She braked immediately, surprised. There were no houses, nothing, along the road.

"Are you going to stay here?" she asked, startled.

"Don't worry. I'm going someplace nearby. I can walk the rest of the way."

"Don't you want me to come pick you up?"

"No. They'll give me a ride back from here."

"Here" was nowhere. Maybe there was a house farther up ahead, Lavinia thought, still uncomfortable about having to leave him on the narrow road, cold, lonely.

"You can turn around here," Sebastián directed, pointing to a widening in the road. "I'll get out to guide you."

He got out and helped her back up in the tight space.

When the car was headed back toward the city, he came over to the window.

"See you," he said, patting her on the head. "Thanks a lot. Don't forget the report. I'll let you know through Flor when we'll see each other again."

"Be careful," Lavinia said. "This is a really lonely place."

Sebastián smiled, waving good-bye as he gestured to her to leave.

"Dance a lot at the party," she managed to hear him say.

On the way back, Lavinia speeded up. The curves came one after another. She liked driving on the highway at night— it gave her a feeling of freedom. She was happy, satisfied with herself. She finally felt useful. Useful for what? she suddenly thought, when she remembered Azucena's face, her vivacious, complaisant eyes, as she was busy smoothing the edges off her sister's roughness, making the fit between the Vela family and the world an easier one.

What would the Movement use information about them for? she wondered, slightly uncomfortable at the thought of how easily detail after detail flowed from the sisters, setting the stage for the family, their habits, their dislikes, their allergies, the conflicts with the teenage son. She'd like to meet him, she thought. (And she noting it all in her mind, passing information...) Felipe had reproached her for caring about the life of the General and his family. But it was inevitable, she thought. Violence was not natural. It was hard for her to imagine Sebastián, Flor, or Felipe firing a weapon. Serene trees taking aim. She couldn't visualize them. She surely wouldn't think that about General Vela when she met him. Military officers had a different air about them. They were trained to see the people as a shapeless, faceless mass. How did they manage to forget that they themselves came from that mass? Most soldiers came from poor backgrounds; they were peasants. General Vela himself was no aristocrat. His wife and sister-in-law must be the daughters of some school teacher or government employee.

Perhaps the process she was going through was that undergone by the Velas except inversely. They would learn to despise their origin and everything that reminded them of their childhood surroundings, the dire straits of poverty.

Once they'd settled into abundance, they would hate the memory of their own kind; they would feel the need to demonstrate the distance that separated them...

The city lights blinked in a long line as she reached the curve on the hill that went back down into the heat. She felt a surge of apprehension. She would have liked to go back to make sure everything was all right along the road where she had left Sebastián. She didn't want to think some General Vela would pierce that smile, immobilizing it forever.

✦ ✦ ✦

The man she fears must be like the captains of the invaders. He must want to baptize everyone. Propagate faith in other gods.

My mother used to tell how in the beginning our calachunis, our chiefs, organized caravans to go to meet the Spaniards. They took them gifts, taguizte, the gold which fascinated them. She went with my father on one of those embassies and she lived to say that said it had been a spectacle. There were nearly five hundred people carrying birds, offerings in their hands. They bore ten pavilions of white feathers. Seventeen women with taguizte adornments marched beside the calachunis, the chieftains.

My mother remembered the Captain. He was standing in the tent where they deposited their offerings. He was tall, with curly golden hair. He spoke with our head calachuni. He asked him for more gold. He told him they should be baptized, renounce their pagan gods. Our people promised to return in three days.

The head calachuni called the men as soon as they had left the encampment of the Spaniards. There were few invaders, and they looked weak and defenseless when they were not riding their four-footed beasts.

Three days later the calachunis returned with four or five thousand warriors, not to be baptized, as the invaders wished, but to wage war. And that was how they fell on them, causing great confusion and many dead and wounded. And other calachunis chased them as well when they fled through their lands, taking back the gifts they had given them, because they were not gods and did not deserve reverence or adoration.

The invaders fled. On long marches where many of them perished from our arrows, they managed to get back to their ships, their huge floating houses. They left. There was celebration, my mother said, and the people drank pulque, danced, played the flying game, volador.

But the Spaniards returned several months later. And they brought more ships, more men with hair on their faces, more beasts and firesticks.

Our people realized it was not enough to win just one battle.

• • •

Ball gowns were taken from her closet. She recalled her mother's joyful face while, traveling through Europe, she prepared her for the "return to Faguas and her debut," with trips to Spanish, English, and Italian department stores. For Lavinia, recently graduated from architectural school, it was interesting from the professional point of view to observe her mother trapped in the buildings overflowing with merchandise, the racks with hundreds of dresses, without any other distractions. It was interesting to see her succumb to the basic architectural concept in stores and modern commercial centers: wherever she looked, there were more and more dresses, rows upon rows of shoes, impeccable islands of cosmetics, beautiful store clerks with perfect makeup, looking like movable mannequins. The range of vision had been carefully studied.

"You have loads of beautiful dresses," Lucrecia was saying, helping her lay them on the bed. "You can go to the ball in any of these."

Lavinia didn't know by what means of association, she thought of Scarlett O' Hara in one of the first scenes from *Gone With the Wind*. Lucrecia was the black maid, spreading out Scarlett's ball gown on the bed.

Except that Lucrecia wasn't fat, nor black. Her brown skin still showed the remains of pallor from the hemorrhage that had nearly killed her. Her broad hips hid her slenderness.

"I'm remembering a movie I saw," Lavinia said.

"Me, too," Lucrecia said, "a movie that was called *Sissi* about a princess who marries a king. That's what you'll look like when you put on one of these dresses."

They both laughed. Lavinia remembered the movie, too: a fairy-tale romance. It had been all the rage when she was in high school. Every girl back then wanted to look like Romy Schneider.

"It must be wonderful to be a princess," Lucrecia said, looking admiringly at the bright-red peau de soie dress that she'd just taken out of the closet.

"I don't think so," smiled Lavinia. "I believe that in real life the king in the movie was assassinated."

"You don't say."

"Besides, remember life isn't just putting on pretty dresses. There are more important things..."

"When you have pretty dresses..." Lucrecia said. "But one shouldn't be envious of what one doesn't have," she added, moving over to make room for the dresses.

"You think being poor or rich is a fate sealed by God, don't you?" Lavinia asked.

"Yes," Lucrecia said. "Some of us are born poor, others are born rich. Life is a 'vale of tears.' If you're poor but honest, you know that when you die you'll have a better chance of going to heaven."

Lavinia sat on the bed, talking to Lucrecia about how numbing Christian "resignation" was, how unfair it was for anyone, no matter how bad they'd been during their lifetime, to be able to be saved just by repenting at the last moment. Not that she didn't respect her faith in God, she told her, but religions were man-made. Didn't she think it was unfair that resignation was always prescribed for poor people?

"Don't you think everyone should have the chance to live better during their lives and not just in Heaven?" Lavinia asked.

"Maybe so," Lucrecia said thoughtfully. "But the fact is that the world's already the way it is, and one doesn't have any choice but to be resigned and think that it will be better in Heaven..."

"But something could be done here on earth," Lavinia said.

"Well, yes. Study, work...," Lucrecia said.

"Or fight," added Lavinia, in a low voice, unsure if she should say it, waiting for Lucrecia's reaction.

"So they'll kill you? I'd rather keep on living in poverty than die. This dress has holes here along the hem where the mice chewed it," Lucrecia pointed out, showing it to her.

"I already took out another one that's been nibbled on," Lavinia said, feeling slightly ridiculous about having such a conversation among party dresses.

"You can cut them off," Lucrecia said, examining them. "They're still good to wear."

Lavinia put the dress on the bed and went over Lucrecia, feeling the sudden urge to make her feel that something could change, as small as it might be, even symbolically.

"Lucrecia," she said. "I'm going to ask you a favor."

"Tell me, tell me, Miss Lavinia." Lucrecia looked at her in surprise.

"I don't want you to call me 'Miss Lavinia' any more. Just call me by my first name."

"But I've always called you Miss Lavinia... I don't think I can get used to it, I don't think I can do it..." she said, lowering her eyes, embarrassed and blushing.

"Even if it's hard for you, try," Lavinia said, "please. I want you to stop treating me as if I were an old lady."

"You're my employer... How can I call you by your first name. It's not respectful. Please don't ask me to do that..."

"Well, if you insist, I'll do the same to you. I'll call you 'Miss Lucrecia.'"

They looked at one another and started to laugh. Lucrecia laughed nervously.

"I can't, I can't," she said. "How could you call me 'Miss Lucrecia'?" and she began to laugh again.

"You'll see."

"Oh, no, for heaven's sake, what's gotten into you?"

"Now we're going to be friends," Lavinia said. "I want us to be friends."

Lucrecia looked at her with a sad light in her eyes. Friends? Her eyes asked, friends?

"Whatever you say," Lucrecia replied, lowering her gaze, not knowing what to do, squeezing her apron as if her hands were wet and she needed to dry them. "I'm going to go get the clothes off the line," she said. "It might rain." And she left the room quickly, looking toward the patio.

They'll never accept me, Lavinia thought, sitting on top of the party gowns, looking at the shadows of the gathering dusk. I shouldn't have said anything to her. Who am I to say things like that?

There was a week left before the ball when the forensic doctor, a key witness in the trial against the warden of La Concordia Prison, was assassinated. Lavinia clearly remembered having listened to the trial on the radio as she was in a taxi on her way to her first day at work. During the days of the trial, she, like many others, had admired the doctor's courage. And like most people, she feared for his life. In Faguas it was inconceivable that there could be an honest soldier who sooner or later did not have to pay for his honesty with exile or death.

Captain Flores had been given the bill very quickly.

Indignation enveloped the city in the cloak of restrained anger. Police cars, alert, multiplied on the street corners.

Dr. Flores had been found dead, riddled with bullets, on top of his car on the road to the provincial city of San Antonio, a city where he used to go to visit relatives. The authorities did not provide an identification of the supposed assassin. Major Lara had been given parole for good behavior that weekend. Nobody doubted that he was the criminal. He was mentioned in the headline of the extra morning edition of the opposition paper, "La Verdad," which was passed from person to person in the drafting room.

The doctor's burial would take place the next morning.

There would be multitudes. The Great General was not going to be able to prevent the hundreds of people from attending the burial ceremony as a sign of protest. How could he stop it, since it was for a military officer? Not even the dead man himself could stop his funeral from turning into—as everything seemed to indicate—the largest demonstration since the famous campaign Sunday for the Greens, where a massacre had occurred.

Felipe was talking on the phone when Lavinia came into his office.

After agreeing to meet with someone at 'the spot' next morning, he hung up and looked at her.

"Ever since the trial we've all known this would happen," Lavinia said. "We knew Major Lara would kill him as soon as he got out of prison."

"But it wasn't possible for those who suspected it to stop it," Felipe replied.

"Are you going to go tomorrow?" Lavinia asked.

"Yes," Felipe said. "I'm going with the students from my class."

"I don't know who I'm going to go with," she said, with determination, "but, anyway, I'm going."

This time she wouldn't have to watch from a distance while the funeral procession marched toward the cemetery. Now it was different, Lavinia thought, remembering the slow voice of the doctor as he gave his testimony. The Great General would have to recognize the people's rejection of this crime, undoubtedly committed with his approval. And now she would participate in the rejection.

"I was talking with Sebastián about precisely that. He told me you were not to go to the funeral under any circumstances. You have to remain 'clean' now more than ever."

"But..." Lavinia said, incredulous.

"I'm not the one who says so," Felipe said. "Sebastián just told me. He asked me to relay it to you."

"But...why not?" she asked, sitting down in front of Felipe's desk. "I don't understand."

"It's easy, Lavinia. If you try, you can see why. The media, a lot of security agents, army patrols, are all going to be there...it's even possible Vela will appear. It's not good for him, or anyone who might tell him, to see you. It wouldn't be good for you to appear on television or in a photograph in the papers."

She nodded her head. It was understandable. She ought to be able to see this, she told herself. But it was cruel. Since she had been in the Movement, trying to assimilate the idea of abandoning her status quo, of trying to become another kind of person, overcome the confining individualism of her class, she was eager for the moment to arrive when she would participate more actively. Break out of the barrier of fear and accept the head-on challenge, not just the theoretical commitment of her decision. But things seemed to work in reverse. She was being told to use her position as an architect to gather information from the Velas, to return to her habitual circles, attend the ball, not to participate in the march. She'd never expected it to be like this, she thought. She never imagined it like that. Apparently, the only way she could be useful to the Movement was by being who she was.

"This is frustrating," she said, slumping into a chair. "I thought my life would be radically changed...that I could participate, not find myself on the sidelines as always."

She remained on the periphery with Sara and Adrián. In their house, expectantly, they sat in the patio following the news, beside the ferns and jalacates garden. In the streets the silent multitude was marching toward the cemetery between a line of soldiers in full battle gear who pretended to be there for the burial.

Silence hovered tensely over the city. Offices and businesses had closed their doors. Nobody had gone to work, even when the official media insisted everything was "normal" and asked people to go on about their business and not to fall into the hands of people trying to "provoke" them and "take advantage of the regrettable incident."

The military deployment had started early in the morning. As she drove to Sara and Adrián's house, Lavinia saw the olive-green trucks crammed with soldiers heading toward the avenue where the funeral cortege would pass. As if in mourning, tanks sporting funeral wreaths on their metal snouts had been posted on the corners near the cemetery.

Acting as if they were conferring military honors upon the dead man, planes had been flying overhead since dawn.

The official radio station and the official television station were broadcasting the funeral, making it into the "honorable funeral ceremony" befitting a distinguished military officer.

The television cameras avoided the throng that would have filled the camera frame, focusing instead on the hearse and the red, tearful faces of the wife and children.

On both sides of the street, flanking the crowded route of those attending the funeral, the line of soldiers was visible, at attention, their bayonets unsheathed.

A single shout, any rebellious movement on the part of the crowd, and there would be a massacre of unimaginable consequences. They were surrounded, forced into immobility, into silent protest. Any other behavior would be suicidal.

Hushed, Lavinia, Sara, and Adrián watched the tiny screen silently, almost without moving, united by the tension.

"I hope nobody does anything, I hope nobody does anything," Sara was saying.

And Lavinia pictured Felipe with his students, marching in silence, waiting for the right moment.

"Nobody will do anything," Adrián said. "The Great General planned it all out. No one can do anything."

The funeral procession was entering the cemetery.

"Look, Lavinia," Adrián said, "that's General Vela."

He was standing near the headstone. A stout man with a protruding belly and shiny black hair carefully combed. The camera focused on him as it passed.

He had a walkie-talkie in his hand. She felt repugnance. He was probably heading up the whole operation.

The coffin was lowered into the grave. A military band played the notes of the National Anthem. The gravediggers set the headstone in place. The crowd was beginning to disperse when the silence of the funeral procession was broken: shouts, slogans came from behind the tombstones. Assassins! Assassin Army! Down with the Great General. Long live the National Liberation Movement! Shots in the air. Soldiers running. People running, Scattering. The television transmission went off. A slide with the photograph of the dead man appeared on the screen, and the announcer's voice said: "This has been the transmission of the funeral services for Captain Ernesto Flores."

Adrián turned the television off. The three of them went out into the street, looking around, pretending they were doing something. Scattered shots could be heard in the distance.

"Oh my God!" exclaimed Sara. "Now what's going to happen? We'd better close the door, Adrián."

They went back into the living room.

Lavinia went into the kitchen to get some water. Her mind projected images of bloody persecution. From afar she tried to send Felipe warning messages so he wouldn't take any risks; it was useless. There were too many soldiers in the streets. It was a losing proposition. Although maybe Felipe wouldn't think like her, she told herself. They didn't think that way. They measured risks another way.

She went out to the living room. Adrián and Sara were sitting in the rocking chairs, absently looking at the garden as if they were not seeing anything. They looked like a posed portrait with their fine, well-cut clothes, in the midst of the furniture, ashtrays and decorations that were carefully placed, the plants with their shiny leaves, the tiny interior garden with the begonias in huge pots. She could have chosen this, Lavinia thought, looking at them as if she were hypnotized, as if she had entered another dimension: this could have been her life. Everything had been designed so she too could have ended up in a house like this, with a husband like Adrián, smoking pensively. Somewhere along the way the path had diverged, and she was on the other side, looking at them as if through a mirror that would never reflect her, imprisoned in anguish that she had to keep secret. that had no place in this other, untouched world.

"I'm leaving," she said suddenly.

"What do you mean you're leaving?" Adrián was practically shouting. "Are you crazy?"

"Nothing will happen to me," Lavinia said, getting her purse. "Nothing's happening near my house."

"But why go home alone?" interjected Sara, standing up, alarmed.

"I don't know," Lavinia said. "I just know I can't stand being here and not doing anything."

"But you're with us," Sara said. "Calm down."

She knew that was the wisest thing to do. Calm down. But she couldn't. She couldn't stay there. She had to leave.

"This is no game, Lavinia," Adrián said. "As long as I'm here, you're not going to leave this house."

"You're not my husband," replied Lavinia. "And it's not up to you to decide what I'm going to do. I'm leaving. Let me go."

More shots were heard. Frantic, Lavinia tried to leave, but Adrián got between her and the door. And he was strong; even though he wasn't very tall, his body was strong and muscular.

"Let's be reasonable, Lavinia, please," Adrián said. "Why do you want to leave?"

She couldn't answer. She just felt the need to get out of there. How could she explain it to them? How could she explain that she didn't want to be in that world she no longer felt a part of? But, little by little, the impulse gave way to reason. Why did she want to leave? She couldn't join the protesters who at that moment must be in the streets, perhaps setting fire to buses, expressing the rage of having had to accompany the corpse through the waiting soldiers in silence... She couldn't do anything except wait. Just like them.

+ + +

Why did I push her? What led me to push her outside, there where the sounds of battle could be heard? I hardly know myself. Did I feel the deep need to measure my own strength? Or was it that the firesticks echoed within me?

It should not have happened. I feel discouraged inside her. I do not know these surroundings, how they work, their rules. I do not know how to measure these unfamiliar dangers.

I thought I was far from the urges of life now. But I am not. When my desire is very intense, she feels it with the strength of my imagination.

I must be cautious. I will quench myself in her blood.

• • •

"I don't know what came over me," Lavinia said later.

CHAPTER 15

• • •

A few days later things returned to normal. The momentary agitation gave way to tense calm. That's how it was in Faguas. Energy accumulated, burst forth suddenly —like an earthquake—and then the landscape resumed its familiar appearance.

Nothing spectacular had happened. Small notations for the dark side of the country's history. Three deaths. A few dozen wounded. Prisoners. Burned busses. Stores with broken windows. The mediation of the bishop. "The army is maintaining order throughout the entire nation."

Felipe and his students returned to their evening classes. None of them had been beaten or jailed. They were not in the ranks of the most belligerent. On this occasion they had kept their risks to a minimum.

"It would have been suicide," Felipe said, admitting for once that Lavinia had been right. "For each one of us, unarmed, there were ten soldiers armed to the teeth. The ones who shouted were provocateurs."

The preparations for the ball continued.

Lavinia went to pick up her dress at the dry cleaner's. "Fresh as dawn in less than an hour," the place announced. It was the only establishment that had such quick service. The owners were friendly, prosperous, blond immigrants from one of the small neighboring countries. A perfect married and business team, moving diligently through the long rows of suits carefully placed in long plastic bags, which had the design of a red flower and the name of the laundry repeated all over them.

From the counter, while she waited, she observed the profusion of evening dresses and tuxedos, proof that the ball was near; demonstrations, deaths and gunfire had already been forgotten.

The clothes looked strange, draped from the rigid hangers in rows on metal bars. While the clerk took her receipt and disappeared into a jungle of clothing, looking for the matching slip, she thought how soon those inanimate fabrics would come to life, how soon they would be wrapped around slender or ample bodies, skin lovingly cared for with almond cream and other delicate things and hidden from the sun in order to exhibit itself as white as milk and ivory.

It would be interesting to see the ball with different eyes, she thought, be inside and outside the show at the same time.

"Here it is," said the clerk, tearing her from her reflections.

When she got home, the telephone was ringing. She ran to pick it up, fearing that it had been ringing for a long time, that it was Felipe and he wouldn't get hold of her.

"Lavinia?" Her mother's unmistakable voice startled her. "Lavinia?"

"Yes. It's me."

"Well, I ran into Sara today, and she told me you're going to go to the ball..."

"So?"

"Well, nothing, I just wanted to know if you're really going to go..."

"Yes, I'm going."

"Oh, honey, you don't know how happy that makes us... You don't know how happy we'd be if you went with us..."

"I can't, Mother, I've promised Sara and Adrián I would go with them."

"But they wouldn't mind, I'm sure. Don't you think it's better for you to go with us than with a pair of newlyweds...it would look better."

"They've been married for over a year, Mother."

"Yes, I know, but that's not a long time. They're still newlyweds... People are going to talk if we arrive separately. There was already enough talk when you left home... You're still a young, unmarried girl."

She should have suspected it. The thought had crossed her mind, but she had put it out of her head. In spite of everything, she hadn't thought her mother would call her, even though she suspected how worried she would be about her daughter showing up alone at the ball.

She should have warned Sara not to say anything to her. She'd never stop being amazed at the things that worried her mother.

"Don't worry about it so much, Mother, I'm grown up now... What can people say that they haven't said already?"

"Your father and I would like so much to take you. It's unnatural for us to be so distant, it doesn't look good at all..."

After so many months of being apart, it had finally dawned on her mother that "it was unnatural."

"But that is the reality, Mother. The ball isn't going to change it."

"But maybe now you will listen to us. After all, we're your parents. We can't go on like this all our lives."

The ball, the return of the prodigal son. One thing led to the other.

"I can't go with you, Mother. I already promised Sara. We can see each other there. I can sit with you for a while."

It wouldn't be a bad idea to sit with them for a while. It would improve her reputation.

"It's just that it's not the same, honey."

"Mother, don't insist, please..."

"All right, all right, but you'll sit with us for a while? You promise?"

"Yes, Mother, I promise. How's Dad?"

"Working, as usual. He hasn't come home from the office yet."

"Say hello to him for me."

"Yes, honey. Are you sure you can't go to the ball with us? I'm certain Sara wouldn't mind..."

"No mother, I already told you no. Let's not fight about it."

"All right, honey, all right. You'll sit with us then?"

"Yes, Mother."

"Good. I'm very happy you're coming to the ball."

"Yes, Mother."

"So I'll see you there?"

"Yes, Mother."

"See you soon."

"See you soon, Mother."

She looked at the receiver, unable to put it back. The shrill sound of the dial tone seemed to spiral up her hand.

Her mother was tall and beautiful. When Lavinia was a child, she felt a vague sensation of wonder and pride whenever she saw her. At school on parents' night, when her friends' mothers were sitting in the rows of chairs, she thought how great her mother would look among them, how much taller, how much more beautiful. But meetings annoyed her mother, and she never attended any of them. "They're useless," she would say, "a waste of time."

Beauty consumed all her free time, before and after playing cards with her friends, or entertaining her father and his friends.

The closest they had ever been was when her mother arrived in Europe to outfit her with the appropriate "trousseau" for the return to Faguas. On that occasion, she'd dragged her on long walks and shopping sprees, talking untiringly of styles and customs, hotels and restaurants.

She was always a distant, unreachable figure for Lavinia.

When she sought the shelter of her mother's arms as a little girl, afraid because of some scary story the nursemaid told her, she was met with an irritated expression and a "don't be a crybaby."

From the time she was a child, she had sensed that her mother didn't love her.

Fortunately she had Aunt Inés, she thought, wiping away the tears that began to well up and blur the outlines of the furniture.

Because her Aunt Inés did like to hug her, cuddle her, give her sweets. She liked to bring her up into her bed and tell her stories while she stroked her hair. Like Lavinia, she had an enormous hunger for affection.

"She's going to spoil her," her mother would say, and Lavinia would panic, thinking they'd keep her aunt away from her.

But her father defended his sister. "She's so alone. Poor thing. The child is the only thing that cheers her up."

"Your aunt rescued you from abandonment," said Natalia, her Spanish friend.

But nothing could rescue one from the absence of a mother.

And that was what her mother was: a permanent absence.

She ought to have known she would call her about the ball. It was impossible for her not to be worried about what her friends would say.

It was incredible, though, that she'd called her only for that.

Only for that.

She realized that she still held the receiver in her hand. The long dial tone had shifted to an intermittent beeping. She hung up and continued crying.

She cried for everything there was to cry for.

She awoke depressed. She got even more depressed after going with Sara to the hairdresser's in the afternoon. The only thing that compensated for the wait and the spectacle of all those women with fine, manicured feet, gathered in the reception area, was her stroke of luck at running into the Vela sisters. They had come in with the air of great ladies, preparing for the ball which the Great General was giving the same night in the recreation club of the armed forces. "My husband has applied for membership in the country club, but he did it such a short time ago, we probably won't be able to attend the ball until next year," Mrs. Vela had said with the tone of certainty she was far from feeling, while Sara looked at her deprecatingly. "The Great General doesn't stop at anything," Sara said afterward, coming over and talking to her under her breath, "since they don't accept his officers in the club, now he holds dances for them the same day at the military casino so they won't feel slighted..."

Lavinia only thought about how perfect it had been to run into them at the smartest hairdressers in the city and be able to tell them she was going to the ball.

When she got home from work, she poured herself a tall glass of orange juice with ice cubes and went into her room to rest a while before getting dressed for the ball. She stretched out on the bed, relaxing her muscles, imagining herself on a raft floating on the water beneath a splendid sun. She needed to relax because she was tense, keyed up. As if in a film, she pictured herself dressed in red, entering the club's large halls: the gazes resting on her, glasses clinking, the sound of the orchestra from the terrace. She would look at them from afar. She would feel the power of being different. She imagined her behavior, her feet moving the hem of the dress with the defiant thrust of a flamenco dancer, the soft fabric brushing across her heels above the shiny marble squares of the dance floor. Boys from her childhood, now grown-up men, embracing her stiffly, with the odor of cologne and cleaning chemicals on the lapels of their tuxedos.

She would smile coquettishly, tell them about her life as an architect, give the conversation the necessary dose of boredom to make them think that the "little girl" had gotten over her curiosity about the new toys "rebellion" and "independence."

She turned in the bed. Her body was warm and sweaty. Solitude was boundless on her bed that afternoon. She couldn't explain to anybody the strange excitement she felt at the thought of sheathing herself in that red dress again with its low-cut bodice. Parading herself would be a pleasure now. Almost a revenge. Showing off now that no one could touch her or penetrate her intimacy, threaten her with endless marriages, servitude disguised as success. It was a sharp, contradictory feeling. There was no denying she felt pleasure at the thought of seeing some of her friends. But it was a Machiavellian pleasure. Just like the one she felt imagining the faces of the young professionals who, in front of her, would discard all their pretensions of civility, the respect they showed prudent virgins, and would allow themselves to be surrounded by her calculated seduction, only to sense finally that they had nothing to hope for, that it had been only a game. She would have nothing to do with them. They swam in opposite directions in the waters of fate and destinations. And the certainty of that, although pleasant, was disquieting, too.

Was she deceiving herself? she wondered. Was she creating for herself the role of a romantic heroine, a pose as stupid as those her friends created, pretending to be prudent virgins? No, she thought. It wasn't the same. For her, going to the ball was a final return, a return in order to emerge from within, enter her original milieu like an outsider so she could abandon it completely, betray it, conspire against it to make that whole tinsel world disappear.

And that was as it should be. She wasn't sorry. She didn't want it to continue, but she still couldn't help remembering the sounds of the milieu that she had belonged to her whole life and that would one day explode, disappear...and when that happened, she would be on the other side, beside the black box where one pushed the detonator, where hands would light the fuse.

And perhaps like Felipe, like the men who were brought up with a definite identity, a tough hide that was difficult to rip away, she would bear her original skin, concealed, crouching behind the new identity she desired.

She closed her eyes and felt a wave of anguish. She wanted to cry for feeling so alone, so lost in this no-man's-land, for not being one thing or the other, for wielding only a wish, a will, an abstract ardor infusing her with certainty—

the certainty that in her magnetic field the needle pointed to a definitive north. She was advancing, stumbling step by step in that direction, shedding her old skin, compelled by a mysterious, inexplicable force.

She finished the last of her orange juice.

Felipe's key turned in the lock.

"Hellooo...hey,...Lavinia?" she heard him call, looking for her in the house.

"Here I am, in the bedroom."

Felipe came in. He was flushed. There were patches of sweat on his shirt. He leaned over to give her a kiss. She smelled his neck. She loved the scent of his sweat. There was something primitive and sensual about sweaty skin, the salty taste, the sea breeze smell.

"Your hair smells delicious," Felipe said, and let his hand glide over her head.

"Herbal shampoo, no less," Lavinia said, smiling. "The problem is most of the women at the ball are going to smell like that tonight! If you were a dog and you were looking for me by my scent tonight at midnight, you might end up running into one of the Vela sisters' hair. We went to the same beauty salon. The Great General also organized his own 'debutante' ball tonight for the army, at the Military Recreation Club..."

"So the Great General is giving a ball, too..." Felipe said, sitting on the edge of the bed.

"Yes. According to Sara, it's a way of compensating them for the historic contempt of the directorate of the country club."

"It's a good move...to entertain them so they don't feel rejected by the aristocrats, to give them their own social life. The Great General is no fool. He knows when a circus is necessary."

"And it's going to be a full circus, according to the Vela sisters."

"It surely will be a juicy topic of conversation at your party. Besides, it will be interesting to know what the aristocracy thinks about it. You have work to do."

"The aristocracy will never accept them. It needs them but despises them. Everybody knows that."

"But until now, they have never competed with each other. They each had their own well-defined territories. The more threatened the Great General feels, the more he strengthens his people. Recently he's given them businesses that compete with the aristocracy. Your friends can't be very happy about that... I'm convinced that as the Great General works to strengthen his military caste, he's creating contradictions even he himself doesn't imagine. Contradictions we need to know how to calculate in order to make them work for us."

"And you think the Great General really feels threatened?"

"I think he's worried. He thought he could root out our presence in the mountains with ease, just as he did with the military efforts of the Greens, but it hasn't turned out that way. We're growing. He's had to send a lot of troops to the mountains. They've had significant losses. And the demonstration the other day...they're nervous."

"But I still don't think he feels threatened."

"No, not yet. But even his men run greater risks now, and he feels he should compensate them for it. Keeping the army happy is becoming more and more important to him."

"I'd love to be a fly on the wall at the dance at the Military Casino...," Lavinia said. "I wonder how things will go with 'Miss Azucena'..."

"I don't think she'll suffer much," Felipe said. "She seems content in her role as Mrs. Vela's sister, at least according to what you say."

"That's true, she doesn't seem unhappy. She has her sister's advantages, without the disadvantages."

"You should get to know her better. If she's not happy, we could even find her a boyfriend," Felipe said, winking mischievously.

"Is that the dress you're going to wear?" he added, going to the closet and inspecting it through the plastic dry cleaners' bag.

"Yes, I should start getting dressed. It's six-thirty."

"But they aren't coming to get you until eight o'clock, are they?"

"Right. But I'm going to take a shower and put on my makeup... I don't like to rush."

Impulsively, Lavinia came over to him and put her head on his chest. She needed Felipe's arms around her.

"I'm nervous," she said, putting aside her joking tone.

"About what?" Felipe asked, holding her away from him and looking her straight in the eyes.

"I don't know...about going to the club again. I feel odd. I don't know who I am yet," Lavinia said.

"You're a member of the Movement," Felipe said. "Didn't you say you were sure of that?"

"You're right, of course. I'm just being silly," and she moved away, going over to get a clean towel. She couldn't talk with anyone about this, she thought to herself. Nobody would understand her. Not one side nor the other. She'd have to deal with her uncertainties by herself.

"When do you have to leave?" she asked Felipe.

"Later," he replied, "after I see you dressed up. I want to see how you're going to look in that 'costume.'" And he headed for the kitchen saying he was going to make himself something to eat because he was hungry.

It didn't seem like a costume to him when he finally saw her dressed and made-up, when she left the house with Adrián and Sara.

He kept watching her as she put on her makeup, constantly joking and trying to hide his discomfort by pretending to be indifferent. When the image that the people attending the ball would see started to emerge, she noticed his silence, his doubts.

GIOCONDA BELLI • 223

Looking at herself in the mirror, Lavinia thought she looked very good. She had lost weight, and the dress fell softly over her body, the red color contrasting with her white skin and the dark hair falling over her shoulders. Her high heels heightened the effect and made her slender figure even more striking.

"You're the living image of the prosperous bourgeoisie," Felipe said with a smile. She laughed unenthusiastically. She sensed in his words the antagonism produced in Felipe by her image of luxury. He had his contradictions, she thought. He looked at her exactly the way the people sitting around her on the benches in the waiting room had that night when she accompanied Lucrecia to the hospital. Perhaps his argument that she "still wasn't mature" had something to do with all of this.

Silently, leaning against the back seat of the car on the way to the ball, traveling along the palm-flanked avenues, she remembered Felipe's amused expression when Adrián and Sara arrived to pick her up, the way he looked at them—especially at Adrián, with his tuxedo—and said good-bye politely. She'd felt the distant tone of his farewell: he seemed to say "see you later" from the other side of an impassable gulf, like the scene from a movie where the earth opens and a man, and a woman who love each other are separated by an enormous chasm.

"Are you all right back there?" Adrián asked. "Do you want me to turn up the air conditioning?"

"No, no," Lavinia said. "I'm fine, don't worry." They were going through poor neighborhoods, houses built with cardboard and strips of wood, the streets unpaved and badly-lit. Squatters settled on the higher ground. They would remain there until they were sent to other areas that were "more appropriate," more secluded, where they wouldn't bother anyone with their unseemly, sprawling poverty, or until the mayor sold the land and kicked them out.

Finally, they turned onto the wide, well-lit avenue, free of slums. A little later they took the private road that led to the club. At the entrance, a line of cars waited to pass the security booth. The cars would stop, show their invitation and the gate—just like the one used at train crossings—would rise, assuring that only those who belonged to that exclusive world gained entry.

The golf course was profusely illuminated with spotlights hidden in the trees: the night lights in the tennis courts were on. Adrián greeted the doorman and the barrier was lifted. At the bend, under the marquee, the chauffeurs of shiny Mercedes Benzes, Jaguars, Volvos, enormous American cars, Japanese models, opened their doors for the couples dressed in tuxedos and evening gowns to get out.

Over at the swimming pool, the orchestra was playing a bossa nova. They got out of the car. Sara seemed exuberant and happy. Adrián stuck his chest out farther than usual. They were nervous, just like her, Lavinia thought, running her hand over her hair and straightening her dress. Adrián took them both by the arm, placing himself proudly between them.

What must Adrián think? wondered Lavinia, thinking how he often reproached her "rebelliousness." He was a curious defender of the status quo, no matter how much he talked of the guerrillas' bravery. He didn't accept her desire for female independence, her "informal" relationship with Felipe. Like her mother, he too considered her coming to the ball a sign of reconciliation, of "accepting reality."

The room was resplendent with light from enormous crystal chandeliers which, adorned with floral garlands, spilled their light over the multi-colored crowd in evening gowns, low-cut dresses and expensive jewelry, flowing from one side to another, waiting for the official opening of the ball.

At the tables surrounding the dance floor there was laughter, mingled with the sound of glasses that tinkled with ice, champagne, and whiskey.

The salon opened onto a terrace beside the immense pool of sky blue water illuminated by submerged lights. Over it a bridge had been constructed for the debutantes to cross. Huge water lilies, real ones, specially imported from Miami, floated on the surface.

Adrián had reserved a table beside the pool so they would have a better view of the debutantes' promenade. They had run into a lot of people they knew as the usher escorted them down the aisle toward their table. "It's been so long since we've seen you, you're looking good, I hope you'll save me a dance" and expressions like "Lavinia! You've finally come out of hiding!" had accompanied her the entire way.

"It looks like you're more popular than ever!" Sara was saying as they sat down.

"I'm beginning to suspect your 'retirement' was part of a plan to increase your value and place your admirers at your feet," Adrián said, amused.

"You picked a good place," Lavinia said, smiling enigmatically and breathing in the cool night air while she looked at the water lilies floating in the pool and the bridge where the debutantes would cross.

Once she was sitting down she looked around. A profusion of elegantly set tables decorated with floral arrangements filled the hall. Most of them were already occupied, while others still displayed "reserved" signs. From one table to the other, glances inspected hairdos and gowns. The female guests, pretending to greet each other from across the room, were checking each other out, identifying the gowns described in telephone conversations or in the comments of the seamstresses they shared. She didn't see her parents. Either they hadn't arrived yet or they were hidden behind the thick pillars covered with flowers and plants. Maybe she'd be able to find them when the promenade began and the guests sat down.

Lavinia recognized and waved to several of her friends from high school at the far end of the room. Some of them were accompanied by their dashing husbands. Antonio and

Florencia waved enthusiastically to her from the group's nearby table. She got up to go over and say hello, elegantly swishing the hem of her red dress.

"It seems now we only get to see you in these despicable places..." Antonio joked when she came up to them.

"You've completely abandoned us," said Sandra.

"No, that's not true at all," Lavinia said, happy to see them. "I'm getting over that serious phase now..."

"And the Felipe stage?" asked Antonio.

"Don't be nosy," Lavinia said, winking at him.

The president of the club crossed the room and went over to the microphone.

"It's going to start," said Florencia, with the tone of a schoolgirl. Lavinia went back to the table with Sara and Adrián. She sat down as the speech began.

"Good evening, dear club members," the loudspeakers blared, causing everyone to return to their tables. The general excitement created by the opening of the ball gave way to silence for the words of the president, who in a tone of solemn rejoicing went on:

"Just as we do every year in the beloved tradition of our club, tonight we have gathered at our annual ball to give a warm reception to the beautiful, distinguished young ladies, daughters of our honorable members, who will be presented to society this evening..."

The speech praised the young ladies' qualities, and their names were read along with those of their parents, to the sound of applause.

"Now he'll read them off one by one," Lavinia thought, remembering when she had been one of those named: the waiting in the ladies' dressing room at the top of the stairway for them to announce her name so she could descend while the orchestra played "La vie en rose." Fortunately, there hadn't been a bridge over the pool then.

Now the president, with a theatrical air and bolstered by the drum roll of the orchestra, announced the first debutante, the club's "Queen." It was Patricia Vilón. (Lavinia remembered her as a noisy kid in the school hallways, among the younger girls). The girl appeared at the runway with a dress of white brocade, covered with beads and sequins, a rose in her chestnut brown hair, walking along the bridge as if she were Miss Universe. The orchestra exploded with the grand march from Verdi's "Aida," drowning out the applause of those present.

His hand extended, the president awaited the "Queen" at the end of her walk. With a smile of satisfaction and importance, he took her by the arm and placed her at his side, in a semicircle formed by the fathers of the other young ladies.

Murmurs and applause accompanied the arrival of those vaporous white apparitions with flowers in their hair, who one by one came to stand beside the president and the "Queen."

Sara and Adrián applauded and made comments to each other. Lavinia clapped, too, remembering Sebastián's instructions to look happy, like a "fish in water." This had been her element, after all, even if she felt out of place now. The sense of absurdity was overwhelming, making her feel like laughing at the initiation rite of those vestal virgins dedicated to wealth and the perpetuation of the species.

Deep down, she was comforted by her decision to join the Movement, to get away from this spectacle: it was impossible to be here and not recognize the folly of a country where with such impunity opulence could co-exist with extreme misery, ignoring it, ignoring the peasants thrown from helicopters because they collaborated with guerrilla forces, the screams of those tortured in the basement of the presidential palace.

The dance began. The president took the "Miss" by the arm and advanced toward the dance floor, where he initiated the graceful whirling of a waltz, joined by the rest of the fathers with the debutantes amid applause and laughter from colored lips, murmurs of appreciation, comments about who was the prettiest, who was wearing the most elegant gown.

The guests got up from their tables, forming a semicircle around the floor where the main characters of the greatest social event of the year were dancing.

Adrián, Sara, and Lavinia moved closer, along with the others.

"Do you remember," Sara said, "when it was our turn? I think the only other time I was that nervous was the day I got married..."

Lavinia remembered everything perfectly. Once in a while she looked at the photo album again and felt embarrassed to see herself on her father's arm, with the same expression she saw now on the faces of the girls who were dancing.

"I remember both of you," Adrián said. "Your expressions were like frightened deer. Thank heaven I wasn't born a woman."

"There's your mother," Sara said, suddenly turning serious. "She's waving."

She caught a glimpse of her mother on the other side of the room, standing in the circle of spectators. She had her arm raised in greeting. Her father was getting out his glasses to get a better look at her.

"She's aged," Lavinia said, raising her arm to reply to the greeting.

She watched them across a mass of heads and hairdos. Her mother had gained a little weight, accenting her gray-haired, matronly appearance. On the other hand, her father seemed to have lost weight. He wasn't much different from the last time she'd seen him.

The circle broke at that moment, when at a signal from the president, the crowd joined the dance. Her father and mother embraced and, dancing, crossed over to her side of the floor.

It was the "big moment." Several people from neighboring tables settled back to witness the encounter, that sort of public-square reunion with a merengue rhythm.

"Honey, how are you?" said her mother, giving her a kiss on the cheek, as if they'd just left the house together. "How are you both?" she asked Sara and Adrián as they leaned forward to greet her.

"How are you?" asked her father, looking her over from head to toe. "You look very good." Then he hugged her tightly.

She slipped out of his embrace, imagining a "Cut!" in a bad Mexican movie of prodigal sons and repenting parents. It was impossible for her to get emotional or respond to her father's effort to be affectionate in that atmosphere. She felt bad for him. At least over the months he had called her from time to time, asking if she needed money, if she was all right.

"Why don't you come over to our table?" suggested Adrián, taking control of the silence after the greetings, overcoming that uncomfortable, tense scene which the noisy merengue of the orchestra threatened to turn into something ridiculous. "Sara and I are going to dance," he said.

They went onto the floor. Lavinia saw Sara talking. She imagined she was reproaching Adrián for having taken her away just when the presence of both of them would have alleviated the tension of the meeting with her parents.

"You look really good, honey," said her mother, as soon as they sat down at the table. "And the dress still looks new. Do you remember I told you it was worth it to buy good labels? You see I was right."

"You look very pretty," said her father.

"And how are you both?" Lavinia asked.

"We're fine," said her father, who was obviously making an effort to take charge of the conversation and avoid her mother's intervention.

"You've caused a sensation at the ball," interrupted her mother. "All my friends have asked me if you're coming back home."

"I hope you've told them that's not the case," Lavinia said, beginning to feel the typical reaction her mother provoked in her.

"How's your work going?" asked her father, quickly intervening.

"Fine, fine," Lavinia said. "And how's the factory doing?"

"Pretty well. I could use a good manager to take over most of the duties. I'm old and tired now. Business is going well although I don't know how things will change when they open the new factory that is being set up by some army officers.

"Are they setting up a factory?"

"Yes. They're getting into more sectors of industry, banking and real estate. Have you heard of the United Bank? Well, they're setting it up with capital from the Great General and several of his officers. They're starting to compete with us as much as they can. And it's unfair competition because they get tax exemptions, duty free materials, and they build with government equipment... They're out to ruin us."

"When are you coming to the house, honey?" her mother was saying. "We could organize a lunch with your friends..."

"What are your plans, what are you going to do with your life?" her father was asking, joining her mother's expressions of concern.

"My life is fine. I've organized it very well," Lavinia said. "I have a job, I take care of my house. You have nothing to worry about." And she smiled without giving any more details, with the expression of having put an end to the matter.

"And that architect you're going out with that no one knows...?" her mother asked.

"He's just a colleague. I see him once in a while. It's nothing serious... Aren't you going to do anything to stop the competition from the Great General?" Lavinia said, trying to return to what her father had begun to talk about.

"Well, we've been having meetings about it, but we can't find any solution."

After they had been sitting together for a while, watching the dancers, her mother commenting on the gowns and the latest gossip, her father on his meetings, her father got up, saying that it was nearly impossible to hear because of the noise; it would be better if Lavinia came to visit them at home.

The three of them stood up, obviously relieved that the conversation had come to an end. Behind the conventional farewells, kisses on the cheek, the "we'll get together soon," they hid what they really would have liked to say. She watched them leave: her father and her mother, both of them looking tall among the others who were dancing, a pair of good-looking human beings, her father with his straight body, his graying yet still abundant hair, strong features, big eyes, moving heavily, smiling unenthusiastically at those who greeted him as he passed. Her mother with her air of a great lady, her thick gray hair shining, her long hands that Lavinia had inherited, her artificially happy expression.

As she watched them, the crystal chandeliers, the lights, took on the bright, diffuse outline produced by tears. She had the feeling she was looking through the wrong end of a telescope. Her misty eyes saw them from afar. Dazzled, she understood that she was finally on the other side, that she had finally managed to swim against the current and was now on the other shore. There were only tears, water, between them, water effacing it all.

"Wouldn't you like to dance? You're all alone here..."

The hand on her bare shoulder startled her. The tables, the dancers, the sound of the orchestra, came into focus again. She lifted her head and saw Pablo Jiménez, a friend from her debutante days, looking at her from above in his tuxedo with a black bow tie at his throat.

He was a quiet, shy man. The tone of his skin, his hair and his eyes seemed as if they'd been faded by the powerful fluid in his mother's womb. She was a noisy, domineering woman. Everyone called him "Pablito." The girls said he was "harmless."

"Hi, Pablito," she answered.

"Hi," he said, holding his hand out to lead her onto the dance floor. "Let's dance...come on, don't stay there in your chair."

She got up, thinking she couldn't have chosen a better partner for this first dance than this mild-mannered, transparent, "harmless" man...

The bolero also smoothed their approach to the dance floor. They created a small space for themselves. The couples danced closely, taking advantage of the music to allow their bodies to touch and to whisper things into each other's ears.

Pablito smelled of cologne. He took her gently by the waist, and they began to sway to the rhythm of the music.

"I heard you are working with Julián Lazo," he said to her. "Are things going well?"

"Yes, very well. The work is interesting."

"But you'd disappeared...people only saw you in the discotheques."

"It's just that after the year I had my debut, I was a little tired of this kind of party. Now I've gotten over it..."

She moved a little closer to him, wishing he would stop talking so she could enjoy the music and dance. She liked to dance. Pablito was a good dancer. "I shouldn't do this," she thought, "I should talk, ask more questions..." Still, she was in a daze. It was hard for her to pay attention, to forget about her parents. She wished the arms holding her were Felipe's. Then she would have been able to close her eyes, let the music lift the weight of her painful relationship with her mother and father.

"So what have you been doing?" she asked.

"I'm working in the Central Bank, in a research office that's just been opened. We do socioeconomic studies, supposedly nonpolitical and independent. It seems the president of the bank has convinced the Great General of the need to have a team which will provide him information that hasn't been tampered with. The government wants to know what the devil is really happening in this country. I don't think it's good for much, but at least one feels maybe, even if out of fear, they'll make up their minds to improve some things...

"But you don't feel bad about working there?"

"No. I think the only thing one can do in this country is try to work from inside the regime, and since we're going to have it for years to come, the most practical thing is to see what can be done so at least some things get better. Besides, as I told you, we're an 'independent' group. No politics. We're economists..."

Being 'apolitical' was a comfortable way of being an accomplice, Lavinia was about to say, but she remembered she was there to create a cover, not to enhance her reputation as a rebel. Besides her comment would be useless. In that milieu, most of the people were in the opposition. It was natural to criticize and complain about the regime, even when tacitly they knew they were allies. Let's criticize it but not change it, was the motto.

That had been her motto, too, until recently.

The bolero was over and the orchestra changed rhythms, beginning a cumbia that put an end to the conversation.

"I'll take you back to your table," Pablito said. "This isn't my type of dance."

Sara and Adrián had come back, too. They were fanning themselves with their napkins.

"This dance floor is an oven... How are you doing, Pablito?"

"Very well, thank you. You also look very well..."

"With all the exercise we've been getting..." Adrián said.

The dance with Pablito opened the way for friends to come over to the table when the orchestra took their breaks.

In an atmosphere of civility and cordiality, conversations exchanging brief news about careers and other activities followed one after another throughout the evening. It was impossible to know what those friendly, smiling faces that stopped by her table were really thinking.

She danced with the ones she knew from her old gang, including Antonio, who kept asking about Felipe. And there was Jorge with his jokes. She had a good time with them. It wasn't hard for her to blink her eyes and flirt vivaciously.

At times the feeling of strangeness returned. In her mind she saw the images of Sebastián, Flor, and Felipe, or the doctor's funeral that everyone seemed to have forgotten. Some of them commented on how lucky it was that the ball hadn't been canceled, the concern they'd felt that the disaster would include them.

Her old high school friends talked with her about their wedding plans, their suitors, fashion, and the latest contraceptives.

From time to time she caught Adrián, amused and intrigued, gazing at her.

She was sure that Adrián noticed she was acting, but he'd never figure out why she was doing it.

He tried to get her to dance with him, but Lavinia, aware that he'd ask her a lot of questions, pretended she couldn't fit him in among her many partners.

"We ought to go," she said at last. "I can't dance any more. My feet are killing me."

Sara, who was beginning to yawn, agreed with her.

"Yes, let's go," she said. "I'm very sleepy."

They went out, taking the route across the terrace so as to avoid the crowd gathered on the dance floor. In the parking lot, she saw her parents in the distance getting into their car to leave. They'd been watching her when she danced near their table, meeting her eyes with indecipherable glances.

"You were charming," Adrián said, when they were on their way home.

"I was nice, wasn't I?" Lavinia said, playing the fool.

"You are nice," Adrián said, "when you act like who you are and don't try to play the liberated, independent woman..."

"I am liberated and independent," Lavinia said. "Make no mistake about it."

"I'll never understand women," replied Adrián.

They were silent, both listening to Sara's measured breathing as she slept in the front seat.

+ + +

Is she feeling nostalgic? I often felt nostalgic for life in my tribe. But in my case there was no possible return. What I left behind dissolved like a worn cloth. The quiet joys of the Calmeac, where we were taught the arts of dance and weaving never returned; never again did I adorn myself for the sacred ceremonies with which we welcomed the return of the sun after the last days of the year, the ominous days when we waited and fasted, and we young people were not allowed to bathe in the river or enjoy ourselves catching fish from the lake.

The feelings Lavinia has are strange, sharp as a dart. A mixture of poison and honey. Everything in her is a tangled fabric, an arm waving farewell, loving and hating at the same time. And this time is indeed confusing. So many disparate occurrences are taking place as if two worlds were existing side by side without mingling. Like her and me, inhabiting this blood.

• • •

She took off her red dress. She threw it over the chair. She saw it crumple into a shapeless wad of folds and sparkles beneath the sliver of light coming from the bathroom. She washed her face, removing the black makeup from her eyes.

It amused her to see Felipe in her bed, waiting for her, pretending to be asleep.

She was sure he was watching her with half-closed eyes. That's why she added a theatrical flair to her movements. She stood naked before the bathroom mirror, now rid of the last vestiges of the ball, before walking barefoot toward the bed. She recalled a fragment of some novel by Cortázar where the man observes the woman watching herself, alone, naked in the mirror.

"How did it go?" Felipe asked, his voice groggy, as if he'd just awakened, as soon as she lifted the sheets to get into bed.

"Fine, really well," she answered, snuggling next to him and kissing him on the cheek.

"That's all? You're not going to tell me how it went...?"

"Let me think how I can summarize it for you...There were a lot of people, lots of colorful gowns, with sequins and beads, a bridge over the pool for the debutantes to cross, water lilies flown in from Miami floating in the water, a lot of useless conversation, two orchestras, the ballroom was full... I danced a lot. I was "nice," like Sebastián told me to be. I ran into my parents."

"And what did people talk about?"

"Not much of anything..."

She always had the impression those people talked just to hear themselves, Lavinia thought. Even before her new awareness had made things like that more obvious, she'd noticed they talked incessantly, as if they had to constantly hear themselves in order to ward off loneliness.

They didn't seem to hear the sounds others made, except as minor instruments in the symphony of their own complacency. Perhaps it's a question of upbringing or class, she told herself. We were all raised to think we were the center of the world, the beginning of the universe.

"That's very vague," Felipe said, raising himself on one elbow and smiling. What did they say?"

"What you want to know is if I got any useful information, right? Because if I start repeating exactly what they said, we'll be going till tomorrow."

"Yes. You're right. What did they say that might be useful?"

She told him what her father and Pablito had said, different comments about the Great General's bad taste in organizing a party for the army on the same day at the Recreational Club of the Armed Forces...

"So they're upset because they're beginning to push into their territory...interesting," Felipe said. "We already suspected that."

Lavinia saw him lose himself in thought, looking as if something had been confirmed for him. She, on the other hand, wanted to analyze the party from a different perspective. She hadn't heard anything out of the ordinary in relation to political questions; what she thought interesting was that she had been able to see the whole thing with a new capacity because order was coming into her life. She felt that the design of her days had meaning now, things were starting to make sense, to have a purpose. She wanted to share her thoughts with Felipe, tell him how she felt she had changed since she no longer got up in the morning with the feeling of facing a shapeless void, a mass of clay waiting for genesis, in order to be filled with fishes or become a tree or an apple.

Now that she knew why she had to do what she had to do.

"It's interesting to see how people of my background act," Lavinia said, pensively. "They all want to call attention to themselves. It's a fierce competition. They use any means they can to be the center of things, monopolize the limelight. And they're amusing, that's for sure! I laughed a lot. But imagine, they had not seen me for ages, and they just asked the usual superficial questions...how are you, what've you been up to? Nobody asked me anything else. They weren't interested in me. The only thing they were interested in was in showing off, being funny, telling interminable stories... As far as I'm concerned, that was all right, but it does show what they're like."

Felipe shrugged. Obviously, she wasn't telling him anything new.

"And who did you dance with?" he asked.

She told him how the men had come over to the table, their questions about whether she had a boyfriend or not.

It was interesting to watch his reaction. He didn't seem to care much what she had thought; he didn't even ask about her parents. After politics, he had a macho interest in knowing who had approached her. He emanated insecurity beneath the apparent indifference he pretended while he fell into the soft sensuality of somnolence to seduce her, to make love to her frantically and violently and thus feel that he possessed her, avenging himself on the boleros and other rhythms.

• • •

CHAPTER 16

Flor reminded her of her Aunt Inés. They were so different, and yet there were moments when Lavinia couldn't help feeling they both had something in common: a certain serious way of talking about life, of perceiving the inner folds of things.

"You worry too much about the business of being accepted," Flor said. "And about identity... Each one of us carries our burden until the end. But we also build. As an architect you should know that. They give you the plot of land when you're born, but the construction is your responsibility."

"Precisely because I'm an architect, I know how important the terrain is..." Lavinia said, smiling. "But what you say is true. I don't know why I worry so much."

"That's right. Don't worry so much. Try to give the best of yourself. Acceptance will come little by little. The important thing is to be honest with yourself. That's what the others learn to respect."

Flor was like that. Not strident, not extreme. Lavinia was always surprised when she discovered, as she got to know her better, the depth and tenderness Flor sheltered beneath her serious, sometimes even austere, appearance.

The two of them, between study sessions and long nights sewing "sausages"—stuffing papers and correspondence that were sent to the mountains, hidden in various objects—had developed a sincere, sisterly friendship. They talked about dreams and aspirations. They shared feminist readings and ideas about "new" relationships between men and women.

Now, while she sat on a high three-legged stool, drawing proposals for the Vela house, Lavinia missed Flor. For several weeks now she'd seen little of her. She seemed to be extremely busy, like Sebastián and Felipe.

As for her, she devoted nearly all her time to finishing the preliminary sketch for the blueprints. Julián had relieved her of all other obligations, asking her to concentrate her talent and energy on taking maximum advantage of the general and his family's delusions of grandeur.

She got up from the table and went over to the desk. It was piled with American magazines. Beside the telephone she saw the post cards of William Hearst's house in California: the Greek pool with inlaid lapis lazuli and gold, the rooms that looked like medieval palaces, forty rooms... It was useful to know the tastes of ostentatious mentalities; when placed on an equivalent scale, they resembled one another.

She settled into the easy chair, prescribing a rest for herself. It was exhausting for her to work on a design where she constantly had to violate the principles of simplicity, and even aesthetics, in order to satisfy Mrs. Vela's voracious taste. She took out a cigarette and lit it, first inhaling the smoke, then exhaling white circles that disintegrated in broken clouds against the neon light of the ceiling lamps. Through the picture window she could see the light May rain, softening the day's glare.

The telephone rang. It was Mrs. Vela. After her initial reservations about the type of terrain her husband had selected, when she understood the potential for building on various levels, her enthusiasm had been growing by leaps and bounds. She called Lavinia nearly every day with ideas for the house.

That day it had occurred to her to give up her sewing room next to the music room as a surprise for her husband.

"He has a gun collection, you know," Mrs. Vela said on the phone. "It occurred to me that it would look really nice to display them on the walls in that room, don't you think?"

"But then you wouldn't have a sewing room," Lavinia said. "Remember he already has the music room, the bar, and billiard room."

"That doesn't matter, that doesn't matter," Mrs. Vela said. "The truth is, I never sew. The seamstress can make do anywhere."

While she talked with Mrs. Vela, Lavinia shuffled the post cards of the Hearst house. She remembered having seen an armory in one of the rooms. She found the multicolored picture. "Secret chamber" was written on the back. Still listening to the woman's voice as she droned on, her imagination began to play with possibilities.

"Could be, could be," Lavinia said. "You're right. The general is going to love the idea. I'm certain of that. I'll work on a proposal, and we'll look at it next week, all right?"

She hung up and thought about it. The need to determine how the weapons would be displayed would give her access to General Vela. She would need details about the weapons in order to determine the sizes, weights, the placement of the shelving. It would be easy to show how important it was to schedule a work meeting with him.

She turned the postcard of the Hearst house over and then looked at the front again. A secret room for the weapons couldn't help but seduce General Vela. She got up enthusiastically from the drafting table.

At dusk she was still making calculations.

A little before quitting time, Mercedes appeared in the doorway, wondering if Lavinia wanted coffee. She came over to the table and looked over her shoulder.

"Why are you drawing rifles and pistols?" she asked.

"Because Mrs. Vela wants an armory," Lavinia replied, "a room to display the collection of firearms her husband has been accumulating since he joined the army."

"Every day she wants something new, doesn't she? That's why she calls you..."

"Yes."

Mercedes was silent. She walked around the table, touching the brushes and pencils absentmindedly.

"You like this job, don't you?"

"Well, yes, it's pretty good."

"I like mine, too, but today I'm depressed."

"What's wrong?"

"I've got problems."

"Again?" Lavinia couldn't help saying. Mercedes occasionally told her about her personal life. Everyone in the office knew Manuel, who visited her and with whom she held endless telephone conversations. He was married. He constantly promised her he was going to leave his wife. He'd been promising her for years, according to Mercedes.

"It turns out that Manuel's wife is pregnant. He told me he was living with her because of the children. Supposedly they hardly spoke to each other. Today a friend calls me and tells me his wife is pregnant..."

"Well, I already told you that excuse seemed pretty flimsy to me..."

"To me, too," she said, looking out the window at the misty landscape, "but I wanted to believe him. I even thought he really did it for his children... I'm certain he adores them. But now I don't know what to do..."

"You're a young woman, Mercedes, you're attractive and intelligent. You deserve something better than being the "other" woman. Why don't you leave him once and for all? You'll see he's not the only man in the world."

"All men are the same."

"That's right, but some of them are single at least."

"But I'm already 'stained.' Single men like to marry virgins. I can only aspire to another lover... That's why married men are always after me."

To a certain extent, Lavinia thought, she was right. The type of men Mercedes went with had aspirations of moving up the social ladder. For that reason, they assumed to an extreme the values that were considered acceptable in the more sophisticated circles of society. After having a relationship with a married man, a woman would have difficulties in that marriage market. They would seek her out as a lover, but for a wife they preferred an innocent creature, easily molded and docile. An "impeccable" woman was considered essential in order to enter certain circles. Mercedes' past could prove embarrassing for them. Still...

"Remember that virgins are an endangered species," Lavinia said.

"But there are still enough around..." Mercedes said, smiling.

"So then you'll end up alone, Mercedes. You're better off alone than you are keeping bad company. If you're unhappy with Manuel, I don't see why you stay with him."

Mercedes looked absently at the magazines on top of the desk. It seemed as if she wanted to solve her problem, but deep down, Lavinia thought, she was trapped in a love affair that was like a spider's web.

She watched her walk toward the door.

"It's that I love him," Mercedes said. "I'm going. I'm holding you up."

And she left in a hurry.

Engrossed in thought, Lavinia looked out the windows at the pink and violet twilight clouds against the gray sky.

She felt sorry for Mercedes. It was practically a curse, she thought, hanging onto love like that. And so feminine. She wondered how men managed to keep those worries out of their daily lives. At least enough to keep their concentration, not to feel the earth give way beneath their feet when their love life wasn't going well. They seemed to have the power to compartmentalize their emotional life, locking it behind solid dams to prevent the rest of their lives from being affected. For women, on the other hand, love seemed to be the axis of the solar system. One deviation, and the melting, the flood, the storm, and chaos were all set loose.

She heard the sounds of quitting time, the switches on the drafting lamps, the keys, the see-you-tomorrows. She had mechanically scribbled on sheet after sheet of paper without paying attention to what she was doing, distracted by the damp caves of life; she looked over the sheets of paper before throwing them in the waste basket: firearms, pistols, rifles

and—how odd—she'd sketched stylized antique blunderbusses and innumerable bows and arrows...

÷ ÷ ÷

Lavinia thinks about the female sex and asks herself
about love.

Time does not elapse: she and I, so distant, could converse
and understand each other in the moonlit night around the
fire. Countless the questions without answers. Man escapes us,
slips through our fingers like a fish in the gentle river. We
sculpt him, we touch him, we give him the breath of life, we
anchor him between our legs, and he remains distant as if his
heart was made of a different material. Yarince used to say
that I wanted his soul, that my deepest desire was to breathe
the soul of a woman into his body. He would say it when I
explained my need for caresses, when I asked for his soft
hands upon my face or body, wanted his understanding during
the days when blood flowed from my sex, and I was sad,
tender and sensitive as a newly born plant.

For him, love was pulque, axe, hurricane. He paced it so
that it wouldn't set his reasoning on fire. He feared it. For
me, on the other hand, love was a force with two sides: one
sharp and fiery and the other cotton and breeze.

My mother used to say that only woman had been granted
the gift of love; that man only knew the basics. The gods had
not wanted to dilute his strength. But I had seen men driven
mad because of love, and I knew that even Yarince, because
he kept me by his side, had been reprimanded by priests and
sages. I could not accept, as my mother did, that men carried
inside them only the obsidian necessary for war. It seemed to
me they hid their love for fear of resembling women.

● ● ●

They agreed to meet in Ceibas Park. For several weeks
now Lavinia had not visited Flor's house because they were

all so busy. She saw her seldom and usually only in public places: parks, restaurants, or while she drove her from one place to another. Flor also visited the road by the hemp brake.

In the park they usually met beneath an immense ceiba. Seated on a concrete bench at the farthest end, they looked like students with their books and note pads. Lavinia liked meeting her there. The tree's long branches formed a circle of shade, a green lace with lines of blue. From there they could watch the children playing in the engine of an old, abandoned train and listen to their distant laughter in the afternoon quiet.

She arrived at the agreed time. Flor wasn't there yet. She left her car in the parking lot, took out the books and notebooks needed for their student "cover," and walked slowly toward the bench. It was hot. The rainless days of the winter season could be extremely hot and humid.

That afternoon only a few children were playing in the old train. They were all very young and wore faded, torn clothes, patched countless times. With their tiny legs they tried to climb to the top of the locomotive. To one side on the grass, the baskets and trays of candy, cigarettes and gum which their mothers had sent them to sell in the park, were abandoned to the pecking of birds.

Later, when the rich children arrived with their nursemaids dressed in neat uniforms, they wouldn't be able to play on the train any longer. They'd have to be content to watch the games from the park curb, while they balanced their wares on their heads, calling out with their little shrill voices: "Caaandy, caaandy..."; "chi-i-clets and ci-i-gar-ettes..."

A few minutes later, Flor came up the path. She carried the knapsack in which she kept her nurse's clothes when she left the hospital. Still visible below the faded jeans were the thick white stockings and austere shoes of her profession, contrasting with her flowered blouse.

She looked tired, bleary-eyed. Lavinia had already thought, when she had seen her several days earlier, that Flor had lost weight; now her sharpened face left no doubt— she was considerably thinner. Nevertheless, her eyes were bright and her movements were energetic, her body rhythms animated by her haste.

"Hi," she said, leaning over to give her a kiss on the cheek and pat on the shoulder. "Sorry for being a little late. I couldn't get a bus. My car is on the blink again. I think its finished this time."

Flor's car, "Chicho," as they called it, had entered a decadent, decrepit old age that kept it constantly in the 'hospital'.

"Did you take it to the 'hospital'?"

"This time I don't think I'll even try. It's not worth it. They fix it and a few days later it breaks down again. Maybe they can sell it for scrap metal. I feel bad because I'm really attached to it, but the truth is it's over the hill now."

"Anyway, we can still use my car," Lavinia said.

"We have to talk about that," Flor said, taking out a cigarette and digging in her purse for her lighter.

Silently, tensely, Lavinia waited until she had found the lighter and finally exhaled a big puff of smoke.

Well," Flor said, with the tone of someone beginning an important conversation. "I imagine you've noticed we're busier than usual?"

Lavinia nodded. Without knowing what it concerned, she'd noticed the increase in activity around her. It saddened her not to be a part of it, but she was aware that the Movement had its unwritten rules, its rituals, and apprenticeships.

"Things are happening..." Flor said. Suddenly she lifted her head and stared at her. "Have you taken the oath yet?"

"No," Lavinia said, remembering how she'd read in the pamphlets those words that were both beautiful and rhetorical, the symbolic pact, the formal pledge to the Movement.

Flor dug again in her purse (it resembled one of those childish bundles full of treasures that children usually keep under their beds) and took out the pamphlet that Lavinia recognized as the one with the Statutes at the same time that a reflex of fear made her look around the park. There were only children playing. She relaxed.

"Put your hand here, on top of the pamphlet," Flor said, placing it on the book they pretended to use for studying.

"Hold up your other hand...just slightly," she told her, whispering with a smile, "and repeat after me..."

She repeated in a low voice the words of the Oath that Flor knew by heart. Both of them, almost imperceptibly, whispered those beautiful, grandiloquent phrases. The park and tree became a cathedral for the ceremony. Lavinia felt a confusing mixture of emotions: fear and strangeness. Everything was happening so quickly. She tried to concentrate on the meaning of the words, to assimilate the fact that she was promising to put her life on the line so that the coming of the dawn would cease being just a dream, to fight so that man ceased being a wolf to man, so that all people would be equal, as they had been created, with equal rights to enjoy the fruits of their labor...for a future of peace, without dictators, where the people were the masters of their own destinies... To swear to be faithful to the Movement, to keep its secrets and protect them with her life if necessary, to accept that the punishment for traitors was dishonor and death...

She was moved, seeing herself as if she were someone else, echoing the firm, passionate tone of Flor's whisper as she finished now, barely raising her voice with the "Liberty or Death!"

"Liberty or Death," Lavinia repeated, while Flor quickly hugged her, then put the pamphlet in her purse, vigilantly observing the quiet park (as she had been doing during the reading).

The quick, tight embrace left Lavinia with the feeling of restrained tenderness. One might think it was part of the ritual, the seal of a natural pact, but something undefined in Flor's nervous behavior called forth a strange sadness in her.

"Well, now you're sworn in. I wanted to be the one to do it," she said, lowering her eyes slightly, noticing Lavinia's vague sadness.

"I'm so glad you were the one to do it," Lavinia said, feeling like she wanted to hug her again, maybe even cry.

Flor ran her hands through her hair, catching the loose strands that hung at the side of her face, brushing them back toward the pony tail she wore tied with a kerchief.

"As I was telling you," Flor continued, visibly controlling her emotion and adopting the executive tone of meetings, "important things are happening: these past few days the joint command of the urban and rural guerrillas have met. They have made decisions of great importance for our Movement. That's what we were busy doing," she added by way of explanation. (She must have guessed I felt like I was being excluded, Lavinia thought, once more controlling the impulse she felt to hug her.)

"I can't give you many details, but we agreed on the need to give compañeros like you some military training. This has to do with matters that you'll be learning about when the time comes; for now, given the importance of your work with General Vela's house—which in fact they consider a priority in your case—we decided to ask you to consider the possibility of some basic training during a weekend."

Moved, she nodded affirmatively. (Rifles, pistols, machine guns, blunderbusses, bows and arrows...)

"As you know, the Movement," Flor went on, "has begun a process of what we've called the 'silent gathering of strength,' That is, we've only taken action in the mountains as a way of keeping up the resistance while waiting for more favorable conditions. We must begin to prepare ourselves to take the pressure off the compañeros in the mountains. We also need to create greater awareness and mobilization in the cities... All this means that there'll be a series of changes and reorganizations. We also need to improve the preparation and capacity of all the members...you understand, don't you?"

She understood. Sebastián, who must have known what would happen, had spent the latest trips to the road by the hemp brake explaining the situation to make her see the need for the Movement to act. He'd explained the importance of acting so clearly that she herself asked him, "And why don't we do something?" which had caused him to break into a big smile.

"Yes," she said.

"I also wanted to inform you," Flor added, "that you'll continue working with Sebastián. I have to take a trip..."

The underground, Lavinia thought. She knew, from what Felipe had told her that in the Movement "to take a trip" meant to go underground.

"Where?" she asked, knowing she shouldn't, but wanting to know if this time it was a real trip.

"I can't tell you," Flor said, smiling and touching her arm affectionately. "But...well, you know what it is about," she conceded.

They were silent. Lavinia thought about whether or not she should say what was going through her mind and heart. Flor interrupted her thoughts.

"Moments like these are always difficult," she said. "In a way they're like good-byes because we don't always have the optimism needed for this business. Neither you nor I should say good-bye with the thought that we might not see each other again, but that's what one feels... Besides, it's a real possibility, even though the possibility that we will see each other again is real, too."

"Do you remember when you used to tell me about how you were afraid?" she was speaking as if to herself, watching the birds fly across the landscape that spread outward from the hill in the park. "When they told me I had to go underground, I felt afraid. I remembered the things I'd told you, what I have told other compañeros who are beginning, what Sebastián used to tell me. But I realize that this is another step and that each step brings with it a dose of fear that one has to overcome. But it so happens that the greater the responsibility, the less opportunity one has to share one's fear. Even though the fear is the same, one is even more alone in facing it. I wanted this. It is a triumph for me. You know there aren't many women in the underground. It is a recognition that we can share and assume responsibilities just like anyone else. But, as a woman, when one is confronted with new tasks, one is also confronted with an inner struggle, a struggle to convince oneself deep down of one's own capabilities. One knows in theory that one has to fight for equal positions of responsibility, but the thing is, once one has the responsibility, one must get over the fear of using it...and, also, take good care not to show one's fear exactly because one is a woman."

"I'm sure it'll be all right," Lavinia said, feeling she was saying something trivial but knowing she couldn't allow her own emotion, her fear, to weigh on Flor's.

"I hope so," she said.

"Just the other day I was thinking how men and women have 'specialized' in different abilities. We, for example, have a greater capacity for affection. They are more limited in that respect. They should learn from us, as we should learn from them, how to use authority in a more natural way. There should be an exchange," Lavinia said, just to say something.

"I don't know," Flor said, pensively. "For the moment the only thing we can do is to suppress the 'feminine' and try to compete on their terrain, with their weapons. Perhaps later on we can allow ourselves the luxury of vindicating the value of our qualities..."

"But we should be able to 'feminize' our environment, especially if we're talking about a difficult environment like the struggle..." Lavinia insisted.

"For me the 'environment of struggle', as you call it, is quite 'feminized.' We need each other, and, for this same reason we create strong emotional ties with the others... It seems to me that our men are sensitive. It's death, danger, and fear that make us create defenses...necessary defenses. Without them, I don't know how we could continue," Flor said softly.

She seemed to have plunged into herself; for Lavinia, her words were only the delicate tip of the iceberg floating in cold waters. Memories, experiences she could scarcely guess at, floated in her eyes, taking her far away.

"I'm going to miss you terribly," Lavinia said.

"Me, too," Flor said, "but I'm happy that you're going to continue working with Sebastián. He's 'feminized,'" she said smiling, "although don't you dare tell him that because he'll think it means something else...! Felipe will help you, too, even if he is such a chauvinist... I think he's better off with you than with some other woman who'd never stand up to him. It amuses me to think how you turned his plans around. You turned the tables on him!"

"Sometimes I think his machismo is contradictory," Lavinia said. "Judging by the women he's been with, perhaps something in him unconsciously gets him into this kind of situation."

"Odd, isn't it? I hadn't really thought about it, but now that you say it... Definitely the German woman wasn't very docile... Yes, Felipe is a good man and wants to change, I'm certain. Theoretically, he's got the right idea. It's in deeds that you can see his true colors."

"He struggles like Yarince," Lavinia said, distracted, unable to concentrate on the conversation, thinking over and over about Flor's passage into the underground.

"And who's Yarince?" asked Flor, curious.

"What?" Lavinia said. "What did I say?"

"That Felipe struggled like Yarince..."

"I don't know who Yarince is. I don't know how that came out..."

"Have you been reading about the Spanish conquest?" asked Flor, and Lavinia shook her head. "There's an indigenous Yarince, chief of the Boacs and Caribs, who fought for more than fifteen years against the Spanish. It's a very moving story. People know hardly anything about the resistance that took place here. They've made us believe the colonial period was idyllic, but there's nothing further from the truth. Even though we don't know whether it's myth or fact, Yarince had a woman who fought beside him. She was one of those who refused to give birth so as not to provide more slaves to the Spaniards... You should read about it. Maybe you heard it somewhere, and the name stuck in your memory. That happens sometimes. There's a medical term, even: 'paramnesia'...it's when something is stored unconsciously in your memory, like when you reach a place and it seems you've been there before..."

"It must be," Lavinia said. "You don't know the strange things that are happening to me; the things I think of... I don't think about them much, but now that you mention it, they're always related to the Indians...with bows and arrows, things like that... It's odd, isn't it?"

"I don't think it's so odd. Maybe something impressed you when you were little... After all, we carry the indigenous heritage in our blood."

"Could be. It could be that my grandfather told me about it when I was a girl."

She tried to remember, to no avail. She couldn't concentrate, and Flor brought her back to the most recent instructions about General Vela's house.

They were in the park for a long time. The neat children with their starched nursemaids were strolling along the tree-lined paths, and the distant swings moved like pendulums, reminding them of the moment of farewell.

"It's time for me to go," Flor said at last. "It's helped to talk with you. I feel calmer. Thanks."

"I'm the one who should thank you," Lavinia said, again feeling the repressed urge to cry. "You don't know what it's meant for me to have someone like you."

"All right," Flor said, smiling. "Don't start that. You're talking as if I were already dead. You'll still have me. As long as you have the Movement, you'll have me, so it's going to be for a long time..."

"I can't believe I won't see you for who knows how long..."

"Life is dialectical," Flor said animatedly. "Everything changes, everything is transformed. Maybe we'll see each other again soon. We have to be optimistic."

"Thanks for giving me the oath," Lavinia said. "I'm glad you're the one who did it..."

"So am I," Flor said. "And now I really should go. It's getting late."

"Don't you want me to take you?" Lavinia said, in the hope of prolonging their time together.

"It's not necessary," she said. "I arranged a contact nearby. Give me fifteen minutes before you leave."

Beneath the tall ceiba, at the far end of the park, they embraced. It was a quick embrace, a kiss on the cheek. It resembled a casual good-bye.

She watched Flor leave, and she remained alone on the bench, listening to the children at play, seeing the day fade, moist and blurry, until the fifteen minutes had passed.

+ + +

CHAPTER 17

I prevented Lavinia from understanding the comment made by her wise friend with the black hair and round eyes. I do not want her to study my past. I want to remember it with her at my own pace, connect her with this umbilical cord of roots and earth.

I am also afraid to think about the death of Yarince. It happened shortly after my own. From my dwelling in the earth, I saw it as if it were a dream...

Terrible and ominous were those final days. We were so tired after so many years of battle, yet the circle was closing more and more tightly around us. Our best warriors had perished. One by one we were dying, without ever accepting the possibility of defeat. We would bury the spears of our dead in the deepest part of the mountain, hoping someday someone would again raise them against the invaders. Yet with each death something irreplaceable was lost, and it tore us apart, a knife of flint tearing the flesh. A part of our lives was lost in each death. We all died a little until, toward my own end, we resembled an army of ghosts. Only our eyes spoke of our furious determination. We came to move like animals from living so long in the jungles, and the animals became our allies, warning us of danger. They scented their own fury in our sweat.

How I remember those days of concealment and hunger!

• • •

The Vela home was in what had been one of the best neighborhoods of the city before the new residential developments in the hills and the surrounding heights, where the new house would be built, became trendy symbols of the good life.

After greeting her at the door, Miss Montes explained to Lavinia that their present residence had already been sold to a young couple from the United States who were professors at the School for Advanced Studies in Business Administration, and who were away on sabbatical.

"That's why we're in such a hurry for the new house," she said. "The owners of this one are coming back at the end of the year."

The noonday sun beat mercilessly on the garden, beside which was a large air-conditioned room that served as a living room.

General Vela hadn't arrived yet, but they were expecting him at any moment.

With the tinkling of her many bracelets, Miss Montes went over to open the wood and glass door to the room, holding it open for Lavinia, who bore under her arm the cardboard cylinders with the drafts of the blueprints.

The Vela residence was as she had imagined it: a mixture of styles, each more gaudy than the other, disparate and ostentatious: mirrors with convoluted gilt frames, matching tables against the wall, heavy furniture with bright damask covers, chrome chairs and tables, enormous urns, rugs of odd pastel colors, reproductions of landscapes on the walls, paintings of gigantic, artificial seascapes.

In the living room, one of the walls was covered by a photographic mural of a forest in autumn.

"Sit down," said Miss Montes. "My sister won't be long; she's finishing trying on a dress. Today is the day the seamstress comes... You know how it is... Wouldn't you like something to drink?"

"A coke, please..."

The woman got up, walking over to a curtain. She opened it and a piece of built-in furniture appeared. Using a set of keys she had hanging from her waist, Miss Montes opened the leaf that served as a cover, making the neon lights buzz as they came on to illuminate an interior of mirrors, crystal, and liquor bottles. She took out a glass and bent over to open the tiny built-in refrigerator, from which she took ice and Coca Cola.

"The general loves built-in furniture," she said as she returned after locking everything up again, placing the cola and the ice-filled glass in front of her.

"It saves space," Lavinia said, thinking about how decadent and tasteless the bar was.

"That's what he says. He's very frugal," she said, "and besides, he doesn't like the servants handling what they shouldn't. You know...leaving liquor within maids' reach is like kissing it good-bye. They steal it. They always have a boyfriend or a relative to give it to. That's why he had this bar built with the refrigerator right here, everything under lock and key. It's the only way. At first it was hard for me to get used to going around unlocking furniture every time I needed something... In my house nothing was ever locked, but of course, it's not the same..."

"How long have you lived with them?" Lavinia asked.

"Oh! Since their boy was born...for thirteen years. Yes, thirteen years it's been. It's incredible how time flies, isn't it?"

"And where's your family from?"

"From San Jorge. My father was the administrator of La Fortuna. You know it, don't you? It's the tobacco farm that belongs to the Great General. That's where my sister and my brother-in-law met... Then he was just the Great General's bodyguard. They often came to the plantation. The Great General liked to take guests on weekends to ride horses and go swimming in the river... We had good times when they came. There were grand parties, they slaughtered cows, pigs, and of course my sister was young and pretty... Florencio fell in love with her. Afterward they got married. The Great General was their best-man. As a wedding gift he promoted Florencio, and that's how he began trusting him more and more until now he's a general... Who would have thought it back then!"

She paused as if remembering. "Since I never married, when they had their son, they asked me to come to live with them, to help them take care of him... My sister has never been very fond of children... I didn't have anybody. My father had died—the poor thing died from asthma—and my mother died when I was born...so I was happy to come. The fact is, my dream was to study to be a nun, but anyway, I serve God the same way in this house...after all, a nun's life is pretty hard, and I like certain things, jewelry, for example," she said pointing to her bracelets and smiling vivaciously. "And I love going to balls and seeing the fancy people dancing... I don't dance, but I love to watch others... By the way, how was the ball?"

Lavinia was just about through with her coke. She had never imagined Miss Montes to be so talkative.

"Ah! It was great. It was a spectacular ball," she said. "Those balls get better every year, fancier, more elegant. I also love to see people, especially on those occasions... I danced all night..." She smiled, enjoying her own sarcasm.

"It's too bad we weren't able to go," Miss Montes said, "but next year we'll go for sure..."

"And what about the casino ball?" Lavinia asked.

"Ah! That one was beautiful, too, but you know, it's not the same; the most famous one is the one at the country club. The one we went to doesn't have a tradition. I think the Great General was right to give it, and it was fine; the food was delicious, the champagne was free, there were three orchestras, a show and all, but only five girls made their debut and they weren't really very pretty...brown-skinned, straight hair, not very graceful..."

The guys would be so disappointed, Lavinia thought, recalling their conjectures about why the unmarried sister was quiet and seemed to conceal something behind her shyness. She probably only kept quiet in front of her sister and her brother-in-law. Now that they were alone for the first time, she talked nonstop of her love of parties, the bright life of the city.

"Could something have happened to the general?" Lavinia asked after some time had gone by, looking at her watch.

"I don't think so," replied Miss Montes. "He called to let us know he was running a little late. He had to stop at the Great General's office for a minute, but he promised he was coming. He hardly ever misses lunch, you know. Only if it's something extraordinary...or when he goes on a mission. Otherwise, he always has lunch here at home. The cook is very good, she knows what he likes. Besides, he never misses his siesta."

The sound of several cars stopping out front and the loud slam of a door broke through the steady hum of the air conditioning.

"He's here," said Miss Montes, getting up as if attracted by a magnet. "Excuse me, I'm going to let him know you're here and call my sister," she said, leaving the room quickly.

In a few moments she would meet General Vela. She nervously ran her hand over her hair, She felt apprehensive, afraid at the thought of meeting him. Flor had brought her up to date about his "brilliant" military career that afternoon in the park. The night before, Felipe and Sebastián had provided her with data about his personality. Various collaborators of the Movement had come to know him during their long interrogations in prison. He played the role of the "good cop," the one who arriving after they had been tortured to ask them not to force him to torture them more. In the mountains, he was known as the "pilot." He was given credit for the idea of throwing peasants alive from the helicopters if they refused to collaborate with the army or denounce the guerrillas. Also attributed to him were the "mud jails" of the North: a concrete pit half-filled with mud, covered by a concrete slab providing only a tiny opening for ventilation, where the peasants were locked up for days on end until they fainted from the stench of their own body wastes or went mad...

He was the Great General's right hand man, as much because of his effectiveness in terrorizing peasants and fighting guerrillas as because of his ability to keep order among his subordinates. The Great General was proud of him because he was a simple man who had moved up in the world. "He's my creation," he was in the habit of saying.

Vela's part in providing the Great General with pretty young women for his escapades ("the jolly times," as Miss Montes had called them) was also well-known.

"Make use of your class," Sebastián had said. "Be serious and cordial, but make him feel you are above him without rubbing it in his face. Be polite, be a princess... make him feel he can trust you as a professional but don't let him get personal..."

The idea of having to pretend to be pleasant and solicitous to such a character repelled her. She recalled her conversation with Flor in the park. This was her first mission. She couldn't be afraid. It had to go well.

The door opened with a strong, brusque movement; General Vela, followed by his wife and sister-in-law, came over to greet her, looking her over from head to toe with the air of a feudal lord.

"So you're the famous architect, eh?" he said, in a tone at once sly and ingratiating.

Lavinia nodded, smiling her best enigmatic smile.

The general shook her hand firmly. His hand was big and rough like his whole body. He was a man whom the nickname "gorilla" fit to a T. His Indian-like features, almost statuesque, could have been handsome if they hadn't been distorted by fat and a conceited expression. General Vela denied his past and his origins, reeked of expensive cologne and wore the impeccable khaki military uniform of the higher-ranking officials; his curly hair, the product of a mix of races, had been tamed laboriously by brilliantine and a strict cut that made it lie close to his head. He was of medium height, and his protruding belly was testament to his love of good food.

He motioned to her to be seated, and sat down himself, while the two sisters, speechless in the presence of the master, smiled at her as if they wanted both to encourage her and share with her the overwhelming effect of the general's figure.

"Let's see those blueprints," the general said in the same authoritarian tone of voice with which he had greeted her. It was a voice of one accustomed to giving orders.

With careful movements, Lavinia got up, trying to ignore the man's sly, lascivious stare. Taking the cardboard cylinders, she pulled out the set of plans and spread them over a round table next to the armchairs where the Velas were sitting.

"I think it would be better if we looked at them over here," she said with aplomb.

"Yes, of course," agreed the general, getting up effortlessly, followed by the two sisters.

She began to spread out the different plans and designs, explaining them: the front, the sides, the interior, the roofs, the furniture, the spaces. The general interrupted her constantly with questions and comments, but Lavinia, replying courteously, asked him to leave his queries until the end because many of the questions would be answered during the presentation.

"I don't like that method," the general said. "I'll forget the questions if I leave them for the end."

And he kept on asking. They were irrelevant questions, more to make her nervous than to satisfy his curiosity...dimensions, materials, colors, the convenience of putting the billiards, music and bar together in the same room because they were used all at the same time... Still he didn't seem too interested in altering his wife's ideas. In spite of the sharp tone of his questions, he suggested only minimal changes. He maintained his cunning, superior attitude until Lavinia unfolded the plan for the armory. Then his expression changed, showing true interest.

Obviously he had never expected anything like the refined details that Lavinia, with great care, had incorporated. The sisters looked at each other and smiled with the satisfaction of accomplices. She noticed the man's fascination when she explained the fanciful idea of the armory's revolving wall. It would have three wood panels, each one with steel rods in the center, supported on individual revolving pivots mounted on a metal track. A mechanism set into the wall would allow them to be locked shut or released so they could turn. On one side the panels would display the weapons collection, mounted on the surface; on the other, the panels would simply be a mahogany wall with lovely grain. This way the General could, as he wished, display one side or the other, just by releasing or locking the panel's mechanism. The rotation area required for this trick would also provide the General with space behind the wall, a sort of "secret chamber" where he could store additional weapons or cleaning equipment.

"Or whatever you want," Lavinia said at last. She had racked her brains over the post cards of the Hearst house, trying to imagine the function of the "secret chamber." She didn't even discuss it with Julián. It was her trump card to win over the general. Her ace in the hole. And it was working. She could read it clearly in the expression on his face when he looked at her now.

"You're very clever, Miss," said Vela, lowering his voice considerably. "I have to admit it's an excellent, original idea... And turning to his wife, he added: 'You finally did something right.'"

Lavinia smiled like a princess, despising him with her whole being. She needed to get some information from him, she said, about the weapons that would need to be mounted.

"Of course, of course," he agreed. "But why don't you stay and have lunch with us? That way we can continue talking during lunch.."

When she left General Vela's house, the scorching three o'clock heat weighed on the city in a air thick with siestas and daytime sleepwalkers.

The Vela family said good-bye to her at the door, flanked by bodyguards in light-colored guayabera shirts and dark glasses, who looked at her amiably as she went by.

At some point during lunch, General Vela had made a joking reference to her family's affiliation with the Green Party. "Our architect has green blood," he said. "It's a family tradition," she had responded. "I don't believe in politics; I prefer not to get involved." The general affirmed his conviction that she was right. In any case, politics was "men's business."

The general's men had looked at her with the same conviction.

One of them opened her car door. She thanked him with a "feminine" smile and, waving good-bye to the Velas, who were holding a lively conversation on the sidewalk, drove quickly away.

On the way back she felt nauseated and had a urgent desire to take a shower. She decided to go by her house before going to the office where Julián was waiting for the news. It hadn't been easy to get through the "succulent" lunch, the extremely greasy food and the general speaking with his mouth full.

It hadn't been easy to listen to his explanations about the "combat capabilities" of the different weapons he showed her, proud of the "rate of fire" and their lethal force.

But she had carried out her duty. The general was thrilled. With a few minor modifications, he had approved the draft of the plans, ordered them to go ahead with the final version, and told her to hire the engineering firm that would be responsible for the construction according to her criteria because he felt "he could trust her."

He had also offered to provide the trucks so they could begin bulldozing as soon as possible. He wanted the house to be finished in December at the latest. He was willing to pay for overtime.

Lavinia stopped at the light, rubbing her hand over her stomach to calm the nausea. The general had succumbed to the idea of the armory—the room they'd call his "private study"—though he didn't completely lose his sly air. Nor did he stop leering at her from time to time. Part of the game, Lavinia told herself. One couldn't expect any other sort of behavior from that man. The important thing was that the Hearst trick had worked. The California millionaire wouldn't believe the service he'd rendered to a Latin American guerrilla movement, she thought. Chalk up one point for Patty.

During the lunch, the Vela sisters had fallen into nearly total silence, only interrupting to agree with the general's opinions or to give directions to the maid. Only their glances told Lavinia how happy and grateful they were. She didn't get to meet the children. They were having lunch at school that day.

The general's chubby hands with short fingers and thick knuckles floated in her memory. She'd had to make an effort during the meal to look away because her eyes, as if with a will of their own, became fixated on the fingers carefully pulling away the flesh from the chicken's bones. She tried to forget so as not to feel the nausea upsetting her stomach.

Lucrecia opened the door. Lately she looked happy, humming songs as she went from one spot to another using the broom and mop. The radio in the kitchen blasted music from the *Sonora Matancera* all through the house.

"What a miracle you're here at this hour!" she said. "Do you feel all right?" she added, looking at her anxiously. "You're so pale."

"Yes, yes, don't worry," Lavinia replied, while she practically ran toward her bedroom. "It's just a bit of indigestion and the heat. I need to take a shower."

She threw her purse and the blueprints on the bed. She went into the bathroom, no longer able to contain the urge to vomit.

She hated to vomit. The body became a hostile entity grabbing the throat But now mind and body were acting as one, furiously rejecting smells, tastes, chubby hands, jangling bracelets, jokes, cold shiny weapons, teeth grinding chicken meat, peasants, mud-jails and feces, torture chambers...

The retching mingled with wretched tears and rage. She didn't want to cry. She would not cry. Instead she hoped this bilious, bitter rage would not go away. She needed it to fight her doubt, the Vela sisters' frightened eyes, the lousy world in which she'd been born.

It was the strength she needed to get rid of her disgust.

She washed her face in the sink. Behind the closed door she heard Lucrecia: "Miss Lavinia, Miss Lavinia, are you all right? Open the door. Can I help you?"

She dried her face with a towel, took a deep breath, and, feeling calm, empty, she opened the door.

"I'm all right now, Lucrecia," she said. "The food didn't agree with me, but I'm all right now. I'm going to lie down a moment because I have to go back to the office. I'll be fine soon."

And she dropped onto the bed. She closed her eyes while Lucrecia went out to prepare her a lemonade. She started to calm down, letting her body relax, letting her breathing return to its slow rhythm so she could get up and go see Julián, tell him the blueprints had been approved, initiate the process so the construction could be completed by December as the general wished.

"So he approved everything?"

Julián, pacing from one side of the office to the other, rubbed his hands in satisfaction.

"I knew you were going to convince him. See? I was right about having you do the design, wasn't I?" he said.

"He's willing to pay overtime so we can have the construction done in December; he asked us to start the bulldozing as soon as possible... Please, Julián, don't go on pacing like that, you make me dizzy. I don't know why you're getting so excited..."

"It's just that it seems almost incredible that they approved all the outlandish things we put in there...the sauna, the gymnasium, the extravagant bathrooms, the four living rooms... I've never had such an easy client."

"And I still haven't told you about my great invention," smiled Lavinia as she sat languidly in the chair.

"What invention?" asked Julián, finally settled in the swivel chair behind the desk.

"A medieval castle's armory with a secret room and everything, which I designed...inspired by the Hearst postcards you gave me."

"But I went over the blueprints..."

"Over a week ago," Lavinia said, roguishly.

"Yes, because there were only a few minor details left..."

"Well, about five days ago Mrs. Vela called with this idea of the armory... Do you remember there was a space for her, a sort of sewing room with a sitting room?"

Julián nodded his head, intrigued, as if he were listening to a detective story.

"Well, she said she was giving it up, she had this idea of surprising her husband...she'd just gotten the idea after looking at a magazine... At first I tried to dissuade her, but she insisted so much, that I designed the armory... The general was really happy," she said, without giving him any more details.

"I can imagine," Julián said, smiling from ear to ear.

"The armory will be in the official blueprints as his 'private study'. The real design will be on a secret blueprint. The conspiratory tone is part of the charm. I thought that it would make it more appealing to him. Vela was like a monkey who's just been given a watch. But this is a secret matter between you and me and nobody else. Don't let me down."

"Don't worry," Julián said, winking, amused.

Lavinia didn't want Felipe to find out. She wasn't sure he'd approve of it.

"Julián," Lavinia said, taking advantage of his good mood. "You know I've never supervised a project. I'd like you to assign me the supervision of this one. I think I deserve it."

He looked at her thoughtfully. "I don't know, I don't know," he replied. "Dealing with engineers and foremen is difficult even for a man... For a woman, it would be almost impossible."

"How can you be sure if you don't try?" she asked without getting upset, keeping the tone of her voice low.

"Because I know the milieu..." he replied.

"Well, I can assure you that the general is going to like it. He was convinced I'm brilliant. He practically told me I was like a man," she said, sarcastically. "He's never seen such an intelligent woman!"

"I don't doubt it, but the general isn't going to have to take orders from you."

"But I designed the damn house!" Lavinia said, raising her voice. "Why does another architect have to supervise it? That's my job! I think it's unfair for it to be any other way, just because I'm a woman! Things have to start changing in this country, as they are in the rest of the world. It's true it might be hard, but when they realize I know what I'm doing, they'll learn to respect me!"

"I don't think it's that easy," Julián said. "What I can do is name you assistant supervisor."

"But..." Lavinia said, ready to launch into a tirade.

"Now calm down," Julián said. "And don't be idealistic. I can let you do almost all the work. Come by once in a while, and that is what matters, isn't it? The rest is theory."

"No, it's not theory," Lavinia said. "What you're talking about is real machismo. You think I can do the work, but you don't dare assign it to me because I'm a woman and the other men are going to feel uncomfortable! I'm just as capable or more so than any of the architects you have here..."

"Including Felipe?"

"Including Felipe," Lavinia said. "Besides, I know you're not going to have Felipe supervise this house!"

They looked at each other defiantly, saying what they both knew, without uttering a word.

"You can't convince me," Julián said, ignoring what had transpired between them, "so let's not wear ourselves out fighting and let's not sour our success. If you accept the arrangement I proposed, we'll go ahead. If not, I'll have to look for another architect."

She was tempted to tell him to look for another architect. Give up right there, throw the blueprints in his face, but she couldn't. She had no alternative but to accept the arrangement. It was terrible to have to swallow one's pride... The things one had to do for one's country!

"Let me think about it," she said to calm herself down, getting up to go out.

"Think about it and let me know," Julián said. "Tomorrow I'm going to call a meeting with the engineers. Leave me the blueprints and don't be like that. You know I trust your professional ability. It's not because of you. It's because of the workers..."

She left Julián's office with dissatisfaction written across her face.

It was easy, she thought, to blame the workers!

She saw Sebastián on Thursday. She took him to the road by the hemp brake late at night. They talked about her visit to the general's house.

"So he wants to inaugurate it in December..." Sebastián said, looking absently at the road.

"Yes," Lavinia said. "And Julián is willing to go along with that. I couldn't get him to assign the supervision of the construction to me, but he named me as assistant."

They drove without saying a word for a long time. A chorus of crickets solidly underscored the silence that surrounded them. There wasn't much traffic at that hour—only an occasional cargo truck forced her to slow down.

"And how's Flor?" Lavinia asked.

"Fine, working hard. Flor is an excellent compañera."

"I miss her," she said.

"You two got to be good friends..." he said. "I miss her too."

"But you see her, don't you?"

"Don't be so nosy," he said fondly. "You love to ask questions..."

"You're right," Lavinia said, "but certain things don't seem so secret to me."

"Things that seem irrelevant can give away matters that are more important."

"But who would I tell?"

"It's not a matter of not trusting you. But we can never discard the possibility that they might capture us. And people can say things when they're tortured. Before we were inflexible. We considered anyone who gave any information to the dictator's security force a traitor. Now, as the torture methods become crueler and more refined, we only ask our compañeros to resist for a week so as to give us time to mobilize the ones who could be implicated... After a week, one can say the minimum so as to avoid a worse punishment."

Lavinia felt her skin crawl and a chill go through her. She tried not to think about that possibility.

"Torture must be horrible," she said.

"Yes," Sebastián said. "I'd rather die than have those bastards catch me alive..."

"When I was having lunch at the general's house, I watched his hands, thinking about what he must do with them..."

"Lately he doesn't do it personally. He only directs things. But there's a compañero in the mountains whom he personally tortured. He buried him in the sun for a week, leaving only his head out of the dirt. Vela would come with a bucket of water and throw it on his head. Our compañero could only drink the bit of water that rolled over his lips. It's a miracle he's alive. He managed to escape when they were taking him someplace, and we had to send him to the mountains because he was completely claustrophobic... You have to work hard," he added after a short silence, "to see what information you can get out of him and have the house ready in December..."

"Don't you think it would be better to delay it?... That was my plan, that's why I asked to be allowed to supervise it..."

"Lavinia," Sebastián said very seriously, "you have to learn that in this matter it's not up to you to make the plans, only the blueprints." He smiled ever so slightly. "Your ideas are welcome, but they have to be approved by the leaders. You're used to acting alone in life, and you have to begin to act in conjunction with others and to be disciplined. I don't want to stifle your initiative, but in the Movement we can't all go off in our own directions, even if we think our ideas are good. You are part of the machinery, and you have to think about the other parts. That's why you have to consult with those who are in charge and who have a wider understanding of the situation... As far as delaying the construction, don't even think of it. We want the general to trust you completely, so you have to be very efficient in your work and have the house ready by December."

"All right," Lavinia said, feeling bad, uncomfortable.

"By the way," Sebastián said. "Flor told you about a military training session, didn't she?"

She nodded.

"We'll do it this weekend. Felipe's in charge of taking you to the contact point."

They were coming to the place where she was to drop Sebastián off. Lavinia stopped, leaving the motor running. A strong cold wind blew through the night, swaying the sharp silhouettes of the hemp brake. Before getting out, Sebastián turned to her. In the shadows, his thin, serene face looked worried.

"We have great plans for you, Lavinia," he said. "The Movement is entering a very important stage. But you have to do your part. None of us is perfect. This is a learning experience, and we know it's not easy. We all have to go through it. Our obligation is to help you train, show you what we've learned... It requires humility and confidence on your part, understanding and firmness on ours... See you soon..."

Before Lavinia could respond, he went off down the narrow road, walking quickly, straight and slender, through the gusting wind...

The wind howled along the road through the half opened car window. She didn't know what to make of the weight pressing her down in her seat. She had deep respect for Sebastián, and his criticism made her uncomfortable, made her aware how far she had to go to be like him, like Flor, even like Felipe.

Perhaps the distances were insurmountable. When did a person stop acting as if the world belonged to her? When would she learn what they seemed to have known forever?

How she missed Flor!

Lately she felt as if she were rebelling against the whole world. Not only because she had joined the Movement, but because being more aware that her own self was stronger, she was beginning to confront her greater self-awareness with more subtle realities: arguments with Felipe, with Julián, Adrián's mocking look, the general, Sebastián's criticisms...the world of men...

Don't confuse what Sebastián said with all that, she told herself meekly.

• • •

CHAPTER 18

The dilapidated jeep bounced along the road, muddy from the recent rain. The driver, a middle-aged man with pleasant good-natured features, whom Felipe referred to as "Toñito," held onto the steering wheel, which spun to and fro as if it had no connection to the wheels.

They had set out in the early hours of dawn. The sun was just beginning to rise. They took the road to the north, turning off at one point towards a mountain-flanked valley.

The landscape was slowly recaptured by the light and displayed itself in pastel colors, pink and green, damp and foggy.

She and Felipe rode in the front of the jeep. In the back seats two men and a woman made themselves barely noticeable except for the scraps of a murmured conversation. They had picked them up at different points in the city.

Lavinia was silent, dreading she might say something she shouldn't, something that might threaten the "compartmentalization." It was the first time she was coming into contact with other members of the Movement, and not knowing the rules of the game in this situation, she opted for silence.

Felipe dozed. Only the driver seemed relaxed, an old hand at the job perhaps. From time to time, he hummed popular songs or old pieces by Agustín Lara.

The sun, as it cleared away the fog, illuminated fields planted with corn and onions. They were in a rural area. Not even electricity reached this far. There were no cross-like posts along the way, nor sparrows on the high voltage lines, as in the city.

It smelled good, clean, like distant cows, horses.

"How much farther is it?" Felipe said, waking up after the vehicle gave a jolting lurch.

"We're close now," Toñito replied, and the two of them returned to their silence.

We're close now, Lavinia thought. She hoped she wouldn't fail the "training." Felipe explained to her about the drills, formations, weapons, assembling and disassembling, target practice, "things you learn in a weekend workshop." Although she'd never excelled in sports or athletics, and the only thing she had to her credit were exercise and ballet classes as a teenager, she didn't think she had to worry too much about the drills because she was a good walker and her body was naturally firm. She was worried about the target practice. Until the day she had lunch with Vela, she'd never held a weapon in her hands. At the general's, she'd scarcely touched the metal, mentioning the usual "feminine" fear of firearms—a fear which she had actually felt that day looking at those mute instruments of who knows how many assassinations. On one occasion, her Aunt Inés, who knew about guns because as a girl she used to accompany her grandfather deer hunting, had shown her an old revolver she kept in the drawer for her "sacred things," along with missals, rosaries and letters from childhood sweethearts. Lavinia had been impressed by the delicate internal architecture, the application of physics to ballistics, the carefully synchronized mechanisms. It was the first time she had seen up close one of those objects that horrified her mother so much. "You're forbidden to touch it, absolutely forbidden to even get near it," she said every time her father took out an old revolver when he thought he'd heard thieves breaking into the house.

And now she was on her way to target practice, to learn to assemble and disassemble weapons. She would learn how to use firearms. Perhaps she would keep weapons in her house. She couldn't imagine herself shooting. How would she feel when she pressed the trigger?

Her parents would never suspect where her life was heading, she thought. Since the day of the ball she had only visited them two afternoons, as if she were a distant acquaintance. They had coffee and cookies in the living room. From time to time they talked on the phone. Her parents inquired about her social life, but they didn't ask too many questions. A wide gulf had been opened between them across which expressions of affection were barely exchanged in gestures and veiled words. That was how she had wanted it. It was better to keep a polite distance. She couldn't risk intimacy and unexpected visits from her parents.

✛ ✛ ✛

She is thinking about her family. Even if she would like to forget about them, their images appear at the most unexpected moments. When she is in danger, I have felt how she yearns for the embrace of her mother and that other woman, who appears in her memories, faded by time. It seems there are unresolved matters in her life. Deep absences. Caresses she never had. Childhood hangs in her fantasy like a region of mist and solitude and at times traps her in a confusing world of silent spirits and bygone days. She never said good-bye. Her parents did not bless her. They did not see her walk off into the distance as an archer watches the flight of the arrow. They have not set her free.

● ● ●

Toñito nudged Felipe.
"We're here," he said, stopping the vehicle.
They were at the end of the dirt road. It ended abruptly at a farm fence. The surrounding vegetation was thick. There were banana trees on both sides of the road.
Felipe signaled for everyone to get out. They obeyed silently, looking uncomprehendingly at that place in the middle of nowhere. They could see nothing but bananas

around them. He told Lavinia and the others to wait for him near the wire fence while he spoke with the driver.

The dilapidated jeep began the return trip down the road, raising dust. "Toñito" lifted his hand to wave good-bye when he had turned around and started back.

"Let's go through here," Felipe said, indicating a place in the wire fence.

They took turns lifting the wire and going under the fence.

They walked for about half an hour, close to one another, silent. Finally they came to a clearing where an old farm house stood.

It was daylight now, but there were no signs of activity in the house.

It looked abandoned, and yet the banana fields...

Felipe went up and knocked on one of the doors: three loud raps, followed by two quick ones.

It was the signal. The door opened and two young men came out of the house, dressed in blue jeans, barefoot, shirtless.

They hugged Felipe in turn while they looked at the small group that accompanied him.

"Are these the 'pupils'?" said the taller of the two, a handsome young man with long, slender hands and feet, light skin, and straight brown hair.

"Yes," Felipe said, "they are," and he introduced them: "Inés," "Ramón," "Pedro," and "Clemencia."

The other one, big and strong, looked at them with a certain twinkle in his eyes.

"Have they come prepared to wear themselves out thoroughly?" he asked, and they all smiled uneasily.

"Let's get started right away," said René, the taller of the two.

They went into the farm house and were shown where to leave their things. Besides some hammocks, the only things they saw were an improvised stove in the corner and several sacks.

The training began on the patio. Lavinia didn't understand the place.

Where were the peasants? Who lived here? she thought while René had them count off and told them they should call each other by number the entire time they were there.

Lavinia was number six, the last one.

Felipe sat on the run-down porch, watching them.

"We're going to have different sessions. I'll give you the elements of forming ranks and military tactics; Felipe will teach the class in field stripping and assembling your weapons; Lorenzo will take daytime guard duty, and at night we'll take turns," said René in a professional tone. "I want no laughter, no conversation, until we take a break. Is that clear?"

"Clear," said the two men and the woman, while Lavinia nodded affirmatively, thinking that the others had more experience.

They were in the patio all morning, learning the "commands," the corresponding movements: halt, right, left, about face, forward march, count off from the rear... "About face!" René would shout and they all pivoted on their heels together.

She couldn't see what good it could do to learn all that, which seemed more suitable for soldiers than for guerrillas, but she applied herself fully, sweating when the physical exercises began until, mercifully, René called for them to be "at eeeeaaase."

She saw Felipe gesturing to her, and, leaving the group, she followed him between the banana plants to a stream that ran nearby.

"You can freshen up here with a little water," he told her, affectionately pulling her hair. "You're pretty dirty."

"And the others?" Lavinia asked. "Why don't we call them? They'll certainly want to wash up, too, and splash themselves with water."

"They'll come," Felipe said. "Don't worry. René's going to bring them. I just wanted to steal a minute with you... We've never been like this together in the country."

"And whose farm is this?"

"As you must have noticed, the house is abandoned. It's part of a farm belonging to one of our collaborators. They've built a new house, and no one comes here anymore because the peasants say it's haunted. They only come by here when it's absolutely necessary, during harvest time, although they've just picked the bananas... Anyway, most of them collaborate with us. This place is fairly safe. I love seeing you dirty and sweaty," he added.

Lavinia smiled. The water was cool, almost cold. The little stream ran among tall reeds, carrying the pebbles along with it and licking the banks with its watery tongue. While she rubbed her sweaty arms and face, she wondered how Felipe's mind worked. Only yesterday, he seemed to disagree with Sebastián about giving her military training. When he was alone with her, he expressed his reservations and said that she was still very "new" in the Movement and that none of her assignments required that kind of preparation.

Determined not to be provoked, she'd listened to him, letting it go in one ear and out the other, aware that in spite of himself, Felipe would have to obey orders. Nevertheless, as always, when she saw him revert to those attitudes, she couldn't help being saddened by his remarks, just as now she couldn't avoid being surprised at seeing him so pleased, as if they'd never argued about it before.

"I've behaved badly," he said suddenly, perhaps reading her thoughts. "I don't know why I get so aggressive, I don't know why it's so hard to accept your participation..."

"It's no use your always feeling sorry," replied Lavinia, splashing water on her hair. "After you've repented several times, it gets boring," she rolled the r in "boring." She didn't feel like fighting. She preferred to smile understandingly.

They heard the sound of the others approaching. They were laughing softly, joking about their rheumatism, their aching bones, their tight muscles—timid jokes among strangers who have suddenly found themselves united by a shipwreck or on an adventure, at the end of which either life or death is lying in wait.

Clemencia, number three, met Lavinia's glance with an expression of understanding and affinity over their shared gender. She was a woman with olive-colored skin, short hair and attractive features. She wasn't fat, but she was stocky, having wide hips that swayed gracefully when she walked.

Lavinia had already noticed the way Lorenzo had looked at her more than once from his guard post.

Together, joking about the ghosts that would come and tickle their feet in the night, they went back to the house to warm a meager lunch over a wood fire.

It was strange what understandings developed between complete strangers in these circumstances. No personal information could be exchanged, but they shared the same view of life and the same quiet determination. That was why they didn't feel like strangers. On the contrary, one might think that they had known each other for ages as they sat on the old porch eating lunch.

Lavinia, with her jeans, sneakers and T-shirt, her hair in a pony tail, without make-up, differed from the others only in the finer lines of her face, but René was also white, pale, and delicate featured. In their attitudes they all resembled each other.

Their lunch consisted of a tortilla with rice and beans and a cup of coffee. Lorenzo, René, and even Felipe ate skillfully, using their hands without being squeamish. Lavinia tried to hide her discomfort, the difficulty she had in eating rice and beans neatly, without silverware, with just the tortilla to help her, unable to help spilling the purple and white grains. She looked at the other three out of the corner of her eye and felt better when she saw that she wasn't the only one who wasn't used to eating without knife and fork.

"From now on, you have to make sure you get more exercise," René had said. "None of you could survive a half hour run, much less a hike through the mountains..."

After lunch, they went into the house and closed the door. Through the windows, a pale afternoon light illuminated the thick-walled enclosure. It was cool inside the high-ceilinged house. Lavinia was familiar with this typically Spanish construction. The thick walls kept out the heat. The high ceilings allowed the stifling air to rise above their heads, leaving a cool comfortable space. In the colonial houses of the cities, the homes closed in around themselves, opening only to an interior of patios and corridors. The hacienda house, conceived for country life, was designed with a different concept: the interior space was only for sleeping; the veranda facing the fields was where the daily activities took place, and where in times past, the masters and their ladies would sit swaying in fancy wicker rocking chairs in the afternoons, observing the plantation.

The ravages of time and disuse had marked the peeling walls. The spider webs, having lost their original transparency, were dusty and clung to the walls, forming designs in the decrepitude.

Felipe brought a brown canvas bag into the center of the room. Out of it he began to take their modest arsenal: an M-16 rifle made in the U.S. and a 9mm P38 pistol. That was all there was. He handled the weapons gently, as if they were loving arms or legs: "This is an M-16 automatic," he began, as he showed it to them, blew on it, softly brushed the dust from it. He explained its properties for combat, its range, other technical data, and began slowly to disassemble it, talking constantly, naming the various parts: firing pin, trigger, hammer, barrel.

They all looked on in silence as he placed the pieces in order beside each other, respectfully.

"It's like looking death in the face," Lavinia thought, staring at the carefully crafted, intricate pieces of metal.

In spite of everything, in spite of her understanding violence differently now, for Lavinia the notion that man would construct those artifacts to eliminate other men was still incomprehensible: the huge factories producing grenades, rifles, tanks, cannons...all for the purpose of destroying each other. It had been like that since ancient times: men had plundered, pursued, and protected themselves from other men, and all because of the need for domination, the concept of property, the mine and the yours...until it became natural, part of the system, part of daily life, the strong against the weak. Even in the twentieth century, the practice of the nomads: to carry off the fire by force. Man's savage state was still not conquered, was apparently unconquerable. And there they were learning to use firearms, with no alternative but to touch them and familiarize themselves with them, learn how to use them. Just as the others knew how to do.

She felt hatred for the Great General, for Vela, for wealth, for foreign domination...everything that forced them to be there, in that abandoned house, all of them so young, kneeling in front of the weapons, motionless, looking at Felipe, hearing him explain firepower, automatic and semi-automatic. She waited for the moment when he would point out the targets, the moment when they'd hear the detonation of the weapon, the dry, hollow sound.

"Now we're going to do triangulation and dry firing," Felipe said.

And that was what they did. They didn't fire a single shot. "Dry firing" was what they learned in sessions like this. Hypothetical shots and salvos. Papers where they drew the trajectory of the imaginary bullet. "I should have known," Lavinia thought. The sound of shooting would have attracted attention. But it was too fantastic to imagine.

At night they slept, fully dressed, in hammocks slung between the beams of the house. In the safe houses, the schools, the mountains, they always slept in their clothes. At times they were allowed to take off their shoes.

Before she fell asleep, Lavinia heard Felipe talking with Lorenzo and René.

René had been in the mountain and was telling him about the mud, the coloradillas (insects that made welts which burned incessantly under the skin), the guerrillas' hunger. "We passed the time talking about food, about what we were going to eat when we came down into the city, when we triumphed." He said he felt strange away from the mountains. It was hard for him to get used to walking in the city. He wasn't used to the sidewalks after so much mud, climbing slopes like a monkey.

She fell asleep listening to them. She dreamt she was wearing a gown with big white and yellow flowers in a place that was like a fortress. In her hand she carried a strange pistol that resembled a miniature cannon. From behind her a woman with braids was ordering her to shoot.

She awoke with Lorenzo shaking her softly.

"Compañera, compañera," he was repeating. "It's your turn to stand watch."

She got up and accompanied Lorenzo in the dark toward a little hill near the house among the banana trees. It was cold and the fourth-quarter moon barely illuminated the shapes of the trees.

Lorenzo handed her the pistol and told her she should listen carefully for the sounds of steps or the movement of human shapes in the underbrush. He showed her how she was supposed to whistle in case she suspected some unusual movement.

She shouldn't shoot unless she was absolutely certain there was a serious problem. If she saw what looked like the outline of a peasant, she should call out "Who goes there?" If they responded "Pascual," everything was all right. That was the password.

He left. At first she didn't feel afraid. Instead she felt important, almost as if she were a guerrilla. However, as time went by, every sound in the night began to seem hostile and suspicious to her. "Who goes there?" she murmured from time to time, without receiving an answer. It was the wind, or insects, mountain animals.

She was cold. Soon her teeth were chattering, and she felt chills through her whole body. She thought of Flor, Lucrecia, and Sebastián to keep her courage up. Once in a while she turned to the memory of General Vela so that rage and revulsion would keep her going. Finally, she thought of her Aunt Inés and later prayed to the forgotten God of her childhood that nobody would come, so she wouldn't have to use the heavy pistol, whose theoretical function she had just learned.

She knew that Lorenzo was also standing watch nearby. René, Felipe, and he took turns accompanying the recruits to the guard posts, but there was nobody in sight. She had to be content with knowing that he was out there somewhere.

Two hours later Lorenzo arrived with number "four" to relieve her.

She went back to the hammock, stiff with cold, shivering. In the doorway she met Felipe going out to relieve Lorenzo. He hugged her silently, quickly, and told her to take his blanket to warm up. Dawn was breaking.

She didn't know why, as warmth returned to her body, she began to feel like laughing. She began to smile at herself at the thought of having survived her first guard duty, and then she laughed quietly, thinking how there, in the hammock, she had become another person, a woman in the middle of her country, on an isolated hacienda which had been abandoned to the ghosts and to them, dreamers who wanted to change the way things were, busy young Quixotes with their spears held high. Or maybe she laughed from nervousness because of the fear she felt while she sat among the big banana leaves, the fear of snakes, the sound of pocoyas in their nocturnal flight, and now she felt the warmth, calming, strengthening her, the strange feeling of power, of being invincible as long as the others were outside, awake, alert.

The next day they practiced "taking" the old house as if it were a military post in the middle of the mountains. They finished, exhausted, around four in the afternoon, after crawling long distances, lying in ambush, carrying out assaults and retreats.

At about five-thirty Toñito appeared once more in his dilapidated jeep. They waited for him, hidden on the other side of the wire fence. They said good-bye to René and Lorenzo and climbed into the jeep. On the trip back there was a lot of conversation, comments on how each one had done, jokes about who had been the best strategist, the way Lavinia had gotten stuck on the barbed wire, giving "the enemy" time to capture her.

Only when they entered the city did the comments cease. The passengers got out again at different street corners.

They said good-bye (maybe they'd never see each other again) and finally Toñito left Lavinia and Felipe a few blocks from her house.

"You were lucky," Felipe said, as they walked down the street. "Your training was easy; conditions were good. Don't think things are always like that. A year ago the army discovered one of our schools and nearly all the compañeros died. Only two escaped."

"Yes, I was lucky," agreed Lavinia, thinking it hadn't been so difficult, in spite of the way her body ached.

"Sebastián watches out for you," Felipe said.

"Do you think so?" she said, pleased, realizing only then Sebastián's invisible presence in the planning of the training.

After a while, she said: "Sebastián always says that the Movement has high hopes for me. I think he says it to make me feel good, but I'm worried I might let him down. I don't know how useful I can be."

"It depends on you," Felipe said, looking at her gravely as they went in and turned on the living room lights.

• • •

CHAPTER 19

The month of July was coming to an end. Lavinia pulled the page off the calendar and went over her work schedule for the next day. Mercedes had jotted down a meeting with Julián and the engineers at eleven in the morning and another with the Vela sisters at four in the afternoon.

She noted other tasks to be attended to between the meetings and, giving a final glance at her desk, straightened the pencils and papers and locked the drawer.

Sara would be expecting her at five-thirty and it was already five o'clock.

She turned out the lights and left the office.

She walked quickly to the parking lot and soon was driving around the corner to merge with the traffic on Central Avenue. The heavy traffic moved slowly because of all the red lights.

She had a lot on her mind and felt a little tired, thinking about the meeting with the engineers. General Vela's house had to be ready on time, and she had to make sure that the builders kept on schedule.

While driving, she could see the people in the other vehicles, shifting lanes, passing, stopping at red lights.

Suddenly she saw Flor in a car a few yards away from her. It took her only seconds to recognize her with short hair, dyed light brown, almost blond. She felt a rush of blood in her heart. There, so close to her, was her friend Flor. She could see her gesturing, smiling at the driver of the car, a man with nondescript features. Lavinia immediately wondered what she could do to get her attention. Beep the horn? Pass them? No. She couldn't do a thing except try to pull up alongside the car, try to make Flor see her. But that was nearly impossible. There was a lane of cars between their vehicles on the four-lane avenue. To pull alongside, she'd have to maneuver illegally, something that was possible out on the highway but hazardous in busy city traffic. When the light turned green, Flor was still absorbed in her conversation without seeing Lavinia, and the car shot ahead in the left-hand lane.

She tried to accelerate, but the cars in front of her were moving slowly. By the time she reached the next light, she had lost them. She managed to see the rear end of the red car disappear around a corner.

Frustrated, she let out a muffled cry and slapped the steering wheel.

It had been almost like a vision: her friend so close and yet so far, unreachable. Once more she felt a heavy sadness, the sensation of loss. It happened to her often. Most of the people she was closest to had disappeared from her life, were now so distant. Even though only the loss of her aunt had been irreversible, the memory of Flor, her Spanish friend Natalia, and Jerome made her feel a poignant nostalgia.

Absence had indelible effects. Faces faded away in the blurry substance of memory. At times she wondered if these people had really existed. Nostalgia clothed them in strange, mythical attire. Time, that traitor, hid the past behind its mists, making it nonexistent, associating it in the mind with fantasy or dreams. The space Flor had once occupied was filled with other images, other experiences. They had ceased to share daily existence, the raw material life. Now there was a sense of loss, an emptiness, a black hole that was swallowing the Flor-star, a shadowy mechanism of the mind trying to protect the heart ever faithful to the pain of absence.

Nothing could keep Lavinia from missing her. She could see her tracks. Her memory simultaneously dissolved her and kept alive the conversations, the empathy, the complicity between them—the unique, special complicity of gender and purpose, something she didn't have with either Felipe or Sara.

To see her, to know she was just a few feet away and not be able to call out to her, not to feel at least the satisfaction of a distant smile, a hand raised in greeting, made sadness bubble to the surface from the wells of her eyes.

All of this was hard. Very hard, she thought. Who would remember to record these struggles, the little, the big, the individual sacrifices when history was being written?

Suffering, tortures, death were all accounted for, but who calculated the separations as part of the battle?

She parked the car across from Sara's house. It wasn't the same with Sara any more. She was growing further and further apart from Sara, her childhood friend, to the point that she felt as if the two of them were in an invisible Tower of Babel, unable to understand each other's language.

Sara opened the door. She was pale.

"Come in, come in, Lavinia," she said. "I have coffee and cookies for you."

"You look as though you need it more than I do," Lavinia said. "Are you all right? You look so pale..."

"I've had a lot of nausea..." Sara said it with an expression of discomfort strangely mingled with a gesture of happiness.

Lavinia looked at her questioningly.

"Maybe you're pregnant. Did your period finally come?"

"No, it didn't. And it's not going to. This morning I took my sample to the lab and I'm pregnant!" She spoke in a rising tone, slowly clutching the words until they burst forth in the joyful "I'm pregnant!"

"That's wonderful," Lavinia said, genuinely happy, hugging her. "Congratulations!"

"It's due in February," Sara said, leading her by the arm over to the table where the coffee was served.

"Did you tell Adrián yet?"

"Oh!" Sara said, sighing and smiling sadly. "Adrián isn't romantic at all. He's been telling me I'm pregnant for days now: 'Your period hasn't come: you're pregnant. It's mathematical,' he keeps telling me. I called to tell him the results of the test and the only thing he said was he already knew it, didn't I remember how he'd been telling me that for several days... It's true you sense it, but, you know, the test is the great event, when you see the 'positive' on the sheet of paper... It's not the same as sensing it yourself. And probably because I've seen so many movies, I imagined he'd come running home and give me a huge special hug, a bouquet of flowers...oh, I don't know! It's silly, but that 'I knew it' made me feel sad."

"You're right," Lavinia said, making a quick mental comparison with what she would expect in a situation like that, surprised she didn't have any preconceived notions. Without knowing why, she returned to the image of Flor in the car. Would she and Flor have children some day?"

"Well, as a friend of mine says, the truth is, pregnancy is a woman's thing. Men don't feel the same way," Sara said, as she poured the coffee into the white cups. "Do you want sugar?"

"No, no thanks," she replied. "I don't know what to say about what men feel. For them, it's something mysterious that happens to us women. They are only observers of the process once it's begun although at the same time they know they are a part of it... Maybe they feel distant and near at the same time. It must seem odd to them. You should ask Adrián about it."

"I'll ask him, but I don't think he'll say much. He'll tell me the usual, that he's happy and that the rest is my usual nonsense."

"It feels strange to think you're going to have a baby...incredible how time passes, isn't it? I remember when we used to talk about all these things locked in my room..." She closed her eyes and laid her head back on the sofa. She saw the two girls engrossed in contemplating the pictures in a book called "The Miracle of Life" that had belonged to her Aunt Inés.

"Yes," Sara said, in the same nostalgic tone. "We've grown up...soon we'll be old ladies, we'll have grandchildren, and we won't believe it."

Would she have grandchildren? Lavinia thought, overwhelmed by nostalgia and the impossibility of visualizing her future with the certainty Sara felt. Maybe she wouldn't even have children.

She opened her eyes and looked, as she so often did, at the house, the garden, and her friend sitting there languidly, sipping coffee. She was always disconcerted by the thought that this could have been her life. It was like standing at a crossroads. Lavinia had chosen a different path, one taking her further and further from those slow afternoons spent contemplating the flowerpots filled with begonias and roses, Sara's delicate white china on the table next to the green inner patio, the grandchildren, the vista of old age with braided white hair. But her choice also distanced her from indifference, from this isolated, protected, unreal time. She was sure she wouldn't have been happy like that, even though she would have liked to think about having children, about a cozy world...

"Have you thought yet about getting married, about having children?" asked Sara.

"No, not yet," Lavinia replied.

"I worry about you all the time. I don't know why I'm always afraid you'll get into trouble; you'll let yourself be led by one of those impulses of yours. Even though you always called me a 'mystic,' I think that of the two of us, you're more romantic and idealistic. You have more trouble accepting the world as it is."

"The world is not any *particular* way, Sara. That's the problem. We are the ones who make it become one way or another."

"No. I can't accept that. We're not the ones who decide. It's other people. We are only part of the crowd, ordinary people... Do you want another cookie?" she asked, holding out the plate of coconut cookies.

"That's an easy way to look at things," Lavinia said, taking the cookie and staring absently at the patio. She often got into discussions like this with Sara. She never knew if they were worth pursuing. Usually she would put an end to the conversation by showing a lack of interest.

"But what can be done? Tell me. Here, for example, what can be done?"

"I don't know, I don't know," Lavinia said. "But something can be done..."

"You don't want to accept it, but the truth of the matter is nothing can be done. Look at you there, with all your ideas, designing that general's house..."

"Yes, well, and what do we know...maybe I can convince the general he should be more concerned about the misery of the poor," and she adopted the kind of joking tone one uses to end a conversation. "Come on, Sara, let's talk about your future child. We'll never get anywhere with this topic."

She stayed and talked to her friend a while longer. On Sunday they were invited to an picnic at some friends' hacienda. It was the host's birthday. The hacienda had a pool and the excursion promised to be fun. They made plans to go together.

"Aren't you going to take Felipe?" asked Sara.

"No. You know Felipe doesn't like parties."

"I've never met a more antisocial person than that boyfriend of yours," Sara said. "But that will be better, because then we can talk more between ourselves."

As she was leaving, she ran into Adrián returning from the office. She congratulated him. He accepted the congratulations shyly, like a cute child. Lavinia smiled to herself, confirming her theory that even if he was truly happy, he didn't know how to handle his own participation in the matter. The surest proof of his excitement was his not having made any cynical or joking remarks. Nevertheless, Sara couldn't perceive it, waiting as she was for the joyful hug like in the movies.

She liked to make love to music. Let herself flow in the tide of kisses with music in the background, soft music like the sinuous body she became in bed. It was amazing, she thought, how the body could be so pliant and versatile. By day, a little tin soldier marching through the streets, from office to office, sitting erect on hard, uncomfortable chairs; by night, as soon as there were music, caresses and kisses, abandoning itself, letting itself soften, become light, relaxed in the anticipation of pleasure, sipping the touch of that other skin, purring.

She couldn't imagine that she could someday lose the feeling of wonder and amazement each time their naked bodies met.

There was always a moment of tense waiting, of threshold and joy, when the last piece of clothing fell defeated beside the bed and the smooth, pink, transparent skin emerged from between the sheets, illuminating the night with its own glow. It was always a primal, symbolic moment. To be naked, vulnerable, with pores open to the exposed skin of another human. It was then time for the deep gazes, desire, the foreseeable actions which were yet forever new: the approach, the touch, the hands discovering continents, palms of familiar skin, known anew each time. She liked Felipe to enter the slow rhythm of a time without haste. She had had to teach him to enjoy caresses in slow motion, the long, drawn out foreplay to reach the point of desperation until the dikes of patience burst, and the provocation and flirting shifted to passion—riders in full gallop of an apocalypse with a happy ending.

Their bodies understood each other much better than they themselves did, she thought, while she felt Felipe's weight settle exhausted on top of her legs.

From the beginning they discovered they were sybarites of love, uninhibited and ingenuous in bed. They liked exploring, mountain climbing, deep-sea fishing, a universe of novas and meteorites.

They were Marco Polos with their spicy essences and saffrons. Their bodies and all their functions were natural and pleasurable to them.

"You never cease to amaze me," he would tell her, tugging her hair affectionately in the morning. "You've gotten me addicted to this business, with those little moans of yours."

"You, too," she would reply.

The bed was their League of Nations, the room where they worked out their arguments, it was where their separations flowed together again. For Lavinia, being able to communicate so profoundly at skin level, when they often got confused on the level of speech, was a mysterious condition. It didn't seem logical to her, but that was the way it worked. It was the terrain where they had achieved equality and justice, vulnerability and trust, where they had the same power over each other.

"It's just that talking gets things tangled sometimes," Felipe would say, and she would argue that it didn't. In fact, she was convinced it didn't, that human beings understood each other best by talking. The way their bodies communicated was something else, a primal impulse, extremely strong but one that didn't eliminate differences, even if it led to tender reconciliations and caresses. It was even dangerous, she argued, to think that conflicts were resolved that way. They could gather beneath the skin, lurk between the teeth, corrode that apparently neutral territory, put cracks in the League of Nations.

It was amazing it hadn't already happened, considering their frequent face-offs. Maybe it was because when they argued, Lavinia actually separated the Felipe she loved from the other Felipe, the one she felt didn't speak for himself but as the incarnation of a sad old discourse: the bad child she wanted to release and expel from the Felipe that she loved.

Flor would always tell her she was too optimistic when she thought she could free her Felipe from the other Felipe, but she conceded Lavinia could hope.

Perhaps hope was the mechanism that allowed her to preserve the music when they made love, although maybe it was just a defense mechanism she had invented to fight off disappointment and pessimism when the thought that change was not possible came over her... How could she believe so fervently in the possibility of changing society and not believe in changing men? "It's a lot more complex," Flor would say, but those theories didn't satisfy Lavinia. She didn't deny the problem was complex, nor was she naive enough to imagine easy solutions. It seemed to her that the heart of the matter was a problem of technique. How could the change be brought about? How should woman behave with man, what did she have to do to rescue the "other"?

She hugged Felipe while he slept and, drifting into sleep, fled from those uncertainties..

• • •

CHAPTER 20

General Vela had called her to a meeting in his office. Ten minutes before the appointment, she turned off the highway toward the gate to the military base.

With an authoritarian gesture, the guard blew his whistle and signaled that she couldn't enter, raising his arm to force her to return to the highway.

Stopping, she stuck her head out the window and shouted that General Vela was expecting her.

The guard, in an olive green uniform and a combat helmet, stopped waving her off and, walking slowly, cautiously, went over to the car.

"What did you say?" he asked, looking at her suspiciously, going over the inside of the car with his eyes.

"I said I've got a appointment to see General Vela. He's expecting me in five minutes."

"Do you have any identification?"

"My license."

"Give it to me."

She picked up her purse. The soldier stepped back a bit, as if he were afraid a weapon would emerge from it. She took out a license and gave it to him.

"Wait here. Don't move," he ordered and went back to the control booth.

Lavinia noticed with satisfaction that she wasn't nervous. On the contrary, she felt sure of herself, animated by her superior motives, and she felt the exaltation of penetrating that bunkered place, of being on the turf of the enemy himself, like a condor reveling in its own ability to fly as it gazes down at its tiny enemies below.

She could see nothing of the military base. A high, solid wall, interrupted only by the black metal gate in front of her, hid it from passersby.

She drummed the tips of her fingers impatiently on the steering wheel. If the guard didn't return soon, she'd leave. She'd tell the general they hadn't let her in, that he should give more specific orders.

Undoubtedly the general would be furious with his subordinates and would reprimand them.

The next time they wouldn't stop her, they'd let her pass quickly.

At first it had been difficult to realize what power came from acting with aplomb, with the assurance of one who is in control and deserves respect. It was always more effective, especially when one was a woman. She had corroborated it in meetings with the engineers and General Vela. If she acted coy and smiling, she was treated in a sexist, sophisticatedly demeaning way. In professional matters, Flor was right: one had to learn from men. And she'd observed them until she figured out the mechanism.

She looked at her watch. Nearly five minutes had passed. She decided to wait no more than five minutes.

Seconds later, the gate opened. Another guard, this time with captain's stripes, came up to her.

"Miss Alarcón," he said, coming over to the car window. "If you don't mind I'm going to ride with you in your car to General Vela's office."

"Isn't it here?"

"Yes, but you'll have to drive across the whole base. I'll go with you so you won't have any problems" And he opened the door and got in beside her.

The gate opened.

Behind the wall, various buildings and barracks formed a citadel, connected by streets where military vehicles were moving about or parked. Uniformed soldiers walked along the sidewalks.

They passed two more check point barriers until they came to a group of concrete buildings. On a smaller scale, they had the same heavy, monumental architecture of the structures in Mussolini's modern Rome: plain gray walls with geometric bulk, rectangular proportions. Mentally Lavinia stored away the details of the structures and the layout of the streets. She preferred to drive in silence so as not to lose her concentration and be able to remember points of reference.

"This is it," the captain said without losing his cadet's expression even for a moment. "This is the Chief of Staff's headquarters. You can park over there."

They got out and, after crossing the lawn, they entered the main building. A gigantic portrait of the Great General's father, founder of the dynasty, presided over the vestibule.

The secretary in a blue suit nodded a greeting to the captain.

Going up the wide marble stairs, they reached another, larger vestibule onto which several offices opened, each one protected by a guard in full regalia. In the middle, the waiting room with its leather furniture was marred by the adornment of plastic flowers on the tables.

General Vela's office offered the same mixture of bad taste and solid, cold architecture. The focal point was a colored photograph hanging on the wall—the Great General smiling a toothy grin from ear to ear. Taken from a lower angle, the photograph tried to invest the small man with the majestic air he lacked. The rest of the furnishings, made of vinyl and chrome, were supposed to be modern. The ashtrays and the shell and snail decorations gave the room a touch of kitsch. Above the filing cabinets the secretary had a collection of matchboxes in an enormous crystal goblet.

She was a bottle-blond, high-strung and slender, middle-aged but trying to look like a teenager. Smiling affectedly, she asked Lavinia to sit down so she could "announce her." The courteous captain, the general's aide-de-camp, left discreetly.

She had hardly gotten comfortable when the intercom buzzer sounded. The secretary lifted it with a little jump that made Lavinia think of a hot line, said "Yes, General," with the tone of a sick bird and then, moving like a wind-up doll, opened the door to Vela's office, indicating she was to go in.

"Good afternoon, Miss Alarcón," the general said, standing behind his solid wood desk, surrounded by photographs of the Great General hugging him, pinning a medal on him, fishing with him, in a helicopter, on horseback.

"Good afternoon, General," she replied, coming over to shake his hand across the desk.

"Sit down, sit down," he told her obsequiously. "Would you like some coffee?"

"I would love it," she said with her most beguiling smile.

"Prettier every day," remarked the general, lasciviously.

"Thank you," she said. "What's on your mind? What's new? What can I do for you?"

"Oh, yes!" the general said, returning from some diseased thought. "I sent for you because I was thinking last night as I was going over the blueprints at home that on the terrace facing the living room, besides the pergola, I'd like to put a barbecue..."

"But we already have one next to the pool..."

"Yes, yes, I know, but it's just that, look, the one for the pool is fine for the summer; in the winter, with the rain, I need a covered area for the barbecue. I already explained to you, didn't I, that it's something I like to do when my friends come over?"

Lavinia took out her notebook and made some notes, nodding her head.

"You want the installation to be the same as the one by the pool?"

"I think it should be a little smaller, don't you?"

"Well, in any event, we'll have to extend the pergola."

"That's my idea, but maybe we could make it a little smaller."

"Yes, a little smaller would be better." Lavinia wrote it down wondering why General Vela would call her to come for something that could have been done perfectly well by telephone.

"Is that all?" she asked.

"Yes, yes. That's all, but drink your coffee...there's no rush. You've just arrived. Tell me how the house is going..."

She was sure the general had something else in mind. She began to think about what she would say to him if he tried to make a pass at her, so she could be polite and firm at the same time.

She explained in detail the agreements with the engineers regarding the bulldozing, the materials, the electrical installation and the sewer. She didn't want to give him the chance to introduce another topic of conversation.

"So do you think the house will be ready in December for sure?" asked the general.

"We'll do everything we can. I think it can be done..." she said.

"We want to have a housewarming party that will coincide with New Year's, invite all our friends...and you, of course..."

"Thank you, thank you," Lavinia said.

"Do you like to dance?"

"Not too much," Lavinia said, thinking 'here it comes.'

"What a pity! I was planning to invite you to a little party some of us officers are organizing...you know, something small just for fun. We work hard, and we rarely enjoy ourselves. It seems to me you're also the type of person who works a lot and doesn't get to relax too often, in spite of the fact that you're so young. You're very serious..."

"No, not at all! What makes you think that.. I'm always being invited to parties and outings..."

"But you hardly ever go," the general said, as if he knew all about her.

"Yes, yes, of course I go. It's just that I don't say yes to every invitation. You know getting up in the morning isn't easy after staying out to all hours."

She began to feel uncomfortable. While she didn't understand the direction the general's questions were headed, she could sense his curiosity, not knowing if it came from his eagerness to seduce her or something more dangerous.

"Don't you have a boyfriend?"

"Well...I guess you could say that. I go out with another architect, someone at work." Did he know about Felipe? Lavinia thought, feeling more and more uncomfortable. She decided to tell the truth. She thought it was less suspicious than denying it. If he was investigating her, he would certainly know about her relationship with Felipe.

"Ah..." the general said, with an innocent expression. "So that's why you wouldn't be able to come to our little party... What a pity! It's just that I've been telling my friends how efficient you are. Pardon me, but I hardly ever meet women who, besides being pretty, are intelligent and capable as well...I'd like them to meet you."

"Thank you," she said, relaxing a bit.

"But what do you say then? Can you go or can't you?"

"When is it?"

"Next Sunday."

"Well, I have plans...an outing," Lavinia answered, thankful it was true.

"But that's during the day and this is at night..."

"You're right, but we'll be getting back late, and you know how you come home exhausted from those things. Why don't we make it for some other time?"

"Well, if there's no choice...another time!" the general said with a forced smile. Obviously he was upset at not getting what he wanted.

He got up, indicating the interview was over.

"In any case—and pardon my insistence—think about it. Maybe you won't be so tired when you get back... If you change your mind, you can call here at the office. I'll order a vehicle to pick you up. Tell your boyfriend you have a meeting at work..."

"You are a persistent man," Lavinia said, making an effort not to snap "Leave me alone!" at him.

"I always get what I want," the general said, returning her smile with a lecherous expression.

Again the cadet, cordial and polite, was waiting to take her to the gate of the compound.

In silence, controlling her anger at the feeling of having been manhandled, Lavinia left the office firmly striding on her high heels.

She noted an expression of compassion in the secretary's eyes.

"You should have told him no and that was it," Felipe was saying, pacing with long strides about the office. He was furious.

"Well, that is just about what I did tell him," replied Lavinia. "You know I can't tell him what I think: I have to play dumb! I don't see why you get like this!"

"It's just that I know what he's after...and there are still several months until the house is finished! You should make it clear to him as soon as possible that you aren't willing to let yourself be seduced."

"Felipe, please, calm down. Why don't we think about how to deal with this without your getting all upset? Don't you see that it's much worse for me than for you? You can't imagine how I felt looking at those lecherous eyes..."

"You see? You see why I didn't want you to get mixed up in this matter?"

"I can't believe what you're saying," Lavinia said, losing her temper. "Everyone—you most of all—agreed that Vela's house was important. Now don't go telling me I shouldn't have gotten involved!"

"Inviting you to a 'little party'! Those little officers' parties are famous! Who does this bastard think you are!"

"A woman. For him all women are the same..." And, lowering her voice, she added: "What do you think Sebastián is going to say? Do you think he'll consider it a good idea for me to go?"

"No, you're not going to go." He snapped with an irate, domineering expression.

"Felipe, you're not the one I answer to. I answer to Sebastián. Calm down," Lavinia said, trying to reason with him. "Remember how many times you've told me the Movement comes first and everything else is secondary... You're reacting like an offended husband."

"And you're very calm... Is it because you want to go?" he said, accusingly.

"I'm leaving," Lavinia said, getting up. "I won't let you even dare insinuate that I want to go to his party. You'd better learn to control yourself..."

She slammed the door as she left Felipe's office, oblivious to the stares of the draftsmen, their heads lifted in unison from their tables, following her until she closed the door to her cubicle.

Almost a whole week went by without her seeing him. They passed each other in the office without saying a word, sunk in the absurdity of their own silence.

The Sunday of the "little party," Lavinia went on the excursion as planned with Sara and Adrián. She returned to her house fearing she'd find messages or an automobile waiting for her, courtesy of General Vela. But she found everything normal: her plants and books, the silent surroundings without Felipe.

She missed him furiously. She couldn't understand him or maybe she didn't want to understand; "understanding" was a double-edged sword. Given Felipe's behavior, it was difficult to simply apply her theory about the "other" Felipe, excuse him from his responsibility in the name of an ancestral heritage. He had continued his behavior for several days, avoiding her in the office, being out, reproaching her with his silence, for a supposed desire on her part to go to Vela's party. It was ridiculous, incredibly absurd and humiliating that even for a moment he could have thought she would have any personal interest in going to the party.

"It's jealousy, don't worry. Jealousy is irrational," Sebastián had said.

She asked—fearing the affirmative reply—if Felipe's attitude had influenced the decision as to whether she should go to Vela's party. Sebastián explained that it hadn't. The Movement wasn't interested in subjecting her to such a difficult and unpleasant task. Rather, they wanted her relationship with the general to be on totally professional grounds. At no time had they thought she should encourage the attempts by the general to seduce her, although they knew it could happen. That's why they recommended that she be distant with him.

The thing with Felipe had nothing to do with it, he repeated.

Absorbed in thought, Lavinia opened the windows to air out the house and cool off the Sunday heat. The patio's silence and peacefulness contrasted with her inner turmoil.

The worst thing was knowing this wouldn't be the end of the relationship, knowing full well that she would accept Felipe's excuses when he gave them to her. She thought Felipe was counting on distance to obtain a more certain victory when he decided to apologize. That idea bothered her, but it made her even more furious to realize that she hoped it was this and not something more ominous and obscure delaying his apologies.

"What can I do?" she said aloud, looking at the orange tree, talking to it as she often did.

She thought she could hear her Aunt Inés, that she could see her deep, light chocolate eyes, telling her: "You have to learn to be good company for yourself." She remembered her conversation with Mercedes in the office, the comments she'd made to Sara. It was so difficult to be coherent, to act logically, when you were in love...

"Aren't you going to reprimand him?" she had asked Sebastián, referring to the need for the Movement to tend to the less than revolutionary attitudes of its members.

Sebastián had smiled sadly, saying: "The revolution is made by human beings, Lavinia, not supermen. The man of the future is still a dream."

And the woman too, most likely, she added to herself.

+ + +

Poor Lavinia, looking at me, so absorbed in her love. She has not even noticed the orange blossoms, the aroma my white flowers give off.

She has been moving about the house like a sleepwalker, distracted and sad.

Her sadness has penetrated me, spilling out through all my branches. Nostalgia is contagious! I often think about being alone. We human beings are so alone. In life and in death. Imprisoned in our own confusions, fearful of showing how thin our skin is, how absorbent and delicate our blood.

Love is but an imperfect approximation of closeness.

I couldn't share Yarince's disappointment every time we lost a battle, and the isolation we suffered deepened every time they conquered another one of our cities, another one of our tribes. It was terrible to return at night to places where previously Pipiles or Chorotegas had given us food to see them dressed in long clothing like the Spaniards, disguised as white people, bent over in servile attitudes. Few dared respond to our encoded messages—imitations of pocoya or güi birds. In some villages, nobody responded any more. Only once in a while we would hear, but only in the night, some lament indicating they could no longer help us, they could do nothing.

We would return from these sad experiences and sit far from one another, letting ourselves be absorbed by our darkening thoughts.

We could say nothing to each other. Nothing could console us.

We knew by then that our struggle was hopeless. Sooner or later, we would die; they would defeat us, but we also knew that until that day we had no choice but to continue.

We were young. We did not want to die, but neither could we accept slavery as the salvation from death. In the mountains we would die as warriors; the gods would receive us with honor and ceremony. On the other hand, if out of desperation to save our lives we gave ourselves up, dogs or fire would dispose of our bodies, and we couldn't even hope for a chosen death.

To defend ourselves from defeat and desperation, we gathered around the fire at night to tell our dreams to one another.

But nostalgia affected us deeply.

We often fell silent, and in our loneliness, each one struggled against fear and sadness in his or her own way. We did not have the strength to face any more ghosts than necessary.

We grew more and more alone.

• • •

At noon, on General Vela's land, the tractors and bulldozers moved around, excavating and flattening the earth. A fine terra cotta dust tinged the workers' clothes red. The engineering company had installed harsh bright lights for the night shifts needed to finish the house on time.

Lavinia got out of her car and went to the shed where the construction boss was with the chief engineer.

She noticed the workers' eyes looking secretly in her direction.

In the middle of the shed were a rough wooden table, several chairs, and another small table where a coffee pot was plugged in. Two men, one young and the other around fifty, were drinking coffee.

"Hello," she said, and addressing the older one, asked, "Are you Don Romano?"

"Yes, that's me. What do you want?" said the man in the T-shirt and denim pants, a pencil behind his ear.

"I'm Lavinia," she said, holding out her hand to greet him, "the assistant architect in charge of supervising this project."

"Oh, you are?" said Romano, looking at her with curiosity. He had a good-natured face, round cheeks and light eyes, big bushy eyebrows with a few gray hairs that stuck out.

"Yes ," Lavinia said. "I see you're already moving along with the bulldozing."

"We'll finish this week," Don Romano said. "May I introduce the assistant engineer, Mr. Rizo?"

"So you and I are going to be seeing a lot each other," Lavinia said to invite the complicity of the engineer's "assistant."

"Seems that way," the assistant engineer said, a young man whom Lavinia guessed might be her age, slender and shy.

She acted self-assured to conceal her fear of possible rejection by the "men" on the construction site, which Julián had predicted.

She asked Don Romano to explain what procedure was being followed in the bulldozing, pointing out the importance of carefully measuring the height of the different levels on which the foundations of the house were to be set, as a way of letting him know the authority and control she had over the architectural plan.

Romano spoke calmly, answering her questions and concerns. She noticed that he looked at her carefully, almost with curiosity, but she didn't feel dislike or rejection from either of the two.

The assistant engineer didn't talk much. He kept his eyes on the blueprints, nodding in agreement to Lavinia and Romano's conversation.

"What luck to get a shy one," she thought.

Then they walked to the construction site and finally Lavinia said good-bye.

Don Romano accompanied her to her car.

"Are you coming back tomorrow?" he asked.

"Yes," Lavinia said. "You're going to be seeing me every day," she added with a smile.

"You know, I had a daughter who wanted to be an architect," Don Romano said. "But instead she got married and died in childbirth... The fact is, I never thought it was right for her to study that sort of thing, but when I see you..."

She didn't quite know what to say: the old man moved her. She patted him on the shoulder, said "Well, I'm sorry" and drove off in her car. Romano's spontaneous and surprising confession returned her to her own nostalgia. She spent the day keeping herself busy so she wouldn't think about Felipe, but things like this reminded her she was still thin-skinned.

Back at the office, she found a brief note from Felipe on her desk: "Come to my office when you get in." Her heart shot up like an elevator in her body. She decided to wait for a while. She didn't feel it was dignified to go running at the first sign. She called Mercedes, requested a cup of coffee and asked if there had been any telephone calls in her absence.

"Look on your desk," Mercedes said, roguishly, going out to get the coffee. She came back almost immediately and while she put it on the desk, she took her time carefully arranging a napkin, saying to Lavinia:

"Did you see the note Felipe left?"

"Yes," she said, hiding her dislike of Mercedes' curiosity. It was practically impossible to hide anything that happened in the office from her. She had mysterious means of finding out everything. In this case, obviously and without any subtlety, she had checked the top of the desk.

"You should get rid of that bad habit of looking at what is on people's desks," she added.

"But I just came to leave you a letter," Mercedes said, playing innocent, "and I saw it. He didn't fold it or anything. I don't go through things, if that's what you're trying to say..."

Lavinia waved her off, indicating she wasn't willing to start a discussion with Mercedes. The secretary left, swaying her hips with an offended air.

"Poor thing," Lavinia thought, feeling bad at having treated her harshly, but everyone had the same complaint about Mercedes. Her curiosity knew no limits. Being Celestina or going around worrying about others' love lives was perhaps her way of compensating for the misfortunes of her own romantic experience. She had started up her relationship with Manuel again. This time, however, it was with an obvious dose of bitterness, almost as if she were giving in to a dark, inevitable destiny.

Lavinia couldn't help noticing a flutter in her stomach when she thought that even with all the differences, she was about to start up her relationship with Felipe again, in spite of everything.

She settled in her chair and lit a cigarette. The hum of the air conditioner sounded loud in the afternoon quiet. It was siesta time. In spite of the cool artificial atmosphere, the humidity was visible on the windows, where it rose like a white veil that blurred the scenery outside.

She wasn't deceiving herself about the imminence of her capitulation, but she had to find a way to get certain things established with Felipe. She wasn't willing to lose the chance to make him see how absurd and disrespectful his attitude was. She wouldn't allow him the victory of an easy reconciliation.

She was practicing her speech when Felipe appeared in the doorway, startling her.

"If the mountain doesn't come to Mohammed, Mohammed goes to the mountain," he said and sat down, lighting a cigarette.

"He's acting like the charming seducer," noted Lavinia, trying to recover her composure, leaning back in her chair again without saying a thing, reminding herself of her decision not to make his apologies easy.

"As you probably noticed," Felipe said, "apologizing is not my specialty..."

Lavinia didn't look away.

"But it was nothing serious," he said. "Don't be like that..."

"And if it wasn't so serious, according to you," Lavinia said, "why did it take you so long to come to apologize?"

"Because, as I told you, I'm no good at apologizing ...especially when my stupidity was so obvious. How could I not feel uncomfortable having to apologize for being so stupid? You have to admit it's hard to accept one's inner demons..."

"And do you think I have to accept them?"

"No, of course not. But as you yourself say, one has to try to be understanding. After all, there are things inside a person that are almost uncontrollable—distrust, insecurity... Machismo, in a word."

"The worst part is having to hear you use my own words to save face. You're hopeless! You're the master of repentance!"

"It's just that you want magical results," Felipe said. "You think that just by talking about these problems and recognizing them, everything should change. It's not that easy. One has almost primitive reactions to certain things. That day, for example, do you think I didn't realize I was acting like a jerk, that what I said was unfair?... But I couldn't help it. It came out in spite of myself. And you slammed the door in my face. You didn't give me time to fix it then. You turned it into a serious matter, so I'd have to make special apologies, as I'm doing now. And it's uncomfortable, difficult to overcome one's pride... But you see I am asking you to forgive me..."

"Still, I can't spend my life forgiving you because 'you're not responsible' for those 'primitive' impulses. I take back what I said. I won't be understanding any more. By virtue of understanding, I'll end up finding justifications for all your actions!"

"I'm not trying to justify myself. I'm telling you that I recognize I acted like a jerk. What else do you want me to say?"

"I don't know why I get the feeling that I only need a priest's robe to be a priest in a confessional and order you to say five rosaries in penitence."

"I'll say them, Lavinia. If you ask me to, I'll say them," Felipe said, kneeling beside her chair in a penitent attitude.

She couldn't hold her smile back, or the embrace, or the reconciliation, made possible by humor. He knew the mechanism. She let him use it. There were no magic remedies against the attraction of his skin, and much less in those circumstances where the whole universe seemed to hang from delicate filaments and every day lived was a day gained against the constant possibility of separation or death.

"Just so you know: that's the last 'primitive impulse' I'll 'understand,'" Lavinia said before Felipe went out the door.

• • •

CHAPTER 21

"Always running. You never stop," Lucrecia said, pulling the dirty clothes out of the hamper in the bathroom.

Lavinia was quickly getting ready to go back to work. The only success she'd had with Lucrecia was that occasionally she would call her "Lavinia" instead of "Miss Lavinia" and once in a while, she'd tell her about the new love affair that kept her singing while she did the housework: he was an electrician, a man about fifty who had done all the playing around he needed to do and had offered her marriage and a home of her own. They were getting married next month.

Lavinia would be the maid of honor. "Because you're my friend," Lucrecia affirmed. And Lavinia had already resigned herself to this "friendship." It had been impossible for her to break the traditional servant-employer relationship.

Maybe in another time, in another type of society, in the future, things would change for both of them. Maybe then she would accept her as an equal, Lavinia thought.

She finished applying her lipstick, reminded Lucrecia to buy bread at the neighborhood store, and left for work.

In the last few months, since the construction of General Vela's house had begun, her schedule had been really irregular. She had so much to do that the twenty-four hours in a day were not enough. It seemed as if everything around her had decided to accelerate its rhythm simultaneously. Not only did she have to battle with Julián, the engineers, the suppliers of construction materials, the carpenters and the interior decorators, frantic with the deadline Vela set but the Movement also seemed to have entered a phase of heightened activity. Suddenly new faces had appeared, silent and smiling men and women, whom she had to take at dawn and dusk to the road by the hemp brake.

Sebastián had sent her out to find strange things: for example, fifteen watches in perfect working order that could be synchronized; party dresses, water canteens.

Felipe, busy with who knew what odd activities, was gone on weekends, returning exhausted Sunday nights.

She suspected he was going to military training because he returned with his nails and hair dirty, and his knapsack full of muddy clothes, which exasperated Lucrecia.

So the months went by in a crescendo of events. The arrival of the dry season could be felt in the November winds. Since October, the rains had succumbed to bright days, allowing the construction of Vela's house to proceed more quickly.

The general insisted on inviting her to "little parties," but Lavinia had now clearly established that the relationship was to remain on a professional level. On Sebastián's advice, she warned him—in the most cordial and diplomatic manner—that either he accepted her professionally or she would ask another architect to assume her duties. It was a tense, uncomfortable moment, but finally Vela seemed to relent and slowed down the rhythm of his sieges to a much more manageable level.

She arrived at the office and quickly went over some problems with Julián to assure the delivery of the wood for the ceilings that were to be installed the following week.

Seated at her desk, looking over the contracts with the curtain and carpet suppliers, she mentally went over the assignment she had to carry out that night, the approach she would take to convince Adrián to collaborate with the Movement.

She had nearly forgotten that there was a time (it seemed so far away now!) Adrián spoke about the Movement often, mentioning it with respect and quiet admiration. He was the one who first explained their objectives in the days of the trial of the warden of La Concordia prison, when she called them "heroic suicides."

Sebastián reminded her of it.

"There were several attempts to approach him at the university," Sebastián had said, "but they were only preliminary efforts. Afterward, he finished his degree, and we lost track of him."

In the dizzying series of events that led her to join, Lavinia had simply not remembered Adrián's comments. It was odd that she had forgotten, especially now that she could recall conversations where Adrián talked of stories he'd heard in the universities about "the boys." She must have been so disinterested at the time that she didn't even pick up on it.

The day she mentioned Adrián's name to Sebastián in relation to a comment about her friend Sara's pregnancy, he asked his last name and when she said 'Linares' said, more to himself than anything, "Oh, really?"

Just the past week Sebastián had questioned her about what Adrián did, how he lived, what he thought. She tried to be fair in her evaluation. As for his political inclinations, she noted the positive comments he usually made about the Movement, even when in practice he seemed so determined to remain on the sidelines, maintaining his status quo. "He's like Julián," noted Lavinia, "he has no hope." She commented that with both Sara and Adrián she avoided talking about political topics. After all, they were her link with the social world. It would have been difficult to maintain the congruency between her socialite personality and the way her new political awareness would undoubtedly have revealed itself in a heated discussion. Adrián was concerned about what he considered her "instability."

His concern was understandable, Lavinia admitted. He had seen her go through an apparent rebellion when she left her parents' house, the club and all the rest of it, and then had seen her return to the social circle of parties and social engagements, which they often attended together. The change still intrigued him. He wasn't convinced of it.

To her surprise, Sebastián suggested she propose the possibility of collaborating with the Movement to Adrián, "without beating around the bush." "He knows what it's about," he told her, referring to Adrián's days at the university.

She wasn't certain what it meant to tell him "without beating around the bush," Lavinia thought while she organized papers on her desk. She imagined Adrián's amazement when she, the "unstable one," approached him, and this produced a feeling of deep satisfaction in her. Nevertheless, she was worried about the way he might react. Adrián had the strange need to make her feel insecure, bad about herself. She had never been able to face his irony and cynicism squarely. She was afraid of hearing him make fun of the Movement for recruiting people like herself, or comments or sarcastic remarks of that sort which would touch her insecurity, the delicate, fragile line of that identity being born within her, which she knew was still vague. In spite of her acceptance by the Movement, she couldn't stop feeling that her class background was a heavy burden she would like to shed once and for all. It seemed like an unpardonable sin to her, a border that perhaps only a heroic death could totally erase.

At the parties and social gatherings she'd obediently attended in recent months, she found sound reasons for the existence of that border. She detested the arrogant and paternalistic behavior of the wealthy and powerful, indifferent to the daily injustice that surrounded them, while they enjoyed their privileges carelessly. She often felt that perhaps she hated them even more than her compañeros did precisely because she knew them so intimately, because she could guess their motives as if they were clearly spelled out. Nothing escaped her, and even in those who pretended to be honest and concerned about their surroundings, she could read the pity and scorn for those who didn't belong to their circles of splendor.

The terrible thing was not being able to separate herself completely from that—from the years when for her things had also been "naturally" that way, to have to accept the burden of a tarnished identity. She feared she would encounter to her horror the legacy of her "illustrious" forebears in herself—would find that she also had those detestable attitudes.

Wrapped in these thoughts which inevitably depressed her, she spent the entire day working in the office and then headed for Adrián and Sara's house. She drove through the streets and tried to raise her spirits. To console herself, she remembered the history of men and women who had also come from privileged milieus who had successfully managed to risk the perilous leap toward the future.

Perhaps her anxiety about acceptance went back to her childhood, she thought; it had nothing to do with the Movement. Maybe the Movement now represented the mother and father whose love she'd always tried to earn, whose acceptance had been so essential because it was so painfully absent. Without Aunt Inés, all acceptance would have been denied her; or paradoxically, perhaps Aunt Inés' desire to make her her daughter had created the distance and silent resentment of her parents... Who could know? There was nothing to do but struggle against ghosts of her past and her subconscious! Her life was now in her own hands. It was useless to try to assign guilt in the pale tribunal of the afternoon, dissolving now into the shadows.

The street lamps, brought to life by an timer that turned them on at dark, almost magically, began to come on along the street where Adrián and Sara lived. She parked her car in the driveway behind Adrián's, and walked slowly to the door, still uncertain about how she should broach the subject. It was only when the bell rang hollowly inside the house that she realized she had not taken Sara's presence into account.

She found them eating supper. Since her pregnancy, Sara had taken on an beatific expression, as if she had found in the embryo growing inside her a miraculous fountain of peace and solace. Her body was growing, expanding in soft, and round lines. Lavinia couldn't help feeling a deep warmth in her womb whenever she saw her, an almost animal desire to be pregnant and a wave of tenderness.

"How's that tummy coming?" she said as she patted her on the stomach and gave her a kiss on the cheek.

"It's growing...see?" Sara said, proudly showing her, stretching her dress against the roundness.

It was true, her stomach had grown a lot. Her five months of pregnancy were obvious now.

Lavinia greeted Adrián and sat down at the table.

The three of them ate between patches of silence, interrupted by comments about the nearness of December, Christmas, Sara's condition. Casual conversation among friends. It was hard for Lavinia to concentrate, worried as she was about finding a way to be alone with Adrián.

"Adrián," she said with sudden inspiration. "After supper, I need to ask you for some advice about the project I'm working on."

"The general's house?" Adrián said with an ironic smile.

"That's the one."

"With pleasure."

"Do you have drawing paper here?" If she managed to get Adrián into the study, the problem would be solved.

"Yes, of course. In the study."

"Would it bother you, Sara, if we worked in the study for a while?"

"No, no, don't worry. If you don't mind, I'm going to bed. I'm very sleepy. With this belly, I'm always sleepy," she said, hiding a yawn.

"She's turned into a marmot," Adrián said, affectionately. "What she should do is look for a cave to hibernate in like a bear until the baby is born."

They laughed jovially. Relieved to have found so easily a solution to the "where," Lavinia, returned to her preoccupation with the "how."

Moments later they finished supper. Sara told the maid to serve Lavinia and Adrián coffee in the study and said good night to each of them with a kiss.

"Don't beat around the bush," Sebastián had said. The expression kept repeating itself in her mind.

They went into the study. It was a small, inviting room, lovingly arranged by Sara, of course. Adrián's diploma and engineering certificates occupied one of the walls. On the others, there were framed illustrations of old blueprints used by the Spaniards during the colonial period to construct cities. Behind Adrián's drafting table was a shelf with books and photographs from their wedding. In the middle of the room were two comfortable sofas and a small table where the maid set down the coffee tray.

Adrián turned on the air conditioning, while Lavinia demurely served the coffee in the little porcelain cups.

"You have done well for yourself in this marriage..." Lavinia said, teasingly.

"Yes, I have, haven't I?" Adrián said. "There's nothing better than being the master of your house and having a good wife..."

"There you go again..."

"Well, you know between us it's become a required conversation. Since we always eventually mention the topic, we might as well take it up right from the start..." Adrián smiled.

"This time I don't think we'll talk about that," Lavinia said.

"Yes, I know. We're going to talk about General Vela's house... I promise I won't be sarcastic, although you already know what I think about the matter."

"I think the same thing you do. My first reaction was to refuse to design the house..."

"Then why did you do it?"

"Because there were people who thought it was important for me to do it..." Lavinia said, casting a veil of mystery over herself, thinking how approaching him would be easier than she had imagined, enjoying it.

"Of course. Julián must have thought it was of utmost importance!"

"I'm not referring to Julián. I'm referring to the National Liberation Movement."

"And what do you have to do with the Movement?" Adrián said, taken totally by surprise.

"I've been working with them for months now," Lavinia said, seriously.

"Oh, woman!" Adrián said. "I knew you were going to get mixed up in something!"

"I'm not mixed up in something, Adrián. You used to say that they were serious, the only ones who acted out their principles..." she said, with slight sarcasm.

"I still do think that, but you... You're not cut out for this sort of thing; you're so romantic, naive, you don't realize the danger. It probably seems like a big adventure to you."

"That's what it was at first, maybe. But now it's different. You can't deny life teaches us..."

"No, I don't deny it, and you're a sensitive woman, but...I don't know, I can't see you in that context."

"Well, let's not worry about me now. The compañeros gave me the task to ask you to collaborate. They say they approached you in the university and that although nothing concrete came of it at that time, they wanted to know if you were still willing to support the Movement."

Adrián rested his head on the back of the chair, silent. Lavinia took out a cigarette, lit it, and blew a dense mouthful of smoke, without looking at him, giving him time to think about her request.

"So they told you about the university?" he said at last, leaning over to take a sip of coffee and looking at her.

"Yes."

"Those were flirtations, a few contacts, nothing more," he said, leaning back in the chair. "At that time we all collaborated by printing underground flyers, distributing

316 • THE INHABITED WOMAN

them...afterward, well, you left the university and you had to start thinking with your stomach...earn money, get well-established, get married... You leave your dreams behind. You become more realistic..." He stared at her.

"But we have to believe in dreams, Adrián," she said softly. "We can't let ourselves be defeated by the horror of reality. Do you want your child to grow up and live in this environment? Don't you want a change for him? Do you want him to have to condemn his parents, like we have, for not having done anything to change the way things are?"

"What I don't want, Lavinia, is for my child to be an orphan. I want to be by Sara's side to bring him up and give him everything he needs..."

"We'd all like that, Adrián. Do you think I don't want to have a child too?"

"But you don't have one."

"But I'd like to have one some day, under other circumstances."

"I congratulate you for planning it. My reality is that Sara is pregnant."

"But that shouldn't be an obstacle, Adrián. On the contrary, that's all the more reason you should help..."

Adrián got up. He went over to the drafting table and began nervously to rearrange pencils, erasers and rulers.

"And so what is it they want me to do?" he said.

"It's no big deal," Lavinia said. "They only need you to lend them your car several nights a week during the next month."

"Do you know what that means?" Adrián said, nervous, coming close to her. "If they catch someone with my car, it's the end. I'd be arrested immediately."

"They asked me to tell you that only 'legal' persons, nobody who is 'burned,' will drive your car... They also wanted to know if they could hide some weapons in your house..."

"That's absolutely out of the question," Adrián said. "I can agree to anything that involves me, but storing weapons here means involving Sara, and there's no way I'll do that. I don't even want to think about what could happen... Do you see?" he added, agitated. "That's the problem with you people. As soon as anybody starts to support you, he is involved in more sensitive and more dangerous matters before he even gets a chance to regret it."

"All right, all right, calm down," Lavinia said, thanking him for that "you people." "Since you're both 'clean,' we thought your house would be a good hiding place... I thought of it, to be honest."

"That's your problem, you don't think enough. You don't realize what you're up against. You've never felt repression anywhere near you! You think this is all like a movie! I did see in the university how they took our friends away, for much less than this, and we never saw them again. They disappeared! As if they'd never existed!"

"Don't get worked up, Adrián," Lavinia said, trying not to get irritated, not to get into a personal argument, trying not to let his words affect her, hurt her. "Forget the part about the weapons. Just tell me if you'll lend them your car."

"What's that about only legals driving it?"

"It means your car isn't going to be used for dangerous things. They're going to use it to transport people. The risk is minimal. I'll make a copy of your key and give it to somebody. Three times a week, you leave your car in a certain place and someone will pick it up and bring it home to you later."

"And how do I explain that to Sara?"

"If you want, I can explain it to her," Lavinia said, relieved. Given the way the conversation had gone, she had thought Adrián would refuse.

"No, we won't tell her anything. I prefer she doesn't know anything. It's safer for her."

"Personally, I think it would be better to tell her, but you have to decide."

"I'm not going to tell her. I'm definitely not going to say anything to her. It's not a good idea to make her nervous with her pregnancy and all. I'll figure out what to tell her about the car."

This time it was Lavinia's turn to lean back on the sofa. She lit another cigarette in silence. She looked at her watch. It was nine o'clock.

"I'm going," Lavinia said. "It's kind of late. Sara must be worried, if she hasn't fallen asleep... I thank you in the name of the Movement."

"Don't be so formal..."

"I'm not being formal. You don't know how difficult it is to find cars, collaborators, these days..."

She got up feeling extremely tired, exhausted from the effort of observing Adrián's inner struggle, feeling his weakness, and understanding it at the same time.

"I look at you, and it still seems incredible to me that you're involved in these things," Adrián said, walking her to the door, putting his hand on her shoulder. "Please, take care of yourself. It's very dangerous."

"I know," Lavinia said. "Don't worry, I know."

"The Great General is frantic because of what's happening in the mountains," he said. "And the struggle to control commerce in the city is costing him the support of the private sector. I don't think he knows how to gauge appropriately the price he's paying for his impulses. But he must have some intuition. Have you noticed how they've stepped up their surveillance?"

"Yes, yes. Of course I've noticed, but I have a good cover. General Vela, at least, doesn't suspect me."

"Don't be too sure. In any event, if he suspected you, you wouldn't realize it. He's an expert in counterinsurgency."

She said good-bye to Adrián. The light from the stars was not enough to illuminate the shadows. The street lights had been turned off. Darkness had fallen like a weight on the street. The cars seemed like strange abandoned antediluvian animals. She felt afraid. It had been a long time since she'd experienced the sharp-edged terror of the early days, but her conversation with Adrián revived the old fears. In recent months, when she had heard Sebastián and Felipe talk about the repression in the countryside, she had felt enough anger and rage to get her through her daily tasks. Considering the siege endured by the compañeros in the mountains, the risks being run in the city seemed small and irrelevant. Besides, recently the political activity in the capital had diminished. The Movement seemed to be lying in wait. Little by little, Lavinia saw signs that something big was being planned. Only this could explain the secret hectic activity she was witnessing, imperceptible to those who didn't know about the hidden world of the underground.

Although Sebastián avoided her questions about it, lately he questioned her constantly, asking her opinion about the possible reaction of the army and the government to a "bold" action the Movement might carry out. From scraps of remarks and insinuations, she suspected a kidnapping, but Felipe denied that possibility over and over again. "In a kidnapping, the action ends up concentrating on individuals," he said, "and we want to broaden the focus of struggle."

The "bold action," whatever it might be, would undoubtedly touch off an asphyxiating wave of repression. Their very inactivity, the Movement's silence in recent months, must have the army worried, even though one could imagine that the brunt of its activities was concentrated in the mountains, where the skirmishes were intensifying. "Our compañeros are making a heroic effort," Sebastián said. "They're making great sacrifices to keep the army busy even though they're extremely short of weapons and ammunition."

But Adrián was right about what he had said: vigilance had increased. Day and night olive-green jeeps loaded with soldiers with combat helmets and machine guns patrolled the city. They were the infamous FLAT. On the other hand, the masses seemed to be building up energy to hurl themselves again defiantly into the streets, to burn tires and overturn buses.

The tension in the air was almost palpable as she drove the car through the silent, dark streets, wrapped in her own thoughts.

Busy with her daily tasks, she usually was not aware of the heavy atmosphere around her. She hadn't felt afraid. She had not felt the fear which now sent a chill though her spine while she added up the bits of information stored in her mind, pieced together the parts of the puzzle, came to conclusions.

Danger was lying in wait, even though her defense mechanisms kept her from intuiting what was to come and allowed her go about her days like a fearless, busy bee.

Fear had not paralyzed her, perhaps because she had enjoyed since childhood the unconscious feeling that people like her were under a special protection in the world: jail and early death was not for them.

Those privileges again, she thought to herself.

Like Flor had once said, a certain degree of paranoia would serve her well. "A certain degree of paranoia is healthy."

She took a deep breath, trying to relax. She was pleased with the result of her meeting with Adrián. As they said good-bye, he had given her an affectionate and concerned hug. He wasn't a bad person. Maybe now they really could be friends.

She found Felipe in her bedroom. He had a suitcase placed on the bed and was packing his clothes and books.

"Where are you going?" she said, putting her purse on the chair, feeling the sting of premonition.

"Don't worry," Felipe said, seeing her turn pale. "I'm not going anywhere."

"But...that suitcase. What does it mean?"

"Well, in a way, I'm sort of leaving."

"Stop the riddles," Lavinia said, nervous and looking for a cigarette.

"You're smoking a lot lately," Felipe said. "It's not good for your health."

"Let me worry about my health, do you mind? Tell me what you mean by 'sort of' going away," she said, going over to look at what was in the suitcase.

"It means that, for your safety and mine, it's not good that I practically live in your house. For the sake of appearances, it's better for us to maintain a little distance. We should have done it some time ago. Even though I'm not so 'burned,' I'm not so 'clean,' either. And lately surveillance has increased. We've relied on your cover. Usually they don't check on people like you too much, but at this point we can't take any chances. The truth is we haven't been that careful. It's not right. We have to step up our security measures, or everything could be ruined."

"And why right now, what is it that can be ruined?"

"Lavinia, please. Haven't you figured out that we're working on something...?"

"Yes, of course I've figured it out...but what is it, Felipe? Tell me what it is. I think I have the right to know."

"It's not a matter of rights. It's a matter of security. It was inevitable you'd realize something is going to happen. But the less you know, the better. Better for you and better for all of us. None of us should know more than what is strictly necessary concerning the work each is doing."

"It has to do with Vela, doesn't it? They're going to kidnap him?" Lavinia said, stubbornly bent on getting an answer.

"No," Felipe said. "It doesn't have to do with Vela, I swear to you. Vela was an initial project, but we discarded that already."

"Then why does Sebastián keep insisting that the house should be ready in December?"

"To disinform you," Felipe said. "I shouldn't be telling you this. I am because I love you, because of our relationship, but I shouldn't do it. Don't you dare mention it to Sebastián. You have to keep on working and following his orders. This is between the two of us, so you'll rest easier. I'm telling you again: I shouldn't have said anything to you, but I don't want you to keep on being needlessly worried..."

Lavinia sat down in the chair and put out the cigarette on the sole of her shoe.

"So now I won't see you," she said, resigned, convinced by what Felipe had confided in her.

"Yes, yes, you'll see me. You'll see me at the office and occasionally I'll be able to come here. We can also see each other somewhere else, taking the proper precautionary measures. But I can't go around doing what I'm doing and always come back to this house. If they detect me and follow me here, it would be fatal."

"But don't you think they already know about your relationship with me?"

"They might, but until now there wasn't much they could discover through me. In the future, that will change. It's already changing. That's why we can't go on as if nothing has happened."

"So you're leaving now?" Lavinia said, in dismay, feeling more and more tired, wishing she could go to sleep and not wake up.

"Yes. They're coming to pick me up in half an hour."

"You're sure you're not lying to me, Felipe, you're not going underground like Flor, are you?"

"No, Lavinia. Believe me. If I were going underground, I'd tell you."

He went over to the sofa and took her hand, pulling her up so he could embrace her. Lavinia closed her eyes and abandoned herself to Felipe's embrace. She breathed the scent of Felipe's chest, his shirt, and began to cry quietly.

"I'm afraid," she said.

"Don't take it like that," murmured Felipe, holding her tightly against him. "Everything will turn out all right. You'll see."

"I don't want to be left alone."

"You're not going to be left alone, Lavinia. We'll still be seeing each other."

"It won't be the same anymore..."

"For a while," Felipe said, stroking her hair, calming her, consoling her...

"I'm afraid," she repeated, pressing against him listening to his heart beat, suddenly invaded by an irrational desire to keep him there, fearing his heart would stop beating, touching Felipe's skin, the muscles of his arm, that flesh which a bullet could leave lifeless, deaf and mute to her caresses. She closed her eyes tightly to try to see Felipe back in her house in a not too distant future. She tried to see herself with him, reading side by side in the placid evening hours. Nothing. The vision would not come. Ever since she was a little girl she imagined she had the power to "see herself" in the future. When something she didn't understand happened to her, she used to close her eyes and concentrate to try to see if she could "see herself" beyond the present. "See herself," for example, in the airplane that was landing (she was afraid of flying). If she managed to have the vision, she felt calmer. It was her way of knowing everything was going to be all right, that she would arrive safely. It always worked. She'd "seen herself" several times. Now she saw nothing.

"I can't see you," she said, crying harder, trying to control the sobs that seemed to emerge from deeper than her thorax, beyond herself even, coming from a greater anguish than the small space within her chest.

"What do you mean you can't see me?" Felipe said softly. "I'm right here."

"You don't understand," Lavinia said. "I can't see you in the future. I don't see us together..."

"Nobody can see the future," Felipe said, holding her away from him a little, looking at her and smiling tenderly.

Lavinia covered her eyes and cried harder.

"Come on, come on," Felipe said. "Don't be so tragic. You have to be strong and optimistic. We can't let ourselves give in to sadness and pessimism. We have to trust that everything will work out all right. It's not good to let our fear run wild. You have to have faith."

Yes. She had to have faith. She couldn't let Felipe leave feeling the flood of her desperation. She had to be strong. She breathed deeply. She couldn't give much weight to childish, magical tricks. They were only tricks of her imagination. She couldn't give in to ominous premonitions. It was her own fear, nothing more than that.

"You're right," she said, "you're right. I'll calm down."

She took several deep breaths. Everything was going to be all right. Felipe wasn't going underground. She'd see him tomorrow at the office. She gradually calmed down.

She went into the bathroom to get toilet paper to blow her nose and dry her tears. Felipe went out to get her a glass of water.

"How did it go with Adrián?" he asked after she was sitting on the bed with the glass of water in her hand and no longer crying.

"Well, I think," she said. "It was hard to convince him, but he finally agreed to lend us his car. I asked him if we could hide weapons in his house, but he said that was out of the question."

"I can understand," Felipe said. "But something is better than nothing."

"He said he couldn't because Sara's pregnant, and it would put her in danger."

"That's natural," Felipe said. "I don't blame him."

He left soon afterward. The dense, clinging silence of the house closed in around her.

She didn't turn out the lights. She left them burning as if in that way she could keep her somber thoughts from breaking into obstinate tears the moment Felipe went out the door.

✢ ✢ ✢

CHAPTER 22

Time, that playful god, that "something" our astrologers searched for day and night from the highest mountains, carefully observing the movement of the celestial bodies, the star-studded dome that also surrounded us then, unfathomable and infinite, is spiraling. Destiny weaves its nets. She is at the vortex of the blooming of life. She watches over the things of the earth. Huehutlatoalli used to sing:

"Care well for the things of the earth.
Do something: cut wood, till land, plant trees, harvest fruit.
You will be able to eat, to drink, to clothe yourself.
You will stand on your feet.
You will truly be.
In this way you will be remembered.
You will be praised.
In this way they will come to know you."

In this new world, simple things give way to complex relationships.
She has not fought with spears. She has battled with her own heart to the point of exhaustion until she has seen her inner landscape shaken by hundreds of volcanoes, until she has seen new rivers, lakes and softly sketched cities emerge. I, quiet inhabitant of her body, see her constructing the solid foundations of her own substance. Now she stands and advances irrevocably toward the place where blood will find its respite.

• • •

"I have a surprise for you," Sebastián said on the phone the next day.

Lavinia was in the office. It was mid-morning. The sun was breaking through the sky, illuminating the distant mountains visible through the picture window. She felt better.

The night before, the tears had been finally overridden by an exhaustion so great that it plunged her into deep sleep. She slept so soundly that she woke late. It was almost ten o'clock when she arrived at the office.

"Good or bad?" she asked.

"Good, good, of course," Sebastián said, "but I don't want to tell you over the phone. I'll wait for you at my aunt's house" (his aunt was a specific address; other addresses were his 'cousins,' the lumber store, simple telephone codes). "Pick me up at five this afternoon" (five o'clock meant six o'clock).

"OK. See you."

She couldn't imagine what "good" surprise Sebastián could have for her. Could it be something related to Felipe? she wondered. She didn't think so. It had been a good idea to move Felipe out of her house. If he had to go on sensitive missions, it was better for them to keep their distance.

She remembered her desperate reaction the previous night. The memory of her fear still knotted her stomach. It had probably been caused by her conversation with Adrián, her thoughts later in the car, her fatigue. She felt ashamed at having behaved so melodramatically. But she was sad. It would be hard to get used to Felipe's absence. She'd seen him when she arrived at the office. Tender and lovingly, he asked her how she had slept. He was concerned about her. She put him at ease, pretending to feel the understanding and strength she would have liked to feel, apologizing for her first reaction, explaining it by her fatigue, the tense time with Adrián, and her surprise at finding him packing his suitcases.

As usual, Lavinia arrived early for the meeting. The 'aunt' was a little-frequented corner along the avenue parallel to the wall of the main cemetery. There was a large jocote tree against which Sebastián would usually lean while he waited for her, biting into the ripe fruit that he picked up from the ground.

When she first drove by it was three minutes before the appointed time. With the usual monotone, the announcer on Radio Minuto said: "It is five fifty-seven." A woman was walking along the sidewalk when Lavinia turned at the corner to take the round-about route that would bring her back to the almond tree at "six o'clock sharp." She thought, as she drove farther, that something had registered in the back of her mind as she passed.

She tried to project the visual image of the place in her mind, searching for the almost imperceptible register.

It was only when she was coming back along the avenue at the exact appointed time and saw the woman leaning against the tree, nibbling on jocotes like Sebastián did, that she realized she'd noticed something strangely familiar about this figure minutes before as she was turning the corner. She had seen her walking along the street, heading toward the place where she was now waiting for her.

It was Flor.

Lavinia saw her smile and get into the car. She noticed her hand held out with a small, ripe, rosy jocote in it.

"I brought you a present," Flor said, while Lavinia, still incredulous, with tears in her eyes, took the tiny fruit from her hand as she felt an uncontrollable urge to cry.

They hugged, and Lavinia gave a little sob. Flor withdrew from her gently.

"Don't cry, sweetie. We can't stop here," Flor said. "Come on, start the car. I need you to take me to the road by the hemp brake. Nibble on your jocote. Its bitter taste will perk you up..."

Obedient, Lavinia placed the jocote between her teeth and began to drive. The simple gesture, the fruit lovingly offered, Flor's unexpected presence, had detonated the charge of strength she had accumulated in recent days. She couldn't stop the heavy tears from flowing. She dried her cheeks with the back of her hand, sucked on the jocote and breathed deeply because now the traffic, the lights, the vehicles in front of her and behind, demanded her attention, forcing her to close the dam that had been about to burst.

"I'm sorry," she said. "But these past few days have been crazy. I've been very tense; I don't know what came over me when I saw you..."

"Don't worry," Flor said. "On days like these when one is going around with so many things bottled up inside, the tiniest thing can unleash the flood... I'm so glad to see you!" she added, patting her hand affectionately.

"I never would have thought that this was the surprise!" Lavinia said, with a sigh. "It was beyond my imagination. Sebastián is incredible... He's like a magician."

"You didn't have any trouble recognizing me, did you? Now that my hair is short and chestnut?"

"No. I recognized you immediately. I'd already seen you, do you know that? About three months ago, I saw you on Central Avenue. You were in a car with some man. It was frustrating to have you so close and not be able to let you know, not even blow the horn, shout, nothing..."

"I didn't see you. When I'm riding in a car, I try not to look outside."

"So how have you been?" Lavinia asked.

"Fine. Great. A lot of work. Fantastic compañeros. I've been running here and there... And you, how's it been going for you?"

"I've had a lot of work, too. General Vela's house is nearly finished..."

"How did your first interview go?"

"Excellent. I managed to 'conquer' General Vela by coming up with a special design for his private study, a room where his weapons collection will be on display. I copied the device from a revolving wall in a California millionaire's mansion. He loved it!

"And what's that about a revolving wall?"

"The wall looks solid, but it's made of wood panels set on pivots. That will allow him to decide if he wants to display his weapons or not. It's like the secret walls you see in the movies. It was my trump card to win Vela over. Only Julián, myself, and now you, know about it..."

"So if there are no weapons visible on the wall, it means they're on the other side of it?"

"Yes, exactly."

"And how does the mechanism work?"

"It's very easy. You simply release a latch behind a sliding light switch on one side of the wall.

"Ingenious," Flor said. "Now I see why it went well in the interview..."

They were quiet. Their prolonged separation made its presence felt. Night was beginning to thicken, erasing the silhouettes of the trees that bordered the highway. Lavinia drove slowly, trying to lengthen her time with Flor. The road looked quiet. Nothing out of the ordinary. Nothing suspicious in the rear view mirror.

"I see you've gotten more cautious," Flor said, smiling, noticing Lavinia's constant glances in the mirror.

"These days, especially. There's an atmosphere of tension. Surveillance has been stepped up."

"There are more skirmishes in the mountains, and the army wants to give the impression of strength. However, their theory is that we are destroyed. They think that once they put an end to the pockets of resistance, as they call them, in the North, they will have annihilated us completely. It doesn't even occur to them that we'd be capable of staging anything in the city. They underestimate us."

"General Vela never tires of saying that 'the subversion in this country is minimal.' He said it just recently in a press conference."

"That remains to be seen. It's good that you're being more cautious," Flor said, nodding her head.

"Felipe moved out of my house," Lavinia said. "It seems there's the risk that he could be detected, and they could follow his trail to my house."

"That's right."

"It had occurred to me. But since I didn't want him to leave, I didn't mention it before. It seems to me that everyone knows what to do; I always have to wait for someone to tell me what to do."

"You're suffering the excessive 'ceremony' of beginners. It happens to many of us, especially in the beginning when we join the Movement thinking we are nobody. And the truth is it takes time to develop trust, the authority to speak and voice an opinion. In regard to Felipe's move, we didn't think it was necessary until now. The fact is, in this country, when you belong to a certain class, you're practically above suspicion. Not even the leaders of the traditional opposition are under much surveillance. They have a very class-conscious perspective on the repression and conspiracy... They are right to a certain extent. Certainly in the future that will change, but it hasn't happened yet. That's why we didn't worry too much.

"Your background has certain advantages, too! On the other hand, Felipe isn't so 'burned.' He was somewhat visible when he taught in the university, but they don't take that much into consideration. They consider all university students 'unruly and hot-headed.' The truth is their security system is based on premises that for a long time were valid, but that are changing at a rhythm that's faster than their own ability to adapt. Nevertheless, it's dangerous to underestimate them. We can't take any risks...now more than ever."

They were entering the dirt road that split off from the main highway. Soon she'd have to leave Flor.

"But," Lavinia said, "we've spoken almost entirely about me. What happened to the doubts you had?"

"It was more or less as I expected," Flor said. "I've had to act strongly, a little 'like a man' if you wish, but in the underground there is a lot of room for closeness and intimacy. Sometimes you have to spend days locked up in a house with other compañeros and compañeras. You get to know each other very well, you lower your personal defenses. People talk about their dreams and uncertainties... You work quietly. Most of the conversations have to do with the future... It's been an enriching experience. I'm more hopeful than before."

"And have you stopped being afraid?"

"I handle my fear better," Flor said, smiling calmly. "You never quite lose all your fear when you love life and have to risk it, but you learn to master it, to keep it under control, to use it when necessary. The problem is not being afraid, I think; the problem is what to be afraid of. Not give in to irrational fear... "

They had arrived at the road by the hemp brake. Lavinia stopped the car in the usual place.

"Drive on some more," Flor said.

Silently they continued for a few more meters until they reached a path that led to a large colonial house barely visible at the end of the path, blurred by the darkness.

"All right," Flor said. "I'm getting out here. I brought you to this place," she added, "because you should be familiar with it. If in the next few days some serious problem were to occur, a really serious one...for example, if they follow you and try to capture you and you can get away...you try your best to come here without their detecting you. You must make absolutely sure that no one follows you here. Throw them off your trail. On the other hand, if you were to be captured, you must keep the location of this place secret, even if it costs you your life. You must not reveal it under any kind of pressure, under any kind of torture, under any circumstances. Ever."

She nodded, gravely. She looked at the house, the surroundings that she knew so well, even though it was the first time she'd come this far, the 'here' where she would drop off Sebastián, and lately other mysterious passengers. She began to perceive the scope of what was going to happen. These conjectures threatened to leave her paralyzed at the wheel, frozen with fear. But Flor was beside her.

"We probably will meet again," Flor said. "So we don't have to say good-bye. Remember the security measures, to the letter," she added, getting out of the car.

When she turned the car around to go back to the city, she saw Flor's extended hand waving good-bye, her white palm like a firefly in the night.

✦ ✦ ✦

Flor is "Xotchitl" in our tongue. Xochitl reminds me of my friend Mimixcoa. She was an artist at the loom. For hours on end she would silently weave beautiful centzontilmatli, multicolored blankets her mother sold in the tiangues. On the day of my water sign, atl, she gave me a skirt and feathers for my hair, with which I adorned myself and celebrated.

We went to the calmeac together. Because of her sweet, grave nature, she was destined to serve the gods when she reached adulthood. We were very different. She always seemed to know her place in the world. On the other hand, I resisted the long hours of using the spindle or kneading the corn in the metlatl. The ichpochtlatoque, our teacher, constantly scolded me and but she loved Mimixcoa, Northern Star, tenderly. Because of these differences, one might think the two of us could not be close. But it was not like that at all. She listened to me kindly when I told her of my wanderings with Citlacoatl, learning to use the bow and arrow. She even asked me to show her how to use it, but the first time she fell on her face and never tried it again. Her eyes were deep as the sacred cenote where she was offered in sacrifice to Quiote-Tláloc, the god of rain. We spoke a great deal during those days before the ceremony. She broke her habitual silence to tell me her magical dreams of dancing stars and her vision of the return of Quetzalcoatl, the god she loved most and the one with whom she dreamed of being united as soon as she looked into the jade eyes of Tláloc, beneath the waters.

I was sad, and she understood how painful the separation was, since we had been like sisters. But she encouraged me to dance my life. She sang verses to me that said: "Every moon/every year/every day/ every wind/comes by and goes away./And all blood as well reaches its place of quietude."

She knew she was going to die. She felt sad because she wasn't going to see me again, never see the flowers in the fields again, the golden maize, the purple tinge of the sunsets. But she was also content because she would live with the gods, she would accompany the mother-goddesses, the Cihuateteo, in their journey toward the place where the sun sets. She gave me wise counsel. She said she would always be with me. Every sunset, I know she sees me. She saw me before. She sees me now. She watches over me.

The day of the sacrifice, I walked with my mother among the warriors who were to carry out the order, up to the sacred cenote. Mimixcoa was brought along with other beautifully adorned children and maidens to the steam baths for purification. My mother and I threw pom and jade pieces into the sacred waters.

The priests received Mimixcoa at the nacom, the sacrificial platform. They removed her feather cape and, clad only in a simple white cloth, she was thrown into the water. Before she was lost in the ever-flowing water, she gave me a long and tender look. Then she disappeared. I stood silently by my mother for a long time, praying for the gods to save her and send her back as a messenger. But Mimixcoa did not return to the surface, and it was then that I cried and screamed, despite the efforts of my mother to quiet me. I did not want her to drown. I could not resign myself to offering her to Tláloc, who at that moment would be contemplating her with his jade eyes.

Little did I know that years later Tláloc would receive me into his breast, would send me to populate gardens, to this tree which I now inhabit, where I now long for my friend Mimixcoa.

• • •

CHAPTER 23

She stood in front of the construction site. General Vela's house was finished. A crowd of men milled about the new building, removing the last vestiges of the work from the surrounding area. The construction company's truck was hauling off remnants of wood, cement and large paint barrels.

Another group of workers was dismantling the shed that had served as an office for the supervisors and foremen. She had spent many hours there during the last few months, with the engineers Rizo and Don Romano, and with Julián and Fito.

It was the 15th of December 1973. The work schedule had been followed with Swiss precision.

The finished house occupied 9000 square meters, distributed among four levels, in the style of the Babylonian terraces, with picture windows on the three upper levels.

The more important entertainment areas, the many living rooms requested by Mrs. Vela, the dining room and the general's music room, had a scenic view. Only the gigantic master bedroom, the private study, the children's and the sister-in-law's bedrooms had been placed in the interior of the house, for fear of thieves and assassination attempts.

The service area occupied the fourth level. There were no picture windows there, but Lavinia had managed to install good-sized louvered windows that, in spite of everything, allowed some view to the outside, plus good ventilation.

All the exterior walls were painted white and were combined with stretches of red brick openly constructed to allow a view of the interior gardens

In spite of the owners' bad taste, the house was a lovely piece of architecture. It seemed to be suspended in space, nestled in the abrupt incline of the terrain. Its spacious interior was light, and each room flowed into the next.

The ostentatious decor was the only thing that bothered Lavinia. It had been impossible to get Mrs. Vela to agree to allow local carpenters to build the furniture. Only the numerous built-in items had been made locally; the living room, bedroom, and dining room furniture, the rugs, curtains, and accessories, that is, all the rest, had been brought in from Miami. The two sisters had spent the last two months traveling constantly, fascinated by the Florida department stores, shipping by air flowery cushions, crystal chandeliers, bronze urns and planters, oddly textured bedspreads, rattan chairs, plastic stools, and pool umbrellas.

But from outside, where Lavinia was, the house was a pleasure to behold, a harmonious eagles' nest on top of the hill. The landscape, her beloved landscape, offered itself without remorse to the sordid inhabitants of the little palace through the crystal eyes of its rooms.

We will reclaim this someday, she told herself. Someday, hopefully, the house would be the site of an art school or would be inhabited by sensitive people whose hearts would be in harmony with the beauty surrounding them.

"It seems unbelievable, doesn't it?" said the voice of Miss Montes behind her.

"You frightened me," Lavinia said, recovering from her start. "I didn't hear you come over."

"You were totally absorbed," Miss Azucena said. "My sister and I arrived a moment ago. She's inside the house. She brought the gardeners to begin planting the interior gardens. We brought so many plants from Miami... They're also going to landscape the outside gardens. The house needs to be ready, with gardens and all, by December 20th. That's the day we're going to have the inauguration. It'll be the first big celebration of the Christmas season..."

"In just five days?" Lavinia asked, surprised.

"At first we thought we'd do it for New Year's, but the Great General isn't going to be in the country then. He's going to spend the Christmas holidays in St. Moritz, Switzerland, so we decided to have the party before that. That's why we bought the grass and a lot of plants in Miami. They sell grass there as if it were a carpet. The only thing that has to be done is roll it out. You'll see—it's marvelous!"

"I can imagine," Lavinia said, thinking about the amount of money they must have spent in shipping charges, given the weight, thinking that General Vela hadn't said anything to her about advancing the date. She scarcely saw him lately. He spent most of his time in the northern part of the country.

"You're going to come to the party, of course. You're an honored guest."

"Of course, of course," Lavinia said. "And when is the general returning?"

"I think he'll be back tomorrow. You know, that poor man has been traveling up and down the country. Luckily, my sister has been traveling, too. She always worries a lot when he has to go out on those missions...those subversives are terrible...and they hate him, you know. Several times they've announced they're going to 'bring him to justice,' as they say when they assassinate people."

"Let's hope nothing happens to him, and he can attend his party," Lavinia said. "He takes good care of himself, anyway. I don't think you have to worry much."

"Let me go get your invitation," said Miss Montes. "We've already begun to send them. I think my sister has yours..."

Lavinia followed her inside the house. They found Mrs. Vela engaged in frantic activity, giving directions to a crew of men who followed her around.

"Miss Alarcón!" she said when she saw her come in. "How are you? Can you actually believe the house is ready? It turned out beautifully! Much better than I ever thought! And as soon as we put out all the plants I brought, it will look sensational! Has my sister already told you about the party? Wait. I have your invitation here in my purse..."

She was euphoric. She carried on an endless monologue. The house, the party, were doubtless the culmination of her social dreams. Her friends would envy her; it would be the event of the year, the height of General Vela's status. And she, as his wife, would receive the credit for having put her woman's touch upon these rooms, the gardens, the decor.

The General's children appeared in the vestibule, as Mrs. Vela extended Lavinia's invitation, a Hallmark card with the picture of a house emerging from a gift box and carefully inscribed inside in Miss Montes' angular handwriting.

The nine-year-old girl, chubby, cute, approached Lavinia slowly with a timid gesture that nevertheless revealed how accustomed she was to excessive attention and pampering. She touched Lavinia's leather belt.

"Will you give it to me?" she asked her, with the tender expression she probably used in order to charm and get her way. Lavinia smiled. In spite of her being Vela's daughter, she was a nice, chubby little girl. A girl, in any event. It was sad to think what she would become.

"Say hello to the lady," Mrs. Vela said. "Don't be rude."

"Hello," said the girl, smiling at her.

"And you, Ricardo, say hello. This is the architect who designed the house."

The boy, who had just reached puberty, awkward and shy like a young and ugly bird, held out his lanky hand. He looked a little like Miss Montes, but he had sorrowful eyes and the air of someone who needed protection from an environment too violent for his dreams. While she designed his room, more than once Lavinia wondered if he, like herself, had dreams in which he flew.

"So you're the one who dreams of flying?" she asked him.

The boy nodded.

"And have you ever had dreams where you see yourself really flying?"

"Yes," the boy said, looking at her with bright eyes.

"He's always dreaming," Mrs. Vela said. "That's his problem..."

The adolescent's expression recovered its opaque, languid air, which had momentarily been brightened by Lavinia's question.

"It's not wrong to dream," Lavinia said, looking at the boy with solidarity and compassion. Maybe in a different environment he could go on dreaming, she thought. Well, Lavinia said, looking at that family scene with mixed feelings, "I think I should go. If you need anything, you can call me at the office. Tomorrow, at eleven, Julián and I will come by with the engineers to go over the final details."

"Very well," Mrs. Vela said. "I hope my husband can be here. Supposedly he's coming back early tomorrow morning."

"If he can't, we can do it later," Lavinia said. "You can let us know."

"Perfect," Mrs. Vela said, accompanying her to the door.

"Wait a minute," Lavinia said before leaving. "I'd like to go over the last touches in the private study. Don't let me hold you up."

"Of course," Mrs. Vela said. "I'm going to continue with my gardeners, if you don't mind."

As she entered the armory, she felt strangely uneasy. During the construction of the house, she had tried to forget the room that had so pleased Vela. It was medium-sized, with orange rugs and a single window with brown curtains that looked out on one of the inner patios.

Two leather sofas with a wooden table were set against the wall. On the floor she saw several unopened wooden boxes. They probably contained the weapons that were to be displayed.

At first glance, the room seemed to end at the wooden wall across from sofas—a wall formed by the three mahogany panels with beautiful grain. She went over to the end of the wall where the nearly invisible mechanism that released the panels was set. She released them and gently pushed one of the panels. The wood panel turned on its axis, revealing the small inner space, the secret chamber with shelves built-in at the center. On the side of the panel that had been previously hidden and that she had just turned, one could see the brackets where the weapons were to be placed. She straightened the panel and then made the other two turn, locking the latch to fix them in place. It worked perfectly. From the general's private room, one could see the wooden wall which before had been smooth now changed to one with the brackets for the weapon collection. Again she released the latch that allowed the panels to turn, and made the smooth side face the room again.

Before turning the last panel, she remained for a moment in the small "secret" room. She felt cold. The place stored the air- conditioning as if it were a refrigerator. But it didn't matter. In any event, nobody would use it for long periods of time.

"Do you dream?"

The boy was standing in the door.

"Yes," she replied. "I dream that my grandfather puts huge white wings on me and lets me fly from a high mountain."

"I dream that I fly without wings," the boy said, "like Superman. Sometimes I also dream that I've become a bird. But my father gets mad. He says the only way to fly is to be a pilot. He wants me to be an air force pilot."

"Parents often make mistakes with their children," Lavinia said. "If I were you, I'd go into commercial aviation. Being a war pilot is very sad. You fly in order to kill. That doesn't have anything to do with your dreams of flying."

Especially if you get to be a pilot for the Great General's air force, she thought to herself, wondering if she weren't being reckless by talking that way to the boy.

"Good-bye," he said, and ran out, disappearing as abruptly as he had appeared.

As she left the house, Lavinia felt the bright noonday sun in her eyes. She rubbed her arms to rid herself of the chill. What sorrowful eyes the kid had!

Felipe was straightening papers on his desk when Lavinia walked into his office. It had been very difficult to change the rhythm of their relationship. They would meet like clandestine lovers, hiding in strange, sordid motels to make love, usually at lunch time.

"The Velas decided to have their inauguration party on the twentieth," she said, sitting in front of Felipe's desk after giving him a long kiss. She took the ugly invitation out of her purse.

"This is the invitation," she added, putting it on the table.

Felipe picked it up without saying anything. He read it and gave it back to her.

"And why would they do that? Do you know?"

"Because they want the Great General to attend. And since he's going to spend Christmas with his family in Switzerland, they had to advance the date."

"And how did the house turn out?" Felipe said, sitting down, looking both worried and distracted.

"It looks beautiful on the outside. Inside...it's awful, gaudy. A nouveau riche house. They even brought the lawn from Miami. Only the built-in furniture looks good, and some color combinations that I managed to get Mrs. Vela to accept."

"Well, that was to be expected..."

"Yes, it had to turn out like that. While I was looking at the house it occurred to me that maybe in the future, when things change, we could use it for an art school..."

"I like your optimism," Felipe said, smiling.

"Are we going to have lunch together?" Lavinia asked.

"Not today," Felipe said, searching for some paper on the desk. "I have to go somewhere."

"But you told me..." She was disappointed.

"Yes, but something's come up..."

"Something bad?"

"No, no. Just urgent," he said while he came over to give her a kiss. "We'll get together later."

She didn't see him again. Not that afternoon, nor the next day. She found a short note at her house saying that he was all right, not to look for him.

Two days without news from anyone. It was night and the December wind ruffled the leaves of the orange tree in the garden.

She had suddenly been left alone in the world. Alone and anxious. She realized how much the Movement had become her whole existence: her family, her friends. For months she hadn't even thought about going to the movies or having a good time. All the parties she'd gone to were missions they had sent her on.

Love and rebellion had managed to absorb her completely. She had gladly allowed herself to be submerged, with a never-before-experienced enthusiasm, in that network of calls, contacts, trips taking compañeros back and forth. Now, suddenly, this silence. She didn't have any means of communicating with them. No telephone number, nothing. Just the address of the mysterious house which she'd glimpsed in the dark.

What was more, the hectic efforts of the last few months with Vela's house had simultaneously stopped. The day before they had officially turned the house over to the general. His wife and sister-in-law, and the children had been present. The whole family going through room after room, space after space, touching the light switches, checking plugs, water faucets, other details. And the gardeners setting out the plants, rolling out the lawn in the garden, the swimming pool company filling the pool and adding chemicals to the water so it would be crystalline.

And Vela's son, with a more opaque expression than ever in his father's presence.

Julián told her she should take a week off, but Lavinia said she would do it later. She didn't know when. Any other time but this one when she didn't have Felipe and the others. What could she do, overwhelmed as she was by loneliness in her silent house, filled only by the December wind? She preferred to go to the office, get out, even if she did nothing more than sit, distant, anxious, waiting.

Even Christmas, which was approaching, the good Christmas spirit, had gone up in smoke for her. It made her uncomfortable. The only thing that cheered her up among the decorations of gigantic Santa Clauses with fake snow in the store windows were the graffiti that appeared on the walls, the product of unknown, invisible compañeros in the sleepless dawn. Graffiti demanding "a Christmas without political prisoners," that had sprung up everywhere during the last few weeks.

Her mother had been calling, asking her if she would come have supper with them. "Please, honey, please." Maybe she had no choice but to go have supper there with those two strangers who, after all, had given her birth. She didn't even have parents, she thought, feeling sorry for herself. They never forgave her for loving Aunt Inés. Nor had she forgiven them deep down for abandoning her to that convenient love which alleviated their parental responsibilities when they were young and didn't have time to devote to an inquisitive, playful little girl who loved books and was caught up in her own little imaginary world of houses and models.

What a combination of incomprehensions and misunderstandings!

And where could Felipe be? Where were Flor and Sebastián?

Adrián and Sara also called to invite her to spend Christmas Eve with them. "Bring Felipe." Sara had commented to her that they didn't go out much at night now because Adrián, who was so generous, decided to lend his car to a colleague at work so he could go to night classes three times a week. With the heaviness of her pregnancy, she didn't mind too much slowing down the rhythm of her social life. That was how Lavinia learned Adrián was holding up his end of the bargain. Between them, since the day she asked him to collaborate, the silence of respect had finally been established. He no longer joked about her feminism or her instability. She almost missed that. Now they limited themselves to boring, meaningless conversations. It was paradoxical, she thought, that just when they should have had more to talk about, when they finally could communicate on more equal terms, with less paternalism on Adrián's part... His machismo again. Those distances again!

The world would change. It would have to change, she thought, thinking about the faceless compañeros fighting in the mountains, the hope that lay within the sadness she felt. What were these bad moments compared with the daily heroism of others? Somewhere in the city a group was preparing to carry out an "assault," some action not yet clear to her. She envied them for being together. Undoubtedly Felipe, Flor, and Sebastián were part of the group. Everyone except her.

She who was alone, abandoned to her solitude, to the creaking branches of the orange tree in the wind.

✛ ✛ ✛

That day we awoke while it was still dark. We had to cross the river before the sun came up. The night before, Yarince and I had talked for a long time, like elders around the fire, recalling the times of our childhood, recalling the years of love and war, the stormy clouds. We went over our whole lives, a tenuous sketch of words bundled together.

Perhaps we would die soon, Yarince had said. He wanted to remember the past because we no longer could count on the certainty of the future.

I rocked him in my slender arms. With those wings, you could embrace the world, he told me. We snuggled together. For so many days our bodies had been a source of inexhaustible joy. They were at times the only strength that kept us from surrendering.

We had been reduced to a group of six warriors. We were skinny and haggard, with the look of hunted animals. That morning it was cool, a soft wind blew, bending the reeds beside the river. We were walking very close to the encampment of the invaders, so we had to cross with great caution in order not to be discovered.

We carried little, just a few wild rabbits we had caught the day before, the hammocks and mats we used to set up camp, and some clay utensils. Tixlitl marched at the head, followed by me, then came three warriors with Yarince bringing up the rear. We were on our way to a meeting with the old priests for the invocation ceremony, to read the auguries and find out what the future would bring us. We felt the need to pray, to commend ourselves to our totems so they would comfort us in the face of so much misfortune.

Tixtlitl had dreamed of Tláloc. He had seen him in the form of a woman with moist eyes, smiling as water covered her. It was a confusing dream that I was able to interpret only later.

Tixtlitl and I were midstream when the Spaniards came out.

They had been waiting for us, crouched in the underbrush.

Maybe they had been watching us since the day before.

We turned back in the water, desperate because we were defenseless.

I heard the shots from their firesticks hitting the water close by. My eyes sought Yarince, while my feet tried to get a foothold on the bottom of the river, on the rocks that helped us cross.

I saw him running on the other side. He had managed to get out of the water.

He did not meet the same fate as Tixlitl, whose blood formed a red spot around me, whose body I saw floating downstream.

He did not meet the same fate I did.

He did not die like me.

I felt a blow in my back, a thick warmth that paralyzed my arms. It was just a instant. When I opened my eyes again, I was no longer in my body: I was floating a short distance over the water, watching myself bleed, watching my body float downstream, too. I heard the warning shouts of the Spaniards and suddenly, from among the trees on the shore, where I saw Yarince for the last time, I heard that long, deep scream from my man, wounded by my death.

It was a blood-chilling sound that silenced the enemy. It terrified them and made them run out of the water, run to hide in the underbrush.

I floated with my body on the river in the current downstream. I barely glimpsed Yarince running along the shore, a crazed deer, following the trail of my blood.

I opened my mouth to shout and the wind howled. I realized then that human sight and sound were being taken from me forever. I sensed sounds and sights, but they were only sensations registered by my spirit, diluted images reconstructed by the memory of life. Oh, gods, how painful it was to feel Yarince without his seeing me, without even being able to move a muscle to touch him, to dry his tears.

At a bend in the river he caught up with me, where the rocks made the water shallow.

He and Natzilitl pulled me out and dragged me to the shore.

Yarince's love fell upon me like a hurricane of cries and lamentations. He shook my shoulders furiously, embracing me. He kept saying "Itzá, Itzá" with the confused language of desperation, of life in the face of death.

I almost couldn't bear it.

It was then that I stopped hearing him. I kept feeling Yarince near me, but I only heard the waves of the water, the sound of the water rushing over the stones, the water licking at the shore of the river.

I know that Tláloc allowed me to be with Yarince at the ceremony when the priests prayed by my body at nightfall. The wise elders conducted the ceremony next to the water until Tláloc gave me over to the gardens.

Then Yarince took my body and brought me here, to this place, where I waited for centuries, as my ancestors had decreed.

• • •

CHAPTER 24

The next day would be the inauguration of Velas' house, and she had no one to advise her whether or not she should go. She decided to take the afternoon off. Go to the movies, visit Sara or her mother. She couldn't handle the anxiety of being alone, her compañeros' silence. Moreover, she didn't want Julián to ask her about Felipe again. She didn't know what to say.

She took the car and roamed around the city, not knowing yet where to go. Suddenly she found herself taking the road that led to the little lookout of her childhood, to the etching of a girl who looked out at a world she thought was hers. Nothing was hers anymore, she thought. Not even her love, her family, her life. She had given everything over to this waiting, ticking like a time bomb. She ought to feel happy, she thought. After all, she had achieved the dream of subordinating her own life to a greater ideal. She was like a woman watching herself give birth, waiting for the contractions of a body possessed by nature to give birth to a new life silently constructed during months of the blood's patient labor. Because that's what this solitude was. Not abandonment, the fear that her loved ones would disappear, swallowed by an obscure dark destiny. This solitude was simply a waiting for birth: somewhere her compañeros must be preparing to uncoil the whip of the voiceless, of those expelled from paradise, and even from their miserable slums. They had not abandoned her, she repeated to herself. It was she who nourished those discouraging feelings. But she should be able to distinguish between reality and her ghosts. Undoubtedly the preparations of so many months were coming to an end. What could she know? What was left for her to do but speculate? Who could know if Vela wasn't really the objective of all that long preparation? Who could know?

She would find out today, tomorrow, in three days, or four, whatever day they chose. She would know by the news.

The road wound upward. The yellow December flowers swayed at the edge of the asphalt. She didn't turn her head when she drove by the dirt road that led to the hacienda. She continued to accelerate, negotiating the sharp curves until she was off the main road and entered the uneven, stone-paved one, full of holes from the rain, that led to the look-out.

There was hardly anybody there at that hour of the afternoon. A few workers from nearby haciendas were walking along the road, but at the look-out there was only the wind blowing. The couples would came later, at dusk.

She got out of the car and walked along the path leading through the grass toward the top. She sat on the boundary stone that marked the limit of the property. The inscription had been worn, erased by the touch of all those who had come to sit here, to talk about their loves, their ambitions, or their dreams.

It was a clear day. The landscape disrobed at her feet, devoid of fog. The tiny houses, the lake, the row of blue volcanoes, were spread out in the distance, silent, motionless, majestic. Up closer, the vegetation in the mountains unfolded in green toward the valley where the city lay. Twisted tree trunks hung dangerously over the edge.

From the nearby plantation came a sweet smell of coffee. The wind mingled the rustling of the leaves with the songs of parakeets in flight.

She rested her chin in the cup of her hand, looking at it all.

It was well worth it to die for that beauty, she thought. To die just to have this instant, this dream of the day when that landscape would truly belong to everyone.

This landscape was hers, her idea of homeland; this is what she had dreamed of when she found herself on the other side of the ocean. This landscape made the most outlandish dreams of the Movement understandable. This land sang to her flesh and blood, to her sense of being a woman in love, rebelling against opulence and misery: the two terrible worlds of her divided existence.

This landscape deserved a better fate. The people deserved this landscape and not the stinking sewers by the lake, the streets where pigs roamed, the aborted fetuses, the mosquito-infested waters of poverty.

Where were her compañeros? In what quadrant, along what streets were they walking? What was Felipe's doing at this moment when she felt at last that she was a part of it all?

Before going to bed, on a sudden impulse, she called her mother.

"Lavinia?" said the voice on the other end of the line.

"Yes Mother, it's me," she said wearily. They always started like that, she thought, recognizing each other.

"How are you?"

"A little sad, to tell the truth." Why was she telling her mother that? she wondered.

"Why? What's wrong, honey?"

"I don't know...I don't know. A lot of things are happening to me. The truth is I'd like to make peace with so many things."

"Wouldn't you like to come over, honey?"

"No, Mother. I'm tired. Don't worry. It was just that I felt like talking with someone."

"We haven't talked for such a long time."

"I don't think we have ever talked, Mother. I think you always felt I didn't need to talk with anyone but Aunt Inés."

"Well," the voice said, growing tense, "she was the only one you loved."

"But didn't it ever occur to you that I loved her because she cared about me, because she loved me, Mother?"

"I tried, honey, but you always preferred her. With me you were always very quiet."

"It's very hard to talk about this on the phone. I don't know why I mentioned it."

"But we should talk about it," her mother said, playing her role. "I don't want you to keep thinking we didn't love you."

"I didn't say that, Mother."

"But you think it."

"Yes, you're right. I do think it."

"Well, you shouldn't think it. You should try to understand us."

"Yes, maybe I should. I'm always the one who should understand."

"Don't be like that, honey. Why don't you come over?"

"All right. I'll come over one of these days."

"Come tomorrow."

"I don't know if I can..."

"Try."

"All right, Mother. Good night."

"Good night, honey. Are you sure you're all right?"

"Yes, Mother. Don't worry."

"You'll come over tomorrow, then?"

"Yes, Mother, I'll stop by tomorrow."

She hung up. It was the longest conversation she'd had with her mother in months, years perhaps. A real conversation. They had talked, they had brushed the subterranean, the fundamental, the things they never discussed. Perhaps someday they could come to love one another, understand one another. Someday.

She felt able to do that now. She could see her simply as a human being, a product of a time, of certain values. In her own way her mother surely loved her, as she probably loved her mother. The impulse to call her when she felt alone had to mean something.

They would never come to understand each other's way of life. Much less now. Much less each day. Her mother would never come to know what she really thought.

She went into the bathroom. She thought how someday her mother, her father and she would have to have the conversation that had always been put off, not so much for their sake, but for her own. Someday she would have to come to terms with her childhood.

She was splashing water on her face, washing off her makeup, when she heard the noise in the living room. A dull sound, like a body collapsing, the door closing.

Her heart gave a quick leap in her chest. Fear paralyzed her. She saw her face whiten in the mirror while she listened closely, trying to control the sudden weakness in her legs.

She began to walk on tiptoe toward the living room, first looking nervously in the closet for the pistol Felipe had given her when he moved out of the house. She heard "Lavinia, Lavinia," as if someone were calling to her from under water. She barely had time to realize whose voice it was when she was in the bedroom doorway, when she was in the living room, where Felipe lay face down on the floor.

"Felipe! Felipe!" she nearly screamed. "What happened to you?"

Still face down, talking with a hoarse voice, as if it required a great effort, Felipe said:

"Go outside, and make sure that there are no stains by the entrance." Then he closed his eyes.

Stunned, she went out to the walk. Stains? There was nothing on the stone slabs.

Near the door she saw the bloodstains.

She went into the house again. She knelt beside him.

"Clean the stains," Felipe said. "Clean the stains first," he said from the floor, without even lifting his head.

She ran to the kitchen and grabbed an old rag. She wet it and ran out again.

352 • THE INHABITED WOMAN

She had no idea how she cleaned off the bloodstains. She moved quickly through the garden, looking everywhere, rubbing her foot on the damp grass where Felipe's blood had fallen.

There was no movement in the street. It was almost midnight.

She came in and locked the door. She locked the windows, too, looking again and again at Felipe on the floor, his arm bent underneath his body, pale. He hadn't moved.

She knelt beside him again.

"All right," she said. "I got rid of the stains. I locked everything. Felipe, what happened to you?"

"Now, help me turn over," he gasped. "Help me see if I can get to your bed. I've been hit," he said, his voice shaky. Hit. Wounded. It was the same thing. She'd heard the expression many times. I have to calm down, she thought. She breathed deeply and helped him turn over. She had to control herself not to let go of him, not to die when she saw his chest, his stomach, the bloody clothes, the floor, and the blood on the floor.

She could see what an effort Felipe was making to sit up. He shut his eyes tight, grimacing.

"I'd better take you to the car, Felipe," she said. "I know where we can go," thinking about the house by the hemp brake.

"No," Felipe said. "No. Help me," he said, the pain distorting his face.

In a time that felt like an eternity, Felipe managed to get to a crouching position. On his knees, practically dragging himself and leaning on Lavinia, he moved toward the bedroom's light. They would never be able to figure out how they managed to reach the bed. Felipe leaned on his side, and she had to help him to lie back on the bed. He was completely exhausted by the effort.

With nerves of steel that she was really far from feeling, Lavinia brought a towel from the bathroom and began to unbutton his shirt, an almost ridiculous gesture because it had been torn to shreds.

Felipe stopped her, putting his hand over hers, indicating she should wait.

A few minutes passed. Lavinia's thoughts raced in her head. She had to get him to the hospital. This wasn't like the time with Sebastián. Felipe was dying, he was bleeding to death, there was a gaping hole in his stomach. He wouldn't last long if she didn't get him to a hospital. She'd have to call the neighbors. Nothing mattered. Nothing except saving his life, even if they put them in jail afterward. Nothing mattered.

"Felipe, this is serious," Lavinia said. "We shouldn't stay here," she said. "I have to take you to the hospital."

You're going to die, she was going to say, but refrained from doing so.

Felipe opened his eyes. Calm had returned to his expression. His breathing was labored.

Instinctively, she put some pillows behind him to prop him up a little, thinking about the blood, the internal hemorrhaging, his lungs.

"I have to get you to the hospital," she repeated, deciding to call Adrián. Adrián would help him.

"Come here," Felipe said. "I'll go to the hospital, but first I have to talk to you...please..."

"But let me call Adrián," Lavinia said. "Let me call Adrián so he can come while we're talking, so he can help me carry you to the car."

"No, no. First, come close. There's no time. Later. Later Adrián can come..."

"But..."

"Please, Lavinia...please..."

He was insistent. He insisted with his eyes, his hands, what was left of him that was still whole. Desperate, Lavinia came close.

"Listen to me carefully. The operation is tomorrow. It's going to be on Vela's house. We're going to take Vela's house.

It's a team of thirteen people. I'm part of that team...or I was..." he said with a half smile. He spoke firmly, as if he'd mustered all his strength to speak to her, the last strength he had. "And everyone is essential. I want you to take my place. You know the house well. There's no time for anyone else to become as familiar with it as they need to be. I want you to be the one to take my place. Nobody else. I know you can do it. Besides, I owe it to you because I was the one who was against your joining...," he breathed, closing his eyes. He opened them again. "I owe it to you. You can do it. You've shown you can. You can do it... Go to the house. Tell them they got me when we were carrying out the taxi operation. Tell them it wasn't the army. It was the taxi driver when I told him to give me the taxi. He thought I was a thief. He fired point blank. I told him too late that I was a member of the Movement. I got nervous. I didn't think he would be armed. I made a mistake. It was my own stupidity! If I'd told him before he wouldn't have fired. 'You should have told me,' that's what the man said."

Felipe smiled ironically at his own bad luck, at the paradox of the unfortunate accident. He coughed, closed his eyes, seemed to catch his breath in order to continue. "He brought me here himself. He wanted to help me. He didn't know what to do. He was going to take me to the hospital, but I convinced him to let me off near here. I told him not to call the police. I even threatened him..." Felipe's voice trailed off. "Just in case."

In her mind she reconstructed Felipe's bad luck. He must have been armed when he turned toward the taxi driver to tell him: "This is a hold-up. Turn over your vehicle." And the taxi driver, who was used to violence, had reacted quickly, shooting him first. Fatal duel. An error. A few seconds.

One sentence spoken in time and perhaps Felipe wouldn't have been wounded. Some taxi drivers were even collaborators of the Movement. Maybe this one wouldn't have shot him. Maybe so many things! They'd never know

now. It didn't matter now. The questions blurred as she looked at Felipe's face, the expression that was beginning to force its way through his paleness.

It was an intense, fixed expression. He was looking at her close yet far away. She had the sensation she was losing him like a tenuous radio signal, dissolving in the air. She kept still, practically paralyzed, listening to him, hearing him say that he had hindered her participation and that now she could take his place. Great gusts of love and desperation intermingled in her breast with frigid winds. She couldn't go on like this. They couldn't just go on looking at each other, telling each other with their glances what there was no long time to resolve. Their eternal arguments ended there, in the face of death, in the face of Felipe's blood flowing from his chest, spreading over the sheets of the bed where they had known love, life, the irreconcilable.

"Let me call Adrián," Lavinia said softly, trying to get Felipe to let go of her hand, the hand anchoring her to the bed where he was bleeding to death.

"You haven't answered me," Felipe said. "Are you going to take my place? Are you going to do it?"

"Yes, yes," Lavinia said. "I'll do it."

"You're not going to let them tell you no."

"No, Felipe, I won't let them tell me no."

She realized she was talking to him like a little boy. Her voice was calm and consoling, like her Aunt Inés' when she got sick.

Felipe closed his eyes and loosened his grip. He coughed slightly and his chest sounded terribly congested.

That sound made Lavinia realize the imminence of his life running out before her eyes, an end she simply could not accept, didn't consider possible. And yet she had to act, she thought, she couldn't keep resisting, thinking that Felipe was going to survive in spite of everything.

She got up and went to the phone, not taking her eyes off Felipe. Felipe with his eyes closed. Felipe's blood forming a red lake upon the bed.

"Adrián?"

The sleepy voice returned a hoarse "yes."

"Adrián, it's Lavinia, wake up, please."

Her urgency woke Adrián. She only had to say that she needed him. She didn't explain anything else. It was an emergency. Please. He had to come to her house right away. It was terribly urgent. "I'll be right there," Adrián said.

She calculated the time it would take him to get there. Fifteen minutes at the most, she thought. There wouldn't be any traffic at this hour.

She went into the bathroom to get another clean towel. She came over to Felipe, kneeling beside the bed. He opened his eyes.

"Lavinia?" he asked, and his look of absence frightened her.

"I'm here, Felipe. Adrián's on his way. We're going to take you to the hospital. Everything will be all right. Rest. Don't worry."

"You're a brave woman, you know that?" Felipe said, with a wisp of a voice, the sound of wind whistling through a canyon.

"I think it's best if you don't talk," Lavinia said. "Be quiet, my love, my love..." She couldn't contain her desire to be close to him, to put her head on Felipe's forehead, kiss him, run her fingers through his hair.

"Baby, oh baby..." Felipe said, as if he were repeating a name, and he coughed again, this time harder, and to Lavinia's horror, a stream of blood began to trickle from his mouth, while his head leaned toward her chest as she bent over him. One slight movement of his head and he was still.

Lavinia bent to wipe the blood from his cheek and saw his fixed stare, his half-open mouth. Felipe was dead. He had died jut a second ago, there, so close to her: his chest, which rose and fell before, almost wheezing, no longer moved.

"Felipe?" she said softly, almost afraid to awaken him, as if he'd fallen asleep. "Felipe?" she said a little louder. No answer. She knew there would be no answer. With both her hands, she leaned on Felipe's chest, pressing hard up and down, as she had seen the medics do more than once in first aid demonstrations. Her hands got all bloody. Nothing happened. Felipe, limp, didn't move.

He's dead, she told herself. Where's Adrián? she asked herself. When is he coming? she thought. Felipe can't die, she repeated to herself over and over, touching him, putting her face up close to Felipe's eyes, to what should have been Felipe's gaze, the sad gaze that couldn't see her any more.

No! she was about to scream. No! she shouted into the loneliness of the night.

"It can't be," she began to say out loud. "Felipe, Felipe, don't die on me," she said. "Felipe, please, come back. Felipe!" And her voice grew desperate, but he didn't move, he didn't try to calm her down, to tell her, "Don't be like that, Lavinia, calm down."

She got up, and without knowing why, began to turn on the lights in the house. She moved frantically. She wanted to do something with her hands. She didn't know what. She didn't know whether she wanted to hit something, pull her hair, or begin to cry. But the tears wouldn't come. She could only think of Adrián. Adrián had to come. She wouldn't believe Felipe was dead until Adrián came. Felipe had fainted. He was unconscious in her bedroom. He'd lost a lot of blood. That's what it must be. She wasn't a doctor. She couldn't tell if he was dead. Adrián had to come. Everything would be all right when Adrián came.

And Adrián arrived. She opened the door and took his hand without saying anything, and led him to the room, and he didn't ask any questions because he saw her covered with blood, her dress, her hands, covered with blood.

He knelt beside Felipe. He touched him and put his hand on his forehead. She saw him place his hand in front of Felipe's mouth, saw him light his lighter and place it before

Felipe's eyes. "Hand me a mirror," he said to her. She gave it to him and saw him put the mirror in front of Felipe's mouth. Then she saw him close Felipe's eyes, running his hand over his face, making sure his eyes were closed, close his half-opened mouth, straighten him on the bed, fold his arms over his chest as it is done with the dead.

He got up from the side of the bed. He came over and looked at her.

"Nothing can be done," he said in a very low voice as if he were telling her a secret. Lavinia looked at him, not wanting to understand.

"He's dead," Adrián said. "Nothing can be done."

"We have to take him to the hospital," Lavinia said. "We don't know anything about this kind of thing."

Adrián put his hands on her shoulders. He looked her squarely in the eyes.

"Yes we do, Lavinia. Felipe is dead," he said; then he hugged her and began to stroke her head slowly.

"It can't be," Lavinia said, pulling away from him. "It just can't be," she repeated. "It can't be!" she screamed.

Adrián grabbed her by the arms again, embracing her once more.

"Lavinia, please don't make it more difficult. Please. It's terrible but you have to accept it."

Felipe was dead. She had to accept it. Why did she have to accept it? Why did she have to accept Felipe's death? She didn't have to accept anything. She slipped from Adrián's embrace. She knelt beside the bed again. She touched Felipe. He was cool. His skin felt cool. He wasn't cold. Only cool. But he didn't move. He wasn't breathing. She had to accept it. He was dead.

"Felipe?" she said, "Felipe?" She was still kneeling, her head bowed, her shoulders slumped, without tears.

Again Adrián came over to her. He put a hand on her shoulder. He lifted her up, led her to the bathroom, made her wash her hands, got her to leave the room, go to the kitchen, sit on one of the kitchen stools while he made her a cup of hot coffee.

"We have to take him to the hospital anyway," Lavinia said.

"Do you know his family?"

"No. I only know they live in Puerto Alto."

"Are you sure we can take him to the hospital? I know it's hard for you, but try to think a little whether it's a good idea to take him to the hospital. They're going to ask questions there. What are we going to tell them...? Tell me what happened? How did it happen?"

"He got in a taxi. He had to commandeer a taxi, take it from the driver. A loan, you know how it is... But the taxi driver didn't understand. He thought Felipe was a thief robbing him. He fired point blank at him. Afterward he brought him here... He was afraid. He said he wasn't going to call the police..."

"What?" Adrián said. "I don't understand. He got in a taxi, the taxi driver thought he was a thief and shot him? But how is it that he brought him here? And how is it that Felipe didn't shoot first? Wasn't he armed?"

"I don't know, I don't know," Lavinia said. "I suppose so. I suppose he didn't fire because the other man fired first, because he didn't think that he would shoot him, how do I know? And afterward he told him he was a member of the Movement and not to turn him in to the police. And the man didn't turn him in, he brought him here.

"I suppose that's what happened!" She sipped the coffee Adrián put in her hand. It was hot. It was good to feel its warmth. She was shivering. She was very cold. Had it rained? Why was she so cold? Felipe's family... What was Felipe's family like?

Adrián got up and returned with a blanket. He put it around her shoulders.

"Felipe's family lives in Puerto Alto," Lavinia said. "His father is a shipyard worker... Do you think we should call them? Do we think we should call them and give Felipe to them?"

She thought: the body, Felipe's body. That's what she thought. But she didn't say it. She couldn't. She began to feel in her stomach a horrible urge to vomit. She put the coffee on the table and, holding her stomach, bent over and put her head on her knees. That's how she wanted to stay. Never lift her head up again. Never see anyone again. Stay there in her house with Felipe.

"Lavinia..." Adrián said.

She didn't respond. She began to think about Felipe's mother. What was she like? Did her son look like her? How awful it would be to arrive with Felipe, dead. She imagined the woman's screams, her pained look. "What happened to him?" she'd probably say. Lavinia's chest began to tighten.

Adrián touched her shoulder. He asked her if she felt ill. She made an ugly sound that she hardly recognized as coming from herself. A dry, hoarse sob.

"Cry," Adrián said. "It will make you feel better."

She lifted her head.

"There's no time," she said. "There's no time," she repeated. Felipe had said she had to take his place. There was no time.

The first light of dawn was beginning to filter through the window. Roosters crowed in the distance.

Adrián would have to take care of Felipe. Felipe who was dead now. She had to leave, go to the house, the house where Felipe should already have arrived. They must surely be waiting for him. The commando team must be nervous, thinking about what might have happened. Something could go wrong if she didn't get there soon, if she didn't let them know what had happened. The taxi driver could report them. She dropped into the chair.

"Adrián, you have to take care of Felipe," she said. "I have to go."

Adrián thought she was upset and didn't know what she was saying.

"Don't say that, Lavinia. You'll see, we'll take care of this together. Don't be like that. Calm down. Have some more coffee."

"You don't understand," Lavinia said. "I'm all right. I'm calm. But I have to go. I have to let them know."

"We can do that later," Adrián said.

"No, it can't wait," Lavinia said. "I can't tell you any more, but it can't wait. I have to go now, before dawn. I have to go."

"And Felipe?" Adrián said. "What are we going to do with Felipe?" He was frightened.

"We have to call Julián," Lavinia said. "Julián is his friend. He'll know how to find his family. And you have to get him out of here without anybody seeing, without the neighbors finding out. Get him out of here and take him somewhere else, away from here. It's very important. I can call Julián, but I can't wait for him. You have to stay here and wait for him. Explain to him about the accident. Tell him I had to go. Tell him not to ask any questions. He'll help you. I'm sure of it. He was his friend. They were very close," she said, and again she felt the urge to stay there, start crying, but there was no time. She had to go.

"But you can't go like that, all by yourself. You're in no condition to go, Lavinia. At least wait until Julián comes, and I'll take you."

"No, I'm all right. Nothing will happen to me. It's just that I have to go let them know. Really, believe me. You can't take me. Nobody can take me. I have to go alone." She ran her hand through her hair. At times she felt she was going crazy. She struggled with herself, against the urge to go back into the bedroom, to stay with Felipe and cry. But the tears wouldn't come. She felt frantic, torn. She wanted to go now, and she wanted to stay. She had to go, she repeated to herself. She had to do what Felipe had asked. It was the last thing he'd said to her, that she was to take his place.

She had to do it. And besides, the others would be worried. The operation might be put off. Everything could fail if she weren't strong, if she started to cry, if she stayed at Felipe's side. But it was terrible to leave him there alone. Horrible to leave him there, all dirty, all bloody on her bed. But she had to go.

She went into the bedroom. Adrián followed her. Felipe was just as before. He hadn't moved. She'd hoped that when she went in, Felipe would be on his side. On his side the way he liked to sleep. But he was still face up, his hands over his chest, just as Adrián had left him. She went to the telephone and looked up Julián's number in her little book. Julián's wife answered with a gruff, sleepy voice. It wasn't five a.m. yet. Julián got on the phone. She told him he had to come to her house, and not to say anything, but that it had to do with Felipe. Felipe had had an accident. It was urgent that he come right away.

Then she went into the bathroom and changed her bloody clothes. She put on jeans, a T-shirt and sneakers. She saw Felipe's denim jacket and grabbed it, putting it over her shoulders. She was still shivering.

Before leaving the bedroom, she knelt beside Felipe. The tears stayed inside her chest like an anguish without a channel, pain beating against every corner of her body.

"I'm leaving, Felipe," she said, putting her face close to his. "I'm leaving now, compañero," she repeated. "Liberty or Death," she sobbed, kissing his hands, feeling for the first time the dampness of tears beginning to flow like wild rivers.

She got up, fleeing from that dampness that threatened to paralyze her, threatened to make her stay, leaning over Felipe's bloody shirt.

"I'm going," she told Adrián, and left the room, almost running.

Adrián followed her to the door. They said good-bye quickly with a strong hug.

"Take care of him for me," Lavinia said.

"Take care of yourself," Adrián said.

She looked at her watch. It was almost five o'clock in the morning. She started the car. She wiped the fog and dew from the windshield. Then she drove off. The streets were beginning to come alive with milk trucks and delivery men on motorcycles hurling the newspapers on people's walks. It was just another day. Another day. Everything seemed normal. She passed houses with Christmas lights in their gardens. Trees with colored lights. Windows where you could catch a glimpse of Christmas trees. Nothing seemed to have changed. The world wasn't mourning Felipe's death. It was as if it hadn't happened. She began to cry. Her tears veiled the road she was traveling, the damp yellow flowers that swayed in the cool air of the December morning.

She felt a sobbing that wracked her from head to toe, giving her a sharp pain in her womb, in her stomach. She breathed deeply. She had to calm down. She couldn't cry like that. She wouldn't be able to drive if she kept crying that way.

Her thoughts unleashed a tangle of images. Felipe laughing, Felipe in bed, Felipe at the office, Felipe the last morning she had seen him, Felipe telling her the operation had nothing to do with Vela, telling her he hadn't wanted her to join, Felipe when she met him, Felipe in her bed, bloody, motionless. The world without Felipe. Nothing had changed. And yet, for her, everything had changed. Rage, rage at his death, so useless, the deaths of so many people, the dictatorship, the Great General, General Vela and his absurd house, the Vela women, imbeciles all of them. She hated them. She hated them viscerally, with her pulsing entrails, with her gut. She could kill them with her own hands, her bare hands. Without remorse.

And she had to keep going, had to go on. Felipe could not have died uselessly. His dreams had to be fulfilled. His and those of so many others. So that their deaths would not be empty, useless. He couldn't have died in vain. They had to triumph, had to do so many things. And Felipe laughing on the beach, Felipe on the ship going to Germany, Felipe as a boy at school... The Felipes she knew and those she didn't know flashed in her mind. Felipe sprite, Felipe bird, Felipe hummingbird, Felipe bear, Felipe machista, sweet Felipe. At the end he'd asked her to take his place. Not because he'd wanted her to do it. Out of necessity. Women would enter history out of necessity. The necessity men feel when there aren't enough of them to die, to fight, to work. They needed women in the end, even if they only recognized it at the moment of death. Why, Felipe? Why? Why did you have to die on me? My love, my baby, my man.

And so she reached the house by the hemp brake. The dark house. She parked the car in front. Lights came on. Movement. A man appeared. He was the compañero on guard. "I'm Inés," Lavinia said. "Do you sell plants here?" That was the password.

"Compañera, put your car in the back," and as she did, she saw other cars. Taxis. The Mercedes Benz taxis. They were there, hidden. There were two taxis. One was in the garage. The other one was outside, covered with blankets. And her car. That would make three cars. So they wouldn't need Felipe's taxi.

At the back door to the house, the glass door that opened onto a porch, Sebastián and Flor had appeared. They were coming toward her. They had jackets thrown over their shoulders. Anxious expressions. She felt a tearing again in her stomach when she saw them. That terrible urge to cry, to scream. She wiped her nose with the back of her hand. Flor and Sebastián came running to her. Sebastián put his arm around her shoulder. "What happened?" he said. And Lavinia couldn't say a word. She started to cry. She hugged Sebastián and cried without uttering a word, feeling she had arrived, she was with her family, with her people, her sisters and brothers. They led her into the house. A large room, practically unfurnished. There were only a few aluminum chairs covered with flowered plastic seats.

Flor said something to the guard, who left the house again. They turned out the lights. Day was breaking through the darkness.

Flor disappeared and came back again with a glass of water in her hand. She gave it to Lavinia. Sebastián had sat her in a chair. He was holding her, half-kneeling at her side. She kept crying.

She drank the water, saying to herself that she had to calm down. She hadn't come there to cry. She had to tell them what had happened, but she felt as if Felipe was going to die in that moment. Only in that moment would Felipe's death be real, in the moment when she would tell them. And the words wouldn't come. Every time she tried to say it, she would start to cry again.

"Did they follow you?" asked Sebastián. "Are they looking for you? Did something happen?"

She moved her head contradicting herself, saying no, yes, unable to utter a word.

"Let her calm down," Flor said to Sebastián. Then she came over to stroke her back and give her more water.

She had to tell them right away. She saw them getting more nervous with every passing moment. She felt that the house was being put on alert. The sound of footsteps on the floor above. Things being moved.

"They aren't following me," she said at last. "Don't be alarmed. They're not following me. Nothing happened with the army."

She took a big gulp of air. She had to continue. Had to mention Felipe. Now. See Felipe die in the eyes of Sebastián and Flor. She had to do it now, now that her sobs were subsiding and she could talk.

"What happened is that Felipe..." She took a drink of water, breathing deeply. "Felipe commandeered a taxi. The taxi driver thought he was a thief. He fired at him point blank. Felipe died at my house. About an hour ago, two maybe. That's what happened."

Now the tears ran down her cheeks, but her sobs were subsiding. She tried not to see Felipe. Every time Felipe's image appeared again in her mind, the sobs returned. She tried to think about something else, the chairs in the room, that inhospitable, abandoned place, its peeling walls. She didn't want to see the faces of Flor and Sebastián.

"You have to pull yourself together," Sebastián was saying, kneeling in front of her chair by her knees and taking hold of her hand. "And you're going to tell me slowly what happened."

She told him as best she could. Taking sips of water, using the big, rough handkerchief Flor handed her while she stood beside her chair, stroking her hair.

When she finished, Flor and Sebastián went to one side. They spoke with each other.

"We're going to send a compañero to help take care of things at your house," Sebastián said, and turning to Flor, said "You stay with her."

"Give me your car keys," Sebastián said.

"Wait," Lavinia said. "Don't go. I have to tell you something else. Felipe wants me to take his place. He insisted. He said that I know the house. That he has confidence in me. That I should do it. That I should take his place."

"OK, OK. We'll see."

"No. I have to do it, Sebastián. Please. Felipe asked me to do it before he died. He told me to insist."

"We'll discuss it," Sebastián said and went out before she could continue.

"Flor, please, you have to help me," Lavinia said. "I have to do it. I know the house better than anyone."

"Yes, yes, calm down. Don't worry. Wait until Sebastián comes back. He didn't say no. It's just that right now there are more urgent things. Drink some more water."

+ + +

CHAPTER 25

He died at dawn. He returned to take his place beside the sun.

Now he is the companion of the eagle, a quauhtecatl, the star's companion. In four years he will return as an airy and resplendent huitzilin, a hummingbird flying from flower to flower in the balmy air. Corn and plants are born in the West, in Tamonchan, the garden of the earthly goddesses of life. Afterward they make the long voyage of germination underground. The gods of rain—Quiote, Tláloc, Chaac—guide them and give them strength so they will not lose their way, so they can rise again in the East, the region of the newborn sun, youth, and abundance, the red country of dawn where the song of the quetzalcoxcoxtli bird can be heard. Neither men nor nature are condemned to eternal death. Death and life are but the two faces of the moon, one bright and the other dark. Life springs forth out of death like the small plant springs from the kernel of corn that decomposes in the breast of the earth and is born to nourish us. Everything changes. Everything is transformed. Felipe's spirit puffed wind in my branches. Now he knows that I exist, that I am watching from Lavinia's blood the signs written in the memory of the future. He will look at her from the cortege of stars that follow the sun until it reaches its zenith. He won't lose sight of her. He will project his warmth to me so that I can sustain her. Lavinia's blood hums like an agitated bee hive. Her stream had to be contained with rocks and her pain transformed to raised spears, just like the pain of Yarince as he knelt before my lifeless body.

Two men overwhelmed by anguish picked up the body of the fallen warrior. They dressed him in clean clothing. They bandaged his deep wounds. They carried him off as if he were a man drunk on pulque.

• • •

Flor took her to a small room with two long, narrow mattresses on the floor. She told her to try and rest a little while she explained to the others what had happened.

A little later Lavinia heard the whisper of voices outside, sounds of people moving. After that there was silence and then Flor's voice saying something about Felipe. She couldn't make out the words. From time to time she heard Felipe's name clearly. The rest was unintelligible. She looked at the greenish walls of the room, dilapidated and peeling. It was cold. She wrapped her arms tightly around her body. She was no longer crying. Instead, she'd fallen into a sort of stupor. She didn't know if she was living in reality or in a time distorted by pain and death.

Flor returned with a small metal mug of coffee and milk in her hand, and a piece of buttered bread.

"Wouldn't you like a little breakfast?" she said. "It'll do you good."

She set it on the floor nearby and sat down on the mattress.

"I can't believe it," Flor said, as if talking to herself. "I can hardly believe that Felipe is dead. It's been happening to me lately. I can't believe the compañeros' deaths. I can't react. I don't know if one of these days I'll start to cry and not be able to control myself. Cry for all those I haven't cried for yet. We say you get used to accepting death as part of all this, get used to seeing it face to face, without lowering one's gaze. To see it naturally. But I think that what actually happens is that we don't accept it. We can't accept it. We simply reject it. We keep hoping to see our compañeros alive.

We think that on the day of the triumph we'll find them all there, that then we'll see they haven't died, they were hidden somewhere..."

Lavinia rested her face on her knees, hugging them, moving her hands nervously.

"Were you alone with him?"

"Yes," Lavinia said. "When I saw him, I thought he was going to die at any moment, but afterward, when we were talking, I refused to accept the fact that he could die. Even when Adrián came and told me, I didn't believe it. Later, I even went into the bedroom to see if he had moved, if he'd changed his position. But nothing..."

"And did he explain to you that the assault on Vela's house takes place today?"

"Yes. He told me I should take his place, that he owed it to me because he had been against my participation. 'You're brave,' he told me, 'you can do it. Don't let them tell you no.'"

"But do you realize it's difficult to bring you in now? All of us compañeros on the team have been training together for two months, simulating the assault..."

"But I know the house better than anybody. I've been there; you haven't. I designed it."

"But that's not enough, Lavinia. We know the house plans, too."

"Yes, I know. I gave Felipe a set of plans, but afterward several changes were made..."

"But the basic design hasn't changed."

"No, but some alterations were made. I can be useful. It's not the same looking at a blueprint as having been there."

She was right, admitted Flor, but they had to wait for Sebastián.

They fell silent.

"You feel a little better now, don't you?" asked Flor.

"I don't know. I don't know how I feel. It seems as if none of this is real."

"You have to be strong," Flor said, "especially if you want to participate in the operation. Sebastián can't see you like this, so low. You have to make an effort to get hold of yourself, to get rid of that lost sleepwalker look. You have to do it. Do it for Felipe. He'd expect it of you."

"It's sad that he only admitted I could participate at the end, isn't it? It's really sad."

Lavinia smoothed her hair with her hands. She tucked her T-shirt into her pants. Flor was right. She had to overcome her pain if she wanted to participate. She put the cup of coffee and milk to her lips and began to take small sips and nibble at the bread.

Flor watched her, silently.

"It would have been sadder if he'd never acknowledged it at all..." Flor said after a long pause. "Lavinia," she added, adopting a solemn tone, "Felipe had his problems. You knew them better than anyone. But the Movement thinks that you have shown ability and courage. We recently decided to grant you 'militant' status. You were to be told after the operation, but I think it's important for you to know it now. I also wanted to tell you that whatever happens, you can count on me. I care deeply for you, I love you like a sister. I know you're going through a difficult time, but I'm sure that you'll come out of this a stronger person. I've seen you overcome your doubts and anxieties, and I know there's good reason to trust you and respect you. You decided to join us, to risk everything, to put your life on the line. That is important, and I promise you I'll fight to get them to let you to participate on your own merits. Not because Felipe asked you to do it, but because you deserve it."

They embraced tightly. Both shed quiet tears without sobbing. Flor dried her face with the back of her hand and went out leaving Lavinia tranquil, serene, a warm, peaceful feeling in her heart.

Outside, the compañeros were getting ready. The atmosphere was charged with anticipation. For two months they had been waiting for this moment. They had trained carefully. Nobody knew exactly what the target of the operation was. Sebastián would fill them in when he arrived. Meanwhile, Flor gave them instructions to leave the house "clean." They burned papers. They put away the clothes they weren't going to use in a sack. They checked their weapons.

Originally the group had consisted of four women and nine men.

Now, with Felipe's death, they would have to see whether five women would participate.

Sebastián returned while she was finishing her shower. Flor had taken her to a small bathroom. "The water's really cold," she told her, "but it'll do you good."

The stream of cold water was like a whip on her skin. Cold mountain water. It made her shudder, brought her back to life. She stood beneath the shower, letting the water run down her face and her long, thick hair. She wanted to wash away the terrible images of the past few hours. Her eyes swollen from crying. But the feeling of water on her cheeks made the tears flow again. Now, however, they were calm, resigned tears that contained both nostalgia and a purpose.

She put her clothes back on again, and Felipe's denim jacket. She was no longer crying. She couldn't cry any more. Not when she had to speak with Sebastián. The sun was high, but the weather was cool in that area, especially this time of year.

She went out to the main room. Nobody was there but Sebastián and Flor, bent over a set of blueprints on an aluminum and formica dining room table.

Sebastián looked up when he heard her enter.

"You look better now," he said.

Lavinia smiled, saying she felt better, that the water had revived her. She looked at him trying to guess from their expressions what their plans for her were.

"Have you decided yet about my participating?" she asked, making an effort to sound casual.

"Yes," he said. "It's approved. You're going to participate. We believe that your knowledge of the house is, in fact, valuable. Nevertheless, we have to give you a crash course. We don't have much time, just about ten hours. "Five" is going to show you how to handle the weapon. You will be number "Twelve." I'm "Zero" and Flor is "One." From now on, we'll call each other by our numbers. You must not mention our names in front of the others. In just a moment, we'll all meet here to go over the details of the operation," Sebastián said. He had taken on his "executive" tone.

She was going to participate, Lavinia thought. They had approved it. For a moment, she felt almost happy.

Sebastián was tense, grave. This time, certainly, there'd be no muffled crying like the primal, mournful roar that night—now distant—in her house. This time, there was neither time nor space to cry. And yet Lavinia could feel the pain enveloping them in a ring of sharp spokes.

"Thanks," she said, relieved. "Just one more thing—was the thing with Felipe taken care of?"

"Yes," Sebastián said. "We found the taxi-driver, too. He swore that if he'd known he was with the Movement, he wouldn't have fired. He says he respects us. According to him, Felipe didn't say anything until afterward. It's strange. Hard to believe. In any case, we have the man under control now. The bastard!" He mumbled the words with rage and impotence.

What was the man who'd killed Felipe like? Lavinia thought. She felt no hatred toward him. She didn't know what she felt. She would have liked to see him, perhaps. But it wasn't important. Why? What use would it be now? The fact was that Felipe had died a victim of the violence in their country. The violence of its dirt streets, the drunks in the canteens, the hovels beside the unhealthy landfills, delinquency, middle-of-the-night detentions, photographs of dead people in the newspapers, the FLAT patrolling the streets, men with helmets and hard, expressionless faces, the elite troops and their terrible orders, the caste and dynasty of the great generals.

The anger and rage had to be directed against them.

Lavinia was distracted. Flor looked at her. Flor's look made her take notice.

"Come," Sebastián said, indicating she should come over to the blueprints. "I'd like you to go over these plans one last time."

She went to the table, remembering the afternoon when Felipe had asked her for them. They had to remove them from the office without anybody noticing in order to photocopy them. She hadn't wanted to lend them to him. She had had to cross another border to agree. Felipe hadn't been able to explain to her why he needed them. "Just to have them," he told her. "You never know when they'll be useful. We need to gather as much information as we can. You recall that when you went to Vela's office, we asked for that floor plan, too."

The blue-print on the table was accurate. A few slight changes had been introduced at the last moment: the bigger pergola on the terrace, the covered barbecue, a sewing room... What was missing, and was important, was the system of automatic gates which the general had ordered to isolate the different levels of the house at night. He did that so that no prospective thief could go from one level to another. Each level could be isolated from the others with the help of a simple system of automatic gates.

"That is very important," Sebastián said. "We were concerned about the possibility of access from the other levels, the traffic from one level to another."

"But we don't know if the general will have them working," Lavinia said. "They're only supposed to be used at night when they go to bed."

"But we can make them work for us," Sebastián said, "when we have the people together on one level... And what about the patio? What can you tell me about it?"

374 • THE INHABITED WOMAN

The patio was walled. It was impossible for anyone to get out that way. The house was a fortress.

"And the device in the wall that you explained to me?" Flor asked, looking at Lavinia.

Sebastián looked up. He wrinkled his brow, intrigued.

"It's here," Lavinia said, pointing to the private study on the blueprint. "The general keeps his weapon collection in this room, set on shelves in the wall. The wall revolves. If you don't see the weapons, it means they're hidden on the other side."

"What are you talking about?" asked Sebastián. "It's not in the blueprints we have."

"No," Lavinia said. "It's in a separate one."

"You'd better call the rest," Sebastián indicated to Flor. "We're going to have the last meeting with closed ranks and give them all the instructions. It's important for them to hear this."

Flor disappeared up a stairway. Minutes later, the group came down single file.

There were seven men and three women. Lavinia recognized Lorenzo and René, the instructors from the training camp she'd attended. She couldn't hide her surprise when she saw Pablito among them, her childhood friend, the one she'd danced with at the country club party, the one who said he worked in the recently inaugurated Office of Social Investigations of the Central Bank, Pablito, the "harmless." According to Sara, he'd left the country to work in a bank in Panama. The surprise was mutual. They were both about to give each other away in the instant they saw the disbelief in each other's face. He signaled her with a glance not to acknowledge anything. She didn't know the four other men, nor the women. One of the women was small and shapely, with long, straight chestnut hair and almond eyes that seemed especially kind. There was another, plump and dark, with a pleasant expression. The other two were serious and a slightly stern looking, older than the rest. The characteristic that stood out among so many different faces was their age: most of the commando members were between twenty-two and thirty years old, except for the two women who must have been in their mid-thirties.

When they were all in the room, Sebastián gave the order to close ranks. They formed two lines. Flor told Lavinia to line up with the rest. She placed herself at the end. She was number "Twelve."

"Attention!" and they all straightened, assuming a military stance.

"Count off!" commanded Sebastián.

The count-off began. Pablito was number "Nine." René and Lorenzo were "Two" and "Five." The young woman with the almond-shaped eyes was "Seven," the pleasant chubby one "Eight." At ease, they relaxed and stayed in place.

Sebastián stood before the group and began to speak. In the Movement it was the tradition to explain the political motives of each operation, reiterating its significance. Like the others, Lavinia paid silent, respectful attention to Sebastián's steady words, which explained how the Organization had put its faith in them and in their ability to carry out the "Eureka" operation. Yes, they were confident that each and every one would know to hold the name of the Movement high and make its force known. He spoke of the struggle in the mountains, the repression and violence of the dictatorship.

With this operation, he continued, the silence that the Movement had kept in the cities for months would now be broken.

"One of the members of this commando group, number 'Two,' died at dawn," he said, after a pause. Lavinia looked at the others' faces, at their sadness.

Sebastián narrated simply the circumstances of Felipe's death—"That's one of our occupational hazards..." he said. Felipe should live on in them, he added. The operation would honor his memory. It had been decided it would be named after him. Felipe's death, the death of so many compañeros, he continued, committed them to turn the dreams for which they'd given their lives into reality.

Sebastián stopped speaking. He looked at the floor for an instant. He lifted his head and said in a loud, throaty voice:

"Compañero Felipe Iturbe!"

"Present!" they all said.

There was a brief silence for recollection and remembrance, in which Lavinia could not visualize Felipe dead, and thought over and over again that all of this was not happening. She heard the echo of that "Present!" distant and terrible, ringing in her ears.

Then Sebastián went on explaining how violence had not been a choice, but an imposition. The Movement fought against the violence of an unjust system that could only be changed by a long struggle involving all the people. It wasn't a matter of selling short-sighted dreams, or of just changing leaders. They were after more profound changes. They were under no illusions that the end of the regime would come quickly. That had to be clear, he stressed, in order to understand and make others understand why the operation would not begin until the Great General had left the house.

The operation, he said, was only the beginning of a new phase. Its purpose was to alleviate the pressure on the compañeros fighting in the mountains, isolated and pursued for months now. It was intended to open other fronts.

Finally, he explained the demands they would make: freedom for political prisoners and broadcasting on all media communiqués explaining to the people the operation's motives. Those demands would not be negotiable.

He said it was a "Liberty or Death" operation. No retreat. Either they were victorious or they died.

"We win or we die!" he said, and in a loud, resonant voice, the slogan, "Patria Libre..."

"O Morir!" "Or Death!" They all responded in chorus.

"Fall out!" Sebastián commanded. He was visibly moved. Felipe's death hung heavy in the air, putting a solemn shadow on their faces.

It must be terrible, Lavinia thought, for them to have to go into action with that death so fresh and recent in their memory. It was hard for her to fall out, to move from her spot. She suddenly saw the enormity of what they were about to do. And she was the only novice among them. She was horrified by the thought that she could make some blunder that would endanger them all, that she could endanger an operation that had been so carefully planned and that was so significant and definitive for the future of the Movement. The trust placed in her comforted her, forcing her to overcome the doubts and fears arising from her own inexperience. She had to be capable, she told herself.

The compañeros were moving about.

"Now we'll form a semicircle around the table. I'm going to explain the details of the operation to you," Sebastián said. "Compañera 'Twelve' was involved in the designing of the house," he added, pointing her out as a way of introduction. "She is going to join us in the operation. She'll fill us in on the details about the interior."

The members of the commando group looked at her attentively, with camaraderie. Now one of them, she stood beside Sebastián as he spoke, pointing to the blueprints.

"Let's go over it," he said, running his fingers over the rooms of the house.

They probably know it even better than I do, Lavinia thought, listening to him.

"The house has a main entry. It's also possible to enter through the garages. On the first level there are three living rooms, separated by interior gardens, a hall, the dining room with a stairway leading down to the second level, a powder room and the kitchen. In the left wall there is a door that allows entry from the garage to the living room..."

She looked at the blueprint almost without seeing it. Sebastián explained the second level, the bedrooms, the music room, the armory, the little sewing room... She lost track. She remembered the months of work, bent intensely over the drafting table designing that house. The house that had caused Felipe's death. Felipe wouldn't have died if the Vela sisters hadn't come that afternoon distant in her memory when Julián asked her to take care of them. She seemed to see them again, both of them. She remembered her first impressions of Azucena, Miss Montes. Impressions that reality later corrected to reveal the frivolous profile of the parasitic spinster, occupied full time with protecting the comfort her sister offered her. The sister, obsessed with belonging to "society," as she called the people with rank and lineage... She thought of Vela's son dreaming about being a bird.

"What did you say the gate system was like?" Sebastián asked, bringing her back to the room, to her comrades' eyes looking at her.

"There are two gates with gratings," Lavinia said, pretending she'd been paying attention to the whole explanation. "The first one is in the dining room; the second is between the private study and the sewing room on the second level. The first one isolates the entertainment area from the bedroom area and from the more intimate family area. The second one divides this area from the service area. All the gates will probably be open during the party. I imagine the general and his wife will want to show the whole house to the guests."

"What about the weapons?"

"The weapons are in Vela's study. There's a wooden wall. The wall revolves. He can have his weapons on display or hidden, as he wishes. If you don't see them, you will have to activate the mechanism located behind a dummy light switch on the wall to the right. Here," she said and they all leaned forward. "To open the switch, you slide a small bolt, and then you lift a tiny lever that activates a lock. That frees the panels. I think it's most likely that during the party he'll have the weapons on display.

"We didn't know anything about this," Lorenzo said.

"Nobody knew," Lavinia said. "Not even Felipe..."

"And the installations near the garden, the sauna, the gymnasium, and the rest?" Sebastián asked.

"You can see them here," Lavinia said, pointing to the design, "beside the pool. This pavilion has two bathrooms with showers, two dressing rooms, the sauna, a gym, and in this space that divides the bathrooms and dressing rooms from the sauna, there's a covered terrace with a bar."

"That place was the one we didn't understand," the chubby one, number "Eight," said.

"There's a direct access. This flagstone path that you see here goes from the pool to both the entertainment and family levels. Those accesses also have gates."

"The house is well-protected..." Pablito, number "Nine," said.

Lavinia continued explaining the accesses, the different rooms. She spoke with confidence. She knew the house; it was her incubus; she had engendered it. The others were looking at her with respect.

"And what weapons are in the study? Do you know?" asked Sebastián, "Zero," leader of the operation.

"There's everything," Lavinia said, "rifles, pistols, submachine guns." Her head ached terribly.

Flor took out a piece of paper and said they would divide into three squadrons of four compañeros each. One of the squadrons would enter from the front, the other through the service entrance, located at the side by the kitchen, the last one through the garage. Since he was in command, "Zero" was not a part of any squadron. He would enter the house with squadron number two through the main door.

"The most important thing," Sebastián said, "is to get in. Anyone who's left outside is a dead man. Squadron two and I will take care of getting the weapons out of that room and distributing them."

Once inside, the squadron leaders had to make sure to close each access. Squadron number one, the one that would enter through the service door, was to join number two, entering the second level of the house; number three was to surround the house, check the pool area, gather up the guests there, and come in the door on the third level, sweeping it and moving the guests and servants they found there to the second level. Then, with the arms they'd captured, they would divide into two squadrons: one to watch over the guests and the other to assure the defense and security of the residence. All the guests were to be gathered on the second level, the most protected one.

The most vulnerable and dangerous point would be when they got out of the vehicles. Sebastián indicated that their intelligence team was already watching the house. They would telephone the information about what security was left in place once the Great General was gone. Sources had told them that several ambassadors would attend the party, in addition to high-ranking members of the armed forces, several members of the country's principle families, and some of the Great General's relatives.

"When we get out, we shoot at anything that moves," Sebastián said. "The occupants of the first two vehicles clear the way to the door. The ones in the third vehicle will also cover them while they make their way in. We have to enter as quickly as possible, in wedge formation."

"Zero," Pablito, number "Nine," said to Sebastián. "I've always been worried that there are too few of us to control the number of people there will be at the party..."

"We estimate that a number of people will leave when the Great General does."

"And many won't attend in the first place," Lavinia added. "General Vela isn't too popular socially."

"The moment we go into action depends on the Great General and how many people are left. In any event, we can't allow the "big fish" to get away on us," clarified "Zero." "It's very important to remember that we shouldn't harm or shoot at any guest unless you're attacked. The ideal result is to come out of there with everyone alive. We can't and don't want to create a blood bath. It's fundamental that the hostages realize they're dealing with revolutionaries, not assassins or thugs."

Even though the commando group had been familiar with the type of action that was to take place, they had not been informed, for security reasons, of the specific target. Nevertheless, according to what Flor had said, they had been training for two months, simulating the assault and familiarizing themselves with their weapons. Now they rehearsed every detail and movement over and over. They continued to ask questions for a long time, discussing them until they were all clear and satisfied, until they were certain they could visualize what was supposed to happen, step by step.

Then Sebastián indicated that they should begin their final preparations for combat.

Flor gave the group instructions to go over the knapsacks, checking the medical supplies, canned food, bicarbonate of soda, batteries, water...the things they'd need in the case of a prolonged siege, tear gas, injuries.

She also had them do a final check of their weapons. She gave instructions to the compañera who ran the kitchen to prepare a light meal early. It was important that they had already digested their food when they went into action in case of a stomach wound, which was more dangerous on a full stomach.

She indicated to Lavinia that she should go to a room at the back with "Five" to receive instructions on the use of her weapon, an old, battered Madzen submachine gun.

The frenetic activity in the house was being conducted in orderly fashion. The men and women checked the provisions in the knapsacks, laying them out on the floor. Sebastián discussed other details of the operation with the squad leaders: Flor and "Three."

It was noon.

✛ ✛ ✛

CHAPTER 26

The day has arrived. The day favorable for combat, marked by the sign of ceitzcuintli, one dog, dedicated to the god of fire and sun. Before the arrival of the invaders, we never used to go to war without warning. Our calachunis would send numerous envoys to the disputed lands, to try to work out friendly agreements. Not only did we give our adversaries enough time to prepare a defense, but we even gave them shields, clubs, bows and arrows. Since the beginning of the world, since the four hundred cloud serpents forgot their mission of feeding the sun and quenching his thirst, our wars obeyed the will of the gods. The judgment of the gods decided the wars and because of that it was necessary that their judgment not be mislead by uneven confrontations or enemies overtaken by surprise.

The invaders imposed new codes of war on us. They were cunning, deceptive. The wars they waged against us were profane from beginning to end. They did not respect the most elemental rules. We realized that we had to face this enemy by night, crouching, with the ingenuity of a quimichtin, a mouse—warriors in disguise that we sent into enemy territory to gather intelligence. Or we had to fight them on terrains only we knew and where we led them by flashing teguizte, the golden metal that fascinated them.

But the art of war has changed so much in the upside-down world of these times. The warriors that surround Lavinia are silent. They have no chimallis to defend themselves against the enemy fire; the atlatl, the bow and arrows, the poisonous tlacochtli have been forgotten. They do not oil their bodies before battle, and I imagine that when they find themselves face to face with the enemy they will not blow their seashells nor rattle their bone flutes to make a thunderous cry.

Oh! But what am I saying? What am I remembering! Even for me, my memories are old. The invaders broke all our laws. They were not satisfied, as we were, with possessing the most important temple of the enemy land, which would mark the defeat of their white Spanish god and the victory of Huitzilopochtli. They razed everything they found in their path.

They did not take warriors, as we used to take the invading soldiers, to offer them in sacrifice, give them the sacred death. They killed without pity or branded their captives like animals, like cattle, then used them to feed their dogs or as beasts of burden.

It was not the custom of the invaders to make truces with the winners or the losers, to reach agreements after the gods had judged the tributes that were to be given to the victorious. They just took everything they could lay their hands on. They didn't leave a stone standing on a stone.

Theirs was a total war.

Their one god, fiercer than all ours, more bloodthirsty.

Their calachuni, whom they called "king," had an insatiable appetite for taguizte.

We were left with nothing but our courage. At the end we had nothing but the fire in our blood with which to oppose them.

With ardor, Yarince conquered death. He looked for caparazones, the hard shells where conches take refuge, and he dressed himself in lime and stone to confront the multiple solitudes of the night.

For days he went on wandering while I, asleep in my earthen dwelling, felt his steps, unmistakable from those of jaguars and deer.

Until the invaders surrounded him. And all this I saw in a dream. Like a puma, he crouched high above on the rocks, and from there, from the top of the mountain, looked one last time at the tresses of the rivers, the vast body of jungle, the blue horizon of the sea, that land he had called his, the one he had possessed.

"You will not possess me!" he shouted to the bearded men who looked at him in fear. "You will not take a single shred of this body!"

"Itzá!" he screamed, forever shaking me from my dream, and hurled himself into space, upon the rocks that kindly took charge of dispersing his remains. The conquerors were unable to recover a vestige of his body: that land of my songs, beloved territory that forever denied itself to the invader.

• • •

Following Flor's instructions, Lavinia and Lorenzo retired to a back room.

As soon as they entered, Lorenzo gave her a big hug.

"I'm sorry, little sister," he said. "I can hardly believe what happened to Felipe! What terrible luck! And how is it the taxi driver shot him?"

She explained it to him calmly. For some reason she was feeling as if Felipe's death had occurred a long time ago, or as if she were no longer herself, the person she had been yesterday, but rather some other woman, strong and decisive, undaunted by danger or death. Maybe I don't care any more if I die, she thought for a moment. Perhaps that was the reason for the cold-blooded way she thought about what would happen in the next few hours.

Lorenzo, gruff and authoritarian during the weekend training on the farm, now used all the gentle kindness he could find in his strong, muscular body.

He showed her the Madzen's secret chambers, how to assemble it and strip it down, its combat qualities, the Madzen's characteristic features as an assault weapon, as if he were talking about a woman's body, a dark, stocky lover. His voice was intimate, soft, soothing; it expressed his conviction that nothing could go wrong. The operation would be a success.

They spent several hours on this training. Attentive, Lavinia didn't miss a detail. The room and Lorenzo's words seemed to be the only lighted area in the darkened universe of her mind. It had to go well, she thought. She was Felipe. Felipe was her.

They melted into each other to take their position in battle. Felipe would live in her hands, in her finger pressing the trigger, in her presence of mind, in her hot blood and cool head, in the "hardening without losing your tenderness," in the words of Che.

"Do you feel like it's a part of you?" Lorenzo asked. "That's what you should feel. You have to feel that the weapon will be faithful in combat, that it will respond like an arm or a leg, like someone who loves you and will defend you to the death... Do you feel it like that?" he asked, coming closer to her, putting one hand on her shoulder and the other on the submachine gun that Lavinia held against her chest.

"Yes," Lavinia said. "I feel it like a sister...or as if it were Felipe."

"That's it. That's it," Lorenzo said. "That's what you must feel. It's your Felipe. Think like that when you fire. Think that way when you use it to defend yourself."

She felt like crying again, like letting her tears fall on the weapon, imagining it was Felipe. But she mustn't think about Felipe as dead. She had to think of him as alive. Alive and agile. Alive and brave. Solid. Strong.

She wiped her moist eyes. Lorenzo looked at her kindly.

"That's it, little mama," he told her. "Don't fall apart on me."

She wouldn't fall apart. There would be time for crying later.

The time was drawing near. Sebastián was out getting the last report from the intelligence team. The group was in the living room, all fully prepared, like runners at their starting blocks, their muscles tensed, making jokes from time to time that were like releases of steam. Some were sitting on chairs and others on the floor with their backs resting against the wall.

What were they thinking about? wondered Lavinia, looking at them.

After she left the room with Lorenzo, Pablito came over to her. They touched in a clumsy, affectionate re-acquaintance, forgiving one another with that gesture for what they knew they each must have thought about the other.

Now, sitting on the floor, she could see him, thoughtful, silent. From time to time, she smiled when their gazes crossed. Unlike the others, they had not had to surmount poverty or humiliation. They came here compelled by the emptiness of abundance, the nothingness of their lives, apparently brimming with wealth, so comfortable and soft. She would never have thought she could feel so content after Felipe's death. But being there, with her back resting against the wall, among these people who dared to dream, gave her a soft inner warmth, the certainty of finally having found herself, of having reached a port.

She felt that finally she had transcended her fears. Finally, she believed; she had faith. She was certain she wanted to be there, sharing with them, with these people and no others, what would perhaps be the last moments of her life.

She was there, part of the group, as if the nearness of danger had suddenly homogenized them. Here the tulle or wooden cradles, the different recollections of childhood, no longer counted. Whether or not they accepted her deep down, she might never know. What was true was that at this moment, in this parenthesis of time, they were one, animals of the same breed. Their lives depended on each other. They trusted each other, they entrusted their lives to the synchrony they shared, their mutual defense, their teamwork.

They would defend themselves and each other, they would act as a single body, moved by the same desire, by the same inspiration.

After so many months, she had the feeling of having achieved an identity with which to clothe and warm herself. Without a surname, without a first name—she was just "Twelve." With no possessions, no nostalgia for the past, she had never had such a clear notion of her own worth and importance, of having come into the world, born to build her life. She was not a whimsical meeting of sperm and ovum. She saw her existence as a search for this moment. Sniffing, without maps or star charts, she had reached this room, to sit on this cold, hard floor, to rest her back on those walls. So many doubts, pains, Felipe's death, had been necessary. Leaving her parents, distancing herself from Sara... She thought about the child to be born to her friend in a hopefully different future.

Her aunt Inés would have been proud of her. She believed in the need to give transcendence to one's passage through the world, to "leave a mark."

And her grandfather, fervent admirer of the indigenous rebellions, iconoclast, supporter of lost causes, pioneer installer of eight-hour workdays and infirmaries for the workers back then almost in the dark ages of slavery, must be watching her, thinking that finally she had donned wings and was flying.

If it weren't for Felipe's death, the future without him, that moment of anticipation would have held the boundless joy of euphoria.

In spite of Felipe, she felt like smiling—she smiled at as many eyes as met hers in the room—and in a vague way sensed that even if he wouldn't be at her side, she would find in their collective love profound answers that would alleviate her loneliness.

Reconciled with everything that had afflicted her for months, she sadly made up her mind to accept the fact that only in her relationship with Felipe had not been a reconciliation. In their face to face combat, only death had made them equal. Only Felipe's death had given her back her rights, allowed her to be there. The symbol was dark and wrenching. But she couldn't accept it as a gloomy omen of love or the old antagonism of Adam and Eve. Felipe was an inhabitant from the dawn of the world, of history. A beautiful, hairy cave man. Later on, things would change. Later on. In the meantime she knew Sebastián was walking around with a promise in his hand.

Were the others going over their lives like she was? she asked herself, running her gaze over the faces that were lost in thought.

Sebastián had said that they would either triumph or die. It was an action that had no retreat.

Perhaps these were the last moments of their lives. Surely they were thinking that, she said to herself. Even when they believed they would be victorious, death was a possible passenger on this voyage. They knew it, even if they turned away from Death's gaze.

But the atmosphere was serene. The serene trees, she thought, evoking the image of the orange tree. She too felt serene, like a tree.

This death wasn't feared like others. It wasn't surrounded by obscure terrors or unknown phantoms. It would happen in an almost predictable way. It was a calculated risk. No mystery enshrouded it. If they died, they would have no vague remorse. It would have been a conscious decision. A freely-elected decision. They wouldn't give their deaths, but their lives. It would be an honorable end. No decrepitude, no emptiness. They would know for what and why they died. That was important. Comforting. Their lives weren't barren plains or thirsty amphoras that needed to be filled. They made sense. Faguas was not a large country where decisions were already made for people, and an individual life didn't mean much. Here the great existential doubts were out of place. It was easy to take sides. In this, her play dough little country, where everything was yet to be done, responsibility couldn't be avoided with arguments arduously developed in long philosophical essays.

One opted for light or darkness.

And yet it was terrible, she thought, to have to put one's life on the line, to end up with no alternative but struggle, to die like Felipe at the height of youth. This was an extreme method, as Felipe had once explained to her. A violent reaction against the violence that was considered "natural" by the privileged.

They all should have had the right to another type of life.

She looked at the women. She thought about what their lives must have been like to end up here, sitting, waiting, in silence. Felipe's death was the price she had to pay. Felipe had had to die to give her his place.

Women would enter history out of necessity.

Headlights shone through the window. Sebastián was returning. They stood up. They picked up their knapsacks. They put the stocking masks in their pockets.

Lavinia looked at her watch. All thirteen of them had synchronized their watches. It was ten thirty at night.

"We're on our way!" Sebastián said as he entered. "The Great General has already left. Also the American ambassador and quite a few guests. But there are plenty of 'big fish' in the tank..."

He called them together in the middle of the main room to explain the security arrangements that remained at Vela's house: a few security guards, bodyguards for the "big fish."

"There are several bodyguards playing cards," Sebastián said. "They don't suspect a thing, so we have to take maximum advantage of the element of surprise. And get in quickly! Don't forget, anyone who stays outside is a dead man!"

"Unless it's a woman," Lavinia thought. When she heard things like this, she couldn't help mocking the language.

The squads grouped.

The squad leaders, Flor, "One," René, number "Two," and "Three," a young fellow of medium height, not too dark, thick mustache, went out to the vehicles parked in the garden.

They were two Mercedes Benz taxis, slightly old, but in perfect condition.

And Lavinia's car.

Each squad settled into a vehicle.

Lavinia formed part of squad number one. Flor was the leader. It was also made up of the woman called "Eight" and Lorenzo.

"Twelve," Flor commanded, "you drive."

Lavinia got behind the wheel. Flor, the chubby "Eight" and Lorenzo quickly got into the vehicle. They started the cars, and soon they were entering the road through the hemp brake. The path and the old house were left behind, erased by the thin fog that covered the night.

"We're going to leave the vehicles as a parapet when we arrive," Flor said as they entered the highway, "in a sort of triangle. "Eleven" is going to position his vehicle at an angle. You leave yours in the middle, straight, and "Seven" is going to form an angle with yours. That way we'll form a kind of trench in front of the door when we get out. Do you understand?" she asked her.

"Yes," Lavinia replied, driving at normal speed, aware of the responsibility of driving carefully so as not to endanger the whole operation. She didn't take her eyes off the road, staying very close to "Eleven" and not losing sight of "Seven."

They left the mist of the hills behind. The night was cool and windy. A December night.

"This Christmas is going to be beautiful," the chubby one said. "Christmas without political prisoners."

"And with good food," Lorenzo said. "I'm sure we're going to eat turkey in Vela's house."

They all laughed at the idea.

"Do you feel all right?" Flor asked Lavinia.

"Fine," replied Lavinia. "If it weren't for Felipe, I would even say I feel happy."

"Felipe is with us," Flor said. "You can be sure that he's going to help all of us."

"And what was he going to do?" she asked.

"He would have been the leader of squad three," Flor said, "and second in command of the operation. 'Two' took his place."

Lavinia smiled, not without irony, making a comment about how difficult it would been for her to substitute for Felipe.

"You're not in this operation to substitute for Felipe," Flor said. "Remember what I told you."

She was grateful to be reminded, although she knew that if Felipe hadn't died, at this moment she'd be in her house, still waiting, nervous, an outsider, not allowed to participate.

"Let's go over our mission," Flor said, turning sideways in the seat to look at 'Eight' and Lorenzo. "First, we get out, shooting, in wedge formation. You shoot at anything that moves and run to the door on the right side, the service entrance. Second, we enter quickly and go down the walk that leads to the pool, on the second level of the house. If we meet anyone, we take them captive, with no shooting, unless they're armed, and we take them to the second level. Remember that we will only attack the security forces. On the second level, we join squadron one. Remember that we need to put our masks on as soon as we enter the house. Is everything clear?"

They replied affirmatively. Lavinia tried to visualize each one of the steps; the walkway to the pool that she often took when she went down to oversee the work was narrow, with flagstone. They were entering the residential road that would lead to the front of Vela's house. She felt the weight of the weapon on her legs, unmistakable evidence of an incredible reality. She'd never fired this kind of weapon.

The only weapon she had ever fired was a pistol. She had been with Felipe on a deserted beach. "Several of us have never fired the weapons we're carrying," Lorenzo had said. It was almost unbelievable, but that's how it was. The operation had been set up with more boldness than resources. There was no use worrying. The three cars separated a little in order to pass inconspicuously by the corner near Vela's house, where there were some security agents with walkie-talkies. They were engrossed, conversing. Several cars were passing by. They didn't pay any attention to the taxis.

The intelligence team had given precise details about the location of all the security agents, and the personal bodyguards, who were closer to the house. Based on this information, each member of the commando group had been assigned a firing sector. They were to shoot even if they didn't see anything. Shoot at the designated sector. Those were the instructions.

When they were just a short distance from the house, Lavinia stepped on the gas in unison with the others.

• • •

CHAPTER 27

Moments later they leaped out of the vehicles in front of Vela's house. They took the security agents completely by surprise. As Sebastián had said, they were playing cards, and only when the team dashed across the security line, did they become alarmed, running in disarray.

Squad one, with Sebastián leading, fired the first volleys. Lavinia was to rush to the right and open fire with the submachine gun. "Grab it hard," Lorenzo had said. She got out amid deafening noise. Shots were ringing out all around her. She ran forward, turned when she calculated she was in her firing zone, and pressed the trigger. She panicked momentarily when she felt the buck of the weapon lifting her hands, the hellish noise buzzing in her ears. She remembered she was supposed to hold the Madzen waist high, gripping it firmly. The discharge had thrown her off balance for an instant, but it didn't make her lose her footing. If she stayed in one spot for long they could hit her, she thought. She ran forward, zigzagging as René had shown her in the training at the farm, and planted her feet firmly to let off another blast. Her ears were ringing. Bullets whistled all around her. She caught a glimpse of Sebastián and René pushing on the door. She removed her finger from the trigger and ran again, crouching and zig-zagging until she reached the service entrance to join the rest. Sebastián and the first squad had already entered the interior of the house through the main door.

"Your masks!" she heard Flor saying. "Your masks!"
Her heart was pounding horribly. She was deafened by the sound of the shots. It seemed to her that everything was

in total confusion. She didn't know if things were working out or not. She was desperate to get into the house. She didn't want to end up outside, as a "dead man."

Lorenzo was pushing on the door with his shoulder, thrusting at it with all his might.

"Quick, 'Five,' quick," Flor said, urging him. "Give it all you've got."

On the grass, a short distance away, she saw two security agents with white guayabera shirts and black pants, lying dead on the ground. They'd been guarding the door that was finally open, letting them inside Vela's house at last.

Lorenzo closed it. He and "Eight" moved a big, heavy flower urn up against the door and fastened the locks. Flor indicated that Lavinia should follow her as they went toward the entrance to the second level, looking on all sides, their weapons ready to fire.

Outside scattered shots rang out. The street was beginning to fall silent.

They had managed to get into the house.

They could hear a car engine as it took off at high speed.

"Quick," Flor said, turning to the other two. "Quick, let's make a sweep of this area."

They had put on their masks. Their features looked distorted and strange beneath the nylon stockings.

She recalled how she'd joked with Sebastián when he'd told her to buy two dozen pairs of nylon stockings.

They were feeling nearly secure when a shot whistled by Lavinia. It came from a bush in the garden. They all fell face forward on the floor and stretched out as flat as they could. Lavinia felt her blood had plunged to her feet.

"Cover me!" shouted Lorenzo, while he zigzagged toward the bush, shooting. "Eight" and Flor opened fire. Lavinia pressed the trigger, half closing her eyes, waiting for the discharge; but nothing happened. The Madzen made a dry sound. The trigger wouldn't depress. She'd been left without a weapon. Without defense. She tried to unjam the submachine gun.

Lorenzo reached the bush firing his Uzi. One of the barrages wrenched a moan from behind the bush, and there was the sound of a body hitting the ground.

Cautiously, Lorenzo crawled over to the spot. He checked it, then stood up.

"This one won't give us any more problems," he shouted, running to join them again.

"Five," Lavinia said. "My weapon won't fire."

Lorenzo took it. He looked at it for an instant and trying to be kind, said to her:

"You have to change the clip. It's nothing."

In her nervousness, her fright at the shot passing so close to her, she had forgotten the most basic thing. Two days without sleep was taking its toll.

They kept advancing. Inside the house there were women's shouts and jumbled sounds of frantic confusion. The garden area through which they were moving seemed ominously quiet, palely lit by garden lamps and a shy, waning moon.

They saw squad three advancing along the back of the pool. Two compañeros were leading two or three guests with their hands up. There had been few people in the garden at the time the assault began, probably because of the darkness and the chilly night wind.

They finally reached the gate that went from the garden to the second level. It was shut.

"What'll we do?" asked the chubby woman, turning her worried face to Flor.

"Step aside," Flor said, pointing her pistol at the lock and firing. The shots, so close, deafened them even more. Lavinia felt as if thousands of bees were buzzing in her head.

"'Five,' throw yourself against the door," Flor said.

"I'm going to apply for a job doing this," Lorenzo said, smiling for a moment and then he lunged against the closed door behind the recently opened gate, with all the strength he had in his nerves and muscles.

The door opened. They burst noisily into the second level.

The scene would have been comical if it hadn't been for the context and the tension that extinguished humor and laughter. There were men and women in stiff suits and shiny gowns facing the wall, hands above their heads. Lavinia also saw several high ranking military officers in uniform. One of them lay dead on the floor. She couldn't help feeling a shiver go up her spine.

"Seven" and "Six" moved among the guests, frisking them, then carefully approaching the officers, from whose ankles they took two or three pistols, while Sebastián and René kept watch, their weapons at ready. Lavinia saw Mrs. Vela and her sister. They were pale, wide-eyed. And there were Vela's children. The girl was crying inconsolably. The boy's teeth were chattering. He clung to his mother like a frightened deer.

There were some thirty people. Too many in that space. She felt sorry for the children.

She looked quickly toward the study's open door. The weapons had been on display. Sebastián and the others had taken them from their places. She wondered if they had opened the panels.

"Nine" and "Ten" came in at that moment from the third level, bringing six musicians, several waitresses and domestic servants, plus three guests.

"Up against the wall!" shouted Sebastián, only to notice there was no more wall available. "Here!" he corrected himself, pointing to the center of the room.

"Go back to the garden," he shouted to "Nine." "Take that one out of here," he added, pointing to the dead officer.

The two compañeros went out carrying the corpse. Only the guests, the staff and the musicians were left.

"Frisk them!" "Zero" commanded Flor.

They came over. Lavinia had seen people being frisked in the city streets. She knew how the army did it. She did it, trying not to be as rough, remembering that they were supposed to show they were different. They weren't thugs, nor members of the army.

The musicians and maids were whimpering, practically in tears. "Don't hurt us, please. We don't have anything to do with this!" they wailed.

"Shut up!" Flor ordered.

Lavinia looked around the room once they had finished frisking and placing the people along the walls and in the middle of the room. Their faces, now turned toward the guerrillas, showed fear. The officers who had appeared to be so sure of themselves, so smiling on the television screen, shifted their glances from side to side. They were war professionals. They must be thinking about what action they could take. In the corner the Vela sisters, their faces livid and distorted by terror, hugged the son and daughter. The boy was whimpering now. The girl kept screaming. She was overwhelmed by a wave of pity for the children. They hadn't chosen where they were born either. They bore the guilt of their merciless father. Perhaps they would bear it forever. They were still unable to understand. And yet they had to suffer because of it.

Lavinia noticed that Vela was not there. "He left with the Great General. He went to accompany him to his house," Mrs. Vela said, whining as Sebastián interrogated her. "What else could be expected of him?" Lavinia thought. "He still acts as if he were a bodyguard."

Suddenly loud explosions were heard outside.

The six of them looked at one another. The officers shifted position, while Flor softly mumbled "mortar shells" to Lorenzo.

"Don't anybody move!" ordered Flor, noticing the officers' subtle shift, "'Five,'" she ordered, "get those soldiers away from the group and take them to that room," she said, pointing to the Vela's son's bedroom. Leave the door open and stay with them. "'Eight,' go with them."

The boy looked toward his room. He had begun to cry.

"Five" pointed his weapon at the soldiers and led them to the room, followed by the woman "Eight."

"Split up into two squads," Sebastián said. "'Two' and 'Four,' you go to the garden. Check the defense of the area!" he ordered.

Sebastián's voice was a bolt of lightning. It traveled the length of her spine, making her straighten. Squad one was then made up of "Zero," Flor, Lorenzo, "Eight," and Lavinia. The speed with which everything had occurred made her dizzy and nauseous. Adrenaline had created a terrible dryness in her mouth. She was thirsty and her lips were cracked as if she had been through a hard, freezing winter. She looked around again. Some of the faces were familiar. There was hardly anyone who belonged to the circles she usually frequented. She only recognized two couples, one of them the manager of the Esso Company and his wife, the other a rich industrial executive who controlled the wood business in the country. His wife was crying. He was nervously gesturing to her to be quiet.

Some of the faces were familiar to her because she had seen them in the newspapers and on television newscasts.

The explosions outside thundered more often. There were sounds of motors roaring. They must be the FLAT forces, Lavinia thought. They would surround and murder them all.

"'Twelve', come over here!"

She went over. It was painful to move. Her body was a dead weight. She felt as if she was observing the scene from some place outside herself. Sebastián whispered in her ear that she was to take Vela's sister-in-law and two other guests into the middle of the room. They were going to send them out with a white handkerchief and the order not to fire or all the hostages would be killed. "If we don't, there's going to be a massacre here," Sebastián said.

Without saying a word, Lavinia went over to the corner of the room where the terrified Miss Montes was hugging Vela's daughter. Will they recognize me? she wondered, telling herself they wouldn't because even she had trouble recognizing her comrades' faces beneath the stockings. She didn't want them to recognize her. She was afraid of being discovered.

She took Miss Montes by the wrist, without saying a word, and pushed her toward the middle of the room. Miss Montes looked at her in panic.

"No, no. Please!" the woman begged.

"Come on!" she said, trying to use an authoritarian tone, and successfully doing so.

She led the three of them to Sebastián. Miss Montes hadn't recognized her.

Only when she turned around to check the rest of the room with the group huddled together in the center and the other guests against the wall, did her eyes run into the astonished, incredulous face of the pale, lanky teenage boy. He was staring at her. He had stopped crying and couldn't seem to take his eyes off her. He had recognized her. She was sure of it. She looked away, startled at her own reaction of surprise and fear.

"You," Sebastián said to Miss Montes, "are going to go out; you are going to go out through the garage door. You will tell them not to keep firing or we'll kill everyone here. Understood? Every single one!"

Miss Montes nodded. She was trembling. In the corner with her mother, the girl whimpered uncontrollably. The boy looked as if he was about to faint. He was watching Lavinia as if hypnotized.

Mortar explosions. Shots. The squad in the garden was firing. The soldiers outside were firing. They must be trying to surround the house. They heard the distant sound of a helicopter.

"Quick," Sebastián said. "Quick! 'One,' take them to the door. 'Six,' you go with them!" And turning to the people in the room, he ordered the women to shout, "Don't shoot!"

"Scream," he told them, "scream as loud as you can. Scream so they won't shoot."

He gave Flor a white handkerchief.

Confusion grew by the moment. The helicopter circled overhead.

Sebastián, "Eight," Lavinia and the woman who was number "Seven," maintained control over the panicked group, the women shouting at the top of their lungs.

Flor went out. Several tense minutes went by. There were shots everywhere. Mortar fire.

Suddenly there was silence.

Flor and "Six" came back. Vela's sister-in-law and the other two were outside the house now.

The boy kept staring at Lavinia.

Two hours had gone by since the beginning of "Eureka."

Leaning against the wall of the study, Lavinia kept an eye on the hostages, trying to avoid Vela's son's eyes.

The room was big, but even so, the number of people was dangerous. Too many people, she thought, clutching the submachine gun. Her hands and jaw ached from the tension. Her head still hurt.

The silence thickened.

"'Six,'" Sebastián said, "go to the garden. Bring me a report on the situation of squad three.

Sebastián looked at the faces in the room. He was speaking with Flor near Lavinia. It was obvious that Vela had left, escorting the Great General, he said. When he returned, he'd find his house had been taken over. His sister-in-law would tell him the details. But they had his wife and children—they would let the children go as soon as the mediators were allowed to enter—two business executives, several members of the Chiefs of Staff, the ambassadors of Chile and Uruguay, the Minister of Public Works, the Minister of Foreign Affairs, and what was more important, the Great General's brother-in-law, the husband of his only sister, a cousin of his... They had enough "big fish". Everything would turn out all right.

But there were too many people.

"We're going to let another group go," Sebastián announced aloud, and he began to select some women, the musicians, the maids.

"They're going to go out four at a time," he said. "Quick!"

They repeated the operation of lining them up to go to the door. The room would be less crowded. The helicopter flew in close again.

"Tell those bastards that if that helicopter flies over us once more, we're going to start sending corpses out of here!" shouted Sebastián to those who were leaving.

Just then the telephone rang. The members of the commando group stiffened.

"You answer, 'Twelve,'" Sebastián said.

Lavinia went over to the telephone. It was terribly kitsch, white with gold trim, like the old ones from the beginning of the century.

She picked up the receiver. The voice on the other end was authoritarian, used to giving orders for generations, and it made her jump. It was the Great General, saying:

"This is the President speaking. Who is this?"

"You are speaking with the Felipe Iturbe Commando of the National Liberation Movement," replied Lavinia with a steady voice.

"What do you want?" the Great General asked.

Lavinia didn't reply. She motioned to Sebastián to come. "Zero" grabbed the receiver. The helicopter flew overhead again.

"Stop any action against this house or no one will get out alive!" Sebastián said. "Tell your pilots to stop flying over the house."

The room was silent. Everyone was listening to the telephone conversation.

"We want Father Rufino Jarquín as mediator. We also want a doctor, Doctor Ignacio Juárez."

They were two people known to be 'apolitical,' but with sterling reputations.

Sebastián was listening.

"We demand the liberation of all political prisoners and the uncensored broadcast on all the media of the communiqués we are going to give to the mediator," Sebastián said. "Otherwise, you will be the sole person responsible for what happens to the hostages. You have one hour to send the mediator."

Then he hung up.

While Sebastián was speaking, Lavinia stood in the center of the room, a few yards from the Vela family group.

The boy was still looking at her, but now he looked at her in a different way. She avoided his eyes, but she still sensed there was something strange in the way he insisted on looking at her. He seemed determined to make her look at him, notice him.

Flor and those who had gone out to take the musicians to the door, were back. Outside there were voices and the sound of cars. Flor went up to Sebastián. Lavinia listened to the whispered conversation.

"'Nine' is hit," Flor said. "Squad three has him in the dressing rooms by the pool. He's been wounded in the thigh near the femoral artery. They've applied a tourniquet, but he's losing a lot of blood."

"We'll wait for the doctor," Sebastián said, his expression steady.

Four hours had passed.

The boy kept staring fixedly at Lavinia. His teeth were no longer chattering, although he looked paler and scrawnier than ever.

"Why was Vela's son looking at her like that?" she began to wonder. He seemed to be trying to tell her something with his eyes. She felt hot. The stocking was bothering her. She was sweating. She was feeling the effects of the tension, of the long vigil. She was still deafened by the shots. Her right ear was still ringing.

Every time the door through which the members of the commando group came in and out of the garden opened, she held her breath. She was waiting for a volley of shots, but nothing was happening outside. A tense silence floated in the night air, interrupted by footsteps and radio communications, the sounds of vehicles.

The boy kept looking at her. She looked at him. Their eyes met in recognition. Lavinia almost smiled at him to reassure him. He shouldn't be afraid. Nothing would happen to him she wanted to tell him. But she remained stern. Once he caught her attention, the boy insistently threw his glance behind her. He seemed to be trying to indicate to Lavinia that there was something behind her back.

She didn't move. It might be a trick. He probably wanted to distract her. After all, he was Vela's son. The boy didn't give up. From time to time, almost imperceptibly, his gaze was accompanied by a slight movement of his chin. Beside him, Mrs. Vela didn't pay any attention, overwhelmed by her own fear, busy with the daughter, who cried intermittently.

The boy kept insisting that Lavinia should look behind her.

Lavinia made an mental effort to visualize what was behind her, mustering almost the last strength she had.

On Sebastián's orders, the hostages sat on the floor. "Zero" had gone out with "Six" to check on Pablito.

Lavinia projected the blueprints in her mind. To the left was the gate leading out to the patio, the music room and the billiard room... To the right, Vela's private study, where the weapons had been. "One" and "Zero" had given them out to everyone. Some of the old weapons they had started with, old pistols and hunting rifles, had failed. If it hadn't been for Vela's weapons, several of them would be unarmed at this point. Now everyone had two weapons. Lavinia had a Magnum pistol tucked into her waist.

Why would the boy be staring toward the study so hard?

Sebastián came back. Pablito was severely wounded. Other than that, the situation in the garden was under control.

Lavinia turned around to go back to her position.

• • •

CHAPTER 28

The telephone rang again.

"Twelve," Sebastián said, "answer it. If it's the Great General, let me have it."

It wasn't the Great General. It was the priest they had requested as mediator. The Great General had agreed to negotiate. The priest was asking for instructions on how to reach the house.

Sebastián spoke with him.

While she was walking back to take her place, Lavinia looked directly in front of her at the wood panels that formed the study walls. The secret chamber. How odd, she thought. Now she understood! That was where the boy insisted she look! But why? she wondered. The weapons weren't there any more. Sebastián and "One" had distributed them... But what if they hadn't opened the secret chamber? she thought suddenly. Perhaps, since they weren't architects, they had only been concerned with checking whether the weapons were on the revolving wall...

She went back to her post and turned around. Intrigued, she leaned her back against the cold wall in Vela's private study.

The boy kept looking at her. She stared at him, questioningly. His eyes gleamed with the same expression with which Sara's brother used to give away the location of the treasure when they organized treasure hunts at her Grandfather's farm.

And then she knew. She knew. Certainty invaded her and left her paralyzed. The adolescent saw her expression, saw her grow tense, straightening up as if the wall had burned her, and he nodded. He bent his head, pretending to look toward the floor, his "yes" perceptible only to her.

Nobody had noticed the exchange between them. The two of them were alone in the world, speaking sign language. Vela was there. He was hiding in the secret chamber! Why hadn't she suspected it earlier? Nobody had guessed that Mrs. Vela was lying, nobody! Not even Lavinia, who knew the dimensions of the room! It simply had not occurred to her. She had believed the woman just like everyone else. It was so much like Vela to be servile, to offer to accompany the Great General to his house. No one had thought it was strange! And now how could she let them know? Vela was in there. The certainty made her freeze. He was there waiting for the right moment to come out and kill them all! He would come out shooting and kill them all! He would wreck the operation!

Why hadn't she insisted they check the secret room? She simply assumed the others would do it! She didn't realize that they would think it was just a revolving wall. Because surely that's what they had thought... Now, recalling the explanation she'd given the commando group only a few hours before, she realized that she hadn't given them the full details about the hidden space. Furthermore, at a certain point at the beginning of the operation "One" had made a comment about the weapons being displayed, and she hadn't thought to ask if they'd opened the panels.

Why? What obscure mechanism made her disregard the importance of revealing the existence of the lair where General Vela was now hiding, like an evil animal, waiting for the right moment?

And how could she let them know? Vela was right there. There was no doubt about it now. That was what the boy had been trying to tell her. He was there.

Lavinia looked at the boy. He was crouched, expectant. Why had he warned her? she wondered. She remembered when she saw him the day the keys to the house were presented, serious, stern, walking behind his father without saying a word, scowling. He probably hated him. His father didn't understand his dreams. He made fun of him and his dreams of flying. For Vela, known paradoxically as "the flyer," flying meant throwing peasants from a helicopter, killing. Did the boy know that? she wondered. Was it one of those terrible children's revenges? She felt a chill. He was giving away his own father! And what would she do? What? "Four" had come in. "Nine" was dead. She heard the code when he told Sebastián. "Nine" was Pablito. Pablito was dead. She had to face Vela by herself, she thought. She was the only one who should risk it. Pablito was dead. No one else should die. She looked around her. Sebastián was leaning against the wall of the master bedroom. "Six" and "Eight" were beside the sewing room. "Seven" was covering the stairway to the first level. Nobody was directly across from the armory area. Nothing could happen if Vela was there. He couldn't fire at anyone except her. Her hands began to feel sweaty. She gripped the submachine gun. With slow, disguised movements, she checked the magazine. It was loaded.

The boy didn't take his eyes off her. He wanted her to do it. It was terrible, but she felt he wanted her to do it. He was urging her on with his eyes. It was hard for her to believe it. Maybe he hoped she would find his father and save his life. Maybe that was it. She had spoken to him about how sad war was. Killing people. Maybe he thought she would protect his father. She had to act quickly, had to wait for the precise moment.

In her mind she went over the mechanism that controlled the panels. She had to release the lock on the wall. Then she could push the panel with her foot. It would open if she gave it a strong kick. One panel would be enough.

From there she could aim at Vela and warn him to surrender. Vela would surrender. At that point he would know he was a dead man if he came out shooting.

There were noises outside. The mediator had arrived. Flor came in to tell Sebastián. He went out, and Flor took his place. She and Lavinia had not exchanged a word since the beginning of "Eureka" an eternity ago.

Dawn was breaking. The guests were sitting on the floor, their faces drawn from lack of sleep. Vela's daughter had fallen asleep. The boy's eyes closed from time to time; he couldn't fight off sleep. He was struggling against sleep, without taking his eyes off her. When he opened his eyes after dozing briefly, he looked at her.

She should do it now, Lavinia thought. Now. When the boy dozed off, she would do it. She clutched the black metal of the Madzen tightly again.

The boy began to close his eyes. He was a teenager. Could sleep be stronger than terror and suspense...could it? Lavinia thought. What did the boy feel?

As soon as she saw him drift off, she began to slip toward the interior of the room. Flor, "Six," and the woman who was number "Eight" were watching the guests. It would be a few moments before they noticed she had moved. It would not take them long. But it would be enough.

The brown carpet muffled her steps.

Once inside the study, she moved quickly. She was calm.

From somewhere a wave of determination swept over her. She had to surprise him, she thought. She had to move quickly.

Stealthily, so as not to alert Vela, she flipped the mechanism of the panel to the far left. It didn't make a sound.

She pushed the first panel with her foot.

"Make the boy sit still," she heard Flor's voice in the living room.

And then, at the exact moment in which Lavinia's eyes could make out Vela's figure crouching came the boy's cry of horror, the long, wrenching, echoing "Noooooo!"

Firmly gripping her weapon, and seeing General Vela in the darkness of that space she had created, Lavinia felt a chill of fright. The two of them stood motionless for a fraction of a second, paralyzed by the boy's horrifying scream.

She moved to one side, shielding herself, making the panel revolve. Vela was ready to fire at her.

Jumbled thoughts with the speed of stars traveling through mad space rained in her mind.

"Noooooo!" the boy shouted again.

⁙ ⁙ ⁙

There stood that man, like the invading captains: his sculpted face like that of an evil god, looking at Lavinia, recognizing her.

And the scream of the boy.

Her blood froze. I felt the images crowd together, shining and dull images, new and old memories.

I saw Felipe's face. I saw the great metal birds launching men from their bellies, I saw terrible prisons, heard screams.

I saw the unborn child of Sara, the dark room where Lucrecia lay, smelling of camphor, saw the shoes in the hospital, the military doctor who had been assassinated.

And I saw the boy. The one who wanted to fly. The boy who denounced his father, hating him. Only at the last moment, realizing that he loved him, did he try to save him with the caw of a wounded bird, paralyzing Lavinia. The boy who had been built with doubt, in whom she saw herself mysteriously reflected.

I did not doubt. I hurled myself through her blood, madly riding the horses of that eternal instant. I screamed from every corner of her body, howled like a wind sweeping away that second of hesitation, tightening her fingers, my fingers, over that metal that vomited fire.

• • •

Lavinia felt in the tumult of her blood the strength of all rebellions, the roots, the violent land of that wild, indomitable country, clutching her entrails, dominating the vision of the boy, the vision of herself that she had seen projected in those adolescent eyes, in the love and the hate, in the Biblical "Thou shalt not kill." She knew then that she had to close the last stroke all those circles, break the last vestige of her contradictions, take sides once and for all. She moved quickly, placing herself in front of the strong, stocky man aiming at her and pressed her fingers—stiff and hard—on the trigger.

The shots thundered, drowning out the broken cries of the boy. The spray of bullets from her Madzen split the air a second before Vela fired, thinking he was the victor, discharging the dark hate of his caste, trained for years to kill.

Lavinia felt the impact in her chest, the warmth flowing all through her. She saw General Vela still on his feet facing her, holding himself up, his uniform splattered with blood, his eyes nitric acid, venom.

Still under Vela's fire, she recovered her balance, and firmly, with no other thought, watching scattered images of her life begin to run like crazed deer before her eyes, feeling the blows, the warmth gathering in her body, clutched the weapon to her side and finished emptying the magazine.

She saw Vela fall, doubled over, collapsing, and only then did she allow death to reach her.

Everything had occurred in a matter of seconds. Flor and "Eight," alerted by the boy's cry, managed to get there at the moment when the battle was being decided.

Sebastián appeared moments later.

The mediator had taken the proposal with him.

They were going to negotiate.

"Eureka" had been a success.
Tomorrow everything would be over.

+ + +

The house lies silent. The wind on my branches seems like the breath of clouds over a dying fire. I am alone again.
I have completed my cycle: my destiny of germinated seed, the design of my ancestors.
Lavinia is earth and humus now. Her spirit dances in the afternoon wind. Her body fertilizes the rich fields.
Through her blood I saw the triumph of the avenging ximiqui.
They recovered their brothers. They conquered hate with serenity and flaming ocote torches.
The light is lit. No one can extinguish it. No one will ever extinguish the sound of the beating drums.
I see great multitudes advancing along the roads opened by Yarince and the warriors, those of today, those of bygone days.
No one will possess this body of lakes and volcanoes,
this mixture of races,
this history of spears;
these people, lovers of maize,
of the moonlit feasts;
people of songs and multi-colored weavings.
Neither she nor I have died without purpose or legacy.
We returned to the earth from whence we will live anew.
We will populate the air of new times with fleshy fruits.
Hummingbird Yarince
Hummingbird Felipe
they will dance above our corollas.
they will make us fruitful forever.
We will live in the dusk of every happiness
and in the dawn of every garden.
Soon we will see the joyous day

the conquerors' ships departing forever.
The gold and the plumes will be ours
the cacao and the mango
the essence of the sacuanjoches
No one who loves will ever die.